Jers   over
Col   nder
mar   crop,
stewi   e of
his pu   t the
boy might have intended to jump, he drives him
home, hoping that his gloomy imagination has
been exaggerating his concern. But when the boy
fails to turn up at school the next day, Colin feels
duty-bound to track him down — thus pitting
himself against the Island establishment, who would
rather there was a little less noise around this
particular absence. In Jersey, where everyone knows
everyone else's business, you must become your
own island, especially when there are secrets to
hide . . .

MAINLANDER

WILL SMITH

ISIS
LARGE
PRINT

First published in Great Britain 2015
by
Fourth Estate
an imprint of HarperCollins*Publishers*

First Isis Edition
published 2016
by arrangement with
HarperCollins*Publishers*

A catalogue record for this book is available
from the British Library.

ISBN 978–1–78541–137–3 (hb)
ISBN 978–1–78541–143–4 (pb)

Published by
F. A. Thorpe (Publishing)
Anstey, Leicestershire

Set by Words & Graphics Ltd.
Anstey, Leicestershire
Printed and bound in Great Britain by
T. J. International Ltd., Padstow, Cornwall

This book is printed on acid-free paper

For Peter.
A rock on the Rock.

CHAPTER
ONE

COLIN

Thursday, 8 October 1987

Hundreds of feet below where Colin Bygate sat on a moss-covered rock, the Atlantic was eating away the coast. Huge surges rolled in to fling up their spray as they hit the cliff-base, then sprang back to collide with the next incoming wave and send a line of water skyward. The sinking sun gave the brilliant white of the foam an apricot tinge, and turned the vapour trails above to threads of fire. It was one of those sharp and clear dusks peculiar to Jersey, with a brightness that belied the approaching dark. A sky that might have hung over Eden.

Since he couldn't climb down to the waves, he dreamt of them rising up to wash the Island clean of all the impurities that so irritated him.

A vast storm, a second Flood: that was what was needed. One that would carry off the bankers, the lawyers, the accountants and all the others who looked down on him from their vertiginous social position, with their sports cars, their boats and their skiing holidays. It was his wife's sensitivity to his low altitude, and his resentment that he should be made to care about it, that had brought him here tonight.

"Rob and Sally have invited us to Chamonix for New Year."

"I don't know if we can afford it. We're stretched enough with the mortgage, and we've got to get your car through a service in February."

"Sally says they'll pay."

"No."

"Why not? She's my best friend and she can afford it."

"You mean he can afford it."

"Don't be jealous."

"I'm not jealous."

"You've such a problem with money, you're really not suited to this Island at all."

"That's not true. You can't just throw that in. Hey, come on, look at me."

"I'd rather not. I don't like your face when you know you're wrong."

Colin wasn't being disingenuous: he didn't have a problem with money. He just preferred it to be earned rather than inherited, but he could live with this inequality on the grounds that people inherit plenty of things that give them an unfair advantage in life — a disarming smile, a propensity for kicking a ball, or precocious numeracy. His problem with Rob de la Haye was Rob de la Haye. He didn't like the way the man laughed at his car.

"Renault 5! Don't drive it too long, you'll grow tits!" Rob had a Porsche 911, which, on an island that had a

2

maximum speed limit of 40 m.p.h., on only two sections of road, Colin saw as a needless display of conspicuous wealth.

Neither did he like his attitude to the local itinerant Portuguese workers.

"Did you hear about the Porko who took a bath?"

"No."

"Nor did I!"

Or his relentless stereotyping of the Scots, Irish, Mancunians and Liverpudlians who made up the remaining seasonal workforce of receptionists, waitresses and car-hire representatives.

"Check your change — Scouser on the till."

In fact, he didn't like much about his world view.

"Take away unemployment benefit, they'll soon find jobs."

It irked him that Rob's horizons were witlessly free of storm clouds. "Keep going like this and in five years I can buy a parish," he joked, after another run of luck on the markets, at which Colin smiled while inwardly praying for a crash.

He shifted on his granite perch, unsettled by the idea that maybe his wife was right, that underneath the layers of antipathy he was just jealous. His own father had died when Colin was seven. Rob's had kept on living and acquiring hotels, one of which, the Bretagne, he'd given to his son on his twenty-first birthday.

The thing that Colin really had a problem with, and which had hit him like a telegraph pole to the chest, was that his wife had dated Rob when they were teenagers. It had come out as a response to his diatribe over Rob and Sally's plans to build a swimming-pool in the grounds of the old farmhouse they were having renovated at a level of expense that Colin found simply incomprehensible. Sally was flying back and forth to London, sourcing furniture and wallpaper, because she was determined that guests shouldn't recognise any element of her house from visits to the few local department stores. Colin was aware that he had to tread carefully because Sally was Emma's oldest friend but, like many such friendships, his wife seemed to spend more time talking about the qualities she didn't like in Sally than those she did. Hence Colin felt on firm ground when it came to expressing his heartfelt but puritanical disdain at the de la Hayes' need for a swimming-pool when surrounded by such beautiful beaches.

"But they won't be living near any beaches in St Lawrence. It's bang in the centre," Emma had pointed out.

"It's an island. You're never that far from a beach."

"It's nice to have your own pool, though. Beaches are full of kids and tourists. And the sea's only warm enough to swim in about one month a year."

"It's refreshing."

"It's bloody freezing."

This confused and annoyed Colin. He was sure that, early on in their relationship, Emma had shared his feelings on public space and the beauty of nature. Hadn't she swooned at his ability to quote huge chunks of Wordsworth's "Lines Written a Few Miles Above Tintern Abbey"?

4

"I thought you preferred the wildness and purity of the ocean to the sterility and isolation of the pool."

"No, that's you. I like swimming-pools. Maybe if I was still with Rob, I'd have one."

"What do you mean 'still with Rob'?"

"I said 'if I was with Rob'. I didn't mean it. Forget it."

" 'If I was with Rob' would have been hurtful enough. But you said 'still with Rob'."

Then it had come out, made ominous by its earlier omission. Colin and Emma had both talked freely of previous lovers, and Colin had no problem with Dave Le Gresley, the man he had unwittingly usurped when he'd first started dating Emma. In fact, he rather liked him, and would have kindled a friendship if he hadn't worried that Emma would find it odd. Rob, on the other hand, had never been mentioned. It now turned out that she had dated him when they were in parallel sixth forms. He wasn't sure for how long — Emma seemed to change it from weeks to months depending on whether she was trying to hurt or protect Colin, which shifted as their argument rose and fell.

"Why didn't you tell me about him before?"

"Because it's obvious you don't like him, and I wanted to avoid exactly this sort of conversation."

"Maybe you never mentioned it because you still like him."

"You're being childish."

"Does he still like you — is that why he's always so bloody rude to me?"

5

"So what if he does? I wouldn't be alone in having admirers outside of this marriage."

"That's not . . . true or fair."

"It's so pathetic, this whole competition you have with Rob."

"You're making me compete! You said if you were still with him you'd have a swimming-pool. Well, I'm sorry, I'm never going to be able to give you that."

"Don't be so bloody smug and virtuous. Earning money is not a crime."

"Precisely. He doesn't earn it. To earn it you have to do something, to contribute."

"Well, your *contribution* means we'll be stuck in this flat for New Year, while my friends are drinking champagne on top of a fucking mountain!"

"Maybe you should have married a Bond villain."

"You are so immature."

"I was joking, but if I'm honest, that's not a lifestyle I —"

"Here we go, Colin the fucking martyr. Could have gone into the City but chose to be a teacher. How bloody noble. And fuck anyone who actually wants to have some fun in their life!"

He'd stormed out after that and driven as far away as he could from their flat in St Helier. He'd ended up at Grosnez, the north-west tip of the Island, which was wedged up in the air as though some sea god had banged his fist on the southeast corner in a primordial rage. Maybe, thought Colin, it was Triton, furious at the discovery that his wife had previously dated Neptune. As he sat on the headland looking down on the churn and whomp of a foaming inlet, he noticed a seagull that kept settling on a sea-besieged rock, then taking to the wing as the water heaved itself over the smooth dome. The bird would not relinquish its perch, but slowly it would be driven off. He felt like the bird: eventually he would be swept from the larger rock. His surname hadn't helped. Bygate. "How long have you been in the Island?" was a question he heard a lot, the implication being that he didn't intrinsically belong there, that he was permanently marked as an outsider. Even the grammar of the question, with the local idiosyncrasy of "in the island" rather than "on", felt loaded against him. His isolation had crept into his home. The qualities for which he felt his wife had initially cherished him were now held up as examples of his shortcomings.

Her reaction to his Bond-villain crack had frustrated him. Granted, it had been said in a row, but it was the sort of flippant comment that used to puncture her dourness and make her laugh. These days, she would take such comments at face value and fling them back at him.

Her birthday, a few weeks before, had been an oasis of happiness that now felt like a mirage. Colin had wrong-footed her by telling her to pack a bag and meet him in the lobby of the Victoria Hotel, an unremarkable establishment on the west coast, which overlooked a beach with notoriously stinky piles of seaweed. He'd led her down into the Tartan Bar, the walls of which were covered with swatches of random tartans and where a man with a Bontempi organ was entertaining elderly couples with an off-key rendition of "The Skye Boat Song".

"You always complain you've seen everything on this Island," he'd said.

"*In* this Island."

"Sorry."

"Doesn't matter, you'll get it eventually. Well, you've certainly opened my eyes. And they hurt! This décor is unbelievable."

"It's like an explosion in a Scottish tat factory."

"I'll say this for it, though. We're not likely to bump into anyone we know."

She'd cheerily gone along with his plan for anonymity in an epicentre of naffness and was proposing a toast to a night away without bumping into friends, colleagues or relations, when a waiter had walked in and announced there was a taxi for Mr and Mrs Bygate. Half an hour later they were making love in a suite at the luxurious Hotel L'Horizon, Emma having been wowed by his extravagance. To Colin, it felt as if they had started over, but when they'd got home the next day, the evening had assumed the status of a one-night stand that neither party chose to acknowledge. Now they seemed further apart than ever.

As the light around him started to die and the temperature made him feel numb rather than refreshed, Colin slid back from his introspection. Further down the coast stood the Marine Peilstand 3 Tower, the silhouettes of its viewing platforms jutting out like the teeth of a key. The Germans had built it as part of a battery to defend St Ouen's Bay from an Allied invasion that never came. He stood up to restore some blood to his buttocks, then turned to the outer wall of Grosnez Castle, caught in the fading rays. Such a bizarre place. Where else in the world could you sit looking at the sea, with a Nazi fortification in front of you and a medieval castle at your back? He fought an unwelcome memory of standing there, watching the subject of his wife's gibe about "admirers" giving a talk to members of the National Trust for Jersey. He had told her he was going to the talk to learn more about the Island, and had neglected to mention it was being given by his colleague Debbie Hamon. Was his deception on a par with his wife's? No: nothing had ever happened between him and Debbie, and nothing ever would. He could erase a possible future; Emma could not erase an actual past that, to his mind, had stained their present.

He remembered that the castle was something of a folly. Although it must have seemed impregnable when built, protected on three sides by the cliffs of the promontory on which it stood, there was no water supply, perhaps accounting for its easy capture and partial demolition around the time of the French occupation in the late fifteenth century. So its current lustre seemed more like fool's gold. Perhaps his marriage, like this castle, had been doomed from its inception.

The granite was glowing pink and orange. On the horizon the white-yellow brightness of the sun had turned to a burning red as it edged its way towards the ceaseless billow of the sea. As the bottom curve melted into the ocean a flickering swathe of ochre widened towards him as it stretched from the point of contact between sea and star. He wanted to get closer to that beam across the water, to get lower to the horizon as the sun disappeared. He set off along a path heading inland and rounded back through the castle, bounding up the steps to the doorway that stood next to the portcullis arch.

As he picked his way through the crumbling inner walls as fast as he could in the swelling murk, he tried to remember the path he had found that went from the headland to a platform further down the cliff. He had wanted to climb down once with Emma, but she'd said it looked dangerous; she was too tired, and she wanted to get home for the *EastEnders* omnibus.

He saw the white railings that led to the automated lighthouse at Grosnez Point, and the route began to come back to him. As the concrete path banked right, he bent down to climb through on the left, and began crabbing his way down a steep, grassy slope as carefully and speedily as he could. The light was waning quicker than he had anticipated and he wasn't sure he would make it. It suddenly felt imperative that he get down there before the sun had gone. If he did, everything else would be okay. As a boy, he had often set himself such meaningless superstitious tasks, perhaps because of the insecurity he had felt when his father had been taken from him — "If I can throw this ball up in the air and catch it ten times in a row I'll get into Cambridge." Sometimes the tasks were subconscious impulses: "If someone as beautiful as Emma marries me, it makes me okay"; "If I can climb down to watch this sunset, I married the right person . . ."

He reached the bottom of the slope and, holding on to two chunky tufts of grass, turned to lower himself down the fifteen feet of jumbled granite that led to the platform. His toes found a tiny ridge, and he twisted round to see where his next foothold would come, but his eyes stayed ahead.

The sun was now winking over the edge of the horizon. Going, going, gone. He felt a calming chill descend in the now colourless dusk. He'd drive the long way home, round the top of the Island. Maybe stop off at St Catherine's harbour and walk along the breakwater, watching the moon on the sea and listening to the creak of the boats.

He looked down at the ledge he'd been making for and, to his surprise, saw a figure. It was a young boy, a teenager. He stood, feet together, right on the edge of the gently undulating rock that formed the basin, looking down the sheer drop to the sea below. He leant back, his face to the sky, arms raised above his sides. The light wasn't clear enough for Colin to be sure, but the boy seemed to be preparing to jump.

Colin was about to cry out when one of the tufts he was holding on to tore out of the loose earth and he was sliding and scrambling down the rock. The boy ran over, helping to break his slow fall as he crumpled at the base.

"Sir?"

"Aah! Ooh! Hello, Duncan," Colin said, rubbing his knees, which had been scraped on his descent. His

11

mind was split between the pain, the general awkwardness of meeting a pupil out of school, and the specific angst that he might have interrupted a suicide attempt.

"Just sit for a second, sir. Don't put any weight on it."

Colin wanted to stand, partly for the sake of his dignity, but also so that he could grab the boy if he had indeed been about to jump and was minded to make a further attempt. "I'm fine. I can stand — better to walk it off," he said, wincing as he got to his feet and hobbled round to put himself between Duncan and the drop.

"It's hard to spot the footholds in the dark," said Duncan. "I can go and get my bike light to help you climb up."

Colin was confused by how normal the boy sounded. He was talking as though they'd ended up stuck there as part of an agreed climb. Maybe he'd been mistaken in what he thought he'd seen. But what if the boy wanted to get away from him so he could fling himself off from another point?

"No, it's fine. The moon's up, I should be okay. What are you doing here, Duncan?"

"Looking at the sunset. It's the best place to see it from."

"You gave me a jump when I first saw you. You were very near the edge." That was as close as Colin felt he could get to the subject.

"I was just trying to get a view without a sense of the Island. You know, just the sun, the sea and me. It's quite a rush."

Duncan's articulacy was no surprise. He was one of Colin's star pupils, an eloquent and sensible boy, the youngest of three brothers. Both of his siblings had excelled in the classroom and on the sporting field, both had been head boy, both had secured places at Oxford. Duncan was matching them in the first two, and was expected to follow them in the others.

"Why are you here, sir, if you don't mind me asking?" he asked.

"Same as you. The sun sinking into the Atlantic. It's an incredible sight. I was hurrying, hence my heavy landing. Don't tell anyone about that, by the way. If I end up limping round the school tomorrow I'm going to say I hurt myself kicking down the door of a burning house to save some baby pandas."

The boy smiled. That was a relief. Colin was closer in age to his pupils than most of the other staff and shared more of a rapport with them. He was open and approachable, and the sound that rang out from his lessons was rare in other classrooms: laughter. But, in the present circumstance, mannered reticence flooded back. "Do you live nearby?" he asked.

"Not really. St Martin's."

"You cycled halfway across the Island? You must really have wanted to see the sunset."

"It's only half an hour or so. I've gone right round it in under three."

"Still . . . everything all right?" As soon as he'd said it, it felt too pointed. Colin retreated. "I mean, workwise. You do history as well as English, don't you?

Not having an essay overload or anything?" He was gabbling now.

"Yes, thanks."

"'Cause you know my policy?"

Duncan nodded. Everyone knew Colin's policy — "If you really can't do it, tell me and I'll give you an extension, everybody has off-moments." It was frowned on by his colleagues and envied by the pupils not under his tutelage.

"Are you okay now? We should get back up," Duncan said. Was this concern about Colin's knee, or an attempt to change the subject?

"Yes, I'm fine. Do you want to lead the way?"

They picked their way up the steep path in silence under the ghostly grey light. Duncan went first, turning regularly to check on Colin and to show him where best to put his hands and feet. When they reached the top, they turned to look at the moon on the water, a cool balm after the searing sun.

"Why don't I give you a lift?" said Colin. "I'm sure if I put the seat down we can fit your bike in the back of my car."

"I quite like the exercise."

"I'd feel better, if you don't mind. It's getting late, and you should be back home. I wouldn't feel right leaving you alone in the dark on the wrong side of the Island."

The boy conceded and they collected his bike, then used the light to pick a way past the potholes and loose rocks to Colin's car. After they had silently wrestled it into the boot, Colin felt an unease that built as they settled into their seats. He had a mild panic over what music to play. One of his most popular lessons was when he told the boys to bring in their favourite songs to discuss the lyrics. Now he felt as if his own taste was on the spot. He ran through the options, hesitating over Springsteen's *Born in the USA* and *The River*. Some people, wrongly in Colin's opinion, labelled Springsteen as a sickeningly bombastic American flag-waver, so he dismissed him as too controversial and polarising. He discarded Dire Straits's *Brothers in Arms* as too ubiquitous and too obvious, something a teacher would play to appear cool while clearly having no idea what that constituted. He decided Erasure were too camp — he wanted to avoid a potentially unshakeable nickname — then became dismayed at the ludicrousness of worrying how his musical taste would be perceived when twenty minutes earlier he'd thought the boy was about to hurl himself to his death. He started the engine and pulled off the track that led from the headland on to a main road. Eventually, to mask the silence, he slid in the cassette tape of Paul Simon's *Graceland*, which was both mainstream and off-beat enough hopefully to score a multitude of points.

"I don't understand that lyric," said Duncan, out of nowhere. "The one about 'lasers in the jungle'?"

"I think he's talking about the double-edged sword of technological expansion. How it affects every area of life, often with a detrimental effect. How we might gain in science, but lose in nature."

"I like 'a distant constellation, that's dying in the corner of the sky'."

"Yes, it's beautiful."

"Makes you feel dwarfed by the futility of it all."

"Well, I suppose it has a poignancy, but that's quite a bleak way of looking at it . . ." Colin glanced across as he was speaking and thought he could see tears glistening on Duncan's cheeks in the staccato glare of the street lights as they headed to the centre of the Island. He was about to stop the car and comfort him, when out of the corner of his eye he saw him wipe his face. The boy began talking, the moment had passed.

"Tom saw him at the Albert Hall in April. Said it was amazing."

"How's your brother doing?"

"Really well. He's got a job at the *Telegraph*. Sports desk."

"He did English?"

"History."

"That's it, and Nigel's doing English?"

"Yes. Finishes next year."

"Any idea what you might like to do?"

"English, but I don't want to copy Nige."

"You wouldn't be copying him. Lots of people do English."

"I just want to get on to the mainland. I don't really mind what I do."

"Do you mind where you go? Are you thinking of Oxford?"

"Mum and Dad are pushing that. But, you know . . ."

"Your brothers went there, so you'd like to find somewhere new?"

"Kind of."

"What about Cambridge?"

"Dad and Grandpa went to Oxford, so it wouldn't go down too well."

"I'm sure they'd be proud. As a Cambridge man, I can tell you it's every bit as good as Oxford. Although there are other options. Oxbridge is obviously fantastic, but some people can find it quite a lot of pressure. Doesn't suit everyone."

"Did you enjoy it?"

"Bits of it. Most of it."

"Why did you come here?"

"The Island? I met my wife. And it's a beautiful place."

"I suppose so, it's easy to forget that."

"We've just gone from golden cliffs and roaring seas through autumn copses and winding valleys. And look at those stars. Won't see many of those in a big town on the mainland. Whereabouts are you?"

They were approaching St Martin's village.

"It's a left after the church, then the second right."

Silence descended again after the flurry of rapport. The mention of his wife had led Colin to wonder whether Paul Simon was singing about him, a "poor boy" compensating "for his ordinary shoes".

"Just here's fine."

Colin pulled up outside a large granite house.

"Thanks for the lift, sir."

"No problem. Duncan . . ." The boy turned back after getting out of the car. Colin wanted to know whether there'd been more to Duncan's comments about futility than the usual adolescent feelings of isolation in an indifferent universe, but how to ask?

". . . your bike."

They hauled it out of the boot in silence.

"Thanks, sir."

"See you tomorrow."

As Duncan wheeled his bike up the path to his house, Colin got back into the car. He watched the boy push it into an annexed garage with a final wave. He had seen the boy home so he was safe now. But Colin would need to keep an eye on him.

He looked at the clock on the dashboard. Seven thirty. He'd stormed out of the flat at half past five. Not much of a statement, being away for two hours. He needed his angst to settle: he didn't want to go back and say things he might later regret. He needed to work out his feelings. He didn't know what to say. Rob was married to his wife's best friend: an end to contact could not be justifiably demanded or practically enforced. They were supposed to be lunching at the de la Hayes' on Saturday — would he refuse to go? Deep down he knew he had to be the bigger person and let it go, but he needed to spend a few more hours stewing, to let the anger and remorse boil out of him.

Also, childishly, he didn't want to see Emma yet because he wanted her to worry about him, to be the first to apologise when he walked through the door. He should go back when she would have begun to worry, but he shouldn't stay away so long that he appeared pig-headed or as if he was trying to induce panic.

He started the car. How to kill time? He thought of dropping in on a friend, but he didn't want anyone knowing his business. He sometimes thought that a Venn diagram of all the interlocking relationships on the Island would have no more than three circles.

He headed down to St Catherine's Bay, where more than half a kilometre of broad granite breakwater reached out towards France, sheltering a mix of fishing boats and pleasure cruisers. The breakwater was unlit, but the moon lifted everything out of the darkness. He got out of the car and walked to the end, where he stood listening to the gentle lap of the water on the leeward side, he thought of what Duncan had said, about looking at the sea and the sky and forgetting the Island. It was a clear sky — the cold silver stars flickered as brightly as the warm golden lights of Carteret eleven miles across the water. *A distant constellation, that's dying in the corner of the sky.* Such should be his anger at the fact that ten years ago Emma had slept with someone he didn't care for; a faraway fading rage. He took succour from the solitude. He walked up and down the breakwater three times, then headed home with his sense of proportion restored. He would talk to his wife; he would talk to his pupil.

CHAPTER
TWO

COLIN

Friday, 9 October 1987

The atmosphere was even tenser in the morning.

Colin had arrived home ready for reconciliation to find his wife had also gone out. He thought he had timed his return just right, at the cusp of where her worry at his having walked out might have turned to anger at his self-indulgence. Their senses of culpability would coincide: as his anger fell and hers rose they could have settled on mutual blame. Now it was his turn to sulk. He moped around and ate a ham sandwich while half watching an episode of *Dynasty* — it served as a diversion from the tastelessness of the ham and the problems with his marriage. He remembered there was a new episode of *Blackadder* on BBC2, but it failed to lift his mood and he turned it off before the end, then sat staring at his reflection in the screen to avoid looking at the wedding photos on top of the set.

In the large left-hand frame was a picture of him and Emma: "The happiest picture I've ever seen of her," her mother had said.

"Thank you for putting a smile back on my daughter's face," her father had said in his speech. "A bit like a Scotsman seeing the sun, I think we'd all forgotten what it looked like!" he'd added, to a big laugh from the marquee. At the time Colin had swelled with pride at his transformative powers. When he had first met her in the last term of his teacher training in Winchester, he couldn't understand how someone so beautiful was so diffident. He didn't think he stood a chance with her so hadn't been intimidated by her sourness, and saw it as a challenge just to make her laugh. She was unused to an irreverent approach from suitors and had been disarmed by him nicknaming her Crusoe ("You come from an island and seem pretty lonely") and his pitch for a first date: "You and me, midday at the canteen, I'll treat you to a Coke and some crisps. If it goes well, I'll step it up on the second date — square crisps." As this went on he began to fall in love with the romance as much as the woman.

Now when he thought of his father-in-law's quip, he wondered if Emma's smile was a rare phenomenon that had simply reappeared independent of his influence. She was smiling, too, in the smaller pictures on the right-hand side of the frame. She was definitely smiling in the picture he was keenest to avoid looking at, the one of them with Rob and Sally. He and Sally on the edges, Rob and Emma in the middle, as if they were the happy couple. As he sat on the sofa, stubbornly avoiding the picture, yet in thrall to its dark message, it felt to him like a tableau that illustrated how he had always felt. Even on his wedding day, he had been an outsider.

He'd felt dislocated from the children on the street where he grew up because he had gone to the grammar school; he had felt different from the other boys at school because they'd had fathers; and he had felt different at Cambridge because he didn't have money. He had had several short-term girlfriends at university, but never lost the sense that he was on probation as one half of a potential power couple. Throughout all this he had learnt to cover his awkwardness by being a listener rather than a talker.

He grew cold, but was unwilling to turn on the electric heater under the mantelpiece. There was no magic in glowing orange coils set before a curved reflective surface. He'd wanted a cliff-top cottage with an open fire, but had been shocked to find that property prices in Jersey rivalled London's. So they had a one-bedroom flat in the capital, St Helier, in a small seventies block. It was mockingly surrounded by the grand Regency buildings that had rippled out from the harbour in the mid-nineteenth century to accommodate the influx of English-speakers, lured by peace with France and the improved communications that came with the new steamships. He wondered whether those earlier Mainlanders had found it as hard to blend in as he had. He'd done his dissertation on nineteenth-century French literature, and had felt an initial connection with the island where Victor Hugo had spent part of his exile, and where a background hum of Frenchness seeped through in place and surnames. But he found he struck a dissonant note amid the hum.

Emma returned at half past ten. He was finally in bed, not wanting to give her the satisfaction of knowing she had won this battle of shammed indifference. If her evening could continue without him, so could his without her. He feigned sleep, hoping she would wake him with the kisses and caresses of an emotional truce.

Instead she got ready for bed and climbed in beside him, her body kept reproachfully apart from his. As she turned off her bedside light his eyes snapped open. He was wide awake. The more he tried to relax, the more trapped he felt in a mode of outward nonchalance and inward rigidity. He turned over, hoping that the movement might stimulate her into some sort of contact, or an enquiry as to whether or not he was asleep. Nothing. She didn't move. Five minutes later he heard her breathing slow into a faint snore.

He went back to the small sitting room, which opened on to the kitchen, and used his sleeplessness to get on with some marking. His dark mood meant he approached it with an uncharacteristic harshness, which began to swell as he noted loose parallels between his own situation and that of the protagonists of Thomas Hardy's "On the Western Circuit", a short story he had asked his pupils to read, then to comment upon the role of Fate. He realised his hackles rose when anyone expressed sympathy for Edith, who writes letters to Charles on behalf of her illiterate serving girl Anna, thereby leading him to fall in love with and marry the wrong person.

He came to Duncan's essay. It was lucidly argued and strewn with apposite quotes, easily worthy of an A minus, the minus being applied only because of a misreading that Colin found troubling: *Hardy wrote that "character is fate". Because of his flaws, Charles can fight his destiny no more than the train on which he meets Anna can leap its tracks.*

"Too pessimistic," Colin scrawled in the margin. "His 'flaw' was that he was trusting; he would be unlikely to make a similar mistake in future, thus transcending his 'fate'." He worried suddenly that Hardy's morose determinism might not be the best choice for emotionally unbalanced teenagers to read in depth.

He awoke the next day to the sound of Emma in the shower, finding himself with a chestful of essays, a chinful of dribble and an ache in his neck from lolling on the armrest of the two-person sofa. He fought an impulse to join her in the shower, or to be waiting on the bed in a humorous position of mock-repentance when she returned. He retained a prideful conviction that he was the wronged party, quelling the thought that he was now prolonging the row.

Emma was out of the shower. He heard her walking back down the corridor into the bedroom. He just lay there, listening to her dressing, then drying her hair. She hadn't come out to see where he was so why should he go in to make amends? In fact, why was he lying out there, feeling like the exiled guilty party? He wasn't the one who had suspiciously withheld information about former lovers. She should be apologising to him.

The bedroom door opened and he heard her walking towards him. Before he knew what he was doing he had shut his eyes and was once more pretending to be asleep, whether to punish her with further isolation or to avoid continued confrontation he didn't know. He was by now tactically awry. He told himself she would no doubt wake him before she had breakfast: it would be a good way of starting again. His fake grogginess could throw a shroud over the row. A wiping of the slate, delayed from last night.

He heard her open the front door. He opened his eyes. She was dressed and ready for work, about to leave. He faked a yawn and a stretch so that she turned round.

"Morning," he said.

"Morning," she replied.

"You not having breakfast?"

"I've got to be in early. I'll grab something on the way."

He refused to take the bait, adding a smile-less "See you later, then." They might have been speaking in code.

As she shut the door he banged his head against the armrest. Brilliant. He'd come home ready to make peace but seemed to be lumbering towards some sort of Cold War stand-off. He looked at the clock on the wall of the open-plan kitchen. Eight. Just enough time for a quick shower and a bowl of Alpen eaten over the sink.

★　★　★

"Good morning, Mr Bygate."

"Morning, Mrs Le Boutillier. Here, let me help you down the stairs."

Colin's departure time of eight fifteen was also the clockwork moment that his and Emma's seventy-two-year-old arthritic landing neighbour began her thrice-weekly toil to the Central Market in the heart of the town. At these encounters there was normally a bit of to and fro between them. Some "I don't want to be a bother" countered by a "Not at all", which would in turn be parried by "No, no, you need to get to school" that would itself be matched with "It's really no bother" until Colin finally dismissed Mrs Le Boutillier's feigned opposition, picked up her shopping trolley and offered his arm as they descended the steps. This morning he lacked the patience for their ritual so he simply picked up the shopping trolley and guided her to the top of the steps, readying himself to supply the usual murmurs of assent to their predictable conversation.

Step 1 — *Got to get to the market for nine. Otherwise the best fruit and veg is always gone.*
Step 2 — *I don't like my spuds too spongy. And cabbage wilts so quick once it's picked.*
Step 3 — *Of course, in the war we hardly had any good vegetables at all. They all went to the Jerries. Cruel people the Jerries . . .*
Step 4 — *You probably don't remember the war, do you? How old are you now?*
Step 5 — *Twenty-seven? Well I never. You look to*

me like you haven't started shaving yet.
Step 6 — My boy Bradley's your age, but I hardly
see him. He's at St Ouen's on the other side of the
Island.

This morning, however, Mrs Le Boutillier remained curiously tight-lipped, and Colin was perplexed. Then he remembered. "I'm so sorry. I said I was going to come and change your light-bulb for you last night."

"Oh, no bother, no bother." It clearly was a bother, though.

"I'll come and do it this evening, I promise. Can't have you cooking in the dark, what with the nights drawing in."

"Well, that would be lovely. I'll get some Jersey Wonders from the market for you."

"Oh, no, I'm happy to do it." It wasn't so much the thought of what a plateful of the local twisted doughnut would do to his waistline but what the time spent chatting might do to his marriage. Given the current *froideur* it might not make much difference, but he didn't want to be accused of trying to avoid his wife. Emma had never been well disposed to their neighbour: her aunt had insinuated she was the same Edna Le Boutillier who had been labelled a "Jerry Bag" after the war for consorting with the enemy. That aside, she had gradually taken exception to Mrs Le Boutillier's semi-regular incursions into their flat and Colin's into hers. At first it had been something of a joke, Emma referring to Mrs Le Boutillier as "the other woman", but it was now another reason why Emma wanted to move. "You're too nice to tell her to get lost," she had said, "so next place we move to we keep the interaction with our neighbours cursory. Nods over the fence, maybe a Christmas card, that's it." She was right: Colin was too nice to ignore the woman, and he was also plagued with guilt.

As the only child of a widow he had been the centre of his mother's life. She hadn't so much as lunched with another man, let alone remarried, maintaining that no one could measure up to his father. Besides, her unshakeable Christian belief meant that she was sure they would meet again, and the presence of a second husband in the afterlife would only complicate it. He had been taken aback by her mixed reaction to his acceptance of an offer from Cambridge. There was pride, obviously, but it was tempered with regret that he would turn down the place at his hometown university of Bristol. He was confused as to why she had reacted like that so late in the process — he would always have taken the Cambridge place if he was lucky enough to secure it. It did little for their relationship when she confessed that she hadn't expected him to get in. He had found himself going back every other weekend for the first year. It was that, or she would come up to stay in Cambridge. Her presence and his absence limited the social impact he had made in that first year, which was already shaky, given how culturally and financially eclipsed he had felt by the people around him. He had stretched his visits to monthly by the end of university but, as a man who shrank from emotional confrontation, he couldn't bear to tell her she was suffocating him. A small but significant part of Jersey's appeal had been that it put 157 miles between him and his mother, including 105 miles of sea.

He couldn't help feeling that to punish him for his callous ingratitude towards the mother who had raised him alone, God had installed a replica of her in the adjoining flat, a woman who felt neglected by her own son and had latched on to him. Mrs Le Boutillier would sit at their kitchen table drinking tea and eating biscuits, and Colin would zone out, then cycle through annoyance, boredom and guilt. Mrs Le Boutillier always seemed to say, "Dearie me, I must be boring you so," at the very moment she was boring him most, which made him cover it with denial and the immediate refilling of the kettle, as Emma sucked in her cheeks in fury at what she saw as his pathetic need to please.

He held open the door to the front of the block and thought of how to approach Duncan, while Mrs Le Boutillier cooed at a ginger cat on the wall. "There's my lovely boy! How are you, Puss-puss?"

How on earth could he ask subtly if the boy had intended to jump off the cliff? That was the sort of question you either asked directly or not at all. And if you were going to ask it, you had to ask it at the relevant moment. To ask afterwards implied you didn't really care, but simply wanted your curiosity satisfied. Colin needed to know that, if the boy had been building up to a jump, it had been a flash of madness from which he had moved on.

He manoeuvred the shopping trolley on to the pavement, deciding he would assess the boy's mood in class.

29

"He's looking thin, don't you think? Probably hasn't had breakfast!" The cat, Marmalade, belonged to the Ozoufs, a middle-aged couple in the ground-floor flat. Mrs Le Boutillier was often coaxing it upstairs for a snooze on her lap in exchange for some raw chicken, a source of tension with the cat's owners. Colin tried to stay out of it. "You get on, my dear, I'll stay and have a chat with my second favourite boy in the block. Poor thing, they don't feed him enough." Mrs Le Boutillier started tickling the cat under the chin as he stretched his paws in front of her. "I'll bring back some bacon, my furry love."

"Have a good day, and I'll pop in later to fix the light, promise." Colin took the get-out. On the occasions he'd walked with her to the market, what would have been ten minutes on his own or twenty with Emma had taken forty. Mrs Le Boutillier, who would need to pause to get her breath, or put on or take off her hat or her coat, and stow or retrieve it from her shopping trolley, would treat the walk as a guided tour, interspersing it with lengthy anecdotes of frankly unstartling local history. All was delivered in the peculiar flat vowels and nasal drone of the indigenous Jersey-French patois that to Colin rendered the accent bizarrely akin to South African.

"This Le Brun's here used to be a haberdasher's back in the fifties . . . The Midland Bank where your wife works used to be the post office . . . Used to see some of the postmen coming back from their rounds in the east of the Island, with fresh lobsters from the pots. This was before we started getting overrun with grockles, what we call tourists . . . Of course, back then there was a train that ran from Gorey to Corbière . . ."

He normally walked to school from the flat, along the main shopping precinct of King Street, with its mix of local outlets, the odd mainland chain, such as Woolworths, and tourist tat shops peddling "Damn Seagulls" baseball caps streaked with fake guano. It was empty enough at that time of the morning for him to hit a long, pounding stride, unlike during the tourist season when aimless milling led to frustrating stop-start manoeuvres. He liked to walk with purpose; Emma liked to mooch. From King Street he would make his way to the bottom gates of the school grounds and up alongside Conqueror's Lawn on a wooded path leading to the top of Mont Millais, where Normandy College presided over St Helier, like the castle of a local baron. He enjoyed the walk — it cleared his mind for the day. Today, though, he was now running slightly late, thanks to Mrs Le Boutillier, and this, coupled with the hollow dread of needing to know that Duncan was okay, meant that he drove.

As he sat in the glacially paced traffic he remembered the other reason he usually chose to walk: it was quicker. The Island had the world's highest number of cars per head of population. This was due to a bus service that was patchy in its reach and erratic in its timetable, and also a culture of flaunting, stoked by the mainly illusory belief that the inhabitants basked in a near-Mediterranean climate, which justified the owner-ship of multiple cabriolets. Colin was stuck in Hill Street, known locally as the Street of Forty Thieves, although he was sure the brass plates of law firms numbered higher than that. He looked around. His car was the cheapest, boxed in by BMWs, Mercedes, the odd Porsche, and other pointlessly overpowered makes. Even the less exclusive vehicles, the Fords, the Peugeots, the Renaults, were models with that extra *i* to the name, which the owner hoped would suggest wealth and sexual potency. It was a sunny day, bright rather than warm, but the air was fresh so windows were open, hoods were down, sunglasses were on, music was blaring. A man next to him in red-rimmed glasses was beating time on the roof of his Mazda RX-7 as he sang along loudly to "Living in a Box". Colin was certain that the man's abode was considerably more opulent than a box. He wound up his window and opted for *Today*.

A sixty-four-year-old man has been shot dead in front of his family in Belfast . . .

He felt relief when he lost the signal as he crawled through the short tunnel that went under Mount Bingham and the Fort Regent Leisure Centre, which billowed on top of it, like a huge white tent. The tunnel cut off a loop round the harbour and supposedly shortened the journey. It didn't seem that way this morning. He snapped *The Joshua Tree* into the stereo halfway through "I Still Haven't Found What I'm Looking For".

He'd thought he had. Now he wasn't so sure. He rewound the track, as though it would bring him clarity. The traffic suddenly freed up. He kept rewinding and listening as he made his way up the hill to the school.

Bono's full-throated determination to spin disappointment into hope and joy chimed with his own feelings of melancholy. He loved how Adam Clayton's bass just kept walking as the Edge's guitars flicked ever upwards like the corners of a smile, while Larry Mullen Jr's drums clattered away, always coming down with a hammer blow at the end of each line. As he neared the school he let the album run into "With or Without You", and he felt a surge of doubt and regret. As he parked, all optimism faded as he remembered the events of the night before. A pupil poised to jump off the edge of a cliff, a husband and wife wrangling over a marriage sliding away.

He switched off the engine and the music, and heard a tap on his window. He turned to see Debbie's impish face smiling at him with a heart-stopping openness. He wound down the window as casually as he could, which took some doing — the handle always stiffened on the second forty-five degrees of the turn. The effort involved always left him feeling as if he was trying to crank-start a car in a silent movie.

"You could just open the door," she said teasingly. "I mean, you are getting out, aren't you?"

"Sorry, not thinking straight. Bit out of it this morning."

"Oh, no, not coming down with something, are you?"

"No, no, just a bit tired. I slept badly." As he said this, he realised she might construe this as a confession of marital discord, which would have felt disloyal to Emma, or a night of monogamous sex, which bizarrely would have felt disloyal to Debbie. She ignored or failed to pick up on either possibility.

"So, you coming? Or are you going to leave me feeling like I'm taking your order at a drive-in?"

"No, yes, coming . . ." He rewound the window as quickly as he could, then tried to get out with his seatbelt still done up. Debbie shook her head. He opened the door. "I meant to do that," he said, with comic severity. "It's important to test the mechanism."

"Hurry up, you clown."

The seatbelt removed, he got out, grabbed his ever-present brown moleskin jacket and swung it on as he nudged the door shut with his left knee. He was on a continual lookout for a new jacket, but the Island shops had a limited range and he was an unusual size, tall and narrow. In this jacket, what he gained in length he gained also in width, leaving it hanging off his shoulders.

Emma had offered to have a jacket made for him by Hamptonne's, the local bespoke tailor, but he had baulked at the price. Debbie had suggested she take it to her uncle, who ran an alterations service, but he clung to a stubborn and no doubt groundless paranoia that such meddling might make things worse and force him to come to school underdressed in a V-neck sweater. Beneath all of this he felt a mild annoyance that the women felt he couldn't dress himself, which Debbie was presently reinforcing as she reached up to unfurl his collar.

"You don't normally drive."

"I was running late."

"Should have taken your time — you might have missed Le Brocq's assembly."

"Oh, God, is it him today?" The headmaster was giving one of his occasional addresses.

"You should be happy, given you need to catch up on sleep."

They made for an odd sight as they went in together, he with his lolloping gait, she pattering along beside him, sometimes turning to walk sideways with puppyish enthusiasm, before the presence and attention of colleagues and pupils demanded a more professional bearing.

The youngest members of staff, their friendship had started on his first day at the school. The austerity of the majority of his new colleagues and the body odour of his overweight head of department meant he had bolted from the staffroom into the playgrounds and corridors to get his bearings. Debbie had found him wandering through the main building, wondering at the names on the doors of the classrooms.

"It's pronounced 'On-ke-teel'," she'd said, sidling up to him. "As in François Anquetil, who left here aged eighteen, and died on his nineteenth birthday at Passchendaele. All these old rooms are named after prominent former teachers and pupils."

"That would be the room to teach war poetry in, then. I'm Colin Bygate, the new English teacher."

"I'm Debbie Hamon, history. If only we had the choice of classrooms! We're stuck in rooms with romantic names like A1 and A2. Do you want the tour of our rather uninspiring arts block?"

"Mr Le Brocq already took me round, but not much went in."

"He does have that effect. Come on, I can tell you who to avoid sitting next to in the staffroom too."

She had been his guide round the school, and latterly his guide round the Island. He had been surprised and confused at his first wedding anniversary dinner when Emma had told him she didn't want them to turn into one of those insufferable couples who did everything together, and that it would be healthy occasionally to do different things at weekends. This had left him at several loose ends. Emma took herself off to try out a variety of short-lived hobbies, such as yoga ("boring"), embroidery ("full of old farts"), and ballroom dancing ("too many creepy men"). She'd laughed when Colin had suggested he could come to the dance lessons to offer a better class of partner.

"I love you, darling, but you're not a dancer."

"But I'd learn. That's the point."

"No. I already have a base level and you'd take ages to get up to that. Besides, the point is we're supposed to have our own things."

Her "own things" had ended up as shopping and lunching, usually with Sally. His "thing" had started as exploring places with intriguing names. One day while he was ambling down to Wolf's Caves he'd bumped into Debbie giving a talk about the eighteenth-century smugglers who'd used them. He'd tagged along, and after that had gone along to her monthly Sunday history walks. Gradually they began meeting before and hanging out after. He realised after a while that he'd only ever told Emma that he was going to history talks, omitting to mention Debbie's presence. He told himself this was an innocent oversight, in no way to be taken as an admission of anything untoward, and told her casually that Debbie, whom he worked with, was one of the key organisers. Emma remembered her from the year below her at school.

"Oh, my God, Velma?"

"Debbie."

"Short, with glasses?"

"Shortish."

"I'm not saying she's a dwarf, Colin, I'm saying she's a short girl with glasses. That's why we used to call her Velma, from *Scooby-Doo*."

"I think the kids do too, although it won't last long. She wears contacts now."

"So she's still banging on about local history?"

"That's a bit harsh. I find it quite interesting. It's very layered, the Island — Neolithic sites, fortifications from the Civil War, the Napoleonic Wars, German bunkers from the Second World War."

"Stop! You're sending me into a coma."

"You don't mind us being friends, though?"

"God, no, she could do with a few."

His friendship with Debbie had continued to bloom, until he'd been plunged into a tailspin of guilt and panic when Emma had spotted her at a school social function at the end of the last summer term.

"Velma's sexed herself up a bit. Trying to look more like Daphne."

"You think so?"

"You said she'd ditched the glasses, but that's a whole new look. She used to be quite the frump."

Maybe because it had been gradual and he hadn't noticed, maybe because he hadn't wanted to notice or maybe because he'd secretly enjoyed noticing too much, Colin had chosen to let Debbie's transformation pass him by. The glasses had indeed gone, the mop of hair had been styled and highlighted, the blouses were now fitted, and the skirts had gone from calf-length to above the knee. And it hadn't just been visual. There had been other signs: the unspoken understanding that they would always sit together in the staffroom, the way she caught his eye in meetings, the handmade invitations to her history talks, but these were signs he chose to enjoy in the moment, ignoring their implications.

"Who's she seeing now?"

"No one, as far as I know."

"Well, she must be after someone. Maybe you. Don't blush, darling — I was only joking. Although it's weird that she's avoided you tonight. Maybe it's because I'm here."

"Don't be silly. You're reading too much into it."

"And you're being too defensive. Relax! I'd be surprised if she didn't like you, but I trust you. You're too good to stray. And if you did leave me I hope it would be for someone hotter. She can't quite carry off that look . . ."

Luckily the deputy head had come over at that point to ask Colin's opinion on Jack Higgins, the Island's most famous resident author, and neither he nor Emma had raised the subject again. He had initially dismissed Emma's suspicions, not allowing anything to threaten the fairy-tale narrative he had constructed between him and his wife. Wife. Divorce was unthinkable to a man whose mother had stayed faithful to the ghost of his father. But why was he thinking of reasons not to divorce? And why, as they walked side by side into the main quadrangle of the school towards the staffroom, was he having to fight an urge to put an arm around Debbie, draw her closer and pour out his heart?

Thankfully, she was chatting away, leaving few gaps, about that night's stay at St Aubin's Fort with her first-year history class.

"The only thing I'm not looking forward to is sleeping in the same building as Mike Touzel. He keeps making cracks about our 'dirty weekend'. I mean, please, the idea of him makes me gag."

Fair enough, thought Colin. Mike Touzel had an unfathomable belief in his own attractiveness to women. He had once told Colin that he wore a fake wedding ring at weekends to repel some of the she-beasts who inevitably lumbered over to him during a night at Bonaparte's, one of the Island's top nightspots. Colin had been there once, for about five minutes.

"That said, he probably is the most eligible man in your department," offered Colin, the other members being Reg Le Marais, a bumbling old fellow in his sixties, with more hair in his ears than on his head, and Frank Ecobichon, who was so right-wing Colin wondered whether he might secretly long for the good old days of the German Occupation.

At that moment Touzel sauntered past, his gait suggesting he had "Stayin' Alive" on a loop in his head. "Morning, Colin," he said, turning to walk backwards as he passed. "Saw your good lady wife last night. Damn, you've done well, man!"

With what might have been a wink at Debbie, he whipped round and continued on his way. It already rankled with Colin that the man was getting to spend the night with Debbie, and he smarted that Touzel knew more of Emma's movements the previous evening than he did. Everything felt wrong. This morning the world had woken up back to front.

"God, tonight's going to be awful," said Debbie, with a roll of her eyes. "How are you fixed tomorrow?" she added, with a quick touch of his arm. "Maybe we could finally do Bouley Bay to Bonne Nuit. It would be nice to have some pleasant memories at the end of the weekend."

"I'd love to, but we've got a big lunch with some friends of Emma's."

There were few things Colin could imagine being more awkward than his duty-bound chat with Duncan Labey, but one was the recurring request for a follow-up walk with Debbie. The north coast of the Island was wondrous: purple-heathered granite cliffs, bursting with green bracken in the spring that switched to ruddy-brown in the autumn. He loved walking its paths. Emma didn't. She'd been dragged there enough as a child and it had completely lost its allure, if it had ever had any for someone who wanted to spend her weekends at her friend's house, so she could bitch later about how much more tastefully she'd have decorated it, given the money, which Colin now interpreted as "husband". He and Debbie had agreed to do the full walk in stages, but hadn't made any progress since June when they had walked from Rozel to Bouley Bay.

It had been a glorious baking blue day, which had culminated with Debbie goading him into a pier jump. In that brief moment of suspension with the bluest sky above and the bluest sea below, and a legitimate excuse for Debbie's hand to be in his, namely that he was too scared to jump on his own, he had experienced some kind of ecstasy. For those brief seconds the universe had made sense. Her hand in his had felt like the missing piece of a puzzle. But that had been before Emma had spotted what Colin had partly longed for and partly dreaded, that Debbie felt the same about him as he did about her. So the puzzle had had to be smashed and the pieces scattered. Once he had realised which road he and Debbie were on, he had flailed against it, terrified he wouldn't be able to resist, that he would fall from grace. He kept to a credo that Debbie, like Emma, had imperfections that would surface if they were locked together, but when he was with her, his credo was in danger of being disproved, which was why he had to pull away, and had deployed multiple excuses not to see her over the last few months. He and Debbie had so much in common, temperamentally, culturally, politically and emotionally. He couldn't stomach any more sense of kinship: he didn't want there to be any more proof of the notion, which he repressed, that maybe he had married the wrong woman too quickly. And that maybe the right woman was the one who wanted to walk up and down cliff paths with him, debating differing interpretations of "Mr Tambourine Man".

"I can't believe you're standing me up to hear a bunch of men boast about boats." She gave him a playful nudge with her elbow, to which he was rigidly unresponsive.

"I'm not standing you up. I mean, I'm not your boyfriend, Debbie." This was not a morning on which to flirt.

Debbie stopped, and he turned towards her, bewildered that he seemed to have stumbled into another major row within a mere twenty-four hours. This time, though, he could see there would be no row. Not just because they were surrounded by pupils and staff but because she had turned pale and seemed to crumple, not knowing where to look.

"What? Where did that come from?"

He froze as she all but limped off, wishing away the words, wishing away the people around them, wishing he could explain that his lashing out had stemmed from his anger at his own desire, that she had done nothing he had not encouraged, that she felt nothing that he did not feel a hundredfold, and that he would rather hurl himself off a cliff than hurt her as he had just done.

Colin's stupor was interrupted as Aidan Blampied roared into the quadrangle in his open-top Jaguar E-type, using the odd rev of the throaty engine and toot of the horn to clear a path through the throng of students loitering towards registration. He cut a cool dash in aviation shades as he parked, but Colin found him a supercilious, selfish jerk. Not just because he usually turned up late, wanting to be noticed. At last summer's Activities Week Blampied had run a course titled "Boat Maintenance", in which eager pupils had given his modest yacht a new coat of varnish.

Colin approached him. He wasn't his first choice of counsel when it came to Duncan's well-being, but he had to unburden himself and get a second opinion, and Blampied was the boy's form teacher. It was the appropriate place to start.

"Morning, Aidan. Have you got a moment?"

"That depends," came the surly reply, as Blampied looked at the sky. "Running late, but what do you reckon? Looks like rain?"

"Um, the forecast says not, but those clouds look like they might be heading over."

"Give me a hand, will you?"

As Colin helped heave the canvas roof back on and line up the poppers, he pushed on with his enquiries. "How do you find Duncan Labey?"

"Good kid. You've got him for English, haven't you?"

"Yes."

"Any problems?"

"No, he's a very capable student. It's just I bumped into him last night . . ."

The roof was reattached and Blampied had walked round and was now face to face with Colin, but the sunglasses made him feel as if he was being unfavourably observed. He couldn't read Blampied's eyes.

"Where?"

"Grosnez?"

"Grosnez? What were you doing there? Arsehole of the Island, isn't it?"

"Don't you mean the nose? Big nose. That's what it means."

"All right, Mainlander, you've done your research. What were you doing there?"

"I was looking at the sunset. So was he." Colin looked around. The last stragglers were entering their classes. He would be late, but this was important, and no one was around to overhear. "He was acting strangely."

"Strangely?"

"He was near the edge of the cliff."

"So? He's a teenage boy. That's the sort of thing they do. They like going fast down hills and leaning out from heights."

"I might be wrong — it was getting dark — but it looked like he was going to jump. I wanted to let you know in case he'd been acting in any way out of the ordinary."

"Other than looking at sunsets, no. I see him for five minutes at the beginning of the day. You see more of him than I do. How does he seem to you?"

"Fine. He's a good student."

"Did you say anything to him?"

"It didn't feel right."

"Then trust your instincts. If you really had seen someone about to do a header off a cliff, you'd know."

"How?"

"Well, they'd probably have done it. I'm guessing they don't normally pause to enjoy the view."

"Will you speak to him?"

"No."

"Why not?"

"What do you want me to say?"

"I just think we have a duty of care to do something."

"This school is full of hormonally rampant adolescents. The thought of topping themselves probably pops into their brains once a week because their football team's gone down, or they're late with homework and can't avoid a detention, or their parents won't let them watch late-night films on Channel 4. They're not going to do anything about it."

"Is it worth taking the risk?"

"There's no risk, trust me. Duncan Labey is fine."

They started walking towards their classes.

"What about you?" continued Blampied.

"Me?"

"What were you doing out there?"

"I told you, looking at the sunset."

"But why? Everything okay with you?"

"Yes, of course."

"There you go. That's what he'd say too. Trust me, he's fine."

After registration Colin and his form made their way up to the main school assembly, which, as predicted, was a monotonous affair. The headmaster, Gerald Le Brocq, gave two addresses each term, the rest being delivered by other members of staff, local vicars and pupils. He tended to draw from one of three rotating talks, and today's was a humdinger about how Jesus was like an invisible parachute we were all unwittingly wearing. Colin was getting close to memorising the addresses verbatim, the other two being a self-penned parable about a bear sharing his food with a field mouse, and an anecdote about the time Le Brocq had sat next to Jeffrey Archer on a train, which he tried to stretch into a lesson about fate: "If my wife had not burnt my toast that morning, I would not have missed my usual train and I would not have had the pleasure of sitting next to the Dickens of our time and drinking deep of his wit and wisdom." Colin occasionally performed versions of these for Debbie's amusement. He'd ridiculed the Jeffrey Archer story to Emma, but she had missed the point and wanted to know the details of the encounter, whether or not Archer and Le Brocq were still in touch, and whether he could get a signed copy of *Not a Penny More, Not a Penny Less* for her father, who was a huge fan and believed the author would make a great future prime minister, having come through the recent libel trial with his integrity restored.

Depressingly he noticed that Debbie was sitting next to Touzel at the other end of the back row.

He scanned the hall for Duncan. It was impossible to pick him out in the massed rows. Although he had distinctive ash-blond hair, Colin reasoned that, since he was of average height, he could be lurking in front of a freakishly outsized pupil, of which there were a few. The boys rose for the headmaster's exit, followed by the staff. Colin hung back to look over the room and stifle a mild but insistent sense of alarm that would not settle until he saw Duncan's face.

His failure to spot the boy meant he was distracted at the start of his first lesson. He began by playing a Chuck Berry song, which loosened the atmosphere and gave him time to gather himself. His mood was lifted by the excitement and interest he generated in explaining the connection between the song and the text — Berry sang of the teenage experience, and *The Catcher in the Rye* was the first novel to give that demographic a literary voice.

He was walking to his A-level class in the sixth-form block when he saw Debbie ahead. He quickened his pace but then slowed. What was there to say? As she headed to the staffroom on the right, he peeled off to the large granite steps that led up to the back of the High Hall. As he walked through it, past walls filled with portraits of previous headmasters, plaques of sporting victory, and lists of pupils fallen in the Boer, First and Second World Wars, his residual unease was supplanted by dread that Duncan would not be in his class. And then what would he do? Wait till Monday and hope the boy returned with a sick note explaining his Friday absence? Or find an excuse to break protocol and get the school to contact the parents now? Colin was hit with waves of anxiety: what if the boy had found another way of ending his life? What if his body was waiting to be found by a dog walker, washed up on one of the eastern beaches, or had been claimed by the tides, never to be found, or was hanging from a beam in the garage into which Colin had seen him disappear last night? The potential enormity struck him like one of the Atlantic rollers he had watched pound against the foundations of the Island. Merely delivering the boy to his front door now struck him as cowardly and futile. Blampied would help to damn Colin, placing him at the scene of the first attempt and forgetting his own dismissive lack of care. Colin would appear a weak, guilty man, who, by his inaction, had as good as pushed the boy off the cliff.

Twelve pupils showed up to his next class. Duncan was not among them.

CHAPTER
THREE

EMMA

Friday, 9 October 1987

Emma's eyes were shut, as much from bliss as from the bright October morning light that flooded into the fifth-floor room of the Hotel Bretagne, turning the white sheets gold and topping up her subsiding glow. As well as her physical nirvana, the smile that uncharacteristically took over the whole of her face had its wellspring in the exchange she'd had with Rob before he had stepped into the shower.

"What are you up to the weekend after this?"

"Whatever you fancy. Sally's off to look at bloody furniture on the King's Road."

She had taken this as a tacit invitation to spend longer than the usual snatched hours with him, and was already weighing up plausible excuses with which to absent herself from Colin. Shopping, lunch with an unnamed relative, plain old wanting some time to herself . . .

She rolled away from the window and opened her eyes to look at the bedside clock: 9:32. Rob had said he needed to start work at ten — but he was the boss: maybe he could cry off and they could spend the day together, or at least the morning. She craved another fuck. In fact, there was time for that and for him to shower again before ten. He was quick and urgent — she loved letting him do what he wanted. Colin's attentiveness in bed, his sublimation of his needs to hers, all of which had seemed too good to be true in those first heady months, now struck her as weak and bloodless. Her former prince had a neediness, a lack of self in his centre, that he filled with duty.

Her musing was broken by a knock. Rob was still in the bathroom, so no need to tell him to hide as was his habit when room service turned up. She always teased him about that: there was no dignity in a king hiding from his servants. She opened the door and a middle-aged Portuguese man with a thick moustache wheeled in a trolley of pastries, cereal, fruit, juice, tea and coffee.

She picked up a croissant, switched on the radio and sat back on the bed. She turned up Tiffany's "I Think We're Alone Now" till Rob barked, "No!" from the bathroom. Laughing, she lowered the volume and fiddled with the channels till she found something more appealing, settling on what she thought was Bryan Adams, or possibly Bruce Springsteen, or that other guy with Jaguar or something as a middle name. It annoyed Colin when she got singers confused like that, the same as getting lyrics wrong. She often did it on purpose.

She fell back to thinking of locations for their mooted weekend assignation. It would be good to get out of this room. They met here as and when they could, maybe eight times since they'd first fallen on the bed back in July. Until then she'd genuinely thought she was over Rob. Their original split had thrown her off balance and she had struggled to regain it. Eventually she'd left the Island for a TEFL course, determined to travel the world and return solely for births, marriages and deaths, only to reappear with Colin at her side and triumph in her breast. He was different from Rob. He was just as handsome, but gentler and less raucous. He was idealistic and unworldly, self-deprecating and no hostage to cool, and above all he worshipped her. By going in the other direction, she had proved she wasn't bothered by Rob moving on to Sally. She would have a purer love, based on intimacy and friendship, not showboating and overhosting. She had pronounced to the world through her marriage that she was finally happy, stable: she had boxed up the past and placed it in deep if not permanent storage. Rob and she had reached a palatable friendship, although she had never seen him without Sally, until that lunch-time when he'd passed her as she was looking in the window of Layzell's, a local travel agency.

"I recommend Barbados."

"Oh, hi, Rob. Yeah, I've been trying to persuade Colin we should go away for New Year. He doesn't like the idea of winter sun, but I go a bit stir-crazy out of season here."

"Well, if you want sun and he wants cold you could come with us. We're thinking of renting a ski lodge in Chamonix with Tony and Becs."

"Sounds great, but might be a little out of our range."

"Well, as a further compromise, you could do worse than stay at the Bretagne. I'd do it for mates' rates, if not gratis."

Emma laughed.

"What?"

"Rob, I want to get off the Island in my holidays. We're already going to be here the rest of the summer, apart from a weekend at Colin's mother's and maybe a week in France."

"Trust me, you stay at the Bretagne and you won't know you're in the Island, apart from the view — which, by the way, is fantastic."

"Yeah, well, I'll bear that in mind."

"What are you doing now?"

"Grabbing a sandwich, then heading back to work."

"You're not eating a sandwich. You're eating at the Bretagne. Chef's running in the new menu before next week's reopening, for a few specially invited guests. Come on, free lunch."

"There's not time to get there and back . . ."

"You forget, I drive a Porsche."

She had laughed, but allowed him to pull her along by the hand. After an above-par lunch of *fruits de mer*, with a couple of glasses of champagne, in a pristine deserted dining room, Rob had insisted on wowing her with the new decor of the rooms before he ran her back into town.

As she had looked out at the rocks of St Clement's Bay from the room she was in now, he had stood behind her and put his hands on her hips. She'd turned to ask him what he was doing, but the fact she didn't remove his hands meant they had kissed, then fallen on to the bed in a near-frenzy. Rob confessed that the memory of their time together loomed larger than its limited duration should have allowed, and that he felt neither regret for what they had just done nor the desire for it to be unrepeated. He had joked about keeping the room free at all times in case they needed it. She wasn't sure whether he was joking or not, and found herself hoping that he wasn't.

Rob came back in, his biceps flexing as he towel-dried the back of his hair, which was longer than the front. A larger towel was wrapped low round his hips, showing off the almost-six-pack for which he'd never had to work. Colin always wore a towel higher up, nearly under his armpits, like a woman.

"Did you tip?" he said, gesturing at the trolley from which he picked up the *Financial Times*.

Emma gestured to the spray of her clothes on the floor. "I don't know where my bag is."

"Tip well and they'll keep schtum."

"None of the staff would say anything anyway. They'd lose their jobs."

"True. Maybe I just like the intrigue."

"You like having a fuck-pad in your own hotel."

" 'Fuck-pad' . . . I like it. Did you come up with that?"

"I don't think so."

"We should have it as a plaque on the door. And another up at Grosnez Castle."

"Why Grosnez Castle?"

"You've forgotten!" yelped Rob, whipping the smaller towel from round his neck and twirling it triumphantly, like a banner. "It's where we first went all the way. Usually I'm the insensitive lunk who forgets significant moments in a relationship."

"We didn't do it in the actual ruins. It was further down, on a ledge."

"Does it matter? I got the general area right."

"It matters! It was my first time," she murmured, stunned that she was feeling the same elation now that she had felt then.

"Mine too . . . outdoors."

"You said it was your first time!"

"It was, it was! I'm kidding! Not sure it's been bettered . . ." He leant down and kissed her. She pulled off his towel and reached for his crotch.

"Sorry, no time for seconds." He straightened and moved to the wardrobe.

"Hey, next weekend, if the weather's good we could maybe take the boat out, pop over to Carteret."

"What do you mean?" he said, as he pulled on the two-tone burgundy Pierre Cardin shirt that earlier he had deftly hung on a hanger with one hand while removing her bra with the other.

"Sally's not around."

"That would break rule *numero uno* — not outside this room."

"Why did you say, 'Whatever you fancy', when I asked you what you were up to the weekend after this?"

"I didn't. I said, 'Whatever *I* fancy.'"

"You said, 'Whatever you fancy.' "

"You must have misheard. Wishful thinking. I'm flattered. And mildly freaked."

Emma sat up in bed and turned away from him.

"Em, come on, we can't risk being found out. You're scaring me."

"We could go on the boat, go to France. Who's going to see us there?"

"Getting out of the harbour unseen is like trying to get out of a prisoner-of-war camp. And Carteret and Saint-Malo are full of Islanders doing the weekend baguette run. That's why we have the rules."

"I don't like rules. It makes me feel you do this all the time."

"Yeah, that's right. This hotel is full of my mistresses. That's the only reason I run it."

"Don't make fun of me."

"But you're being . . ." He trailed off.

"What? Ridiculous? Crazy? Say it."

"Paranoid. And demanding. We should just enjoy what we have."

"I'm a little confused as to what that is right now. It feels like no-strings sex."

"Well, I don't know what you're complaining about. It was me adding strings that split us up the first time."

Emma stood and headed wordlessly to the bathroom. She felt a slam rising through her arm as she reached for the side of the door, but knew instinctively that the same cold pseudo-normality she had used against Colin last night and earlier that morning would be more cutting, and so closed the door gently.

She began her second shower of the day, annoyed again with the man in the other room. This shower was powerful, enveloping: she could lose herself in it, unlike the electrically heated unit at home that whirred and buzzed to produce a trickle akin to that of an emptying watering-can. She always took long showers after sex with Rob. She supposed he might read guilt into this, that she was undertaking the kind of instinctive baptism people do when struggling with shame, but she felt none of that. She just liked the shower.

What was bugging her, though, was that Rob had been right. Their affair could only ever remain behind closed doors, and closed doors upon which no one was likely to come knocking other than room service. Everyone knew everyone else's business in the Island. Wipe a tear from your eye on leaving a supermarket in a cold wind, and expect your partner to ask why you were seen sobbing in public when you made it home.

He was also right that she had ended their earlier coupling through fear of constriction. While they had seen themselves as being together for ever, in the endless love peculiar to teenagers, they envisaged it happening in different parts of the globe. Emma was a big and beautiful fish in a small pond: she had designs on larger waters. London, New York, Paris, Los Angeles, they would all fall to her charms, in what industry she wasn't yet sure. She should be able to rise to the top of whichever pile she chose to climb: acting, music and fashion were all easy options for someone with her looks and instinctive knack for trailing broken hearts behind her, as evidenced by the legions of solitary doe-eyed boys pounding the beaches, pining for her, with "Please, Please, Please Let Me Get What I Want" on their Walkmans. Rob saw their future differently. It was to be Island-based. He would provide a large income and they would be the Island's "It Couple". They would live in a converted granite farmhouse with a pool, and a garage for as many cars as they wanted. Labradors, horses and, after a time, two children, one of each, named Hugo and Holly, who would go to the same schools as their parents had attended and follow the same paths laid out before them, leading to lives of stress-free luxury.

These opposing visions of the future were as distinct as high and low pressure, and the result was as inescapable as the storm that had broken a week before the end of the summer holidays. They were about to start the last year of their respective sixth forms, where they were each deemed the coolest and most attractive of their peers. Rob had shown Emma the broken-down St Lawrence farmhouse he wished to buy one day and restore for her. She suddenly felt restricted, as though her life was being mapped out for her without her consultation, so her response was less than exuberant. Rob was hurt, declaring her ungrateful.

"Ungrateful? For you telling me how my life's going to be? There's a whole world out there, Rob! It's nice to have options."

"Options on houses, or options on guys?"

"Both. This is all too much."

She convinced herself that the split was for the best, which was easier than admitting she might have overreacted. She knew it would sting to be dropped off by her mother on the first day of term, rather than by Rob in his open-top white VW Beetle. She would no longer feel like the unofficial Princess of the Island, and would need to control the agenda when news of their breakup rippled through the common rooms. The sting had the added barb that on the first day of term it was her best friend Sally getting out of his car at the school gates. Sally, whose gawkiness threw her own elegance into even greater relief, Sally, who only got her cast-offs, Sally, to whom boys talked so that they got to talk to herself. Sally had explained that she'd started dating Rob only after Emma had dumped him, in fact just days before term started. When Emma's anger had increased, she had become defensive, citing Emma's proclamation that she was unfazed at the demise of what had been a golden coupling, and her declaration that she could "do better than Rob". After weeks of antipathy, Sally had admitted at a tearful café summit that she should have told Emma that Rob had asked her out, but she hadn't known how to go about it: she'd felt awkward and guilty, paranoid that it wouldn't last, and was scared of jinxing it. Emma and she had made up, unsure as to how the new power shift would affect their worlds but still best friends because, at their age, these things seemed cast in stone.

Over their final year at school Sally's status and confidence grew until she had become the cool beauty everyone wished to associate with, while Emma seemed to lose her bloom and momentum. Her bitterness and confusion seeped out, and her face hardened. Her eyes seemed permanently narrowed, which gave her the intimidating look of someone predisposed to disapproval.

She became aware that the short-term boyfriends she acquired thereafter were facsimiles of Rob. She wasn't sure whether she went for yachting alphas because she wanted Rob or simply to outdo Sally. They treated her badly, perhaps encouraged by her own lack of self-esteem. The only exception had been Dave Le Gresley, who had begged her to maintain a cross-Channel relationship when she had set off for the TEFL training college, even promising to follow her round the world if she went through with her travel plans. Dave had been too doting and would do anything for her. By then she had known only how to come second.

And here she was, still coming second.

Rob was on the phone when she came out of the bathroom.

"Christophe, Louise on the front desk, she's got to go . . . No, not because she's Scouse, I don't have a problem with that, but my wife will . . . Yeah, you know. Cheers."

He raised his newspaper and immediately made another call. "Rick, it's Rob. How's tricks? . . . Great, I want five thousand worth of Acorn . . . Because they're going to replace the BBC micros in schools . . . Yeah, not just in the Island, across the UK . . . And a company called Exotech . . . Mainly copper . . . I want fifteen thousand of that . . . I don't care how much it is, it's going to go up . . . Because it's in electrical wiring. Trust me, the amount I've spunked away having that farmhouse rewired, not to mention the bloody kitchens here, means I know what I'm talking about . . . Good, speak soon."

He hung up and began making notes in his Filofax, while she sat on the bed and combed her wet hair. Provoked by his silence and knowing time was short, she opened her mouth to resume their argument, then closed it. A lump in her throat had choked her off. There was only one sensible way their affair could end: lifelong silence between them. If she pushed him now that would be it. She hated herself for accepting the little he could give, but she needed it.

She hid behind her hair. "You should get some monogrammed towelling robes."

"That's all phase-three stuff, icing on the cake. We'll scare the working classes off first, then go upmarket. Robes cost more than towels and one in five gets nicked. More, if it's Scousers staying."

"How's the restaurant doing?"

"Not great. Refurb overran so playing catch-up from opening mid-season. Bar's doing well, and at least Sammy Dee hasn't come back. Had a major fight with Dad over that, but times change. Who wants to see some fat dick with a perm and a velvet jacket singing out-of-tune Sinatra in front of some tinsel?"

"The guests presumably. Some of them come back year after year to see him."

"They'll be dead soon, and until then they can stay at the Victor Hugo or Golden Dunes or one of the other morgues. I'm looking at the next generation, and they want something different. The Royal Barge have that guy who does Eagles covers — at least that's only ten years behind. Right, done."

Rob put down his Filofax as Emma switched on the hairdryer.

"You need better hairdryers too. This always takes ages."

"They're all new."

"They're no good."

"No more upgrades till I've paid off a chunk of the refit bill. Need people to tuck into those surf-and-turfs. Such a good mark-up on lobsters. I'd start pulling ahead a damn sight quicker if that's all they ate."

"You were just buying and selling in tens of thousands! You can afford some decent bloody hairdryers."

"I need those tens of thousands to keep afloat."

"Women need a decent hairdryer."

"Are you complaining about the facilities in the free fuck-pad?"

"I'd be complaining if I was paying."

"The old dears we get are happy to spend half the morning drying their blue rinses, and it gives their husbands time to lie on the bed and stare at the walls."

"You've got to invest in your business."

"I am investing in my business — too fucking much, as it happens. Can we not talk about this? It's stressing me out."

Emma switched off the hairdryer. "I give up. I'll let it dry on the way."

Rob reached for her hand. "Em, what we're doing, it's okay, you know. We're just working through a bit of unfinished business."

"You're tagging this on to when we were together before."

"Yes. It's part of what happened then."

"As opposed to now."

"Now is different. We're in different places."

"Do you think I'm a slut?"

"What?"

"I've slept with more people in this Island than you have. I mean, you've been with me and Sally. That's it, isn't it?"

"Are you trying to make me feel inadequate? What's your point?"

"I'm a girl you sleep with but don't marry."

"I can't marry you because I'm already married. So are you."

She crawled across the bed and draped her arms round his neck. "I'm sorry . . . I don't know what I'm saying today."

"If it's too much, we can cool it . . ."

"It's not too much. It's just enough. A little bit of fun in these four walls that no one knows about. Just as we agreed."

"Yup. Only Christophe."

She withdrew her arms. "What?"

"Christophe knows. About the room. And why I need it."

"Jesus, Rob."

"I can't keep it from him — he's my eyes and ears in this place. Trust me, he's a locked safe. He's French so he knows how these things work."

"I thought he was Corsican."

"Same thing."

"Oh, really? So a Jerseyman's the same as an Englishman."

"Fine. He's Corsican. You win. Point is, I trust the guy."

Emma started picking her clothes off the floor. "Colin knows too."

"What?"

"About us."

"Fucking hell! Why are you telling me this now?"

"He only knows about the first time."

Rob threw his head back. "Oh, Jesus, you nearly gave me a heart attack."

"Unlike Christophe, he's very much an unlocked safe. Should make tomorrow interesting."

"Tomorrow?"

"We're coming for lunch."

"Are you? Sally never tells me anything."

"Sorry — you annoyed me about Christophe."

"It's fine. Look at us, sniping like an old married couple."

"That's not funny."

"I take it back. Are we okay?"

"Yeah."

"I'd better get to work."

"Me too."

Thinking that they might have spent the day together, Emma had called in sick immediately after confirming her rendezvous with Rob. An empty day now yawned before her. The weather was fair but she couldn't face a walk. There was the risk of bumping into someone who knew someone from work and, in any case, she was dressed in her Midland Bank navy skirt and jacket, and court shoes. She set off driving round the Island, on the same roads, past the same houses, with the same faces at the same windows and the same shrubs in the same gardens. Every corner, every street lamp, every tree-shrouded lane was primed to trigger a memory. She felt as if she was driving through her own theme park.

She passed her parents' St Clement's beachfront house where she'd spent an awkward New Year following the announcement that her first term at Birmingham University was to be her last, and where Colin had written "Marry me" in seashells outside her bedroom window on the first Christmas Day of their relationship.

Further along the coast road was the flat at La Rocque that she'd rented during the years of idle temping and dating, years of confusion and anger. There were natural laws in the universe that she had never imagined could be defied, and one of them was that she would marry sooner and better than Sally.

Gorey Castle was where Sally, sprawled against the outer battlements after a pub crawl on the last day of school, had told her she didn't care about her exam results and had decided to turn down her university place: she wanted to be Mrs Rob de la Haye. It was also where Emma had first kissed Rob after they had rolled down the castle green, a sweeping slope edging the castle's northern wall.

St Catherine's Breakwater was a compound memory: multiple family walks in the rain, disappointing her father with her lack of enthusiasm for sailing, her younger brother Rory nearly falling off the edge during a tantrum, Colin boring her with his superior knowledge of the history of the breakwater.

As she drove up the east coast she remembered sitting alone at White Rock, bereft and broken after fulfilling her duties as Sally's chief bridesmaid. She had been convinced that Sally was trying maliciously to emphasise her recent weight gain with the cut of the dress. At the end of the evening a drunken Sally had told Emma that she knew how hard it must have been to watch her and Rob walk down the aisle, but that she, too, would soon find her prince. Emma had played it cool, denying it was even an issue, while struggling to understand why it still was and why she was maintaining a friendship that served only to undermine her confidence and self-esteem. As she had watched the sun come up that morning, disappointed that its sickly rays still left her shivering under her car blanket, she had known she had to leave again.

On skirting the top of Bouley Bay she was reminded of Colin, and how on his first visit he had eulogised about how the purple pebbles matched the heather on the cliffs then wondered why she could ever want to leave such a place. She had come back to work for the summer to earn some cash before she set off on her TEFL travels. As their love grew and his stay extended from July to August, his enthusiasm made Emma see the Island in a new light and her travel plans receded.

When the job at the school had come up in September, she had allowed herself to be swept up in his sense of Providence. Now she resented Colin for having cheated her out of other, possibly better, options. She could have been off this rock and married to an architect in New Zealand, sending round-robin Christmas letters detailing their idyllic life spent flitting between their beachfront mansion and thousand-acre farm.

Nearing the brown-brackened outcrops that loomed over Bonne Nuit, she realised that she was halfway round the Island. She was literally going round in a circle. She turned into the centre, determined to find an unfamiliar road. She veered left down a lane, remembered it led to her cousin Yvonne's house, so took the next right, then another left and a right, all along lanes that she knew by sight if not by name. She took three straight lefts in a row, then discovered she had doubled back on herself and went into a frenzy of random turns, speeding as fast as she dared, pushing herself to near panic as she imagined the hedgerows folding over and swallowing her. She came to a crossroads. Straight ahead lay the Carrefour Selous, another crossroads at the middle of the central parish of St Lawrence. The right cut across to the top of St Peter's Valley and the airport, dense copses lining the slow curve up to a plateau leading to the broad beaches of the west coast. A pleasant drive but one she'd made many times before. The left led back towards St Catherine's and Rozel. She rested her chin on the steering wheel and a fugue descended, until an estate car stopped behind her and beeped. She pulled out quickly to the left, then noticed a smaller road just off it that led up a steep incline. To make it she had to swing on to the other side of the road, which caused an oncoming van to brake hard and blare its horn, but she had found her Holy Grail: she did not know where this road led. Her mood lifted, along with the land's elevation, as the lane banked left and right.

She turned on the radio for a further boost but the nimble-fingered riff of Dire Straits's "Romeo and Juliet" conjured a heart-tugging combination of jauntiness and despair. She turned the dial blindly, desperate for another song, one she hadn't listened to endlessly as part of the compilation tape *Bounce Back* that she'd made around the time of Rob and Sally's wedding. As she flicked between stations, she laughed at her misplaced fury with the station programmers. They hadn't chosen to mock her with their selections. There was no conspiracy: this was the Island getting on top of her.

As the road rose she found a French station, which was accessible from various points on the Island. The song that was playing was the one she had chosen as the climax of that tape, a song as high in the air as "Romeo and Juliet" was down on the floor.

> *Baby look at me,*
> *And tell me what you see,*
> *You ain't seen the best of me yet,*
> *Give me time I'll make you forget the rest.*

For some reason it unlocked within her a deep-hidden joy. She slapped up the volume and jigged in her seat, beeping her horn in time with the music, partly out of the need to warn any oncoming drivers of her presence as she rounded fern-laden corners, and partly out of an unexpected frenzy of optimism that could not be held back. As she sang along, "Fame! I'm going to live for ever", she started to believe it, only a kernel of her feeling ridiculous, but that was part of her revelry: the ridiculous was far more fun than moroseness. Rob was just something she was working out of her system. She'd needed to go back to him to grasp that she didn't really want him. Their affair was benign, a boon to her marriage as it would help her see the good in the husband with whom she lived on a beautiful island. She would not be drowned by the past. She would spring on top of it, laughing as it drained away. She stopped the car, her elation snatched away, as if a magician had pulled off a tablecloth leaving everything on it in its place.

She had driven this lane before. She must have. There in front of her was the farmhouse that Rob and Sally were having renovated. The same farmhouse that Rob had promised her when she was seventeen. Sally had taken her round the empty shell at a celebration barbecue following the successful purchase, pleading with Rob to replace an oak on the front lawn with a circular drive and a fountain, and expounding on the dilemma of deciding between a swimming-pool or a tennis court or both, but then having a limited garden space. Emma had been inclined to make sure she was not around for the work's completion.

Builders were plodding around the house now: it was coming together. Emma leant her head against the car window, crushed by the epiphany that it wasn't just the ghosts of the past that she had to wrestle and evade but the ghosts of the future. She could fool herself no longer. She had to leave, this time for good.

As she trudged up the stairs to the flat, with nothing to look forward to except sitting in the tainted glare of framed wedding photos, wondering if she'd ever smile like that again, Mrs Le Boutillier's door opened. Emma's mood deflated further.

"Hello, Mrs Bygate, not at work today?"

"No."

"Have you got that bug that's going round?"

"I think I probably have, so best keep back. I don't want to give it to you."

"Very thoughtful of you — got to be careful at my age."

Emma turned to put her key in the lock.

"Oh, silly me, I've got this for you — you must have just missed him," Mrs Le Boutillier went on.

"Colin?" replied Emma, confused.

"No, the boy. He had a letter for your husband. I said I'd make sure he got it. Things get awfully messed up in the pigeonholes. Not everyone in this block takes as much care as I do, making sure the right letters go in the right places." She held up an envelope with "Mr Bygate" handwritten in the centre.

"Right, thanks." Emma tried not to sigh, but was weighed down by yet further proof that any interaction with her neighbour took at least five times longer than she might have predicted.

"He was ever so helpful. I'd just got back from the market and he helped me in with my trolley. I offered him a cup of tea to say thank you but he said he was in a rush. Maybe I put him off, talking too much. That's the thing when you live alone. If you get the chance to talk you probably do it too much . . ."

"Right. I'll make sure Colin gets it. Did he say who he was?"

"He said he was a pupil."

"He should be at school then."

"I hadn't thought of that. I get so confused by what holidays they have, these days. Not like in my day . . ."

"Wonder how he knew our address."

"Well, it's an odd name. Only one in the phone book."

"I suppose. Thanks again."

"Let me know if you're feeling up to a cup of tea later. I bought some currant buns at the market that need eating up . . ."

Emma had shut the door.

CHAPTER
FOUR

LOUISE

Saturday, 10 October 1987

The first coffee had pierced the fug of her hangover. The second had helped her assemble the jumbled pieces of the previous night. The third unbuttoned the Scouse lip that Louise O'Rourke had used sparingly since she'd come to the Island.

She had held back yesterday morning when she'd been fired from the Bretagne halfway through her first day. Initially this was because she was reeling from the shock. She had just about got used to the fact of having landed a job at one of the Island's top hotels, the first rung on a ladder that would take her to higher levels previously denied. For a moment she had thought she was about to cause a monumental scene, but as she processed what was happening she decided on a cannier move.

Though she knew him by name and reputation, she had not met Rob de la Haye before she started working on the front desk of his hotel. She'd caught his eye as he walked up the main staircase that Friday morning, but she had recognised him as Doug, the yacht salesman, "in the Island for one night only", who had bedded her at the end of a day's carousing at the Bouley Bay Hill Climb in July, an annual event in which bikes and cars took turns to roar up the tree-fringed bends from the harbour to the top of the bluffs.

She hadn't been sure it was the same man so once she'd finished dealing with a guest she had checked the register for anyone staying named Doug or Douglas. There was none. Later that morning the inscrutable Christophe had taken her into his manager's office and told her that, due to circumstances beyond his control, he would have to ask her to leave. He offered her three months' wages, a glowing reference and a hint to refrain from pursuing the matter, which she declined to take.

"Shame. I never even got to meet Mr de la Haye. Or his wife." She still wasn't sure whether Rob was the man she had slept with.

"I could make it six months' wages, if your need to meet Mr de la Haye or his wife were to disperse." That was all the confirmation she needed.

She'd taken the money, met some friends at lunchtime, told them she'd jacked in her job after a modest win on the local lottery that would see her right for a while, and drunk the day away. Her friend Danny had joined her for last orders once he'd finished his kitchen shift and they'd sat on the walkway that led out to the Victorian tidal bathing pool at Havre des Pas. It was opposite the café outside which she now sat, insulated from the fresh October air by her body warmer, and a stagger away from the bedsit where she'd been woken by sunlight streaming through the dip in the sheet that hung as a makeshift curtain. It hadn't helped her mood to find Danny on the floor; that meant they'd started off sharing the bed platonically, then he'd either mentioned the L-word or had started grinding against her with an erection while they were spooning. Either way, she'd literally kicked him out of bed. He had a characteristic that marked him out from other men she had known, which drew her to him as a friend but repelled her as a lover: dependability. She'd enjoyed sleeping with him initially, but she was not conditioned to be attracted to men who posed no challenge, so had made it clear some months ago that they were to proceed as friends. He'd protested but they had stuck to it without any tension, except on those odd occasions when Louise had been drunk on the wrong side of the Island at midnight without a taxi fare and they'd ended up sharing a bed. Her girlfriends had taken to referring to him as "Danny Doormat", which she resented. If he chose to put her on a pedestal and make an unasked-for pledge of romantic servitude, that was his look-out. She'd made clear to him where they stood.

The café was starting to fill for lunch. A family of four stood on the pavement, the parents eyeing the menu with distaste.

"It's a rip-off place for visitors. I mean, look at the people," muttered the father, in peach-coloured linen trousers and boat shoes. Louise looked around at the out-of-season tourists. They were her kind of people: Mancs, Scousers, Scots, working-class families in search of a bit of sun in a place where you could order a decent cup of tea in your own language.

"Oh, please, I'm starving," moaned the elder son, lanky for his age.

"You said it was our choice, Dad, and this looks fine," put in the daughter.

"There's no room anyway," said the mum, whose taut features were mostly hidden behind a pair of outsize sunglasses.

"I'm going if you're looking for a table," piped up Louise, broadening her accent to intensify the awkwardness.

"Oh, no, we're fine, actually," replied the dad. "We're running late for a thing anyway . . ."

"They serve really quick," said Louise, getting up. "Hey, Mick, I'm leaving two quid for the coffees. This lovely family needs to eat and go!" A waiter in his fifties with smeared tattoos on his forearms and a beer belly like a balloon came straight over with menus and ushered the family, who were divided between relief and annoyance, to their seats.

"I recommend the chip butty," Louise added perkily, as she passed the mum, who looked the type to wonder why ten minutes a week in front of the calisthenics video didn't shift the pounds accrued at aimless social teas.

She crossed the road and stood at the railing, looking down at the beach. The dark blue water was smooth and gelatinous. She inhaled deeply. She loved the saline scent that permeated the perimeter of the Island. Very different from the stench of the diesel-skimmed brown water that lay in the port of her home city. The sound of the wash was calm and hypnotic. It wasn't the kind of tide that felt like it was trying to take the Island, unlike the late-autumn swells that beat over the edge of the sea walls. It was nuzzling the sand about twenty feet down from where the high tide had left a rim of seaweed. She looked at her watch. Midday. Twelve hours earlier she and Danny had bought a bottle of whisky from behind the bar and sat on the walkway staring down at the reflections of the coloured bulbs strung above that glinted in the roll of the black water. She had found herself admitting to him that she had been sacked. She regretted telling him the specifics: mention of her sleeping with another man reinforced the boundaries of their relationship, but he spiralled into a monosyllabic gloom of hurt. She remembered ignoring this and declaring that Rob de la Haye would regret the fucking day he'd crossed her.

A toddler punctured her reverie by bursting into tears as a seagull attempted to mug him for his doughnut. She remembered crying last night. Fuck. Danny was so loyal to her, carrying a torch that might have been mistaken for a lighthouse, that she tended to steel herself against the revelation of any vulnerability, but last night she had broken down, and he had put his arm round her. A pass dressed up as gallantry. He had made her a promise. She had talked about packing up and going home. The best a Mainlander like her could hope for was to serve at top table: she was never going to get a seat at it.

"Get your own place then, like you wanted," Danny had slurred. When they first met, at the St Aubin hotel where she'd started as a cleaner, she'd talked of her grand plan to buy a little hotel or B and B and build up a business. Her fellow expats were happy to use the Island as a source of casual labour and casual sex, but not her. She didn't like the way its people looked down their noses at her. Forty-three years ago and seventy-one miles away her granddad had run up Normandy's Gold Beach into the jaws of death while these petty Islanders were waiting out the war with nothing more to complain about than a shortage of sugar.

"I'm not allowed to fucking buy here, Danny," she'd spat back. Her grand plan had been shattered: without local housing qualifications she wasn't eligible to buy any property, commercial or private, until she had rented for twenty years. "I can't wait till I'm forty-two."

"Use my quallies then."

"What are you talking about?"

"We'll do it together. You find the money, I'll buy it for you."

"Buy what, though?"

"The Crow's Nest is for sale."

"How much?"

"Sixty."

"So I'd need a six-grand deposit. Plus another four or so for the refurb. That place hasn't been touched since the seventies. Anyway, that would make you my boss. I don't think either of us could handle that."

"We'd be partners. Mine on paper only. I run the restaurant, you do the rest. And we split any sale fifty-fifty."

"Oh, Christ, Danny. This is some weird future fantasy you've worked out. How many times? I don't need you to save me."

"I'm looking at it as a business proposition. You're bright, Lou, brighter than me. And tougher. I don't want to spend my life chopping carrots and reheating shepherd's pies so some hotelier can own three cars and a pool, but that's all I've got ahead of me. You can pull me out too."

"Pull you out of what? You're Jersey born and bred. You're fine."

"We're not all fucking millionaires and tax exiles. Some of us work bloody hard, same as your lot."

"Do not compare yourself to my lot. My lot have been shat on. How many of your school-friends have been stabbed or banged up?"

She started to feel hungry so opened her purse to check how much cash she had left. She found two pounds and a scrap of paper scrawled with *Le Petit Palais, La Rue de Grassière, Trinity*. Rob's home address. She had surreptitiously obtained it from the office before she left the Bretagne. She hadn't known why. A vicious letter to his duped wife? An anonymous threat? A dog turd in a box? She looked back at the café where the parents of the local family were wolfing their food, the wife clutching her handbag on her lap rather than risk putting it on the floor against her chair. What did she expect would happen? That it would be hooked and tossed into the throng of the great unwashed who would close ranks like a League of Thieves from a nineteenth-century romance? This Island had branded her since she had first touched down, a two-star accent in a five-star town: Scousers were thieves, untrustworthy. Very well, if that's what the Island wanted, maybe that's what the Island should get.

She strode back to her bedsit and used the communal phone in the hall to dial a cab, then went back to her room and took a tenner from Danny's wallet, leaving him an IOU and a promise to be in touch in the week.

On the way into the belly of the Island, sunbeams darted through the spindly branches of the wind-stripped trees, adding to her headache. She shifted to the other side of the car and wound down the window to let the cool breeze enliven and narrow her sense of purpose. This had the bonus of drowning out the insinuations of the prying local driver.

"Friend's house?"

"Yeah, going for lunch."

"Nice houses round there."

She wanted to say, "Keep the car running while I rob them," but settled for "Hm."

The houses on the hawthorn-edged lane began to thin out and swell. As, she imagined, did the hair and girth of the male owners, fattened by the confluence of middle age and wealth. The waists of their wives would slim with the need to retain the attention and resources of the tailored sloths.

"Just pull up here," she said. She paid and got out in the road.

The white house looked big but, then, anywhere looked big compared to the council flat in which she'd grown up. It had had two windows: the front and the back. This house had twelve on the front, all with wooden shutters painted gold to match the fake Victorian gas lamps that lined the snaking drive at intervals too close for the desired effect to work.

A metallic green Renault 5 approached, its indicator flashing to turn in, so she continued walking towards the next house to muster her courage. After it had pulled into Rob's drive, she snuck back to see who it was. She knew who it wasn't: there was no way that the man she had fucked would drive a car like that.

She peeked round the trunk of a beech tree that stood at the edge of the front garden and saw a rowing couple get out of the now parked car. The woman was attractive, in spite of her frown, which looked to Louise as though it had become the default setting for her face. Their raised voices drifted over.

"I can't believe you only mention this now. Where's the letter?"

"Back at the flat."

"And he said he was a pupil? I've got to go back now."

"You can read it later. This is embarrassing."

"No — I've got to go now. I'm sorry . . . I'll come straight back — we're just down the road."

"Fucking hell, Colin, why does everyone have to come before me? Fine, piss off. And don't bother coming back. I'll get a taxi."

"I'll be back . . ."

As he jumped back into the car and began to reverse clumsily at speed, Louise ran forward to hide behind one of the large bushes that pocked the garden. He headed out of the drive and back the way he had come, while she spied on the woman she supposed was Colin's girlfriend or wife. She watched her collect herself, then ring the bell. The door was opened by a blonde woman in a Breton top and white jeans with a gold chain-link belt. She was pretty, but the kind of pretty you could buy. Rob hovered in the background. Louise bristled at the sound of indiscriminate shrieking. She knew their sort: they were finicky orderers and bad tippers. As the door with its large fish knocker shut behind them, she thought of how people like that didn't know they were fucking born. She'd love to choke the forced shriek in that stupid bitch's throat and give her a real howl of pain.

She collected herself. The wife wasn't the enemy. Rob was. She pitied the poor cow. She looked at the cars parked in front of the house and in the open garage. A Porsche, a small jeep, some kind of classic car, an old soft-top VW Beetle and a sporty yellow cabriolet. More cars than her dad had owned in his life.

The phone was ringing as she eventually approached the house. She heard Rob yell that he'd get it and caught a glimpse of him through the glass panels at either side of the door that looked on to the front hall, which was bigger than her living quarters. It sported an oak sideboard the size of her bed, on which sat a large pink conch shell, a piece of white coral and a golden bowl overflowing with sunhats and sunglasses. He had picked up the phone and had his back to her.

"Hi . . . Oh, hi, you going to be joining us eventually? . . . Sure, I'll get her." He held the receiver away. "Emma, Colin for you!"

As Emma approached, her view of Louise blocked by Rob, he pointed at the phone with his spare hand, motioned "ssh", then opened his arm for an embrace. Emma allowed him to kiss her, while Colin waited at the other end of the line. Louise stood still and smiled: this prick couldn't be asking for it more if he tried. As Rob moved aside and Emma took the call, she spotted Louise and pointed, then turned her back, terror in her eyes.

"Hi . . . I put it on the coffee table . . . Well, you must have moved it without knowing what it was . . ."

Rob caught sight of Louise and his jaw dropped, as if he'd just been told he had thirty seconds to live. She moved in front of the door, which he opened, then stepped through, shutting it behind him.

"What the hell are you doing?"

"What the hell are you doing? She's not your wife, is she? I'm pretty sure your wife was the blonde who opened the door. And Emma has a husband, or at least a boyfriend. Called Colin. I was over there when he dropped her off. And I heard him ring and saw you two kiss while he was waiting to talk to her. Classy."

"What do you want?"

"Let's talk about what you want. I assume you don't want a divorce, or at least a couple of long nights in the doghouse. Mind you, a doghouse round here might be roomier than most people's flats."

"Look, I'm sorry about what happened. I was drunk and —"

"Drunk when you fucked me, or drunk when you sacked me?"

"I understood you were well compensated."

"Now you're just making me feel like a whore."

"You're the one making you feel like a whore. You already got us to double the offer."

"We can keep insulting each other like this, but I'm just worried your wife might hear and wonder who I am. You're already going to have to explain me to Emma."

"What do you want?"

"Well, now that I've seen your cars and your house, I reckon I can name my price and you wouldn't feel it."

"Fuck off."

"Cheaper than what happens if I tell your wife about us, and also tell her about you and Emma. And Colin. Quite a lot to lose."

Rob tensed. He didn't look the sort to hit her, but you could never tell. Let him try — she'd go straight for the nuts.

He breathed out. "Just go, I'll be in touch."

"Why not make a date right now? Tomorrow night, the Black Dog, for old times' sake. This time just drinks, though, no need to book a room. Be there at nine."

Louise turned and walked all the way home. She arrived forty-five minutes later, pride restored, hangover vanquished. Danny was still sprawled on her floor. She nudged him awake. "Morning," she said, "I've been thinking about the kind offer you made last night, and I'd like to accept."

CHAPTER
FIVE

ROB

Saturday, 10 October 1987

"Sorry, Sal, got caught up with a lost tourist looking for the zoo in our driveway."

"The zoo? That's bloody miles away! Why can't grockles read a map?"

"On the plus side, the more they drive, the more they're spending on our petrol. Right, where was I? Drinks. Emma, what's your poison?"

In the twenty seconds it took to walk back to the lounge following Louise's departure, Rob strained to conjure his charm and mask the depth charge of panic that she had set off. Emma was just sitting down when he walked back in. He quelled a second wave of horror at the thought that she might have hung around to hear what Louise had said to him, then segued into suave-host mode, regaining the cocksure aura of a man who wasn't going to remove his hand from a wall at a party without a kiss, all wrapped up with the smile women told him reminded them of Tom Cruise. He told some of his conquests that by coincidence his surname was "Maverick", Cruise's handle in *Top Gun*. Underneath, he was reeling from the seismic shock to his swagger. What had just happened? How had it happened? He was used to sailing close to the wind, but this was a capsizing.

With the drinks orders in, he went to forage for ice. He thought of feigning a lack of lemons and jumping into the Porsche to burn some rubber and clear his mind, but knew he had to maintain an air of normality. He returned to stand in front of the chrome drinks cabinet, where he fixed Emma a gin and tonic and Sally a Malibu and pineapple juice, all the while thinking, What the fuck? What the fuck? What the fuck? Luckily the women were engrossed in a conversation about the ageless beauty of their former French teacher, so he could take his time with the drinks and steady his flayed nerves with a Jack Daniel's and Coke.

"How old was she when she was teaching us, then?"

"She must have been in her fifties."

"No way, Em. She looked thirty, if that."

"But she is actually French, and they just age better. They don't give up like we do. She was always dressing younger, but not in a muttony way."

His extra-curricular fucks were not supposed to know his name or address. Most of them thought he was from Guernsey, for Christ's sake. To his way of thinking, he hadn't been lying the day before when he'd told Emma he hadn't slept with anyone but her and Sally. She'd specifically brought up her tally of sexual partners "in the Island". And in the Island he'd slept with just those two. And Louise, but she wasn't *from* the Island, so he reckoned he could transfer her to the off-Island tally, a considerable number that nobody needed to know about. When he went to France with his mates on a jolly, or flew to conferences on hotel management, or just went to look at upmarket establishments in Saint-Tropez or Monte Carlo, the sort of places he wanted Jersey to compete with, that was another matter. Off came the ring, and more often than not the name would change as a secondary precaution. It wasn't that he didn't love Sally: he really did, even though she could give him a hard time. He had only started dating her to hurt Emma, but Sally's devotion had knocked him out. She worshipped him — at least, she had at first. Probably because she was punching above her weight, although she really had morphed into a stunner. But they'd been together since they were seventeen, and there was a whole world of women out there. She was great as a homemaker, but it felt wrong to put that homemaker on all fours and pound into her in time to Robert Palmer, as was his wont.

"So now she's, what — fifty?"

"No, Fee told me she's retiring, which makes her at least sixty."

"Must be early retirement. I'm still convinced she's forty."

"I'll get Colin to check — he knows a couple of the teachers there — but I'm telling you she's sixty."

Why, oh, fucking why had he broken one of his three rules with Louise?

1. Never go lower than a nine.
2. Never in the Island.
3. Never fuck them more than once.

This last rule stopped anyone forming an attachment, and also made for rather frenetic sex; he always aimed to have them in all positions so that he wouldn't feel the need to go back for more.

"I saw her a few months ago in Voisins. My God, if I look that good at her age it'll be a miracle. Never married, though, did she?"

"Far from a spinster . . ."

Emma sounded perky. Thank Christ Louise hadn't spooked her. Tough girl, Emma. If she could front out their affair before their partners, adding Louise to the mix shouldn't be a stretch. Although if Emma knew he'd slept with her that could be tricky, but not insurmountable. The bigger question was how to deal with Louise. He was buggered if he was going to give her any more money. It would feel like he was paying for sex, and he'd never do that — might as well hang a white flag on his dick.

"Bit of a goer, was she?"

"Well, again according to Fee, she did that French thing of taking a series of lovers."

"Not just a French thing from what I hear. Ironic that Fee should say that."

"What do you mean? Sally, don't pull that face! Come on, spill!"

"I heard she was shagging Eric Le Maistre."

"You're kidding! But he's a Jurat, and married! Can't afford the scandal. And such a bald little thing. How do you know?"

"Can't remember, but whispers turn to roars in this Island."

"Not that I'd ever cheat, but if I did I'd make sure I did it off the Rock."

Christ, what did Emma mean by that? Don't talk about how you'd have an affair, you dumb bitch! Unless she was doing that thing of hiding in plain sight? Yes, clever girl. Oh, God, what had he been thinking, starting an affair with her? That had broken rules two and three. Pity initially. There was something about Emma that was so down, so unfulfilled, and so palpably unfucked, that he had seen it as his duty to do what Colin couldn't. Plus, since Colin would never grant him the last word in any argument, he took immense pleasure in claiming the ultimate, if silent, victory by unmanning him in the arena of his own marriage. And he couldn't deny that Emma was an amazing fuck. Maybe the whole double-guilt thing of betraying her husband and friend meant she really put her back into it. He himself had no guilt, only fear of being caught, which was very different.

"Here you go." He turned round with the drinks.

"Are you okay, sweetheart?" asked Sally.

"Yeah, I'm great."

"You look like you're sweating a bit."

"Oh, I had a quick peek at the chops, got a blast of hot air."

"For God's sake, Rob, I've told you not to open the oven when the meat's in there. You lose the temperature."

"Not with that oven."

"Right. It can subvert convection, can it?"

"Con-what?"

"Convection? Movement of heat through gases and fluids. Honestly, Em, he bangs on about his cars and his hi-fi but he hasn't a bloody clue how they work. I know more about them than he does, just from home economics. And, as you remember, I hardly paid any attention in that class. Or any class, come to think of it!"

"Men just won't ask for help, will they?"

"What's up with Colin?" asked Rob, anxious to throw the attention on to someone else. He hadn't even opened the stupid oven and he didn't give two shits how the bloody thing worked. He was used to enjoying these lunches, seeing the victim of his cuckoldry at close quarters, not having his two lovers hold him up as an example of an idiot man. He was fucking them both: how could he be an idiot?

"Some work thing. A pupil dropped something round yesterday and I forgot to pass it on."

"Right." That had bought him nothing. Fucking Colin. Such a useless prick. He didn't even need to be there to kill the mood of a room. Just the mention of him cast a dreary pall that had everyone shifting in their seats. "Well, let's not wait for him to start the party." Rob pressed PLAY on the remote control of his new Technics SL-P1000 CD player. He'd let slip the price and specs when Colin arrived — be good to get a rise out of him. Stupid cunt was still using tapes.

"Oh, not this! I hate it — it gives me a bloody headache," moaned Sally.

"Gave the band a headache too. They recorded each individual string of the guitars separately. I think it sounds bloody amazing."

"Who is it?" asked Emma.

"Def Leppard."

"Put something else on. Not boys' music. Let's have Belinda Carlisle."

"Why don't we let Emma choose?"

"Here's a test, darling. You can have your music on your new toy if you let me take the oak down at the farmhouse." Sally turned to Emma. "He still won't budge. I mean, why would you prefer a ghastly tree that blocks out all the light in the front rooms to an illuminated fountain in the centre of a circular drive?"

"Apart from the cost of plumbing and maintaining this faux-Versailles water feature you've set your heart on, which would involve the removal of the old cider press that I want to get working again, I've always loved that tree. I'm thinking tree-house for the kids, when they come along, plus Christmas lights. Right, Emma . . ." Rob gestured to her but caught himself just in time. In his head he was asking her for confirmation that this had always been his dream for the house, which would have been a giant misstep. He changed his tone mid-sentence. ". . . why don't you choose the music? Then we can delay the tree-versus-fountain decision to when my wife has come to her senses."

"I really like Tiffany."

Shit. She had semi-seriously lobbied for "I Think We're Alone Now" to be their song, but he hated it and had banned it from his earshot. This was her sending him a signal that she was upset. Christ, she must have heard what Louise had said.

"Colin won't be long, will he?" asked Sally.

"Shouldn't be. Said he was popping straight back."

"I'd better put the veg on, then." Sally got up to head to the kitchen.

"I can do that — means I can escape Tiffany," said Rob, standing to change the CD and desperate not to be left alone with Emma.

"I think we've established you're not to be trusted with the oven, darling," twinkled Sally, who gave him a kiss on the cheek before skipping off.

Rob took as long as he could loading the CD, trying to pretend he couldn't free the disc from the central hub of plastic teeth, when in fact the sodding thing had popped out first time. Realising that any further delay would be transparent, he turned to Emma with a "Crazy, huh?" shrug. His overarching strategy in business and in his personal life was to say what the other person wanted to hear. Right now he possessed neither the time nor the clarity of mind to read Emma: he was in the middle of a mental whiteout.

"Who was that at the door?"

"Told you, tourist." Always start with a bluff.

"No, you told Sally it was a tourist. I was the other side of the door, Rob. I heard what the girl said."

Rob turned up the music so Sally couldn't hear from the kitchen. Just when he'd thought he couldn't hate Tiffany any more, she became the soundtrack to the single worst moment of his life so far.

"She said you fucked her. And that you sacked her."

This was a first for Rob. He'd never thought he'd find himself having to deny infidelity because, apart from Louise, his extramarital conquests were literally

91

oceans apart. He certainly never imagined he'd have to be denying infidelity to someone with whom he was already being unfaithful. This was ridiculous. Why was Emma getting so bent out of shape? First: he had not cheated on her when he'd slept with Louise; he'd cheated on Sally. If anything, Emma should be grateful he'd slept with Louise, since the ease of the experience had made him lower his guard and consider a further Island-based fling. Second: Emma couldn't really express any legitimate affront, given that she was cheating, too. None of this was of any particular use to Rob at that moment. Emma wanted an explanation, and Sally would be back from the kitchen at any minute. He was pretty sure Emma wasn't going to blow up in front of Sally, but not sure enough to tell her to shut the fuck up. That might be like trying to defuse a bomb by whacking it with a hammer.

"She's mad."

"Mad."

"Yeah, she's a fantasist. She worked at the hotel, she made a pass at me. I turned her down, and obviously her pride was wounded, because she started making accusations, telling people we'd had an affair. We had to pay her off to get rid of her."

"Why would you pay her off if you hadn't done anything?"

"Hm?"

"Why would you pay her off if you hadn't done anything?" Emma repeated, at a lower volume but with a more insistent tone. The focus of her questioning left Rob feeling like a lobster at the fish market, wriggling on its back and wondering how the hell it had gone from piddling round on the ocean floor to being prodded on a tray with its pincers tied shut.

"I didn't mean pay her off to shut her up. I meant pay her off as in sack her with enough redundancy that she'd go. You know, make her an offer she can't refuse."

"That's blackmail."

"What is?"

"Making someone an offer they can't refuse. That means blackmail."

"Look, I don't know the ins and outs of whatever deal she took. Christophe dealt with it."

"Christophe, the only person who knows about us. Until she turned up."

"Someone else is going to find out if you don't shut up," said Rob, nodding towards the kitchen.

"Are you threatening me like you threatened her?"

"I didn't threaten her."

"You called her a whore. Is that what you think I am?"

"Of course not!"

"How many women have you fucked behind your wife's back?"

"How many men have you fucked behind your husband's?"

Emma threw her drink at Rob's chest. "Oh, my God, I'm so sorry!" she said loudly and coolly, for Sally's benefit.

"What's happened?" Sally yelled back.

"I tripped and managed to spill my drink all over Rob." She leant in close to Rob. "Don't ever fucking touch me again."

There was a knock at the door.

"Rob, can you get that? In between changing your shirt!" yelled Sally, from the kitchen.

"Will do." Rob was already on his way, anxious to get away from Emma, but with his arteries under renewed strain at the thought that it might be Louise returning for more. He opened the door and experienced a hitherto unknown reaction to the sight of Colin: relief.

CHAPTER
SIX

COLIN

Monday, 12 October 1987

"He shouldn't be much longer. He does know you're here."

"Sure, no problem."

"I heard you sighing."

"Just a breath that got echoed. A hiccup would sound like a firework in this corridor."

Colin's quip was dashed against the permanent frown of the implacable Mrs Bisson, the school secretary, who waddled back into her office, with her own sighs of exertion and irritation as she squeezed her squat frame sideways behind her desk. Colin thought it was a bit much to accuse him of impatience, given that she saw the most basic of duties as an imposition on her day, to the point at which she would joke with sparse irony that her job would be easier if she worked at a school devoid of both teachers and pupils.

Colin leant his temple against the grey granite pillar that formed part of the benched alcove in which he was sitting outside the headmaster's office. Even in summer the granite felt cool and damp. Today's oppressively low clouds and clinging drizzle meant the school was pervaded with an atmosphere of dank gloom.

Footsteps echoed from the flagstones in the corridor. A fifth-year pupil whom Colin knew by name and reputation appeared round the corner, followed by Debbie. His heart thudded and he hoped his rising colour was not distinguishable in the dim light of the windowless passage.

"Morning," he said, "what's going on?" Debbie had not been in assembly and they had not spoken since his outburst on Friday.

"Someone would rather instigate a ruler fight than learn about Tudor Britain."

"It was a historical re-enactment, miss," the boy said breezily. Colin repressed a chuckle.

"Be quiet, sit here and wait till he sees you, then come straight back to class."

"Yes, miss," replied the pupil, perkily, sitting next to Colin and giving the confusing impression that they were waiting to see the headmaster together. This was typical of what Colin knew of John Duval, who possessed preternatural confidence. He held himself like an equal of the teachers, and remained regularly unbowed in the face of his frequent punishments. From what Colin could make out he was bright and bored, stirring up lesser minds than his to greater mischief than he was prepared to undertake.

"Mrs Bisson, Duval is waiting to see Mr Le Brocq again," Debbie said, through the doorway. Colin could see Mrs Bisson interrupt her phone call and huff her way to finding a pencil.

"Yes, okay. Will there be any more to join the queue?" she hissed.

"Possibly, I don't know," replied Debbie, with a smile, refusing to be cowed by Mrs Bisson's confrontational tropes.

"How was the night at the fort?" asked Colin, as Debbie made to leave.

"Good. Everyone behaved," she said, with a pointed glance at Duval.

"Including Mr Touzel?"

Debbie was already stepping through the small gate set within the vast oak entrance door, which remained closed during inclement weather.

Colin had prepared a jokey summation of his weekend with "men boasting about boats", as she had put it, but the door shut behind her and his Touzel enquiry remained unanswered. Of course, it was unprofessional to expect her to switch from disciplinarian to friend in front of a pupil, and to be publicly flippant about another member of staff. Plus she had a class to get back to. Or maybe she was still hurt by what Colin had said. The likelihood was that all of these factors had come into play. He pondered how to make it up to her, whether to make it up to her. Wasn't this the disengagement he'd been working towards anyway?

"You can go in now, Mr Bygate," barked Mrs Bisson, as various coded lights came up on her intercom system. Colin stood up and pushed open the door.

"Come in, Colin, come in. Take a seat. Sorry to keep you." Le Brocq was normally a somnolent figure, whose slouch exaggerated his hunch and his pot-belly, but this morning he had an almost skittish air about him as he welcomed Colin into his office. "I had a rather important phone call that ran on somewhat . . . I may as well tell you — in fact, you shall be the first to know. We are to have a visit from our Duke!"

He beamed expectantly. Colin smiled, registering that this was cause for good cheer, without grasping the specifics.

Clearly Le Brocq sensed the vagueness behind Colin's pale smirk. "Ah, I forget, you're not an Islander so you don't know who our Duke is. Care to hazard a guess?"

"I didn't know Jersey had a duke."

"Normandy had a duke. William the Conqueror was his name. He became King of England, but here in this Island his descendants retain the title of Duke of Normandy. Our Duke is the Queen!" Confusion still swirled in Colin's eyes despite this flourish.

"The Queen is coming to visit!" Le Brocq yelped, with a hint of exasperation.

"Oh, fantastic," said Colin. "When?"

"June next year."

"Terrific. Is she just coming to the school?"

"No, it's an official visit to the Island, but the school has always retained a place in her heart, and the afternoon she will spend here will doubtless be a highlight. The foundation stone was laid by her great-great-great . . . Actually, I'm not sure how many greats, better look that up before she comes, but the foundation stone on which this school was built was laid by her ancestor, the Prince Consort."

Le Brocq looked off into the middle distance. It would be an awkward segue, but Colin steeled himself. He took a breath. "Sir, there's something I need to —"

"She's such a delightful woman. A real inspiration." Le Brocq had still not finished enthusing. His features relaxed into a wide smile that made his face seem to deflate. "How can I help?"

"It's a rather delicate matter . . ."

"Will it take long? I should really talk to Mr Boucher about the security arrangements." Mr Boucher was the caretaker who, for some reason, was allowed to indulge in the affectation of a uniform that from a distance resembled that of a policeman: black trousers and jacket with silver buttons and epaulettes. Colin was certain that the Queen would have her own security team, and that they would be considerably more effective than a middle-aged man with a line in foul-mouthed "Porko" jokes.

"I'm worried about a pupil in my A level English class."

"Worried how? If it's to do with his UCCA application, or any kind of academic issue you should speak to his form teacher."

"I've mentioned it to Aidan — Mr Blampied — but he was rather dismissive."

"Who is the boy, and what is the problem?" Le Brocq's tone had shifted to one of wary focus.

"Duncan Labey. Last Thursday I chanced upon him at Grosnez —"

"Why were you at Grosnez?"

"I was having a walk, looking at the sunset."

"And Labey?"

"He said he was doing the same. However, without wishing to be melodramatic, it looked as if he might have gone there to, er, jump off the cliff."

"Really? Why do you think that?"

"He was standing at the edge, he'd raised his arms —"

"He could have been about to do some star jumps."

"Why would someone do star jumps at the edge of a cliff? He could do star jumps at home."

"Maybe he was cold. They're an excellent way of restoring the circulation."

"He really wasn't doing star jumps. I think he would have said if that was what he was doing."

"So you spoke to him."

"Yes, of course. I ended up giving him a lift home."

"There you go, then. All's well that ends well."

"He seemed distracted, absent. He might have been crying."

"Might have been?"

"He was crying. I saw him cry. In the car."

"This is all very . . . circumstantial. I simply can't imagine why a boy like that would contemplate such an act."

"That's what Mr Blampied said . . ."

"Well, he's the boy's form teacher so he probably has a better overview than yourself. How's Labey been since?"

"He didn't come in on Friday. He brought this letter to my home — I didn't read it till Saturday because my wife forgot to give it to me . . ."

Le Brocq leant across and took the letter that Colin held up from his jacket pocket.

"He'd wanted to meet me."

"To meet you?"

"It's probably best if you just read it."

The headmaster put on his half-moon glasses and read through the side of A4 in silence.

Colin's thoughts turned to when he had first read it two days ago. He'd had to go back to Rob and Sally's, but had been inevitably distracted. Duncan had asked to meet him back at Grosnez on Friday evening at seven, saying he had something to tell him. He had felt furious at Emma's forgetfulness, and awful that he had let the boy down further. Still, it meant he hadn't been as focused as usual on how irritating he found Rob, who had himself seemed unnervingly subdued at points. Sunday had seen something of a rapprochement with Emma. Neither had offered any apology, but they had at least muddled forward with renewed civility. Emma had made a real effort to pick up as though nothing had happened. This had been threatened by the revelation that she had gone to the cinema after he had stormed out on the Thursday, where she had bumped into Mike Touzel. Colin had silently seethed that she could do something vaguely social, even in a solo capacity, following a row, rather than worry about him. He was also annoyed that she had gone to see *The Untouchables*, which he really wanted to see, and further piqued by her telling him that it was "crap".

He hadn't spoken to her about Duncan. When questioned in front of Rob and Sally he had said that the letter was an overdue essay dropped off during a suspension for smoking. He'd shied away from telling the truth to Emma to retain some mystique over his post-row whereabouts, and also because of an oft-repeated accusation that he cared more about his pupils than he did about her.

Le Brocq looked up. His previous playfulness had vanished and instead of his usual befuddlement there was a coldness that Colin had not seen before. "Where is he now?"

"He didn't turn up for my class, which is why I came straight here."

"Who's looking after your class?"

"I set them some reading."

"You'd better get back, then."

"What are we going to do about this?"

"Wait for him to come back and knuckle down."

"He says he won't come back to school. Not without speaking to me."

"He says a lot of things. There's a lot of nonsense here. There's a paragraph about a boy in a bubble."

"That's a Paul Simon song. We listened to it in the car."

"It's incoherent babble. As his English teacher, you should be more concerned with his inability to construct lucid prose."

"It's a cry for help. I think we should speak to his parents — they need to know he's truanting."

"I'm sure his parents are well aware of his situation, and are acutely embarrassed. As we speak, his mother is probably trying to prise him from his bed or the sofa or wherever he's chosen to sulk."

"What if they don't know where he is?"

"Then they would have rung us." Le Brocq stood up to usher Colin out.

"He could be leaving in the morning in his school uniform and coming back at night and doing God knows what in the day."

"This is the Channel Islands, not some inner-city drug zone. Please don't project your experiences of the mainland on to us."

Colin took a breath and stood. "Okay, but I want it noted that I raised this. And I'm going to speak to Blampied again."

Le Brocq rose to his feet, holding the letter. "You'll do no such thing. I will speak to Mr Blampied."

"About what? You just said there was nothing to be done."

"You'd be advised to watch your tone, Mr Bygate."

"Apologies, sir, but I can't sit back and do nothing. He contacted me directly, asked for my help. I feel a sense of responsibility."

"Really? You received this letter on Friday . . ."

"Saturday."

". . . then waited till Monday morning to do anything about it."

"This is the first opportunity I had."

"No. The first opportunity would have been when I arrived at half past eight. You waited to see if the boy turned up first. Because then you could have dismissed this for what it is — embarrassing nonsense best forgotten."

Le Brocq handed the letter back to Colin and opened the door. Colin stepped out as the waiting boy was ushered in.

"I just had a call from Duncan Labey's parents," wheezed Mrs Bisson from her doorway. "They came back from a weekend away this morning and it didn't look like he'd been at home. They want to check he's here."

"He's not," said Colin.

"Not in front of . . ." Le Brocq gestured to Duval. He then addressed the boy. "Why are you here?"

"I hit someone with a ruler in Miss Hamon's class, sir."

"Right. That was obviously an extremely foolish thing to do. You'll come in this Saturday afternoon for detention."

"I was defending her honour."

"You can come in the Saturday after as well for that cheek. Now get back to your class."

"Yes, sir."

"We need to speak to the parents, and we need to call the police," said Colin, once the boy had gone.

"Will you kindly refrain from telling me how to run my school? This is an internal matter, and will be dealt with as such."

"It's not internal. We have a pupil who has run away from home."

"Please return to your class."

Le Brocq withdrew to his office and slammed the door. Mrs Bisson stared disapprovingly at Colin. "You'll never make head of department with that attitude," she said.

He wondered what conversation she thought she was commenting on.

He headed back through the quadrangle, where the Edwardian extension, on a smaller scale than the main building, offered an attempt at architectural consistency, before the separate arts block threw in the towel, skulking alone with its faded sixties minimalism.

He was boiling over with frustration at Le Brocq's response, which was even more lamentable than his own. As he approached he could hear that chaos had enveloped his class. Before he reached the door, Blampied sprang out of the adjacent room in a rage.

"It's all right, I'll deal with them," said Colin, quickening his pace.

"Would you mind? How can I tell my class to keep quiet when your lot are jumping round like the damned Beastie Boys?"

"I'm sorry, okay? I was checking on Duncan Labey. He's still absent."

"Right. Is there a law against illness on the mainland? Because over here we let pupils recover in their own time."

Colin stepped in closer. This time Blampied was without his shades, so Colin could see him blink away something: doubt, fear, guilt, he wasn't sure. "His parents rang. He's not at home, and he's not here. So where is he?"

"Somewhere. It's not a big island. Nine miles by five, if memory serves correctly. So he'll show up. Now, how about you show up to class, and do your job?"

"I intend to. And, unlike some people's round here, my job doesn't stop when the bell goes."

"Right now, you're not doing your job at all."

Blampied stalked back in. Colin was about to enter his own class when he spotted Duval behind a pillar opposite the door. "You should be back in Miss Hamon's class," he said, as he passed him.

"What's going on between you two?" leered the boy.

"Are you looking to come in every Saturday from now till Christmas?" asked Colin, his blood fully up.

"Why? Oh, you thought I was talking about you and Miss Hamon," said Duval, with mock affront. "I meant you and Mr Blampied."

"Come on, Duval, why are you doing this? Have you become so institutionalised that you can't cope with life outside detention?"

"Or you and the head. Mind you, I know what his problem is. He doesn't like the idea of one of the golden Labey boys falling from grace."

"Whatever you heard from outside that office is private."

"I didn't hear anything from the office, sir. But I hear other things round the school. I heard squeaky Duncan Labey sold his halo for some ganja from Mickey Rouain."

"Who's he?"

"A guy who sells ganja and other stuff. I've never met him."

"Why are you telling me this?"

"Because this place likes to blame all its problems on me. And there are worse things going on than ruler fights. You should speak to him too."

"Who?"

Duval nodded at Blampied, who was staring through the glass of his door with a look of exasperation at the continued disruption. Colin waved him off and turned back to Duval, but the boy had made himself scarce. Blampied re-emerged.

"Do I have to speak to Mr Le Brocq about your lack of control?"

"However you like to do things on the Island," retorted Colin, and burst into his class with a fury of which his lawless pupils had not believed him capable.

CHAPTER
SEVEN

ROB

Tuesday, 13 October 1987

Christophe put down the phone and allowed his eyes, if not his mouth, to smile. His eyes were his great asset: they took in more than most people's, and let a great deal less out. If the eyes were the windows to the soul, then it was as though his were fitted with mirrored glass: they let people see themselves as they wished to be seen, while concealing his own agendas.

His office was opposite Reception, and he turned off the light before opening the blinds enough to observe. He could see Rebecca, Louise's replacement, giving the bell a polish before carefully using Sellotape to remove the lily stamens threatening to fall where a guest might lean when signing in or out. Very impressive that she chose to attend to such minutiae at a quiet moment when most in her position would have stared blankly across the foyer or glanced through a concealed magazine. But it meant he would have to upbraid that morning's cleaner, whom he knew without having to check the roster was Juanita. It was unusual for her to be so lax. He opened the door a crack and could hear from the Hoovers that the dining room was being cleaned after breakfast and, from the squeak of a wheel at the top of the stairs to his right, that the cleaning cart was making its way down the first-floor corridor. Not that in either case there was a great deal of cleaning to do, the current occupancy being frankly minimal. But what he had just learnt on his phone call might change that.

His eyes narrowed as he caught the glint of what he suspected was a sliver of cellophane from a cigarette packet. Just as he was about to stride out and stand with his toe pointing towards it while glaring at Rebecca, she came out from behind the desk to retrieve it. On a certain level he regretted having had to fire Louise: she'd had a certain brio to which he had responded, even as she had ramped up her price. But realistically she could have no place in his current sphere. Rebecca would work out perfectly, provided his boss could stop himself rubbing up against her, which Christophe was fairly certain he could. The two men were natural compartmentalisers. He was about to step out and congratulate Rebecca on her attentiveness when she turned to greet whoever was walking towards her down the corridor that ran alongside his office.

"Good morning, gentlemen. Have a nice day." She beamed as the two men from NatWest hove into view. She was ignored by the larger man, whose double-breasted jacket wafted around his distended belly as he waddled at an angle, bowed down by his oversized briefcase.

The second man, a skeletal figure who always refused tea or coffee in favour of water, responded in a whiny tone. "Why would I try otherwise?"

Rebecca laughed along, but as Christophe slid out of his office door, once the men had passed, he saw her face register "Prick". She looked startled to have been caught in this act of private insubordination. Christophe let the moment hang. He liked to use silence as a weapon, but he was also momentarily distracted by Rob's absence. The men had been with him for nearly an hour and it was unusual for his boss to leave guests to find their own way out. He preferred to glide across the foyer in the manner of a king escorting visiting dignitaries to the boundaries of his lands.

"Miss Pallot. You appear to have cleaned the bell and trimmed the flowers." Rebecca smiled. She had fallen for his feint.

"I would, however, prefer you keep smiling even after the guests have departed, no matter how onerous they may be."

"Yes, Monsieur Fournier." She nodded, chastened.

"Tell Juanita I need to speak to her, once I have finished with Monsieur de la Haye."

Christophe headed down the corridor to Rob's office, which, in another unusual occurrence, had been left half open.

"Monsieur de la Haye?"

Rob was staring out of the window of his office, but his gaze didn't reach the sand, the rocks, the sea or the boats on the horizon, his focus stopped at the glass, its

rainbow smears of detergent and flecks of dried salt.
Two high tides a day that, with the help of wind, would
send up spray as the waves pounded the sea wall below.
That was why he paid a window cleaner. Fucking Porko
was taking the piss. Were the windows in the restaurant
as dirty? No wonder no one was coming, no wonder he
was fucked. It was the bloody window cleaner's fault.

Christophe stepped inside and shut the door behind
him. "I have some news that may be of interest."

"Have I won the lottery?"

"Potentially. I have just heard from a contact at
Tourism. The Queen is due to visit next year."

"Yeah, I heard something about that. She always
stays at the L'Horizon."

Christophe frowned. "Your father has a good
relationship with the Bailiff. Surely he could persuade
him to advise the Palace that there is now a superior
establishment to the L'Horizon."

"No . . ."

"Or at the very least that there is no finer place in
the Island to dine. If she were to eat here for one of the
official dinners then maybe it would lead to a future
stay. The publicity we would get from a visit, even just
for a meal, would be invaluable."

Rob slid a fan of accounts across his desk. "Have a
gander. There may not be a hotel by the time she turns
up."

Christophe scanned the columns. As manager he
was aware of the day-to-day running costs, but the
figures concerning the long-term loans and commercial
mortgage were new and horrendously bleak.

"As you can see, I'm fucked."

"That has to be an exaggeration. To my mind. It has just been a slower start than anticipated."

"That's only half of it. They're looking at the whole picture. I'm building a fucking house, Christophe."

"I understood it was a renovation."

"Well, the walls have stayed. Some of them. Others were either structurally unsound or my wife didn't like where they were. There was no running water. These people were real Jersiaise. Proper English-as-a-second-language-don't-marry-outside-the-parish types. Spoke Jersey French better than English. Electricity was from some generator powered by cowshit. I'm not kidding. I'm building a bloody house. From scratch. And it keeps changing. Bathroom's where the kitchen was going to be because . . . I don't fucking know."

Rob continued to stare out of the window.

Christophe began, "Costs often escalate —"

"Last night I agreed to a changing room for the swimming-pool. Christ knows why people can't change in the bedrooms, or in one of the summer houses. She gets a changing room, and I get to keep my tree, the one in the driveway. And you know why I agreed to this? Because I needed to leave in a hurry, and didn't want to get into an argument. Oh, yeah, I am quite the businessman."

"These figures are far from catastrophic."

"I was relying on the profits from the hotel to pay off the loans I've taken out to pay the builders, the architects and the structural engineers. I'm not even thinking about the mortgage on the property. And it turns out the income from this place isn't even paying off the interest on the money I owe for redesigning it."

"We reopened late in the season and most people book ahead. It will pick up from the spring."

"That's the hotel. The restaurant should be full all year. It was supposed to soak up any losses. Why aren't people coming?"

"We may be outpricing ourselves for the local market."

"This Island shits money, Christophe. Why aren't they spending it in my Cordon Bleu sea-view restaurant? I mean, where else is there? This is the best food in the best location. It's the place to fucking be."

"It takes time to build a clientele . . ."

"Should I not have been in the adverts?"

"No."

"Stop being so bloody diplomatic — you're coming across as more Swiss than French. What the hell do I do?"

"Some offers on the food and the accommodation would attract —"

"Wait-wait-wait — cut the prices? When we're losing money? No, that's batshit. Plus, this is the dog's bollocks. Do they have offers at the Ritz or the Waldorf? I say we go the other way, charge people a damn entrance fee —"

"That would be unorthodox, and would choke off the numbers even further."

"How can we get them to spend more at the bar? That wasn't too bad in the summer, but not according to these figures! I mean, what the fuck? You oversee the bar staff. Are they just serving tap water?"

"We have to match our expenses to the demand."

"Meaning?"

"At first glance, I would advocate a programme of outwardly indiscernible belt-tightening. Both here and, if I may say so, in your private finances. No one will be aware of it."

"Private finances? Right. First up, I need ten grand by Friday. Cash. As you can see, I don't have it."

"For the house?"

"No. For our recently departed employee."

"I thought the compensation was agreed."

"No. She turned up at my house on Saturday. Handily, just in time to clock the situation with me and Emma. Threatened to blow the whole thing open. Her and me, me and Emma. And, amazingly, it's not the worst thing to happen to me in the last twenty-four hours. Right now, it's pretty much bottom of my list. Have you got a gun? Would you shoot me? If this is a bad dream, I'll wake up, and if it's not, I'll be dead. Win-win."

"She is blackmailing you?"

"I prefer to think she's providing a service, in exchange for a fee."

"The service being?"

"Not sex — don't look at me like that. Silence. The service is silence."

"Did you meet her last night? Was that what I provided cover for?"

Rob nodded. He'd felt increasingly relaxed leading up to his summit with Louise: they would meet with cooler heads, and laugh it off. He was not going to pay, of that he was certain. Not because he couldn't, but because he baulked at being forced retrospectively to pay for sex. Himself, the Casanova of the Channel Isles, being held to ransom by one of his conquests? It was a bewildering phenomenon. She was a conquest damn it, claimed and subjugated. Failure to quash this singular revolt would be a mojo-threatening dent to his self-esteem. She would be crushed with charm.

The first ratchet of unforeseen pressure had been finding Sally at home preparing supper at seven on Monday evening. His practised flair for dissemblance meant he expressed seamless delight at her unexpected presence: she was supposed to be at the theatre with her mother, who had been taken ill with a stomach bug. "Poor thing, give her my best," Rob cooed, while hoping the inconsiderate old cow shat herself inside out. He made much of the bonus of an evening with just the two of them, then snuck off to make an undetected call to Christophe. This prompted a call back that he had made sure Sally answered, which led in turn to him rushing to the hotel to deal with an unforeseen and too-complicated-to-explain emergency, and agreeing to the changing room to abate the relentless campaign against his beloved oak.

He had driven to Bouley Bay in the least conspicuous vehicle in his portfolio, the Mini Moke. It had been bought on a whim, the nearest thing to a beach buggy, but in two years it had clocked up barely a hundred miles. A moderately observant acquaintance, let alone your standard-issue Island busybody, would have spotted the Porsche or the Morgan, the former with its giveaway "J007" number plate, and the latter with the Jersey flag painted on the bonnet. As it was, a thick sea fog blanketed the end of Bouley Bay pier, a squat granite spar sheltering a small harbour, where he took the space furthest from land, next to the sprawl of buoys, nets and lobster pots cluttering the tip. Fog clears, though, and it would not have been an unknown coincidence for him to find himself parked alongside a colleague, cousin, relative of a neighbour, or some other agent of doom, who might, at some later and inconvenient moment, potentially pull at the threads of the swiftly woven alibi he had presented to his wife.

Luckily, his instinct that his set were unlikely to be frequenting a north-coast pub on a Monday night was proved right, and his equilibrium was partially restored. Under the sickly glow of the street lamps the other cars revealed themselves to be three Fiestas with the white on red "H" for hire car, grockle-mobiles, as he called them, plus a purple Volvo and a beige Capri. The vehicles outside the Black Dog, which sat at the bottom of the hill two hundred yards from the base of the pier, were similarly unknown. He suspected Louise thought he would be on edge coming back to the scene of their crime, but on walking in, he couldn't think of a better location. He'd never normally come here, so the staff wouldn't know him and neither would the regulars. This was bandit country. He and his mates had only popped in after watching the Hill Climb because there was literally nowhere else to drink. Unless you wanted to knock at one of the cottages set back from the road and see if they had any home-brewed cider.

His main stress on walking over to sit opposite her in the corner booth was the damage the sticky carpet was doing to the soles of his Gucci loafers. Her demeanour was, thankfully, less deranged than it had been two days ago. She looked beautiful, corkscrew curls and dimples, with a glow that brought back exactly why he'd broken his "never in the Island" rule. Her calm stoked his hopes for an amicable resolution based on flattery, while disallowing the possibility of a second fuck. Not that he didn't want one: on the contrary, he found all that stern pride a massive turn-on, and would love to bring it low. No, he didn't want to give any hint that an ongoing affair was possible. In the forty-eight hours since she had turned up on his doorstep, Rob's ego had de-emphasised the fact he'd had her sacked, and inflated a spurious fantasy that located the primary source of her rage as jealousy at the discovery of his wife and regular mistress.

He had been instantly disabused of this notion. The strident histrionics were gone, but they had been replaced by a simple certitude that disconcerted him even more. He prided himself on knowing how to dance around what he saw as a woman's desires and contradictions, staying ahead of where the demands would land; he dealt in below-the-surface signals. But what Louise presented to him wasn't surface: it was as solid as a sea wall. Although he was not a stranger to this negotiating tactic in business, he was unable to soften the defences of his adversary over drinks, dinner or golf.

"Here we are again."

"Ten grand, or I ring your wife."

"Look, let's talk about this as adults."

"Two nine one seven four. That's your home number. Is your wife at home?"

"Let's leave her out of this."

"Doesn't matter. I saw you had an answering machine."

"Listen, I apologise, but what happened, it's kind of a compliment. For me to risk my marriage by sleeping with you, doesn't that tell you how special you are?"

"Jesus. You're actually going with that? I was going to walk to the phone, be all cold and purposeful. But, fuck it, I really want to hear what you're going to say next."

Rob had loaded his silver bullet, and had no option but to fire. He adapted a go-to line for when his mark was wavering over the morality of a one-night stand or the existence of a boyfriend or husband. "Do I regret the deception? Yes. Do I regret that we're sitting here arguing, and reducing an amazing night to something as tawdry as money? Yes. But it's nothing compared to the regret I would have felt on my deathbed if I'd passed up the chance to wake in the arms of a woman as beautiful as you."

"But you didn't wake up with me. You fucked off as soon as you could. Supposedly to sell yachts in the Caribbean."

Bollocks. His silver bullet was made of tinfoil.

"Last chance, Romeo."

"My wife and I have an understanding."

"Really? Then why didn't you invite me in on Saturday? We could have fucked in the spare room. Or in your bed, if she's so understanding."

When Rob was seven he had fallen off his father's yacht after disobeying his command not to lark about hanging off the side as they sailed out to the Écréhous. His father had come around but refused to extend a hand to help him up the stern ladder. In the roll and pitch of the sea he'd found it hard to swing his legs on to the bottom rung, and he lacked the strength in his arms to pull himself up. His panic had brought him to the edge of tears, which flooded out when his father pretended he'd spotted a shark to give him the impetus to shimmy up. He felt like that now. Helpless against the buffeting of a larger force, but this time without his mother to intervene and pull him up blubbing into her arms. He had nothing. The honeyed words refused to pour out of his mouth and get the woman in front of him to do what he wanted. All he had was a weak counter that he didn't believe. "It's your word against mine."

"True, and if that's all it was, you might be safe. All your mates will back you up."

Absolutely they would, steel traps to a man. They'd all gone by the time he and Louise were getting down to it, but even if they'd been in the room watching he could rely on them to say he'd left with them for midnight mass and a stint at the homeless shelter. "But will Emma cover for you? 'Cause I'm going to tell your wife about that snog you had with her, as well as the fuck you had with me. Time's up."

With that Louise had got up and strode towards the payphone on the wall in the corridor that led to the toilets.

Rob had stayed sitting, stunned. If Louise made that call, what she revealed would feed the beast of Island gossip indefinitely. There would be nowhere to hide from the unravelling of a marriage whose tentacles were wound round relatives, friends, business associates. There would be no place to show his face in comfort. His shining surface would be ripped off, his shell cracked and the dark meat within pecked at and flung by the carrion gulls over whom he had long lorded his golden life. This was his Island, the garden in which he had created himself in his own image, and it wasn't going to be fouled. Terror outweighed pride and he sprang up to follow Louise, affecting a nonchalant saunter that he knew was more of a speed walk.

When he caught up she was at the phone, the receiver lifted, 10p lined up in the slot, and had started to dial, her thumb poised to push in the coin as soon as Sally answered or the machine clicked in.

"Stop. Okay, I'll pay."

He could hear his thin recorded voice down the speaker. "This is the de la Hayes, leave a message for Rob or Sally after the . . ."

Sally picked up. "Hello?" He felt like he was looking over the edge of the world, where the oceans drained into space.

120

Louise replaced the handset and took back the uninserted coin.

"Okay," she said. "Let's sit down again and, as you said, resolve this like adults."

They settled back in the booth. Rob abandoned charm in favour of assertion.

"I need to know that if I give you this you're not going to come asking for more. This is the end of it."

"It will be. You got my word."

"That's not good enough."

"You judging me by your standards? How telling."

"I'm not going to pay only to have you ruin my life anyway."

"Maybe I went in too low at ten."

"We had a deal."

"Good. You're treating this like a proper business exchange."

"Is it enough for you to leave the Island?"

"No. I like it here."

"Then if we meet again, it's as strangers."

"Are you quoting Bob Dylan?"

"What? No, fucking hate him."

"Another reason we can't be together." This was bizarre. Now he'd agreed to pay her off, she was flirting with him.

"I'm going to say it again. If we meet, we pretend we've never met."

"Suits me."

"How do you want it?"

"Cash. I don't think either of us wants to risk a bouncing cheque."

"I'll need a few days."

"Friday lunchtime. Here."

"End of the breakwater. Actually, there are steps over it, which get you on to a little bay. There."

"Midday. On the dot. Or I head to your house."

"See you then."

He had driven round after that, to give truth to the lie that he'd been called into the hotel for something substantial, which he'd decided would be a bill dispute with an irksome and untraceable Mainlander. He'd pulled into the car park at La Corbière lighthouse, then driven straight out again on spotting Pippa La Motte's Lotus Elise. She was one of Sally's myriad cousins and a grade-A blabbermouth. In the end he spent longer driving round than he anticipated and Sally had been asleep when he returned, so in the morning he added being pressed into general hosting duties to the lie of his previous night's whereabouts.

That morning, ten grand hadn't seemed too big a deal, given the hassle he'd saved himself. He was used to it as a figure he could fling around, move from column to column, take from one part of his business and put into another. Now here he was, in front of a dirty window for which he paid twenty-five pounds a day to be cleaned, having been told that even an extra tenner in the red could seize the whole thing up.

"Okay," said Christophe, authoritatively, after a pause. Rob was used to him stepping in with solutions: the older man filled a father-shaped void in his life — he would always offer a hand when Rob had fallen overboard. Still, he doubted he could save him this time.

"You need this money by Friday? No extensions?"

"No. She's not going to believe I don't have it. She's a fucking maniac. I want her off my back."

"It is possible."

"What is possible?"

"For me to get you that money."

"Ten grand? Where from?"

"You pay me well, I have free board and lodging here at the hotel. I am not a big spender."

"Christ, you'd do that?"

"Monsieur de la Haye, you have given me everything. I was a waiter and now I am manager of the finest hotel in the Channel Islands, which I have no desire to see closed."

"Well, your ten grand will save me, but it won't save the hotel. I mean, Jesus, I don't even know when I can pay you back."

"If you'll put me in charge of your business affairs, you'll be able to pay me back by this time next year."

"You want to run the hotel proper?"

"It strikes me that your strength is your vision, your commitment, your business relationships and the capital you put into projects. You are not so concerned with minutiae, and why should you be?"

"Yeah, I guess I'm a big-picture kind of guy."

"Yes, you are macro. I am micro."

"Absolutely. Wait, which one's which? I get confused."

"Macro big, micro small."

"Of course. Sorry, I'm very tired."

"I would also want to assist regulation of your personal finances."

"So you'd be, what? My business manager?"

"Exactly."

"In return for what?"

"I would like a five per cent stake in the hotel, and a rise commensurate with my new duties, to come into effect only if I deliver what I have promised, that I can turn things round in a year."

The two men shook hands, then at Rob's instigation, hugged.

Christophe locked the door of his suite behind him and opened his wardrobe. He tapped in the code for the room safe and grabbed the half-empty bottle of his favourite cognac, Forgeron 1974, from beside it as the lock sprang open. He fetched a tumbler from the bathroom and sat on the edge of the bed. A smile flitted across his usually impassive face as he poured himself a measure, which he couldn't stop turning into a grin. His natural sombreness then reasserted itself as he raised a silent toast to the skimmed notes bulging out of the safe.

CHAPTER
EIGHT

COLIN

Tuesday, 13 October 1987

Colin looked at the dashboard clock — 7:15. He was
sitting in his car outside the Labeys' house. He'd pulled
up at six thirty, told himself he'd give them time to
finish supper and knock on the door at seven, then
crashed through his deadline in a paralysing fog of
doubt. A light rain was falling. The scattered drops were
backlit by a lone streetlight, turning the windscreen
into a mini-constellation that he occasionally cleared
with the wipers to pass the time. The ignition key was
in its first position, to allow for heating and music.

Mark Knopfler's guitar was delicately cascading
around his gruff voice, like a mountain stream tinkling
through rocks. Colin imagined the protagonist was
singing about him in the chorus, which also gave the
song its title, "The Man's Too Strong". After today's
battering he felt a rising resilience, which he would
need to ford the Rubicon that lay before him: Duncan's
front door.

Following the boy's continued absence that morning,
he had power-walked out of school in the lunch-hour to

the police station at Rouge Bouillon, favouring a face-to-face over a fobbing-off on the phone.

In the event it had been a fobbing-off. The desk officer had told him that since no crime was being reported, there was nothing he could do. Colin insisted on speaking to the detective who dealt with missing-person reports.

There was no such person. "We don't have missing people in Jersey."

He then requested any available detective, adding that he had only twenty minutes, and was told, "Policemen have to have lunch, you know." He refrained from retorting that he wasn't aware of having advanced a contrary position and instead stated calmly that he would wait before settling into an orange moulded-plastic chair with one leg marginally lower than the others. He spent his time being incensed at the askew angle of the poster on the wall opposite him, the unnecessary apostrophe in its exhortation to "Think twice before leaving valuable's in your car!" and finally his own anal tendencies, which prevented him relaxing.

Five minutes before he had to leave, an officer had emerged from a door behind the desk, crisp shards dusting his sandy moustache, and ignored Colin to banter with his colleague.

"You all right there, Ted? You're sweating like a Guernseyman doing his times tables."

"It's too hot in here — it's like my wife's in charge of the thermostat."

"Tell me about it. I risk losing a hand if I go near mine when Eileen's in the house."

126

"I thought my heating bills would go down when my old girl got the hot flushes. Not a bit of it."

"So, who's pulled me off my pasty?"

The desk officer had nodded at Colin, who had stood up and offered his hand across the desk.

"Colin Bygate."

"Detective Sergeant Vautier."

There was the usual flicker at the oddity of Colin's surname, then his own twitch at the strength of Vautier's grip. The man's stomach was large enough to render the buttons of his jacket redundant, and those on his shirt were surrounded by tiny fault-lines from the strain of holding things together when he sat. Colin quickly reattributed his physique as muscle gone to seed rather than out-and-out fat. A weightlifter who'd lost his drive.

"How can I help you?"

"Well, as I explained to your colleague, I'm a teacher at Normandy College, and we have a pupil who hasn't turned up."

The man snorted. "You've given me indigestion over a registration issue?"

"He's not at home."

"So why aren't his parents here?"

"I don't know."

"You've taken it upon yourself to report this?"

"Yes."

"And when was he last at school?"

Colin hesitated, then answered. "Thursday," he said, omitting the Grosnez encounter.

"Domestic issue. He's not been gone long enough to raise concern."

The desk officer coughed himself into the conversation. "I did point this out, Barney."

"I thought it was two days. On the mainland I'm pretty sure it's two days. Before people can be considered missing," said Colin, with an accusatory tone he instantly regretted.

Another look between the two behind the desk. "We're not on the mainland, though, are we?" said Vautier, any warmth in his smile negated by the sudden hardness behind his dull eyes.

"No, I know that. I didn't mean —"

"We're on an island. Know what that means? Surrounded by water. No way off it. So he's not really missing. He's just not where he's supposed to be."

"Shouldn't we try to find him?"

"He'll turn up. Kids run away from home occasionally. They can't go anywhere, they come home."

And that had been that. He'd walked back up to school, too agitated to eat. Twenty minutes into his first class of the afternoon Le Brocq's face had loomed at the door's window and he'd found himself in the corridor getting a hushed dressing-down.

"I've just had a call from an officer at Rouge Bouillon police station."

"Really? Is he reporting me for reporting a possible crime?"

"The only crime here is that you have wilfully disobeyed my instructions. The situation will be dealt with internally."

"The 'situation' involves a missing child."

"He's not a child, he's a young adult, and I'm sure he's perfectly all right."

"I'm sorry, I find it hard to square the fact that you show more concern about my liberal attitude to homework deadlines than you do a pupil going AWOL."

"Bandying about over-the-top phrases like AWOL serves only to heighten your sanctimoniousness. You don't seem to understand the ramifications of creating a song and dance about nothing."

"No, I don't. Say we look for him, and he turns up anyway, what exactly is the problem?"

"Do I need to spell it out? This kind of unpleasantness could cast a pall over Her Majesty's visit, maybe even cause her to abandon it."

"But you said he's fine. What unpleasantness are you imagining?"

Le Brocq's index finger rose, like a baton. "This is the last time we shall speak of it. Do I make myself clear? Those are the wishes of myself, and the wishes of his parents. Nobody but you wants to draw attention to this matter, which will resolve itself."

Colin flinched at the tone and gesture. "I am a teacher here, not a pupil."

"And if you are unhappy with the way I run my school I am sure there are plenty of establishments back on the mainland that would welcome you. Although on current form you would be unwise to expect me to provide the most glowing reference."

When the bell rang at the end of the day he had walked home in a drizzle that was not discomforting enough for him to bother opening his umbrella. He preferred to grasp it in the manner of a weapon, ready to strike out at anyone who crossed him. He just wanted to go home, shut the door and scream.

As he approached the entrance to the block, he saw Ian Mourant, from one of the upstairs flats, caught in the tractor beam of Mrs Le Boutillier's conversation. Colin took an immediate right and two lefts to work his way through the back-streets and come up behind the entrance, near his car. He knew from experience that if he passed them, Ian would slip away, leaving him stuck in an exchange for which he did not have the energy. He would sit in the car and wait till he could get home unimpeded. Ten minutes or so would do it. The damp of the drizzle had begun to chill him so he started the ignition to get some warm air going, and before he knew it he was pulling out, passing the entrance where Ian was still nodding blankly, and heading out west round the curve of St Aubin's Bay. As he had neared Grosnez, he was gripped by a defiant determination to do things right and headed for St Martin, retracing his journey of the previous week.

The impulse had faded when he found the house and saw the lights within, but the sense of duty remained as an ache.

Now he gave himself to the end of the album, turning up the volume on the long fade of "Brothers in Arms", a song of bravery and loyalty, savouring the full intensity of the solo, then sat staring ahead as if hypnotised by the tape hiss. The cassette clicked to a stop and he switched off the electrics, got out of the car and walked towards the front door.

Three firm knocks led to the wide, low burgundy door swinging open under its sagging frame and a small woman, her greying hair held back in an Alice band, peering out at him.

"Mrs Labey, I'm Colin Bygate, Duncan's English teacher."

"Oh, yes, I remember you from parents' evening. You said he had a flair for practical criticism." She smiled sweetly but firmly, giving no sense of disquiet.

"Yes, he does. Very bright son you have. Is he back yet?"

"No. We've still no idea where he is."

"I presume Mr Le Brocq told you I saw him at Grosnez on Thursday, and that he also wrote me a letter."

"He did. He said you bumped into him looking at the castle."

Colin hesitated. He couldn't bear to tell her his awful suspicion. "Yes. And then the next day he wrote me a letter, saying he wouldn't come back to school unless he talked to me. Unfortunately I missed him and —"

"You look awfully burdened, Mr Bygate. Please don't be. Especially now he won't be going back to school at all."

"Why is that?"

"Apologies, I see you've not been kept fully informed. I'd rather not discuss this further if it's all the same . . ." She began to close the door.

"I went to the police earlier. They seemed very blasé."

The door stopped halfway. "Why ever did you do that, you silly man? Come in — I don't want next door hearing all of this. Their bloody curtains are twitching already."

Colin stepped inside. "I have a similar problem with my neighbour."

"Everyone does, affliction of the Island. I'm afraid I've never quite got used to it."

"You're not born and bred, then?"

"No, I'm a Somerset girl."

"Ah, I'm Bristol."

"Fancy that."

She took him through to the drawing room, the walls of which were hidden by a cram of pictures that gave the effect of a mosaic, featuring seascapes, naval vessels, old maps and engravings of Victorian Island scenes.

Duncan's balding father put down the paper and stood up from his green velvet winged armchair. He had one eye that stared out further than the other, as though he was missing a monocle, although Colin couldn't be sure whether this was an effect of the low light, which came from a reading lamp and the flickering of a fire.

"Arthur, this is Mr Bygate, Duncan's English teacher."

The father offered his hand and a whiff of hair tonic.

"I'm sure he meant well, but he's been to see the police about Duncan," she continued.

"Hell's teeth, man, what did you do that for? Is this Le Brocq's idea of keeping a lid on things?" exploded the man.

"Mr Le Brocq has just kept saying that the situation will resolve itself, which to me seemed . . . irresponsible."

"Duncan will turn up, and he'll face the music from us," intoned Duncan's mother, with an odd resignation, as though she was talking about unavoidable frost damage to a rose. "Le Brocq will say nothing provided Duncan is moved to another school, probably on the mainland. Which is best for all concerned. So, you see, there really is no cause for concern, Mr Bygate. Matters are in hand."

"I don't see why Duncan should have to move schools, and board on the mainland, simply for truanting."

"Truanting's just the tip of the bloody iceberg," fumed the father. "And here's the rub. If Le Brocq would take him back, I wouldn't send him there. I would not want my son at a school that overlooked cannabis peddling. My son's a bloody drug runner. He's damn lucky Blampied didn't call the police."

"Arthur, please, how is that keeping things quiet?"

"I think once Mr Bygate realises the seriousness of the issue it'll stop him making it worse by trying to involve the authorities. The reputation of the school is at stake here. The Queen is not going to show up at a place where pupils deal drugs, then threaten to accuse teachers of touching them up when they're caught bang to rights."

"Duncan said Mr Blampied assaulted him? Sexually?"

"He told Blampied that was what he would say if he went to Le Brocq or to the police," said the old man, staring wistfully at the fire.

"When was this?"

"Caught him with it on Thursday, apparently. Idiot. First Labey in four generations not to finish at that school."

"Poor Mr Blampied didn't know what to do," enjoined the mother, sympathetically. "Once Duncan had disappeared, of course he went straight to Le Brocq. We only found out all of this yesterday."

"Shouldn't we be trying to find Duncan, to hear his side?"

"What do you mean, 'his side'?" sneered the father. "There are no sides. There is only the truth."

"But we have only Mr Blampied's version of events."

"You would doubt a colleague?"

"You would doubt your son?"

"Of course I would, if he said something ridiculous. Which in this case he has. I was at school with Aidan Blampied's father. The man was not raised a liar."

"Duncan obviously panicked at what a mess he'd made of the situation. He'll come back when he realises there's nowhere to go. But, like I say, we'd rather all this was kept within the four walls, Mr Bygate," added the mother, her eyes wide with admonishment. "Now, if you don't mind, I have a quiche in the oven that will be burning."

Half an hour later, Colin walked into his flat to see Emma sitting on the sofa, her face set against him, he presumed because of his unexplained absence.

"Sorry," he began, "I know you don't like me going on about work all the time, but there's a pupil who's missing. I went to see his parents, who are just weird, so

134

cold. Don't repeat this, but it sounds like he was caught with drugs by a teacher he then accused of making a pass at him. It's a total mess."

"Sounds bad," she said neutrally. "You have some post — I opened it by mistake. Thought it said 'Mrs Colin Bygate'." She gestured to a card poking out of its envelope on the coffee table.

"Fine, no worries. What is it? One of Mum's epics?"

"No, I know her writing and, besides, I don't want to read anything negative about myself."

"Come on, she really likes you. That was one day, and everyone was a bit tired." Emma had once overheard Colin's mother refer to her as "abrupt". "It was my fault — I forgot to spike her tea with gin."

Emma was unmoved by his attempt at levity. "You should read it."

Colin picked up the card, which had the image of a little girl walking by a stream with a hand on a protective-looking bear, and felt himself colour under the affronted gaze of his wife and the recognition of Debbie's handwriting. He scanned it quickly, praying for nothing incriminating — but how could there be? There had been no crime. Yet something had to explain the smart of betrayal that Emma clearly felt.

Dear Colin,

I thought it best to write as you seem to be avoiding me at school and there are things I really need to say to you. I haven't slept well since you rebuked me for behaving as your girlfriend, out of guilt, embarrassment, shame, and the realisation

135

that feeling like that was what I enjoy about our friendship, and that I have been fooling myself into hoping that you felt the same way. I realise that I have emotionally overstepped the bounds of friendship, which is not healthy for either of us. For you, because you are married, and for me also because you are married. Allow me to say this once on paper, for I shall never summon the strength to say it in person: I wish that you weren't. But you are, and I need to remember that. However, I do not think I am entirely to blame. The way you are with me made me forget that you are a husband to someone else. Like I say, I overstepped the bounds, but I always felt that you were beckoning me on. I'm not accusing you of deliberately misleading me, rather of a minor carelessness that has resulted in a major heartbreak.

That said, maybe this honesty, combined with a little bit of time, will enable us to renew our friendship on an acknowledged platonic basis. That is my hope for, if you will allow me one last moment of disinhibition, I miss you greatly.

Your friend,
Debbie

Colin's hands fell to his sides. "Emma . . ." he began, trailing off in the expectation that she would interrupt with a tirade, but she just stared at him. "This is awkward, but she makes it clear, nothing ever happened . . ."

"That's because you're a fucking coward."

"No, it's because I'm your husband."

"That's all that's stopping you, though, isn't it? If you weren't married to me, you'd be with her. Is that why you hate me?"

"Of course I don't hate you."

"Well, you don't love me. You haven't made me feel loved for a long time."

"That's not true! I love you —"

"You don't make any effort with me —"

"What about your birthday?"

"When you took me to a flash hotel so you could fuck me? Like some kind of whore?"

"Hey, listen —"

"Were you thinking of her? Is that how you came? Imagining you were in her cunt rather than mine?"

"You're being horrible. Don't use that word."

"How about from now on you fuck me from behind, make it easier to pretend it's her, or should I get a mask made? And a tit job? Is that why you like her? Because her tits are bigger? Or do you like me because I'm flatter, so you can pretend I'm a boy, you fucking faggot?"

"Shut up! All right? Fucking shut up! What are you talking about?" Colin screamed, as he lunged towards her.

"You want to hit me? Is that what you want to do?"

"Don't be ridiculous! I would never hit you!"

"Your fists are clenched. I think you want to hit me. Go on, hit me. I deserve it,"

"What are you talking about? Let's just calm down."

137

"So you can sweet-talk me like you did her? No fucking way. Stop being so spineless — make a choice. If you want her, go have her. At least have the guts to tell me you don't love me, that you love someone else."

"What is this? Do you want me to leave?"

"Oh, you'd bloody love that, wouldn't you? That would suit you just fine, let you off the hook!"

Colin crouched with his hands on his head. "This is insane! We both need to take a moment, get some perspective . . ."

"I agree," snapped Emma, and headed for the bedroom, emerging moments later with a small suitcase. "I'm going to my parents. You need to think about what you've done, and whether you deserve forgiveness."

"When did you pack?"

"What's that got to do with it?"

"You had that bag packed already. You've been sitting here, waiting for me, knowing that you were going to judge me whatever I said and walk out."

"Oh, I'm sorry. Is there some miraculous defence that would explain all and restore your fucking angel's wings? Because it seems you've had the chance to offer one, and you've said nothing."

"You've been looking for a fight for weeks. Months. You want to go and this is your excuse. You're the coward."

"Don't try your pathetic psychological insights on me. You think you're so wise and full of insights, and 'Oh, I've read lots of stupid books so I know about human nature.' Well, I'll tell you one thing your books can't tell you. How to fuck me so I'd forgive you anything."

With that she was out of the door, and Colin found himself lying on the floor, too numb to cry.

CHAPTER
NINE

ROB

Wednesday, 14 October 1987

Rob gunned the engine of the Porsche, then added four blasts of the horn in time to the keyboard stabs of Van Halen's "Jump".

"Bloody grockle," he muttered, at the Ford Fiesta hire car squatting on St Clement's Coast Road, its hazard lights blinking as the driver peered between La Rue de Samares on his left, Green Island car park on his right and the map lying in his passenger's lap.

Two miles up the road, Rob had pulled out from the Bretagne brimming with the euphoria of second chances. He'd spent the morning hunkered in his office with Christophe, rowing his personal and professional affairs back from the financial storm, by whose advance gusts he was already being rocked. Item one on the agenda was the liquidation of Rob's share portfolio, which Christophe insisted was done as a matter of urgency. That money was to be ploughed straight into the business in order to turn zero from a mirage to an actual point on the horizon.

"Jesus," Rob had said, "you know you're in the hole when it'll be a relief to be classed as having no money."

That agreed, Christophe had confirmed he could help him assuage his vengeful one-night stand by providing him with ten thousand pounds in cash on Friday morning. His marriage saved, Rob concurred that he would have to make clear to his profligate wife that the era of "Whatever you want, darling" and "Rip it out and start again" was over. The shiny new concepts of "budget" and "time frame" were to be introduced into her dream-home project.

Having played to Rob's victim status in helping him bring the women in his life to heel, Christophe had then tried to balance the books of his personal life, cutting a swathe through his indulgences and sparing the playboy no blushes: he didn't need to be a member of three golf clubs and two tennis clubs, he didn't need to run the Porsche, the Morgan and the Mini Moke and, given that he had never enjoyed a single theatrical performance in his life, his ownership of a box at the Opera House was nonsensical. Rob protested that having it was about being seen, but conceded that since he never went this was a far from cost-effective self-promotional tool. Christophe had ended on an upswing, pointing out an unused mooring buoy in the bay overlooked by the hotel. Rob could make a considerable annual saving if he was to move his motorboat there from the exclusive marina at St Helier harbour. Rob was delighted by this blatant appeal to his vanity, so much so that having a flash car parked out back and a flash boat moored out front barely registered as a sacrifice. He saw it as a ballsy move, pulling away from the herd, implying they needed his kudos more than he needed theirs.

"Yes-yes-yes, love it!" he had exclaimed, giving a little two-punch to the air and a triumphant handclap. "Bloody Richard Carrière is such a patronising old shit. I mean, he inherited that marina from his dad anyway. What's he got to be so snooty about?" Rob thought he saw Christophe's lips twitch in a smile. "Yeah, okay, I know Dad handed me this place, but look what I've done with it — will do with it." Christophe had assured him he had been smiling at the idea of Carrière losing such a prominent client.

They had spent another couple of hours restructuring the business plan for the said hotel, although this had largely consisted of Christophe talking and Rob filling the gaps with nods and assertive phrases like "Yup, action that" and "Bang. Done. Next." His sole contribution, thrown in as he headed off, was the idea of altering the menu in the wake of the putative regal booking.

"Name some shit after her — the Royal Steak, Windsor Pie . . ."

"What is Windsor Pie?"

"I don't know — pie with the word 'Windsor' in front of it. Leave that to the chefs. This is all about image. We should get her to have afternoon tea. Then we can announce the 'Royal Cream Tea' afterwards. Scones and sarnies cost fuck-all, but *Telegraph* readers with crazy eyebrows will chuck tenners at it, especially if they think they're sitting in a seat where the Queen once sat. In fact, wherever they sit, tell them it's a secret but they're on 'the throne'."

He had then set off on a grand mission of financial streamlining. He would visit the sports clubs to terminate his memberships, the garages to arrange the sale of his cars, and the marina to give notice on the berth. He'd also drop in on his stockbroker and quietly close his account, then go home to steer his wife away from the "simply must-have" ranges towards the compromise of overpriced but affordable. Cancelling the theatre box might be tricky — Sally still liked that kind of crap, and her mum was a big noise on the local drama scene. He might present it as something that had to go, which could then be granted a reprieve in return for some compromise on her part, like not spending more on the curtains than the bloody window frames.

While Christophe had been doing the grunt work, talking through the figures, Rob had been working out how to mitigate the embarrassment of these public financial climb-downs. He'd spin it that the golf clubs were getting the heave because an associate had given him lifetime membership of Gleneagles, that there was no point in belonging to two tennis clubs when he was having his own court built at the house, that the Porsche's sublimity meant his arse only made biannual contact with the seats of his other cars, and that he wanted to be able to see his boat from the window of his office. The disposal of his shares would never become public knowledge: Rick was bound by confidentiality. Sally he would come clean with. All riches were finite. Even Croesus had had to tell his wife, "Stop." He was pumped and ready, the sun had shone, the traffic had flowed and he felt the hand of Fate beckoning him forward, like a policeman telling him to cross a junction. And just when he should have been opening up the throttle while Eddie Van Halen demonstrated why he was the world's greatest guitarist (Clapton and Knopfler being close second and third) by hammering up and down the fretboard, like Bach with a Gibson, Rob's mojo was being crushed by the chicken-headed tit blocking the road in front of him.

"In what fucking country is it okay to just stop for no reason on a bend?" He sighed, pulling out to overtake while adding another horn blast. As he lurched forward, so did the hire car, the driver having decided to blight Rob's day further by taking up a halting vanguard on his route.

"Oh, screw this!" cried Rob, and took the freed-up left turn, heading for the inner coast road and hopefully a run out east to Gorey and the Royal Jersey Golf Club in which he never slipped under third gear.

As he bombed up the road past the new estates with their creamy exteriors and orange roofs, the converted granite farmhouses with incongruous uPVC windows, the Edwardian houses, whose grandeur had been smirched with pebble-dash, and the occasional field of tomatoes, he realised this detour would take him close to the Samares Tennis Club. He would go there first, then the Royal. Although, thinking about it, maybe he should retain just one of his three golf-club memberships and, as the most prestigious, the Royal was the one to keep. They all had their merits, though.

The Royal was the closest to the hotel, but St John's was closer to the new house, and Les Mielles way out on the west coast was the furthest away but had the best course. Maybe it would be better to take a breath and make a decision in the clear light of day. Go to Samares, though, he thought, taking the left back west towards town, a wider road whose sizeable properties on one side were dwarfed by the manor house and grounds that they overlooked on the other.

Yup, death to the tennis clubs, stay of execution for the golf clubs — he needed places to drop in for a drink where the right sort were relaxing at two or more of the Island's compass points. You couldn't put a figure on that, much as Christophe might try.

Both the tennis clubs could definitely go, though. He would do that right now. It was a no-brainer: he would have his own court. That was a fact . . .

But, damn it, there was a queue for the car park! What with all there was to do that day, Rob decided there wasn't time to sit in traffic, and actually, now that he thought about it, if he pulled out of both Samares and Les Landes, he wouldn't have anywhere to play tennis in the short term. His logic snagged: he didn't own a functioning racket, and hadn't for two years, but it was less about the tennis and more about the social scene, not forgetting the ample opportunities for seeing women in short white skirts working up a sheen of sweat. So, on balance, probably better to wait until his own court was built and functioning before he pulled out of the clubs. Over the thirty seconds it took Rob to reach this conclusion, the queue had dissipated, but he'd made up his mind and roared off, fully intending to drop in on his old pal Rory Sarre at Five Oaks Garage and see what kind of price he'd get for his surplus vehicles.

He wasn't ditching Christophe's plans wholesale, just reconfiguring those elements that concerned him directly. The changes to the running of the hotel, well, that was different: a lot of it made perfect business sense, but in truth it was hard to separate the two. Christophe wanted Rob to pull every string he could to secure patronage for the upcoming royal visit, then spread the word that it was happening. But how could he do that without working his contacts at the golf and tennis clubs? That was the clincher, no question. Those would have to stay, at least until the visit was secured. Ditching the *Royal* Golf Club felt less like a bad omen and more like suicide. To realise Christophe's plans to stabilise the hotel's future, he had to modify them for his own financial future. That's what Christophe didn't understand: the "perks" and "indulgences" that he was seeking to exterminate were precisely the kind of living advertising that drove Rob's business. Success breeds success. Act like a god and the world will worship you. He could spin the relocation of the boat as an extension of his hotel, but there was no way he could, say, sell a car without buying a new one and not have it perceived as what it was: a frantic and necessary restructuring of the debts that had suddenly loomed above him, like a wave in the dark.

He was looking forward to the righting of the ship — he loved a bit of slash and burn. Staff would be cut by a third and the remainder made to work harder; Rob's largesse would be replaced with the pragmatism of a man who had worked himself up from fifteen-hour shifts in Marseille bars and Paris kitchens to running one of the swishest hotels in the Island. And Rob was thrilled with the idea of kick-starting some buzz by offering half-price accommodation to bands playing the Fort Regent Leisure Centre: Marillion, Big Country and the Stranglers were all lined up over the next six months. They would make up the loss on the rooms with money spent in the restaurant and the bar by the bands and crew, as well as the locals hoping to mix with the stars. His only panic was the presence of potential groupies and his inability to resist, but he was fairly certain Louise had stopped him ever going off-piste in the Island again. The restaurant would get on its feet with a weekly tasting menu and matching wines for the well-to-do set, and a brasserie menu for those wanting a taste of the high life without the dent to the wallet. All told, everything was back on the straight and narrow, so really no need to dispose of the extra wheels. More to the point, the new house was going to have a four-car garage, and they'd already laid the concrete for the floor, so to change his mind on that would be a false economy, and to have a garage running at 25 per cent occupancy was kind of nuts.

He took a left rather than burn up Mont Millais and on to Sarre's garage, heading instead through town to the marina. He was still going to cancel the berth, once he'd swung by his broker. For one he would enjoy making Carrière feel like yesterday's man. Maybe he'd

147

wind him up by implying he was starting his own exclusive marina in St Clement's Bay. But also, if he didn't take up the mooring outside the hotel, it would be clear visual proof to Christophe that he had agreed to do one thing, then done another. The fact was, cutting all these membership fees and cars was small beer compared to the big chunk of debt his shares sale would clear, but he had to show willing. He didn't want to upset his lieutenant, especially when he was about to loan him ten grand to make Louise go away.

He pulled the Porsche into the car park of an old grey granite building with peeling red window frames, the frumpy aunt of the sexy new buildings at either side, with their reflective glass. Behind this run of offices loomed the south-east face of Mont de la Ville, which, at its modest tabletop peak, was garlanded by a huge wall of large granite blocks, akin to the stones of a pyramid. These were the foundations and walls of Fort Regent, now converted to the venue whose bands he hoped to snare.

Bounding up the narrow stairway, he wondered as ever why the centre of such an awful lot of money should feel like the offices of some provincial theatrical agent. Most of the business was done on the phone, but that didn't excuse the pervasive shoddiness of the place where the phones were answered. Rob had occasionally toyed with moving to one of the flashier brokers, with chrome-pipe furniture rather than the MDF desks that he imagined had been reclaimed from a bankrupt sixth-form college, but he'd never popped into the offices with enough regularity for it to be an issue.

Above and beyond that, Rick was a financial whiz-kid and therefore the one member of Rob's circle for whom he suspended his usual standards of physical deportment. At school the younger boy had taught Rob how to win at poker, and the patronage of the older, cooler, leaner pin-up had signalled a dwindling in taunts about weight and given him the confidence to get his much-commented-upon odour problem under control.

"Hello, how can I help?" asked the pudgy girl on Reception.

Rob decided she must be either new to the business or of limited memory not to recognise her boss's most important client. He was about to deliver a withering introduction when the bulbous Rick Leverrier leapt out of his office to stride open-armed towards him, pausing after the hug to retuck his shirt, which had been lifted out of his brace-pinioned suit trousers by the raising of his arms.

"Robertram!" he declaimed. Rob had acquired this nickname by being head of Bertram House in his final year at school.

"Ricky the Hutt!" Rick's moniker came from his rotundity, which was akin to that of *Return of the Jedi*'s slug-like crime boss. He had cultivated it to replace such unasked-for playground alter egos as "Lord Lard Arse", "Fatty Bum Buckle" and "Tryer Fuck", the latter a particularly cruel reference to both his weight and the late loss of his virginity.

"Julie, drinks, please. Tea, coffee, something stronger?"

"Coffee, black."

"Add a nip of the old barley water? Make it a Mick's coffee."

"Too early for me, Rick."

"Hey, I don't know whether this is the start of the morning for you, or the end of a long night. I'll have the same, love — I've got a head on me today like Captain Langville. 'Declension — *der, die, das, die. Den, die, das,* what?'" He delivered the "what?" with a puzzled furrow, and Rob chuckled at the memory of the elderly teacher of German whose questions in his final years had seemed directed more to himself than his pupils.

"Poor old boy was really losing it by the end. I was in his last class when you could answer him in French and he wouldn't notice." Rick shook his head. "Shouldn't take the piss, really. Did you see his obit in the *Island News*? He was a bloody translator at Nuremberg. Never mentioned it. Imagine dealing with that and then having to put up with us little shits. Anyway, come through. Hold the calls, Julie."

"Sure. Just a reminder that you have Alan Le Motte coming in at three."

"Ooh, see if you can shunt it a bit, till I'm done with Rob."

Rob went in and sat on an orange S-shaped plastic chair, which sagged worryingly under his weight, as Rick shut the door and lumbered to the executive chair behind his desk, his one furniture extravagance.

"She new?"

"Julie? No — been with me years. Why?"

"She didn't seem to know who I am."

"Rare indeed for a woman in this Island. Good call on Exotech by the way — copper's already gone up three points. You don't mind if I keep an eye on this while we wag, do you?" Rick motioned to a small green-screened computer monitor on his desk.

"Not at all. There'd be something wrong if you didn't have one eye on it."

"Exactly . . . Bollocks. Dow Jones is dropping like a stone today."

"August the twenty-fifth was an all-time high, though, so it's still well up."

"Yeah, nothing to worry about long-term. How can I help?"

"Well," said Rob, "I've reached a point financially where —"

"Oh, Christ, I'm getting canned, aren't I? You're moving to Varden's just like every other bastard."

"No."

"Who, then? Don't tell me you're going with one of the UK branches? You won't get the personal touch there. Come on, we have a history . . ."

"Between you and me, I need more money, which is why —"

"I'll up your leverage to fifty per cent."

Rob paused imperceptibly. "Fifty?"

"Yup. I'll take that risk to keep you. I'll be honest with you, having you as a client brings a lot of people in."

"You've always told me forty per cent leverage is the safety line. Most of the time we've walked a steady thirty. I've always pushed for more, and you've pushed

151

back, saying look at the long-term margins, that's where I want to be."

"The markets have changed. Okay, there's that blip today, but we're on a rising curve."

Rob chewed his lip.

"Hey, if you don't want to take the risk, then fine. But I'll make you more money than anyone else can. You know that's the truth."

Rob laughed and extended his hand. "Can't argue with that. You never lose, Rick. You never lost a single game."

"Well, that was poker, and most of the time we were just betting with porn mags."

Julie came in with the coffee and Rick scrambled for something to fill the agonising echo of the last phrase.

"Great, coffee. Nothing like it. They'd ban it if it came out now. Same with alcohol. Read that somewhere. How's the hotel by the way?"

"Awesome. You should come down — it's the only stop-off for the City boys. Hang in the bar with your ears open, you'd pick up a fair few tips."

Julie handed Rob his drink. "It was milk, wasn't it?"

"No, but never mind. We're kind of wrapped up here. I've got to swing by the marina. Unlike you, pal, they are definitely getting canned!"

Hugs, handshakes and promises of untold riches complete, Rob pounded down the stairs two at a time, alive with the certainties of resurgent success. He doubted his heart could have taken that coffee — it would have beaten its way through his sternum. He'd gone in to cash in, and come out with a higher stake.

By expanding his portfolio he'd soon bring in more than he'd have got by selling. This was why he owned a hotel, whereas Christophe was an employee. Big picture, risks, balls, verve, that was business, not piddling around trying to cut costs by using cheaper napkins. He got back in his car, cranked up the ZZ Top and roared off in the direction of the harbour. Seeing how Rick had panicked at the thought of losing him, Carrière and his cohorts were bound to beg him to stay, but he wouldn't. Without his name on the books, any members' club in the Island might as well shut up shop.

He drew up in the club car park and got out to look over the marina. It was low tide so the pontoons were floating thirty feet below him in the water trapped by the sill, beyond which lay the shelter of the Albert Pier, where the passenger ferries and fishing vessels deposited their cargo. It always knocked off the glamour, having to pass those big iron buckets with their rust streaks, although the hydrofoils had a certain futuristic something. In the distance beyond, the Victoria Pier stretched out a second protective pincer on which sat fat yellow and red cranes waiting for the tankers that brought the things the Island couldn't produce itself in sufficient quality or quantity: clothing, alcohol, white goods. The tops of the highest masts nodded slightly at his eye level. Rob never understood why people bothered with sails when technology had moved on. Might as well decline anaesthetic on the grounds you preferred "the old ways".

153

He walked round the clubhouse to the entrance on the other side and glanced down at the drying moorings in the Old Harbour, where the smaller, less ostentatious craft lay on their keels. The draining tide had left ledges and rivulets in the wet sand, greyed over time by oil leaks. This place was not quite dying, but was certainly leached of life. It was definitely time to move on, he thought, as he pushed open the double swing doors to the marina clubhouse as though he was entering a Western bordello.

"Hey, Sheena." He winked at her — a fortysomething woman with a smoker's face and coarse blonde hair — as he signed in at the front desk. "Richard around?"

"He's in the bar, I think," she replied.

"Cheers, doll," he replied, with a grin he mistakenly thought had made her day.

He went into the dark oak bar and saw Richard Carrière sitting on a stool leafing through *The Times*, his trademark red jeans clashing with the orange tan that gave his white hair a tinge of neon.

"Afternoon, Richard," boomed Rob, disappointed that only a few members dotted the bar to witness his withdrawal from the old boy's monstrous clutches.

Carrière swung round. "Rob," he replied, with a tight smile. "Not seen you for a while."

"Yeah, well, I've got more pies than fingers right now."

"That's nice for you. You taking her out today, or just dropping in as part of a roving one-man ad campaign?"

"Ha! Actually I've come to cancel the berth."

154

Carrière's face lengthened, revealing white crow's feet left untanned from a sea-squint.

Yes, thought Rob. That rocked you.

"Oh. Selling her, are we?" The old stag refused to follow the young buck's script.

"No. Why would I do that?"

"To help pay for all those empty rooms. I'm joking — everyone's had a bad season. Isn't that right, Stanley?" Carrière called, to a man with slicked-back grey hair in a yellow polo shirt and blue blazer, who was nursing some kind of pink drink in the corner.

"No, Richard, we've had a boom year at Victor Hugo's. Surprising, 'cause young de la Haye there referred to it as feeling more like a retirement home than a hotel."

"Did I? When did I say that?" asked Rob, puzzled at the bristling atmosphere.

"When you announced the relaunch of your dad's place. The announcement, not the actual relaunch. There was quite a delay between those two events as I recall."

"I don't remember saying that."

"Well, you did."

"To whom?"

"To someone within earshot of a good friend of mine."

"Like I say, I don't recall. But I've no reason to denigrate the Victor Hugo. There's more than enough grockles to go round."

"Not by the look of your front-desk register!" Stanley added, with a laugh. He glanced around for others to

155

join in, but they either weren't paying attention or didn't care.

"Well, filling a hundred rooms is more of a challenge than . . . What have you got? Twenty-five?"

"Thirty-two."

"So even at thirty per cent occupancy, I'd still be fuller than you."

"True, but you'd also be paying a bunch of extra staff to sit around scratching their arses while they wait for a reason to clean and launder the seventy-odd rooms you've got gathering dust. My gaff may feel like an old people's home, but yours is like a bloody stately home you can't afford the upkeep on."

Rob let out a laugh. "Well, I'm going to miss this place."

"Where are you taking her?" asked Carrière, flatly, presenting Rob with some paperwork to sign.

"There's a spare buoy in front of the Bretagne."

"Okay if you move her now?"

"Right now?" queried Rob, blowing on the glisten of his signature.

"My waiting list is in double figures. Someone else will be in by sunset."

"It's a little tricky to do it exactly now."

"Need someone to help you start the engine?"

"I drove here. I'd have to leave the car."

"Well, you've just cancelled the berth and I need to fill it. So if you don't move her, I will."

"Fine, I'll move her now. And then maybe I'll buy up some of the other buoys in my bay . . ."

"Your bay?" echoed Stanley, mockingly.

156

". . . maybe slap in a jetty," continued a stung Rob, "start a nice little marina of my own."

"Be my guest, son. I'm sure it'll be as successful as your other ventures."

Rob left reeling, as though he'd been mugged. He'd show them, stupid old bastards. As he stomped down the gangway to the pontoons, his eye was caught by a large moored sailing boat hidden from his previous vantage-point, and by the young blonde woman in jeans and a hooded sweatshirt lounging on the deck reading the local paper. He stood in front of the stern where he could see her face hovering over the headline "Teacher Concerned For Missing Normandy College Pupil". Big deal, he thought, while waiting for her to acknowledge him. He'll turn up, nowhere to go. She was tanned, and his thoughts turned to the perfectly sized breasts that, given the right weather, she had no trouble displaying for him. He knew that behind the Ray-Bans she was perfectly aware of his presence, and that she was now probably not reading the paper but staring him down, willing him to make the first move.

"Hi," he said, his appetite for games drained for the day.

She put the paper down and sat up. Her sea-salt-knotted blonde hair spilt out from the back of her weathered baseball cap. Rob seethed at her capacity to appear to him so deeply fuckable, even though she was one of the people he most loathed on earth. "Oh, hi," she said. "You surprised me."

"And you me. How long have you been back?"

"A week. We've been sleeping on the boat, though. Doesn't feel right sleeping on land after so many months."

"You did the whole thing from Nice?"

"Yup. Amazing."

"Well, whether you've been sleeping on the boat or not, you've been back in the Island a week, and it would have been nice to hear from you."

"I'm sorry. Have I been a bad mummy again?"

"You're not my . . . I'm not doing this. Is he below?"

"He's just had a shower. His second of the day."

Rob held her gaze, ignoring the allusion to sex. "Can you call him for me, please?"

The woman smirked, stood up and walked to the bow where she called below deck, "Russ, we have a visitor."

A lithe, greying man loomed up from below and kissed her as she went down in turn. He smiled when he saw Rob, climbed on to the pontoon and extended his hand. "Rob, nice to see you."

"Dad."

"How are things?"

"Good. I didn't know you were back."

"Got here a couple of days ago."

"Rachel said it was a week."

"Could well be. Been so many people to catch up with, it's all a bit of a blur."

"Were you planning to catch up with me?"

"I didn't know if you'd be around. You jet about more than I do."

"No, I'm here. Be good to have lunch or dinner. The two of us."

"Absolutely. We're probably back for Christmas."

"What's wrong with before then?"

"We're off to the Caymans tomorrow. Got a bit addicted to the sun."

Rob took a breath, but changed tack. He couldn't bear to articulate what he knew to be true: that if he hadn't bumped into his father he would never have known he'd been back in the Island. "Right," he stumbled.

"How's business?" asked his father.

"Good, really good. Long-term, things are looking like they'll explode." He took a breath. He had faith in Rick, but it would be good to add a belt to his braces. "Medium-term I could maybe do with a bridging loan —"

"That's great to hear," interjected his father, cutting him off mid-hint. "I'm happy it's working out. Glad you're taking the place to new heights."

"Yes, although, since you brought it up . . ." Rob tailed off as Rachel came back on deck, this time in a camisole with her hoodie draped over her shoulders. He could see she wasn't wearing a bra. As she settled back with the paper, he drew his father aside. "Why don't you walk with me? I'm moving the boat."

His father fell in beside him. "Why the move?"

"Easier to have it moored in front of the Bretagne — I'm there more than here. Plus, between us, I'm making economies, talking of which —"

"I'm not giving you any money, Rob."

"I don't want you to give it to me. It would be a loan."

"I made my way, you can make yours."

"I am making my way. I've got plans. Big plans. You know the Queen's coming?"

"Yes, I heard."

"Well, if you won't help financially, maybe you could get Henry to put in a word —"

"Rob, I told you, I'm off tomorrow."

"It would just be a phone call."

"I'm not calling the Bailiff to sort your business problems out. You shouldn't rely on gimmicks. Stick to what works."

"I know you still think I shouldn't have got rid of Sammy Dee . . ."

"This isn't about Sammy, although I hear he's hitting the sauce now he doesn't have a regular gig. It's about change for change's sake."

"The world is changing, don't you know that?"

"I know I started with nothing and that I ended up with some hotels. I gave you one, and you've decided to turn it back into nothing."

"That's not true. And how would you know that anyway?"

"An Islander doesn't have to be in the Island to hear the news, you know."

"Please — have you been listening to those old farts in the clubhouse? I mean, maybe I overstretched at the start, but I've adjusted my business plan. I'll be fine, but any help would be welcome. It would just get me there quicker."

"Sorry. I've helped enough."

"You'd help Rachel. You were going to buy her that stupid café."

"She's my wife."

"I'm your son."

"You're not a little boy any more. When I was your age —"

"Don't bring up age, okay? I'm going to end up saying something I'll regret."

"Your attitude towards Rachel doesn't help. It's been five years."

"So she's twenty-seven now. Still younger than Mum was when she had me."

"She's very mature."

"And I'm not?"

"I didn't say that. Is this you?"

They had arrived at Rob's boat, and both men saw fit to change the subject.

"Yeah. Have you not seen her before?"

"No, don't think I have. She's new, is she?"

"Got her last year. Traded in the old one. Like to update the model."

"Hm." Neither man could decide whether Rob had just made a crack at his father's third marriage.

"If you fancy taking her out, you could help me move her."

"Love to, but you know me. More into wind-power."

"Well, maybe drive the car back for me. Make it a race, winner buys drinks."

"We're due to have tea with Rachel's parents. Good to see you, though, love to Sally."

161

A brief handshake and Rob was abruptly left to untie the boat and cast off alone. He had a humiliating thirty-minute wait till the tide came in enough to allow him to pass the sill, which resulted in some jeers from above that he declined to acknowledge. Ten minutes after that he arrived at his new mooring, then rowed ashore in the cruiser's dinghy to be met by Christophe, blaming his tear streaks and reddened eyes on the wind and spray.

CHAPTER
TEN

COLIN

Thursday, 15 October 1987

Colin stared silently at the staffroom carpet, willing himself to become engrossed in calculating the total number of tiles, anything to distract from the isolation he was feeling from his colleagues. The downcast eyes, the wide berths, the lack of conversation with each other, let alone with him, made him feel they were waiting for something. Whether it was for him to break the silence with an apology or the signal for some preordained attack was impossible for him to determine from his addled cocoon.

Following Tuesday's revelations and walk-outs, he'd woken with a surprising sense of vigour and attack. He'd skipped Wednesday's assembly to give a phone interview to a journalist at the *Island News*, who was delighted to feature Colin's anonymous concerns about an unnamed absent pupil, including his shock at the apathy of the authorities. The paper didn't come out till four o'clock, by which time he was at home. The phone rang at ten past. Colin had supposed it might be a truce-seeking Emma, and had been taken aback to hear her father's voice. He had expected a rebuke for the way he had treated her, knowing it was too much to expect an off-the-record acknowledgement that, while Jack had to take his daughter's side, he had every sympathy with his son-in-law and knew exactly how she could go off at the deep end. But he had not expected to be berated for the article, or for the motives of the journalist to be so impugned.

"Do you know where Paul La Cloche went to school?"

"No."

"Ogiers — so, of course, he wants to make trouble for us. They don't even have a uniform at that hippie coven."

"Jack, a boy is missing."

"Your wife is missing from your home and you didn't alert the media to that unfortunate titbit."

"A missing child is not a titbit."

"You've made it a titbit by not giving his name. Surely you know how this Island works. Everybody will be trying to figure out who it is."

"Good, because no one's given a damn up till now."

"And what happens when they find out he was dealing drugs in the playground? Yes, I know about that! Know his name too, but I'm not going to say it in case I'm overheard. We have fees and an entrance exam so parents can rest easy that this kind of thing doesn't happen."

"The boy needs help."

"It's a bloody witch-hunt, but it's the reputation of the school that will go up in flames. Yours, too. You think Le Brocq's not going to know it was you who spoke to the press? I worked it out in about five minutes."

164

"You mean Emma told you."

"That's not all she told me. It seems your conduct with pupils *and* staff is unbecoming, these days. And I'm speaking to you not as Emma's father but as a member of the board of governors."

"I've done nothing wrong. Emma and I are just having a little difficulty."

There was a pause.

"Aren't you going to ask to speak to her?"

"I didn't think she'd want to speak to me."

"Well, if you need prompting, I'm sure she doesn't."

With that Jack had hung up, leaving Colin to another long late afternoon and evening caged in the flat, apprehensive about handling the shards of his marriage and the barbs of his colleagues.

As he now perched alone and Jonah-like on the staffroom sofa, while his peers stood or milled at a distance, a pair of yellow cork wedge shoes entered the top of his field of vision and paused. It was Debbie — he knew from the ankle, the shape of her calves and the shoes that brought her mouth within kissing range. He knew, too, she was waiting for an upwards glance he refused to bestow. He had no wish to break the silence that hung over the room, certainly not with an argument over the row that her letter had precipitated.

She moved off as the door opened behind him and he felt the swagger of Blampied before he heard his leer. "Well, if it isn't Woodward or Bernstein."

Colin sat back and raised his head, but refrained from turning round. He felt like a kid at the cinema who, having been pelted with a chewed sweet, was hoping time would prove it to be an accident, despite knowing it was deliberate.

"You're awfully quiet, Bygate. Couldn't shut up yesterday, though, could you? Blessed with uncharacteristic loquacity — 'I believe that our duty of care is not limited by the boundary of the school gates,' said a 'member of staff'. You may as well have given your name and bowed, had your photo taken, flash off obviously, else they might catch some flare from your halo."

"Why are you so unconcerned, Aidan? Why is it just a joke to you?" said Colin, speaking softly, determined not to match Blampied's antagonism.

"You don't know what you've done, do you?"

"I don't know what you've done. I'd like to find out from Duncan Labey what it was."

"There you go again, making private stuff public, adding little smears and hints. You actually want people to know what Duncan Labey is running from?"

"I'd like to hear it from him."

"You know, some people could be mistaken for thinking you're calling me a liar. Some people, rather than asking why I'm so laid back about the situation, might ask why you're so uptight. Is everything all right at home?"

Colin shot up from the sofa and turned to face Blampied, with only the furniture to stop him lunging at the man. "That's below the fucking belt."

"Language. That's not a very good example. I hope you don't speak like that in class."

"You found drugs on him, but you took no action."

166

"Why are you so intent on washing dirty linen in public?"

"Why are you intent on washing it behind closed doors?"

"He threatened me with unfounded accusations."

"Why would he do that?"

"To avoid punishment."

"And now he's God knows where."

"Are you sure your time wouldn't be better spent trying to find your wife than your pupil?"

From the edge of his vision he saw Debbie blanch and couldn't stop his eyes darting to her. The flickered smirk on Blampied's face told him he had clocked it too. Colin rounded the sofa and stood nose to nose with him, the other man annoyingly refusing to flinch.

"Where are the drugs, then?"

"What?"

"The cannabis you found on him. Where is it?"

"Are you calling me a liar, just because I don't have it in my jacket pocket? I'm not going to walk round with it. It's illegal to possess it. Are the laws on drugs different where you come from?"

"Where I come from, we tend to let the authorities deal with the laws, rather than hiding it away and fucking it up ourselves."

"Again with the inappropriate language."

Colin seethed with a surge of adrenalin that made him feel he could have picked up the sofa and smacked Blampied round the head with it.

He heard the click and squeak of the door again, and Le Brocq's voice pre-empting whatever snipe would have come next.

"Mr Bygate. Please step outside."

Colin's eyes remained locked with Blampied's. He had never come this close to hitting another human being in his life.

"You are not a good person." To Colin, this was the vilest insult he could have given, but Blampied just snorted as Colin walked off to his fate with Le Brocq. As the headmaster shut the door behind them he heard a collective release of breath, followed by the whooshing hubbub of gossip. He walked alongside Le Brocq in silence through the milling ranks of pupils awaiting the registration bell. When they arrived in the headmaster's office Colin saw the *Island News* on his desk.

Le Brocq stood in front of his chair. "Don't sit, this won't take long. What have you got to say? Doesn't matter, won't change things. You've disobeyed my instructions three times, Mr Bygate. You contacted the police, the parents and the press. You are suspended, Mr Bygate."

Colin shrugged. He had expected as much. "For how long?"

"Indefinitely. Feel free to explore other options during this period. Possibly consider a career away from teaching."

"I'm a good teacher."

"You almost attacked another member of staff just now. And I hear that you may be amorously attached to another. None of this will do. I will discuss your future with the governors at the end of the month. As I said, it is far from rosy."

"May I go?"

"It would be my pleasure if you would do so."

Colin stopped at the door. "You haven't even mentioned Duncan Labey."

"The police are confident they will locate him soon."

"Oh, they're bothering now. Well, that's something. Must have worked their way down the to-do list, washed all the squad cars."

Colin left the front door of the school, passing Mr Boucher as he rang the handbell for registration on the steps. As a final act of childish transgression he strode directly on to the out-of-bounds Conqueror's Lawn and headed for the lower gate, elated by the intrigue among the staff and pupils this was clearly creating in his wake.

As he reached the exit Debbie overtook him and glided to a stop on her bike, having freewheeled down one of the tree-fringed paths that ringed the lawn. He strode past her with a nod.

"Colin!"

He stopped and turned. "What?"

"Look, what's happened to you is completely unfair. You're doing the right thing. But why are you angry with me? Did you get my card? I want us to be friends again."

"Yes, I got your card. Unfortunately so did Emma. Which is why she left. So thanks for that. Next time I find myself with a chip-pan fire, maybe you could come round and pour petrol on it."

Debbie wilted. "Oh, God, I'm so sorry. I didn't mean to be any trouble. I can speak to her, if you like, and explain —"

"Not sure she'd want to speak to you right now. I know I don't." And, having vented his frustration with Emma at the woman he resented for superseding her in his affections, he strode off.

He had little recollection of the walk home as he became lost in an ebb and flow of fury, numbness, outrage and indifference. As he mounted the stairs to his flat he was jolted from his thoughts by the sight of Barney Vautier, the detective he'd spoken to at the station two days before, and a younger man, with dark shiny hair and a beaky nose, chatting to Mrs Le Boutillier.

"Here he comes now, Officers," she said.

Vautier walked down the stairs to meet Colin halfway with a proffered hand, an easy smile, and a day's worth of stubble to add to his moustache. "Mr Bygate."

"You've made me look a pretty fool now. I told these officers you'd be at work," said Mrs Le Boutillier, wearily.

"I was. Why are you here?"

"We heard you might be leaving work early, sir."

"What is this? East Germany?"

"Look, we obviously got off on the wrong foot last time. I apologise. I was unprofessional and dismissive. I'd like to make that right."

Colin shook his hand. "I just want this followed through."

"We all do. Your headline set off some tremors. Our orders have been written on stone tablets and hurled down from the top of the mountain — find the boy."

"Is that the boy we were talking about? Is he the one in the paper?" asked Mrs Le Boutillier, already attempting to descend the steps for a better notion of what was going on.

"Why don't we discuss this somewhere more private?" said Vautier to Colin, turning to gesture to his colleague, who immediately began the slow task of leading Mrs le Boutillier back to her flat.

"What's Mr Bygate got to do with it? He's such a nice young man. How old are you? I don't see a wedding ring. I bet all the ladies find you so dashing, being a detective . . ." She was returned to her abode with her queries unanswered.

As they descended to the street they could hear her moving about, drawing curtains and blinds, and when they made it outside she had opened a window and was beckoning to Colin. "Sorry, Mr Bygate, I forgot to ask, have you seen Marmalade?"

"I'm afraid I haven't, but I'm sure he's fine. Cat," he said, turning to the officers.

It was a short walk to the station. The other man, introduced as Detective Fauvant, proved taciturn, and Vautier seemed keen to focus on small-talk as they ambled along in the brisk sunshine.

Vautier led them into a dingy café just as the station came into view. "You might want to grab a coffee here, Mr Bygate. Not to put too fine a point on it, but the coffee served by the Island's constabulary is bat's piss. That's no lie, is it, Gerry?"

"Not tasted bat's piss myself, Barney. Can't comment."

Vautier turned to the short round man behind the counter. "Two coffees, Mario, one black no sugar, one white three sugars."

"I know the bloody milk and the bloody sugars, boss, you coming in here every day," snapped Mario, in semi-serious rage.

"Easy. I know what your memory's like. Look around, you forget to clean this place. Might have to shut you down. What can I get you, Mr Bygate?"

"Nothing. I'm fine, thanks," said Colin, curtly, frustrated at the delay.

"You all right? You seem a bit on edge."

"No, it's just I'm keen to get things moving."

"Oh, sure, sure, we will. But they'll move a hell of a lot quicker when I've got my caffeine to wake me up. I had a long night. Setting up this investigation. Pretty much five minutes after the *Island News* came out the Bailiff himself rang my super and called him all kinds of things. Five minutes after that I was in the super's office, getting what I can only describe as a right bollocking. Apparently it could be heard two floors down."

"I heard every word, Barney," added Gerry, "and I was in the car park."

"I think they were both so touchy, being old Normans. Don't like to see their hallowed school getting any bad press."

"I'm sorry if I caused you any trouble, internally," offered Colin, uneasy at the tone of the conversation, which had taken on an edge that was noticeably harder yet still deniable.

"Oh, I'm not having a go at you, sir. I just want you to be aware of how seriously we're taking this now. Five minutes after that I was out of the super's office, and I've been playing catch-up ever since. Hence my need for coffee and, come to think of it, breakfast. Mario, slap on a bacon sarnie for me, would you? Gerry?"

"I'm good, Barney, had me some Weetabix."

"Mr Bygate?"

"I've had breakfast. Look, shall we go over what we know —"

"Best we follow protocol and do it at the station. We've got pens and tape recorders and everything there. We shouldn't really discuss it here, in a public place."

"Okay, I get it. You didn't like me going to the paper. I'm sorry, but it has at least got everyone looking for Duncan."

"Ooh, you shouldn't have said his name, Mr Bygate. Naming a minor at the centre of an investigation, that breaks all sorts of rules. Still, I'll let you off with a caution, if you agree to refrain from talking about the case until I indicate that you should do so."

Colin was pretty sure that he hadn't broken any laws, and that it was just Vautier throwing his bulk around, but he grasped the underlying message the detective was conveying: we're doing this my way, not yours.

While Vautier waited for his bacon sandwich, Colin looked over the posters for departed summer-season shows, whose age was given away as much by the grease of the Blu-tack showing through as by the out-of-date itineraries. The three of them then headed for the station in silence, broken only by Vautier cursing at the butter that had dripped on to his tie. Colin hoped that by now he had had his fun and that they could go forward on a more even footing. This seemed to be the case: they treated him with formality and courtesy at the station, and ushered him into an interview room where they insisted they would take his statement and begin the search for Duncan in earnest.

They left him there for an hour.

When they finally unlocked the door and entered the windowless room, his anger had subsided and he had accepted that he had no choice but to play by their rules. They had broken him.

"Sorry about the delay, Mr Bygate. Some information came in that we had to factor in ASAP. Has anyone asked if you want a tea or coffee?"

"No."

"Can I get you one?"

"No, thanks."

"I know I slagged off the coffee, but the tea's not bad. I mean, how can you mess up tea? Bag, hot water, milk, done."

"Tell that to my mother-in-law," added Gerry. His statement had the form of a joke, but his face betrayed no sign of humour.

Colin shifted in his seat, their obfuscating schtick pushing his irritation back up to previous levels. "Do you need the loo there, Mr Bygate?"

"No. I'd just like to get on."

"Really? Is that 'cause you have somewhere to be?"

"He doesn't have to be at work, Barney. He's been sacked."

"Suspended," corrected Colin.

"You should have remembered that, Gerry. We just spoke to Mr Le Brocq and he clarified the situation," said Vautier, closing the door and sitting opposite Colin. Gerry joined him and they laid out various folders, notebooks and a tape recorder.

Colin clenched his jaw, determined not to ask if they'd dragged him in here knowing they were going to leave him to sweat for the last hour.

"You look worried, Mr Bygate."

"I'm not worried, just tired."

"We wanted to get you in here to sort out the timeline of events. We've spoken to other concerned parties, such as Mr Le Brocq just now, and Duncan Labey's parents last night, so we have a pretty good idea of the movements of the key players. We'd just like to see how you fit into that."

Colin nodded, not wanting to say another word. Vautier pressed PLAY and RECORD. "Thursday, the fifteenth of October 1987, preliminary interview with Colin Bygate. Present are myself, Detective Barney Vautier, and Detective Gerry Fauvant. Interview begins eleven ten a.m." Vautier sat back. "Just a bit of background first, if you don't mind. You've been in the Island how long?"

"Three years."

"And before that you were teaching where?"

"Nowhere. I was training to be a teacher. Normandy College is my first job."

"And what is your relationship with Duncan Labey?"

"He is a pupil in my A-level English class."

"Do you see much of him out of class?"

"Not at all. I mean, I see him around the school, might stop for a chat, but no contact at all outside school."

"And you noticed he was missing when?"

"He's been absent from school since last Friday. I mean, I told you all this on Tuesday, and I'm sure Le Brocq has told it again to you just now. When you had me in here waiting as part of your mind games."

"Mind games. You think that's what this is?"

"Totally. You're giving me the runaround because I made you look bad in front of your superiors."

"I'm not sure we're the ones in this room playing mind games. You see, when you first came to see me, yes, you told me that Duncan Labey had last attended school on the Thursday, absent since the Friday. But when we spoke to Mr Le Brocq just now, he told us that you had told him that you'd seen Duncan Labey out at Grosnez on the Thursday night. Yet you never mentioned this to me."

Gerry took the invisible conversational baton. "Didn't mention it now when we asked if you had any contact with him outside class."

"I don't have any regular contact."

"You said 'no contact *at all* outside school'. I can rewind the tape if you like."

"You were asking me general background questions. Obviously I was going to mention it when we came to the specifics of his disappearance."

"And why didn't you mention it to me when we first spoke?"

"As you've acknowledged, you were pretty dismissive. There wasn't time to go into details, and I didn't want to overcomplicate things —"

"You think it would overcomplicate things to let us know you were the last person to see the boy alive?"

"No, that would be his parents on the Thursday evening. I dropped him home."

"Yes, so we gather. Again, not from you. Thing is, his parents were already away that night. So that really does make you the last person to see him alive. Unless someone's had some contact with him since."

Colin felt faint. "He dropped a letter at my flat on Friday."

"You know, you're the third person to tell us that. After your neighbour Mrs Le Boutillier and your headmaster Mr Le Brocq. I'd have thought you'd want to be the first person to tell us. Why did you hide the fact of the letter from us?"

"He been to your flat before?" Gerry took another cue.

"No. Look, can we accept I made a mistake in not being up front from the beginning, and talk about what I've found out since then?"

"Still got the letter?"

"It's at home."

"And what does it say?"

"That he wouldn't come back to school, that the boy needed to step outside the bubble —"

"What?"

"It's from a Paul Simon song. We listened to it on the way to his house. He wanted me to meet him back at Grosnez on Friday evening, but I read the letter too late. My wife forgot to give it to me."

"And why do you think he wanted to meet you?"

"He said he wanted to tell me something."

"Why you?"

"I like to think it's because he trusts me."

"You don't think he blames you?"

"For what?"

"Hard to say without reading it. Guess we'll have to take your word for it."

"You can read it. I can go and get it, or you can send someone."

"And how will we know for sure that he wrote it?"

"Who else would it be from?"

"Maybe somebody wrote it so it would look like they were trying to help."

"You think I forged the letter?"

"Did you?"

"No. Why do you think I would do something like that? It makes no sense."

"If people only did things that made sense, then I'd be out of a job." Vautier leant back in his chair and put his hands behind his head. "You too probably, Mr Bygate. You teach books, plays, that sort of thing, correct?"

"Yes."

"And if people only did what was expected, well, you'd have some pretty dull stories. Everyone would be exactly as you find them."

Colin found himself digging his toes into the soles of his shoes.

"Indulge me if you don't mind, Mr Bygate. Say you had a villain in a drama, someone who'd done something really quite bad, he might try to cover that up by looking like a good person. Gerry, you're a cultured man — well, his wife drags him to all the local am-dram plays — you know what I'm on about."

"Yeah, saw an outdoor Shakespeare with something like that."

"You see, Mr Bygate, we even have Shakespeare on our little *arland*." Vautier gave "island" the local pronunciation with a leer. "Outdoors as well, just like they do in some of the parks in your big old London. What was the play, Gerry?"

"I don't recall, Barney. I was dozing on the mulled wine. Had a chappie blacked up."

Colin couldn't help himself. "That's *Othello*. He's a Moor. An Arab. But the character you're referring to is Iago."

"Why, thank you for that, Mr Bygate. And he would be a villain, would he?"

"The audience see him as a villain, but Othello is oblivious."

"What a devious bugger. Well, I can tell you it's not just in plays. Oh, no. Plenty of times we find a wrong 'un hiding in plain sight. Go to a house fire, most likely the arsonist will be there offering to start a bucket chain. And are you aware that most killers are known to their victims? They're the ones who sob the loudest. At least, that's what my colleagues on the mainland tell me. We average one murder a decade here. Which brings me to you. You've been making a song and dance about this Labey boy from day one. What are you hiding?"

"Nothing."

"Nothing? Aside from the fact you met him on a cliff, dropped him home and then he delivered a letter to your flat. Doesn't strike me as nothing."

"I didn't meet him on a cliff. I bumped into him. You're making it sound prearranged."

"What were you doing on the cliff?"

"Looking at the view. Thinking."

"We understand that your wife has moved out," said Gerry, blankly.

"Yes."

"May I ask why?"

"You can ask, but it's a private matter."

Vautier brought his fist down on the tape recorder, which stopped with an echoing click. "There are no fucking private matters, you stupid piss-slick." Vautier leant forward, his eyes narrowing.

"It concerns a relationship. That's all I'm saying."

"With a pupil?"

"No. Turn that tape recorder on again, please. I'm not comfortable with this."

"Two things I hate — queers and liars. I think you're both."

"I am neither."

"I think you fell in love with Duncan Labey and he wouldn't suck your cock so you pushed him off that cliff."

Colin choked down a scream of denial, and forced it into a hoarse and emphatic "I told you, I drove him home," discarding all attempts to conceal his contempt for the man who was taunting him so viciously.

"We don't know that. His parents were away that night."

"I'm telling you the truth."

"Maybe I'll send some divers down to see if you are."

"Oh, Jesus, this is ridiculous. He's not down there, and if he was the currents would take him somewhere else."

"You an expert on bodies and currents?"

"I'm not saying anything else."

"You want a lawyer?"

"No, because I've done nothing wrong. Why the hell are you treating me like this? You should be speaking to Aidan Blampied."

"Why?"

"Because he allegedly caught Duncan with cannabis, which is what sent Duncan off the rails. And Mickey Rouain."

"Who?"

"I've been told he sold Duncan the drugs. He's some kind of local dealer."

Vautier turned to Gerry. "You heard of a Mickey Rouain?"

"Could be Alain Rouain's boy, Michael."

"Oh, yes. Well, he's no choirboy, but he's no dealer either."

"I've heard differently," insisted Colin.

181

"These are very serious allegations you're throwing about, Mr Bygate."

"So are the ones you're throwing at me."

"Mickey Rouain picks up the odd parking ticket. Aidan Blampied I've no time for, he's a preening pillock, but Mr Le Brocq tells us he's behaved with the utmost discretion and professionalism. Unlike yourself."

"Is Le Brocq still here? Get him in this room and let's have it out."

"We spoke to him on the phone."

"So you haven't interviewed him officially? This is ridiculous."

"I told you, my super and the Bailiff are Old Boys. You think I'm going to drag their headmaster in here in public? Imagine the grief I'd get!"

"Well, what about Duncan's parents? What did they say about Blampied? About what happened between the two of them? Because something did, and you should get them both in a room and find out what."

"The Labeys want their son back. What they don't want is private matters being splashed across the front of the *Island News*."

"I didn't name names."

"You didn't have to. Anyone with half a brain can work out who you're talking about. Do you think all us Islanders have half a brain?"

Colin and Vautier stared each other down, till Vautier jutted forward suddenly, causing Colin to flinch. The detective laughed, then pressed PLAY and RECORD again.

"Interview concludes at eleven thirty-two a.m."

182

He pressed STOP. There was a further silence.

"Now what?" said Colin. "Are you charging me?"

"You're free to go."

"Why would you do that if I'm under suspicion?"

"Like I said before, it's a fucking island, dick-splash. There's nowhere for you to go. That's why Duncan Labey will turn up and you'll have wasted my fucking time and dragged a beacon of education through the mud."

"I thought you were accusing me of killing him."

"Not sure you've got it in you. But I want you to learn a lesson from this — shit sticks."

CHAPTER
ELEVEN

BARNEY

Thursday, 15 October 1987

Later that evening Barney Vautier lifted up his vest and sucked in his stomach, turning to the side for another angle from the bathroom mirror. Not bad. If he held it in he looked close to his fighting weight. He reckoned he could still get the pump in his biceps — they retained their dormant power. Maybe he couldn't get a single knockout, as he had when he'd boxed for the Island. "Jersey born, Jersey bred, strong in the arm, thick in the head" used to be the taunt. His supporters had adapted that to "strong in the arm, he'll take off your head", which he nearly had on a number of occasions. That big Guernsey donkey Bichet had gone down ten seconds in, the Roman nose the ladies loved spread all over his face like a pizza. The Alderney boy had put up a fight — he'd liked him, let him dance around a bit before he'd knocked him right across the canvas so he'd slid off the edge, like a net full of cod. No, his one-punch days were over. He'd need three to five now, depending on his opponent and whether or not they knew he was about to hit them.

There was something so majestic about taking someone down in one, though. He felt almost wistful at the thought that he would never again see that look of stunned humiliation in another man's eyes, the confused registration that the hand they had shaken earlier, a soft and pliable dangle of digits, could transform into some kind of asteroid, slamming into their world and casting it into years of darkness. Like old Paul Coutanche. He'd seen him shuffling round Fineprice supermarket the other week: big gut, food stains on his cardigan, half his hair migrated to his neck and shoulders, a right state. They were the same age, but you wouldn't know it to look at them, less still that in 1965 they'd slugged it out for the inter-Island under-21 championship. Both proud Jersey boys, it had been insularly hyped as East Coast versus West Coast. Paul had made him work for it, knocked him down four times, damn near broken his jaw, which still made a click if he ate when he was tense — that was how Eileen always knew if he was in a mood. Paul had bottomed out after that defeat, felt he'd let down his dad, his parish, his side of the Island. But Barney had had his own disappointments. He'd wanted to turn pro, make a go of it on the mainland. The offers were there, but his dad wouldn't hear of it: still hated those backstabbing ponces for leaving everyone to Jerry in the war. So much that he wouldn't acknowledge Liberation Day: 9 May was like any other day in their house. "They turned up eleven months after D-Day, which was a bloody boat ride away. Put the French, who were cowards to a man, before their own. Damn them all."

185

And that had been that. Eileen hadn't wanted him to keep fighting anyway, so he'd taken a job where he could hand out the occasional beating in return for a wage. But he sometimes thought, Am I the best man I could have been?

He let his stomach slide back to its natural shape. Jesus, another ten years and he'd be playing Santa at the Christmas party. He blamed it on Eileen's lasagne — he'd had two helpings for supper, then some crumble.

"Stop it!" she called from the bedroom.

"What?" he called back, squirting paste on his brush.

"Looking at your stomach," she said.

"I'm doing my teeth."

"You are now, but before you were looking at your belly. You're not twenty-one any more."

Smart woman, Eileen. She'd have made a damn good copper. He finished brushing and headed through to her, after a detour to draw the curtains in the room where he kept his weights, the room they'd earmarked as the nursery they'd never needed.

Eileen put down her book. "My tits and bum have been heading south for a while now but you still love me, don't you?"

"Course I do, Princess."

"Then stop worrying about your weight. We're getting old, that's all."

"Never been this big, though. Might have to get a new suit."

"You're not that big, Barney. Flabby Labbé's big. We'll start worrying when you need a wheelbarrow to carry your gut."

Barney smiled. She always made him feel good.

She flung open his side of the duvet. "To be honest, I prefer it, means you can't run away as quick when I want a cuddle. Come here."

Barney slid into bed and Eileen put her arms round his chest. The frequency and length of cuddles had been one of the only causes of discord in their marriage. Barney would always get overheated or want to change position. "The old bull, tethered at last" had been the opening line of his wedding speech. Even though he and Eileen were both twenty-two and had been together for five years, it did feel like the end of something, not just his boxing career. It felt like the end of having to worry. With her at his side, he always said he felt like a champion.

The phone rang in the hall.

"Leave it," pleaded Eileen. "Must be a wrong number at this time of night."

"Or work," said Barney, swinging his legs out of the bed.

He stomped down the stairs, grabbed the receiver and gave his phone number.

"What? . . . Where?" He turned to see that Eileen had followed him down and was heading for the kitchen. "Okay, okay. I'll be there in forty-five minutes . . . Because it's half ten . . . Because I'm in my pyjamas."

He put the phone down and called through to the kitchen, "Mugging. Out west. Sounds nasty. They want the bugger found by morning. Not good for tourism."

"I'll do you some sarnies."

"I'll be fine, love. Back in a flash."

"You just said they wanted the guy caught by morning. You'll need something to keep you going. I'll box up some of the crumble. Will Gerry be there?"

"Should think so, usual crew."

"I'll do some for him as well."

"He'll be fine. Janet'll fix him something."

"No, she won't. She'll leave his pyjamas on the landing and ask him to sleep on the sofa so as not to wake her when he comes back."

"Okay. I'll go and get changed."

An hour later he pulled into the undulating clay car park at Noirmont Point. The beams from his headlights darted up and down as he hit the potholes, water spraying out across the lights as if caught in a strobe. The car park was deserted, except for a battered Fiesta and a bin. The pilot lights of St Helier harbour winked at him across the bays of St Brelade and St Aubin.

He took a torch from the glove box and began to pick his way inland through the gorse, leaving the wash of the sea behind him. He wouldn't have needed the torch if the moonlight hadn't been blunted by clouds, and could probably have followed the route blindfolded, but he needed to keep an eye out for a loose root or freshly dug rabbit hole. The air was still, broken only by the caw of the odd gull as he reached the lip of a concrete trench four feet wide that sloped down to the boarded-up entrance of a German bunker. He clambered down, sidestepping the occasional hanging bramble and cursing at how the trench was treated as a giant bin; his feet clattered through drink cans and glass and plastic bottles. He pulled out a bunch of keys and unlocked the grille that covered the boarded-up entrance. He gave three knocks and the partition was lifted back, then replaced as he stepped inside. He swung his torch round on a pallid young ponytailed man in a lumberjack shirt.

"Bloody hell, Barney, point that somewhere else, you're blinding me."

"I don't think you want me to put the torch down. That would leave both hands free. And I could happily strangle you, Mickey. Happily. You rang my home in the middle of the fucking night. You're supposed to call the office number."

"I followed the rest of the protocol. I still used a payphone. It couldn't wait till morning."

"Just tell me what it is so I can go. This place stinks of fox piss."

"We don't have any foxes on —"

"Mickey, get on with it, or I will break your neck for resisting arrest."

"I was mugged —"

"We don't need to stick to the fucking code, okay. There's no one else here."

"I was fucking mugged! For real!"

"What are you talking about? The local lowlifes know anyone who lays a hand on you gets that hand broken."

"It wasn't a local, it was a Scouser."

"Fucking Scousers. Okay, talk me through it." Barney cast his torch around for something to sit on: a wooden pallet, the remains of a fire, a broken bucket, beer cans, used condoms. Who the fuck would fuck in

189

here? Gays maybe, nowhere else to go. He stayed standing. "We need to change our meeting place. Or change the locks. Anyway, go on."

"I was out at Sands, having a drink, watching a mate's band. Davey Ricard turns up, asks for an eighth. I have it on me, but I'm not doing it there — I know the rules, you don't want it in the clubs — so we meet out back, in the alley by the oil tank. He pays, I hand it over. Then I take a piss —"

"Fuck's sake, Mickey, you can piss in the clubs, just don't sell your drugs there."

"I was bursting, okay? Anyway, mid-piss this guy punches me right in the kidneys. I go down — I've pissed all over my trousers now — but before I can move, he's pulled me up and slammed me against the wall. Look!" Mickey shone his own torch on his grazed temple.

"He took the money? Rest of your stash?"

"No. He stuck a knife in my mouth."

"He did what? A knife?"

"He fish-hooked me and stuck the flat end of a knife against the inside of my cheek. He said I stop selling drugs in the Island or he'll slit my face from mouth to ear."

Barney stared at the floor.

"Barney? Did you hear me?"

Barney lurched towards the pallet, wedged it against the wall and the floor and with five quick kicks had split it into broken planks.

"Barney, I'm sorry —"

"Shut the fuck up, Mickey. I'm thinking." Barney gave a boot to the bucket, which ricocheted off the walls. "Where was he coming from? I mean, is this turf? Is he seriously making a play for the business, or is he some fucked-up anti-drugs vigilante?"

"It was a pretty short conversation. One-sided. He had a knife in my mouth. Didn't feel like he wanted me to talk."

"So he just said stop, and left?"

"Yeah, he took the knife out of my mouth, pushed me down, kicked me in the balls from behind, and went."

"You get a look at him?"

"No. I was scared to turn round. What do we do?"

"Any of your boys been hit?"

"No. I've told them to look out."

"We don't want a panic. But tell them to pair up."

"So we're not going to stop for a bit?"

"Of course you're not going to fucking stop. I'm going to find this guy, and he's going to be airlifted off the Island on a gurney."

"You can't arrest him for attacking me, though. You and I, our arrangement, we don't want anything official . . ."

"Then I'll arrest him for something else."

"What?"

"You ever met a Scouser without a prior? I sure as shit haven't."

"Come on, some my best clients are Scousers. I've got Scouse mates . . ."

"Not the sort that stick knives in people's mouths. Trust me, that's not someone's first move into crime. Now, think. Anyone been watching you, following you?" Mickey shook his head. Barney sighed. "I don't want to be too obvious here, but any new Scouse clients?"

"No, business as usual. The only thing's been a teacher, asking about the boy."

"You what?"

"This afternoon he turned up, asking if I knew anything about the boy that's missing. From the paper."

"What did he look like?"

"Tall, late twenties, Colin, odd surname."

"Bygate?"

"Yeah, that's him."

Barney laughed drily. "The backbone on that man. He will not stay down. How did he find you?"

"I don't know. There was a boy in his car. I watched him get back in and go."

"A boy?"

"Yeah, teenager. Normandy College uniform, I think."

"So what did you tell Mr Bygate?"

"Nothing. I told him to fuck off, didn't know what he was talking about."

"And do you?"

"No. I've never heard of this Duncan, um . . ."

"Labey. Duncan Labey. You're sure?"

"Yeah, why?"

192

"Well, Bygate mentioned you when I interviewed him this morning."

"Why would he do that?"

"I don't know. I was imagining it was crossed wires because you don't sell to kids. I remember being very clear about that."

"Is that what you told him?"

"Of course I didn't fucking tell him that! I'm not going to lay out my terms of business with a drug dealer while I'm taking a statement. I told him you were a rogue but not a wrong 'un."

"Right. And do you know where the kid is?"

"He's playing hooky. He'll be fine. Bygate's stirring it up, but the school say there's nothing to worry about. Someone who's going to have a lot to worry about is you, if I find out you sold to him."

"Barney, I swear I don't sell to kids, and I don't know the name Duncan Labey."

Mickey blinked away as Barney brought his torch right up in his face. "Look me in the eye and say that again."

"It's too bright."

"Say it."

Mickey squinted at the beam. "I don't sell to kids, and I don't know Duncan Labey." The torch came down. "But some of these teenagers look older than they are. He comes up to me out of school uniform, gives a different name, that's on him, not me."

"No, Mickey, it's on you. I promise. Those tears in your eyes?"

"It's the light, made my eyes water."

"I'm going now. Give it five and get yourself together."

"You going to look for this Scouser?"

"I'm going to see Bygate, keep him away from you. Then I'm going to bed."

"So what do I do?"

"Business as usual."

"What if he attacks me again?"

"Then I'll know where to find him. Try and get a punch in this time."

CHAPTER
TWELVE

COLIN

Friday, 16 October 1987

Colin woke and looked at the kitchen clock: 7:05 a.m. He'd had about two hours' sleep. The sofa wasn't as comfortable as the bed, but he hadn't been able to sleep in it since Emma left. Her smell was still on the pillow, and while they'd been keeping to their own sides recently, he wanted to reach out now more than ever.

The evening before he had found his mind active but unable to focus, leaving him tired and frustrated. He'd heard Mrs Le Boutillier shuffle across the landing to knock on his door, and had shamefully pretended to be out. She had returned ten minutes later to slide a note under, asking whether or not he knew for sure that Ian Mourant was right and that the Ozoufs were away. She hadn't seen Marmalade now for a few days, and if they'd cruelly put him in a cattery, at least that would be better than him having disappeared completely. He didn't know and he didn't care, but he promised himself he'd try to put her mind at rest, then left it too late as he didn't want to take on the responsibility of locating a missing cat as well as a missing boy.

He'd been woken from a shallow slumber at 1:10a.m. by a visit from Detective Vautier, whose muddy footprints he noticed had now just about dried out on the carpet. Colin rolled off the sofa and crawled towards a cupboard from which he retrieved a dustpan and brush. He crawled back to the stained areas and began brushing off the dirt.

Vautier had been more reasonable at night. Whether or not it was genuine, or a charm-offensive tactic, Colin wasn't sure. But at least there had been a more open exchange of views.

"You think I'm a heel-dragging bumpkin."

"You think I killed my pupil."

"I was trying to show you that that accusation is as crazy as the ones you're throwing about. There's no conspiracy here. You think I'm complacent, but maybe I'm someone with enough experience to know how things play out. Now, you're a bright guy, but you're a stubborn bastard, and you have to let me do my job."

"Are you going to speak to Blampied?"

"Le Brocq says I have no cause to."

"Le Brocq told Duncan's parents Blampied found drugs on him."

"None of them are saying that to me."

"That's because you're not asking them."

"I've told you how the totem pole works in this case. My boss and my boss's boss are friends with your boss. So I can't make Le Brocq do anything he doesn't want to. And the parents are standing behind him."

"So what are you doing?"

"We're checking guesthouses and hotels, campsites, even the dolmens. His picture's been given to staff at the harbours and the airport. Beyond that, what can we do?" Vautier cut Colin off as he opened his mouth. "Before you say it, I paid Mickey Rouain a visit this evening. I believe you made his acquaintance earlier in the day."

"I presume he was more forthcoming with you than me."

"Yes. I can tell you that I've eliminated him from your enquiries. He was never seriously on mine. He doesn't sell drugs, trust me. I know the people who do, and I put them in La Moye. And he doesn't know Duncan Labey. So he can't have sold him drugs on two counts — he doesn't sell drugs, and he's never met Duncan. Happy?"

"I'm still not convinced he's an upstanding member of society."

"That's a separate issue. You want a second-hand car with a doctored mileometer, he can probably sort that through his brother. That's the extent of Mickey's wrongdoing."

"Another shot?"

"Thanks."

Colin had opened a bottle of Dalwhinnie for this nocturnal peace summit, in part because he needed a drink to sleep but the prig in him frowned on imbibing on his own.

"Now what I have to ask you, Mr Bygate, is — who was the boy in your car outside Mickey's?"

"Not Duncan, if that's what you're asking."

"If I thought it was Duncan I wouldn't be here sipping your very fine single malt. I'd be putting cuffs on you, and making sure you banged your head as I shoved you into the back of a panda."

"Then why do you care who it was?"

"Christ, mate, I've come here off the record to apologise and try to reassure you I'm not the Devil. Play the game, get off my back, stop muddying the waters. Otherwise I can go the other way, the way I was veering this morning."

"The last two times we've met, you've apologised and said you want to make things right, then treated me like a piece of shit, so forgive me if I'm not completely won over by this sudden honesty. I'd rather we just cut to the chase. The genuine chase."

"All right. Back off. You're not from here, you don't understand the way things work. You may have lost your job, and your wife's not here in the middle of the night. If you want things to get worse, they will. Your choice. Thanks for the whisky."

With the evidence of Vautier's visit removed, Colin crawled again to the kitchen, knelt in front of the bin to empty the dustpan, then lay down on the floor, the cold of the lino seeping into his bones.

The doorbell rang. He looked up at the clock again — 7:23. He got to his feet and slouched towards the door, adjusting his pyjamas so that nothing unexpected popped out of the fly. He didn't want Vautier to come back and arrest him for flashing at the postman or a delivery person. Actually, who would be calling this early? Maybe it was a set-up by Vautier — maybe he'd decided to make things worse anyway. No, it was probably Mrs Le Boutillier, obsessing about a cat that wasn't hers.

He opened the door and blinked at Debbie, momentarily unsure as to whether she was real.

"Hi."

"What are you doing here?"

"Looking for you?"

"Why?"

"Can I come in?

Colin sighed and held the door as she entered. In his depleted mood he began to wonder why he had found her attractive, noting blemishes on her skin, and how lank her hair was tied back, a far cry from the elegant bob from whose curtains her dimpled smile had once enchanted him.

"Sit down. Do you want tea or coffee?" he asked, not feeling able to face another dramatic showdown.

"Tea, please," she said, sitting.

Colin remained motionless. "Why are you here, Debbie?"

"I wanted to check you were okay."

"I'm great, never better."

"Le Brocq's an idiot, and the way you've been treated is crazy, appalling."

"Well, everyone seems to think Duncan will turn up."

"You're not going to do any more."

"Nope. Nothing to do."

"Why did you take John Duval out of school yesterday lunchtime?"

"Who says I did?"

"I saw you drop him back on College Lane. A3 looks down on it."

"I called up pretending to be his dad, told him to meet me outside the bottom gate at lunchtime and paid him twenty quid to take me to Mickey Rouain."

"Who's he?"

"No one apparently. Duval said he sold drugs to Duncan. Rouain told me to fuck off. And a policeman came to see me in the middle of the night to politely tell me to fuck off. He'd told me to fuck off in a more aggressive way earlier. I think he was trying to reason with me. Which I'm thankful for, because he's the sort of guy who looks like he could put me through a wall."

"So you're just giving up."

"I'm tired, Debbie. I haven't really slept much and, as you may be aware, I have some personal issues to deal with."

Debbie looked down. Colin blew out his cheeks. "So, if it's okay with you, I'd like to —"

"Why are you being like this?" Debbie looked up, her eyes pooling with tears. Colin froze. "You're a monster, an absolute monster." The tears fell, and she wiped them away quickly, as though unable to keep up with their flow. "I love you, okay? I know you don't want to hear that, but that's how it is. It's not something I can just turn off, like a tap. I will turn it off, or the tap will run dry, and your behaviour is certainly helping with that, so thanks. But everyone around you has turned their back on you, your colleagues, your wife, but I'm still here. I don't think you have any other friends.

200

Maybe you do but you just don't talk about them. You're so bloody lonely! And it kills me. It kills me to be here and see you so angry and so bitter. I don't want you to be like that. It wasn't easy for me to come here, you've made it plain you don't want anything to do with me, but I don't want that, so just — just —"

She broke down sobbing. Colin faltered, walked over to the sideboard, grabbed some sheets of kitchen roll and handed them to her, standing in front of her.

"Is this all you've got? Kitchen roll? Why don't you hug me? Do you hate me that much? I'm in pieces here!"

"Debbie, if I hug you, we're going to end up in bed. And it's the bed I share with my wife."

The sobs slowed.

Colin took a breath. "You're right, I've been horrible. But it's because I feel things that I shouldn't. I'm married, that's a big deal for me. And we work together. I can't —"

"I thought you'd been sacked." She shuddered.

"Not completely. And anyway —"

She reached up for his hand and pulled him down to sit next to her. He left his hand in hers, but his arms remained rigidly by his sides.

"I know." She sighed.

"I wish things were different. But they're not. And I don't know what's happening, whether I still have a job or a wife, and I just need not to do anything crazy."

"Being with me would be crazy," she hacked, in a cross between a laugh and a cry, but with enough lightness for Colin to risk a playful shoulder nudge.

"Stop fishing for compliments." He frowned warmly. "You'll have to be content with my silence speaking volumes."

She laid her head on his shoulder. "I miss being friends."

"Me too," he said. "I could use a friend. Friends again?"

She lifted her head to nod. He withdrew his hand and stood. "I'll get that tea."

"Actually, make it coffee. I didn't sleep that well."

Colin went over to the kettle. "Well, the weekend's nearly here. Just today to get through. I imagine the pupils are talking about me."

"They're missing you."

"Really?"

"Yeah. Perchard's filling in for you, so it's pretty dry. I've heard them moaning."

"Christ. His favourite author is Disraeli. Do they know Duncan's missing?"

"They know something's going on, but they're not sure what. Obviously they've clocked he's not around."

"They'll find him soon. The police are searching the hotels and B and Bs. And they've got the airport covered, and the harbours. And Le Brocq will make it all go away and sack me instead of Blampied."

"What if he's already left the Island?"

"They have passenger records. I presume they've checked those. I mean, he could have given a false name, but a teenager travelling on his own would stand out. And he'd need a passport to get to France."

202

"You can leave the Island and still be in the Island. I was last weekend."

"What do you mean?"

"I stayed at St Aubin's Fort. And there's also the towers — La Rocco, Seymour, Portelet and La Tour de Vinde. All accessible at low tide."

"Would Duncan know about them?"

"Why wouldn't he?"

Colin picked an old *Island News* off the coffee table. "We've just missed low tide, have to wait till nine this evening."

"Certainly for Seymour Tower — that's over a mile out. But we can get to some of the others sooner. In the meantime we could check out the Martello and Conway Towers on the land. Plus L'Etacquerel Fort."

Colin rubbed his temples. "Okay. Yes. We should. We can ask him about Blampied before he gets sat on. You should call in sick."

"And go home and change."

"There's no time for that, the amount of places we have to get through."

"I'm not clambering over Napoleonic fortifications in heels and a pencil skirt."

"Grab some clothes of Emma's."

"Sure."

Colin couldn't tell whether this was a question or a confirmation, so he covered the awkwardness by telling her to phone the school while he got dressed, then headed to the bedroom.

Twenty minutes later, they left the flat, Debbie in a fleece and Barbour jacket of Emma's, and a pair of her jeans rolled up over the hiking boots that had stayed in the box since Colin had given them to her two birthdays previously. It was eight fifteen so they ran straight into Mrs Le Boutillier.

"Morning, Mr Bygate. Hello, dear."

"Hello," said Debbie, hesitantly, not sure whether to introduce herself, or follow Colin as he barrelled down the stairs.

"Did you get my note?" Mrs Le Boutillier called after him.

"Yes, sorry, not seen him."

"Marmalade? Or Mr Ozouf?"

"Neither. Sorry, I'm in a bit of a hurry. See you later." Colin and Debbie stepped out of the front door. Mrs Le Boutillier stared sadly after them, then pulled her trolley to the top of the stairs and began her careful descent.

CHAPTER
THIRTEEN

LOUISE

Friday, 16 October 1987

Another perfect fist-sized purple pebble shattered against a ruddy granite rock that was jutting out of the rising tide. Louise was in a rancorous mood, dully furious at the unheralded obstructions that had altered her plans not just for the day but, by extrapolation, the rest of her life. Someone was going to suffer for this, and the coloured stones of whatever unpronounceable bay she was sitting on were nearest to hand.

She was supposed to have met Rob here bang on midday. That had been her stipulation. She had got here at quarter past. He hadn't waited, if he'd even shown up in the first place. She'd already had a scare that morning, panicking that the copper who'd knocked on her door just as she was about to set off was there at Rob's behest. Maybe he'd come clean with his wife, spun himself as a drunken, wretched fool and Louise as a professional honey-trapper, thus gaining not only forgiveness but a fervent ally who wanted to assuage the hurt her husband had dealt her by punishing the Jezebel who had cruelly exploited his momentary weakness. Maybe she was one of those fucking fools so lacking in self-awareness and -esteem that she blamed her partner's bed-hopping on her own sexual reticence. But, no, that fat filth, with his seventies 'tache, had come looking for another man in her life.

"Louise O'Rourke?"

She'd known he was police before he even produced his ID. The cheap suit, the shapeless hair — he even had the piggy-eyes to go with his nickname.

"Detective Vautier. Mind if I come in?"

He was blocking the door so she couldn't make a run for it. Best ask him in, then go to the loo on the landing, climb out on to the flat roof below, jump down and then, what? He knew her name: she wasn't getting off the Island without feeling his hand on her shoulder.

"Sure. I was just heading out, but . . . What's this about?"

"Just a little chat about a friend of yours, nothing to worry you."

She'd stood back and beckoned him in, catching herself just in time before she said, "Yeah, you guys normally come in twos if there's a problem", not wanting him to think she had any familiarity with police procedure beyond the plot lines of *Juliet Bravo*.

"Surprised to catch you in in the middle of the day. Day off, or in between jobs?"

"The latter." Front it out, pretend you've nothing to hide. "I was at the Bretagne, but things quietened down for the winter."

"I heard they've quietened down there full stop."

He'd looked around for somewhere to sit. She gathered up a bunch of clothes from a folding plastic chair and dumped them on the unmade bed. "Here," she said, settling herself on the bed, trying to size him up. So, who was he? An emissary of Rob's bringing a compromise — back off and there'll be no charges? She hadn't broken any other laws recently. Okay, there'd been that piss in front of the door of the Five Oaks pub on Wednesday. Closing time meant closing time, the arsehole landlord had said, blocking her way to the toilet out of sheer malice, or possibly revenge for her repeatedly mocking the local accent and beer at the apex of her drunkenness in the final hour. She realised she probably had her fierce face on. Best play it sweet to start. "Can I get you a brew, Officer?"

"Yes, thanks. Milk, three sugars. And, please, Barney."

"Right you are, Barney," she'd said, springing up. "Just fetch some water from the well." She went out to the landing with the electric kettle and filled it from the sink in the loo, pausing to ponder and reject again escape from the window. She needed to leave soon, but maybe he was about to tell her the rendezvous was off.

Vautier was scanning the room when she returned to set the water to boil on the small table next to the hob and toaster. "Live here alone?"

"Not really room for two."

"Where do you wash, if you don't mind me asking?"

"There's a communal shower down the way. Queue starts at six." The kettle clicked off. "I'll get the tea," she said. Further silence as she added water to the bag.

She walked over to the window, drew back the sheet that masqueraded as a curtain, and opened the sash. "What do you think of my fridge?" She smiled as she brought in the milk from the sill. It also afforded her a look into the street, to see if he'd brought back-up. Was he taunting her into making a run for it? Why would he do that, though? She returned the milk and handed him his tea.

"Thanks, love," he said. Maybe it was nothing, she'd thought, calming herself as she sat back on the bed. Maybe this was a case of mistaken identity.

"I want to ask you about your ex-boyfriend. Billy McCaffrey."

No, it wasn't.

"Ah," she replied, with as much nonchalance as she could muster.

"I can see he's not staying here. I just wondered if he'd made contact."

"How would he have done that? He's doing time."

"He got out two weeks ago. Now, either that's news to you or you're an extremely good actress."

"It's news to me. He got seven years."

"I'd say that was light for what he did. Pistol-whipped that kid."

"Well, they never found the gun."

"Doesn't really matter whether he used a bit of metal or his fists. Boy's in a wheelchair for the rest of his life. He was in a coma for six months. Lucky he came out of it, otherwise there would have been no one to testify. Everyone else in that nightclub came down with a severe case of 'I didn't see nuffink'."

"Jesus. Why is he out so soon?" She'd felt a rising panic, the shock of Billy's release blending with the agitation that while this guy wasn't here officially to stop her meeting Rob that was exactly what he was unwittingly doing. The taxi would arrive any minute.

"I don't wish to denigrate your fine home city, but a fair chunk of the constabulary seems to be on overly cosy terms with the likes of Billy. Same goes for the screws. He got time off for good behaviour. Although I find it hard to believe. Can't see him spending his time inside campaigning for more books in the library and putting on the Christmas panto. You visit him much?"

"Never."

"Not once?"

"I was with Billy since I was fifteen. I'd wanted to leave him for a while. Him getting banged up made it possible."

"So that kid getting beat half to death was a bit of a result for you. Every cloud."

"I wanted another life."

"One where your dad's car doesn't get torched."

"That wasn't Billy. It was a rival. Like I say, it's another life. I've moved on."

"You think he's happy about that?"

"He knows the deal. You go away, some people can wait and others can't. It's just the way it is." The beep of a horn: that would be the taxi.

"Well, if you see him, give me a call."

"I'm not going to see him. I'm not going home, and he's never travelled further than Manchester."

"To torch a pub as I recall."

Louise had shrugged. "There's nothing for him here. I don't think you or me have anything to worry about."

Barney nodded as he cradled his tea, then sat back in his chair. "We had an incident last night — pretty unpleasant by the standards of our Island. I've got a friend in Liverpool CID. One of the good guys. We've ended up liaising a lot over the years because of the odd undesirable that washes up here from the Mersey. So when I ring him this morning and say, 'Scouser, likes to stick knives in people's mouths', it takes him all of two seconds to reply, 'Billy McCaffrey.'" Vautier stood up, looked around for somewhere to put the mug, then placed it on the chair he'd vacated. "He's here, Louise. Watch yourself."

He'd left her rooted to the bed. Further angry horn blasts had broken through her stupor. She'd gathered her coat and bag and run out of the bedsit, waving to the cabbie from the window on the way. But she'd been too late to meet Rob, losing not just ten grand but her future as a hotel owner. At least he hadn't called the police. Although just because she was wrong earlier didn't mean she was wrong now. He could be down at the station right at this moment while she sat here smashing rocks. Maybe she should cut her losses and get off the Island, go back to Liverpool. But what if Billy was there? She didn't doubt he was out, but she couldn't believe he'd come to the Island. Thinking about it, the attack didn't prove anything. Billy was the adopter not the originator of his signature attack. The Glasgow Grin, the Chelsea Smile: he wasn't the only psychopath in Britain. Even if he was here, that

210

detective had him in his sights. He'd get in a fight and be back inside before he could ruin her life again. But what life did she have on the Island? She shrugged. It was still a better life than back home, where there'd be other Billys waiting for her. That was why she'd left, running from a queue of hard men looking to humiliate Billy by taking his woman while he was away. She was her own person, not a sexual pawn in a grim power struggle. She called the shots now.

She heard someone clattering over the stones and turned. Rob was walking awkwardly towards her, his ankles rolling in the pitch of the pebbles, his arms windmilling to keep his balance, almost going over with the weight of the briefcase in his right hand.

"Sorry I'm late, so glad you waited . . ."

"Where the fuck have you been? I was that close to heading for your wife!" spat Louise, springing up and flinging a stone at his feet.

"Hey! Stop that! I got stuck with the police."

"What?"

"They wanted to check all the rooms, looking for this missing boy, said he might have checked in under another name or stolen a key. I didn't want them freaking out our guests and ended up having a bit of a set-to. My uncle sacked Gerry Fauvant's dad, and it was pretty obvious he was enjoying bossing me around. Although I shouldn't have said that to his face . . ."

"I don't care. Give me the money."

"Here," said Rob, holding out the briefcase as he stumbled up to her. "It didn't help my nerves, standing around with a case of cash. Shit," he added, looking down, "my shoes are fucked."

Louise sat down and opened the briefcase. It was full of money.

"It's all there," said Rob, licking his fingers and trying to smooth over the scuffs on his shoes with saliva. "Got this new counting machine. Put the notes in, it flicks them through, gives you the total. Don't know how it works. Seems like magic to me."

"Why are you so happy? It's freaking me out."

"Just glad to get this over with, move on. All good?"

"Yeah."

Rob stood there expectantly.

"What are you waiting for? A goodbye kiss?"

"No, the briefcase. It's mine."

"What do you want me to do? Stuff ten grand in my knickers?"

"I thought you'd bring your own bag."

"I've got a handbag and a purse."

"It's my actual briefcase, though — look, it has my initials on it."

"I don't give a shit. You should have brought it in a sports bag or something."

"I didn't want to arouse suspicion. I go round with a briefcase, not a sports bag."

"I thought wankers like you all played squash?"

"Are you going to give me my case or not?"

"How about I buy it off you? Take a hundred quid back."

"It's of sentimental value. It was my dad's. He gave it to me for my eighteenth birthday."

212

"I thought you said it had your initials."

"His are the same as mine — he's Russell."

"Cheapskate present, then."

"It means a lot to me."

"I'll drop it by the hotel."

"No. We're not having any contact after this."

"Okay, I'll get a friend to drop it off."

"Promise?"

"Yes."

"And promise that that'll be it? You and I, we're done, yes?"

"Yes. Now piss off."

"Sure. Just thinking if I should take my shoes off to get back. No, they're ruined anyway."

Rob made his way back to the steps and on to the breakwater. She glanced over occasionally to make sure he was going, then lay back hugging the briefcase. Ten thousand pounds. She shut her eyes and listened to the sloshing and sluicing of the waves as they landed on the shore and drained back, dragging and clattering the loose lighter stones on their way. She lifted her head and opened her eyes, squinting. It was a grey day but there was still brightness in the sky. The sea was now only a few feet below her: it had come way up since she arrived — must be nearing high tide.

She got up and walked back to the breakwater, the road and, more importantly, the phone box at the bottom of the hill from which she called Danny. Not wanting to set foot again in the Black Dog, she sat on the sea wall, looking down at the water. The bay got so deep so quickly that the sea had a navy hue, dark purple even, broken up beneath her feet by the yellows, greens and pinks of the seaweeds that softened the outcrops on which the wall was built. It really was a beautiful island. Now she could buy her way in.

Half an hour later Danny arrived in a cab. They shared a hug, restrained and fraternal so as not to arouse Danny's libidinous hopes or the suspicions of the driver. It wouldn't do to start punching the air and crowing about what she had just pulled off. They took the car to Rozel, a smaller, calmer bay, less grand and more homely, where at the base of the pier stood the Crow's Nest bed and breakfast, dilapidated, uncared-for, and for sale. They knocked on the door, were shown round by an old man shrouded in a thick grey cable-knit cardigan, with a dense spray of nostril hairs to match.

Louise was in a daze, tuning in and out of the guided tour. Luckily Danny was attentive enough to provide the requisite nods and noises of concurrence.

"Shut up for the season . . . thank God . . . Too much at my age . . . Bloody grockles . . . Up at five to get breakfast . . . The young ones come in past midnight . . . They've got keys, but the noise on the stairs . . . Carpet's seen better days . . . Washing, washing, all I do is washing . . . Wife can't help, what with the arthritis . . . She's downstairs . . . Separate flat . . . No privacy . . . Edith! Edith! You okay, my girl? . . . Showing people round . . . I said showing people round . . . Not to stay, to buy . . . BUY! . . . Deaf as a week-old baguette . . . Beyond us both now . . . Good opportunity for a young couple like you . . . You are

214

interested, yes? . . . I said on the phone, 'No bloody time-wasters' . . . Fed up of getting my hopes up . . . Okay the roof leaks, I can't lie, you'll catch it on the survey . . . Can't use top two bedrooms right now . . . But I'm not dropping the price, not for this location . . . You'll take it! Oh bloody wonderful . . . Edith, we'll be in the cottage by Christmas! . . . I said, never mind, I'll come down in a mo . . . I'LL COME DOWN! . . . Let me shake your hand, my son. So glad it's going to a nice Jersey boy too . . . Keep it among our own, eh!"

Louise found herself back outside not having uttered a word. Unusually for her, she had felt no need to puncture the old bigot's giddiness with a "thank you" Scoused up to near-unintelligibility.

"What are you thinking?" asked Danny, nervy at her stillness.

"It's a tip. It's perfect. It's perfect!" She exhaled, breaking out in a smile.

"And it's ours!" He beamed, raising his arms in what she knew was a request for a hug dressed up as a gesture of elation.

"Let's go and get pissed," she said, keeping her arms by her sides. He'd had his hug for the day.

Another phone call and another taxi ride found them back in town at the Soleil Levant pub. Danny had bought a canvas bag from the general store at Rozel while Louise was ordering the car, assuming she'd find the briefcase too conspicuous. But there was nowhere private for them to transfer the cash and, besides, she wasn't going to junk the case: she'd promised to return it.

215

"Why should you give him his stupid case back?" Danny asked, clearly puzzled.

"Because I said I would. If I stick to that, he'll know I'm serious about leaving him alone."

So they sat drinking with an empty Îles de la Manche zip bag and a black leather briefcase full of money nuzzling between their feet under the table. They toasted Jersey, Liverpool, grockles, Scousers, adulterers, slags, each other, and their about-to-be-acquired establishment.

"What happens now?" she asked.

"I've got my head round it. I give half of this to a lawyer so we get a Preliminary Agreement of Sale."

"You're going to give him a briefcase of cash?"

"Her. She's my best mate's sister — Heather, you met her at that Hallowe'en thing? Never mind, it's fine. I've said I've been saving under the mattress, like the old farmers who don't trust the banks. I'll pop in at five."

"Jesus, this Island, it's like a bloody gypsy state. All ritual and blood oaths. What next?"

"I sort a mortgage — shouldn't be a problem. I've got a cousin at Midland. He says it's just a matter of filling out some forms. In a couple of weeks I go to the Royal Court on a Friday to pass the contract of conveyance. I get the keys on the Monday or Tuesday. Scuse, I need a piss."

Louise sipped her beer, then shut her eyes. Her head was spinning, from drink, change or bewilderment at local practices, she couldn't tell.

216

When Danny came back he sat on the bench next to her rather than the stool opposite. His eyes were bloodshot and his breath stank. He never could hold his drink. "I can't believe it. We've done it."

"I did it. I was the one who fucked him, in all senses." She frowned, hoping to remind him of the ground rules of their agreement. He was too drunk to notice.

"I don't know whether to tell my boss to stick his job now, or when I get the keys."

"When *we* get the keys. Stop saying 'I'."

"Well, it will be me. You can't show up. In person, or on paper, you're not allowed to buy property here."

Louise bristled. "Don't think I'm going to be a silent partner. Behind closed doors, I'm in charge."

"Yeah, yeah. The kitchen is the limit of my domain."

"What about the rest of the money? For the refurb. Where are we keeping that?"

"I thought in my account. We don't want it lying around."

"So you hold all the purse strings? I don't think so."

"Come on, Louise, what are you worried about? You know how I feel about you. Why would I do you over?"

"Because that's what men do," she almost said, but she didn't want him to start droning on about how he was different. "I'm sorry. I guess I'm just jumpy. This time last week I had a good job at a nice hotel."

"And now you're about to buy one. You can trust me. You know why? Because I'm scared of you. I'm not going to cross you, Lou. You're the toughest person I know."

217

She smiled. "Aw, Danny, you say the nicest things."

"I love you, Lou. In the way you want me to."

She was softened by drink and touched by his respect. "I know you do. And I love you too."

She opened her arms to him and he leant in. As he tilted his head she pushed him back.

"What?"

"You were going to kiss me."

"On the cheek."

"My cheek's not under my nose."

"I thought you wanted me to."

"Why do you have to do this? You always push it."

"You just told me you loved me and opened your arms."

"And that means you can do what you want with me? If I want to kiss you, I'll kiss you."

"You're being really mean, considering what I'm doing for you."

"Is this how it's going to be?"

"How what's going to be?"

"You buy me a hotel and I'm expected to give up my snatch in return?"

"You're being mental."

"Fuck you," she hissed, reaching under the table and grabbing the briefcase.

"What are you doing?"

"Taking what's mine."

"Lou . . ." Danny rose unsteadily to his feet. The other drinkers were staring now at what was clearly becoming a scene. Louise put her hand on a pint glass.

"Sit down," she whispered, "or I'll stick this in your face."

Danny raised his hands and did as he was told.

"Stay away from me Danny," she said quietly. "I need to think. Maybe I don't want to put the money down on this bum crumb of an island. Maybe I don't want another man telling me what I can or can't do. Maybe I've had enough of being threatened."

"You threatened me!"

"Stay away from me."

Louise strode out, not looking round because she knew he didn't have the guts to follow her straight away. He'd send her a whining letter or make a bleating phone call or come scratching round her door in the small hours. The skies were darkening, the wind had picked up and she was cold. It was a fifteen-minute walk home, and she kept swapping the case between her hands to stop it pulling so much on her shoulders.

She got back to the bedsit, flung the case on to the bed, threw the remains of Barney's tea out of the window and poured a slosh of vodka into the dirty mug.

There was a knock at the door. Maybe she should have looked behind her. Maybe that simpering fool had followed her after all. "Danny, if it's you, fuck off!" Another knock, louder. Jesus Christ, when would he get the message? She yanked the door open, her teeth bared in a snarl.

"Hey, Lou, who's Danny?" said the one person in her life whom she wished with all her heart she had never met.

"Billy."

CHAPTER
FOURTEEN

CHRISTOPHE

Friday, 16 October 1987

Christophe looked in on the dining room at about six o'clock and spotted the broad back perched on the barstool at the far end. It was a back not dissimilar to that of Jambo, the silverback gorilla up at Jersey Zoo, a back that looked like a blow from a cricket bat would be brushed away, and a second attack warned off with a glance. Last year Jambo had stood guard over a boy knocked unconscious by a fall into the enclosure and protected him from the advances of the rest of the group. Christophe was pretty sure Barney Vautier would stand guard over a fallen child. But when that child came to, he would find himself in Vautier's indeterminate debt.

"Detective Vautier."

"What the fuck's going on here, then?"

Christophe held his gaze and offered a quizzical smile, hoping this was just one of the detective's usual brusque opening volleys rather than a specific enquiry.

"There is something wrong with your drink?" Christophe asked, nodding towards the bottle of Sol that sat on the bar encircled by Vautier's massive right hand, which to an inebriated patron might look like the hand of a giant nursing a miniature.

"That's the least of it, but since you asked, one, you've stopped serving beer in pints, and two, that daft prick put a piece of fruit in it." He picked out the lime from the top of the bottle and slung it down the bar top to where the Portuguese barman was standing as far away from him as he could. The barman looked to Christophe, who dismissed him with a lift of his fingers.

"This used to be a nice little bar, loads of character for the visitors, and now look at it."

Vautier had not visited since the relaunch. Nelson's Bar had been totally ripped out and renamed Skyliners, its faux-nautical theme abandoned. Gone were the ceiling nets and ship's wheel chandelier, the plastic crabs and lobsters, the anchor in the fireplace, porthole windows and mermaid fresco. It was now twice the size and included a dining area, with a bar of black marble offset by chrome-pipe edging, silver walls, angled pink and lime neon strip lights and a mirror-backed bar with a transfer image of night-time Manhattan.

"Know your market. You think northern wrinklies want to feel like they're in New York? They hate New York. It scares the shit out of them."

"Eventually the older market will die off. Businesses need to look to the future."

"I blame you, bringing your poncy mainland ideas over to our island. This is Jersey, not fucking Paris or wherever you're pretending to be from this week."

"I merely carry out Monsieur de la Haye's instructions."

"Bollocks! You're the power behind the throne — anyone can see that. That boy couldn't shit proper without you leaving a note in his pants. 'Wipe arse, use paper.' Well, congratulations. You've turned a nice little bar into a wanker magnet."

Christophe forced a good-humoured chuckle, longing to add that the Island had no shortage of wankers, and that maybe he was looking at the biggest one right now. But Barney Vautier had him on a small but unretractable hook. He moved round behind the bar.

"Perhaps I can fix you something else. We have many fine wines, cocktails —"

"Cocktails? You trying to compete with Roy's?"

Christophe faked another laugh at the reference to Roy's Theatre Bar, the twenty square feet of which made up the Island's entire gay district.

"We only want one of those," continued Vautier. "That way we know where they all are if we want to enforce the sodomy law. Although I don't mind the queers myself. Fought one, back in the day, the Minto boy. You'd never have known, the way he punched."

"Then perhaps a spirit," said Christophe, ploughing on with relentless goodwill.

"Nah, shouldn't drink on duty anyway."

"So this is a professional visit?"

"We don't have a social relationship, Louis."

Christophe flinched at the mention of his real name. Vautier was pushing him harder than he had since their first confrontation. He hoped he was not the source of the man's rancour, just his punchbag. "Please," said Christophe, "maybe we should go to my office."

Vautier smirked and cast his head around comically. "So we're not overheard? There's no fucker here. Your stupid prices and crazy furniture have seen to that. Seriously, this stool is so uncomfortable I'm going to feel like I spent the night getting rogered at Roy's. Don't look so bloody serious — I'm trying to lighten the mood. Although I'm in such a terrible mood to begin with, it might not feel that light to you. Come on, let's sit on one of those chairs. They are chairs, right?"

Christophe nodded and walked with the detective to a window table. The dining chairs had disproportionately high wrought-iron backs, as if someone had attached a ladder to a stool.

"Looking for someone, need you to keep an eye out."

"I always have an eye out."

"This is specific."

"The boy? Your colleague has already been in —"

"Yeah, Gerry's doing the rounds on that. The guy I'm looking for is Scouse, in his twenties, bit of an animal. Should be an easy spot for you."

"As per our agreement, I don't move in those circles. My work is strictly in the hotel industry."

"He might turn up looking for his ex, Louise O'Rourke."

Christophe repressed another flinch. "She no longer works here."

"So I gather. What happened?"

"Things were not working out. Her manner was . . ."

223

"Too Scouse?"

Christophe inclined his head.

"What about her behaviour? Was that Scouse too?"

"What do you mean?"

"Was she on the take?"

"Not to my knowledge."

"And you'd know. Well, long term, probably a good idea not to have her around. Anyone who used to hang out with this piece of shit is bound to have picked up a few bad habits." Vautier unfolded a black-and-white faxed photo from his pocket and threw it on to the table. Despite the blurred quality, the eyes cut through and Christophe could see defiance and unrepentance; the look of a man who would not bend the knee. It was a look he had been relieved not to deploy or receive for several years.

"Got tats too, declaring his loyalty to the fraternity. Like you used to. Never got that myself — like an undercover copper wearing his helmet."

Christophe didn't react.

"You've still got your tat?"

"This Island is not exactly overflowing with removal clinics."

"And I guess you don't want anyone talking about what you're getting removed."

"It's not as if it's a swastika or the number 666. It is of no significance to most."

"I suppose. You were just unlucky with me." Vautier stood. "This guy, if he comes in here, makes any trouble and you put him down hard, it won't be a problem."

224

"I'm not sure that would be good for the image of the hotel or for myself."

"What I know about this guy, you might not have a choice. He finds out you fired his ex, or you won't give up her address, he could get nasty."

"I provide you with information. I'm not your muscle."

"You're whatever I want you to be. Otherwise I might have to tell your friends back in the Unione where you washed up."

Christophe had indeed been unlucky to ping on to Barney Vautier's radar. He had blamed himself for lowering his guard, for his prejudiced assumption that such a dull backwater was unlikely to produce many sharpened minds. But over time he had absolved himself and instead ascribed his unmasking to a chance misfortune, which in time he could perhaps turn to his advantage.

The night Vautier had first noticed Christophe had also been the night Rob had spotted him. That night he had begun to serve two masters.

Earlier in the day Rob's father had handed his son the keys to the Bretagne. Russell de la Haye had overseen thirty-one successful years of ownership, transforming it from an old-school into a two-star bed and breakfast and, later, a solid three-star hotel. Christophe was a recently appointed barman, who had caught Rob's attention when, in response to his new boss's braying declaration that he had a snowball's chance in hell of getting a Slow Comfortable Screw

Against a Wall in the bar, he had delivered not just a perfect Slow Comfortable Screw but also a Snowball.

He had been appointed head barman on the spot, a post that, previously, had not officially existed but had had a de facto holder in the elderly Alfonse, who sniffily remarked that Christophe would not see any extra wages. Christophe secured the old man's support by giving him a rise of his own, once he had control of the budget.

He had also served Vautier that night, and thought of him as a glum man in the corner gamely trying to celebrate the anniversary of a troubled marriage, unaware that the man's sourness was being stoked by the voluble revelry of Rob and his hangers-on, and soothed by the redoubtable Eileen.

One member of the party, a thirty-four-year-old estate agent called Jan, whom Rob told Christophe was "on the prowl" and "an open goal", draped her arm round the Frenchman's neck when asking for a fifth Piña Colada, and managed to tip the icy remains of the fourth down the front of his shirt. As she had dried it with the edge of her shawl a dark patch had appeared against the wet white cloth on the left of his chest.

"What's that — a bruise? Looks nasty . . ."

"A youthful folly, a tattoo of the Moor's Head, the symbol of my home island of Corsica."

Sally had ushered Jan towards a sobering coffee while mouthing, "Sorry," to Christophe, who, as he turned to head for a new shirt, caught Vautier's eye, which was registering a curiosity Christophe could well have done without.

226

A casual enquiry days later had alerted him to the man's profession, but as the weeks went by he attributed the look the detective had given him to disdain for public drunkenness rather than any wider suspicion of Christophe's origins.

Three months later Christophe was on his steady rise to the position of Rob's lieutenant, sharing his enthusiasm and vision for the hotel, and perfecting the knack of presenting his next step up the ladder's rungs as a fait accompli to his boss. To Rob's mind, Christophe was another element in his own success story, a weapon he chose to deploy, marking out his genius as a strategist. From Christophe's point of view, Rob's character failed to match the position Providence had bestowed: he was a man arrogant enough to place his faith in his own potency, neglecting the part that fortune had played in his cushioned existence.

There had been a knock at his office door and Alfonse had told him that a gentleman in the bar was asking to see the Corsican. Christophe had asked Alfonse to show the man in, and was not surprised when Vautier strode in and splayed himself in the leather chair on the other side of the desk.

"Mr Fournier, I'm Detective Vautier. Hope I'm not disturbing you."

"Not at all. How can I help?"

"Just looking into something, could do with your expertise."

"I'm not sure I have any."

"Well, you know France better than me."

"Not all of it. It is a big country."

"Yes, it is. I think this Island's the only place in the world where if someone goes, 'Oh, you're from Jersey, you must know so-and-so,' and you actually do."

"It is a small place."

"But beautifully formed."

"So where or who or what in France do you want to know about?"

"I'll give you the background. I have to go on these conferences with my English and French counterparts, bit of a jolly to Weymouth or Saint-Malo or, if I'm lucky, London or Paris, so we can put names to faces, work out better liaison procedures, you know the sort of thing."

Christophe nodded.

"I did one a while back, in Rouen as a matter of fact. Know it?"

"I know of it."

"Not missing much. Nice cathedral — we don't have one of those over here. Anyway, I ended up sharing a few Cointreaus with this . . . I was going to say 'cop', but I think the term you would use is '*keuf*'."

" '*Keuf*' is actually street slang. It is quite derogatory. A closer translation of 'cop' would be '*flic*'."

"There you go. I'm learning already, and I haven't even got to the big question. So this *flic*, he can't really hold his Cointreau. In truth, he's a right state, great fat gut, blood vessels all burst in his nose, like a tramp dressed up for court. Obviously the job's getting to him. He's from Marseille — you must know Marseille, main sea link to Corsica. That's where you're from, right?"

"Yes."

"Yes, you're from Corsica, or yes, you know Marseille?"

"Both."

"Spent much time there?"

"A little."

"Sounds wise. Not a place to hang around, by all accounts, Marseille. I mean this guy, he was so jealous of me being from Jersey. 'Cause we have, what, a murder every ten years? This guy's patch had one a week. And what really got to him was he knew who was pulling the triggers and wielding the knives — this gang, from Corsica as it happens, but no one would talk. Said they all had the same tattoo. Said he could cut crime in half if he went out with an armed unit one night and shot every cunt with a Moor's Head. Good job he didn't, you might have got caught up in that. By mistake."

"The Moor's Head is the symbol of Corsica. It is on the flag, and most of the souvenirs. Having a tattoo of it is not a crime."

Vautier tapped his chest. "But having it on the heart's a big deal. Only members of the Corsican Mafia are allowed that. And if you ever leave or turn, I heard they cut it out, take your heart with it."

"Please don't take offence, but your friend, the *flic*, was telling stories, the town mouse trying to frighten his country cousin. You are familiar with *The French Connection?*"

"The film?"

"It is based on true events. The Unione Corse were running heroin from Marseille to New York. They got caught, after which they fell apart."

"So who's running the bars, casinos, hookers and dope on the south coast now, then?"

"I wouldn't know."

"I think you would. And I think if you were to roll up your shirt I'd see a wound just there under your ribcage," said Vautier, leaning over to jab at Christophe's right side, "where your old friends tried to shiv you on the inside."

Christophe felt his face harden into a long-abandoned expression, that of a man who was facing both fight and flight.

"I'm happy to be proved wrong. Roll up your shirt."

"I have served my time."

"Unclench your fists, pal. As it happens, I wouldn't have sent you down in the first place. The guy you half killed was the worst kind of scum."

"He was selling wraps of smack to fifteen-year-olds for blowjobs."

"And you were selling them to sixteen-year-olds for cash, so you're no fucking angel."

"The organisation I was in did not allow you to opt out of tasks you found unappealing."

"No, and it likes its own justice. You beat up your boss's son, the cops turned up and you both went down for possession."

"He threw the first punch. From behind too. He was a coward, who relied on his name for protection."

"Hey, I don't disagree. But beating the heir to the throne and getting him sent down? I bet they've got a long, slow death planned for you. Probably glad you didn't bleed out in that prison corridor."

Christophe held his gaze, wondering whether to hear him out or break his jaw. He decided to let him run on and fully show his hand.

"That's why you didn't hang around when you got out. Took the first new identity you could find, no time to shop around. I asked a friendly gendarme and he was pretty sure Fournier is a name from the Nord-Pas-de-Calais, near the Belgian border. I can tell you myself there are no Fourniers on Corsica. I mean, I know it used to be Italian, that place, so maybe they're a little slipshod on the census, but you'd think they'd at least get it together for the birth registers."

"What can I say? I'm reluctantly impressed."

"That drunk slag really landed you in it, letting me see that tattoo, having you blurt out your Corsican connection."

"So what happens now? Is this where you tell me I have twenty-four hours to get off your island?"

"Maybe. There's another way, of possible mutual benefit."

"I have committed no crime since I arrived here."

"Other than living under a false identity."

"What do you want from me?"

"First, I want an assurance that you really are a reformed character. You're right, you've done nothing wrong in my backyard so I've no reason to pull you in. It needs to stay that way."

"Why would I want to draw any attention to myself? You're well aware of what will happen if they find me."

"I am. And I can push that button."

"Unless I do what?"

"I want you to be my early-warning system. No one can spot a villain like another villain. You picked here because it's small and sleepy. You could have tried to lose yourself in a big city, but big cities have friends of friends of friends of the wrong sort. I don't want that sort here, and neither do you."

"Okay."

"Specifically I want you to keep your ear to the ground among your own."

"By 'own', you mean foreigners?"

"We don't pay the Portuguese enough for them to get any rackets going."

"That is usually how rackets start, an isolated community trying to make its way."

"If you spot anything, great. But in my experience the Porkos want to get their heads down, pick the potatoes and go home. Your lot are another story. They've always had their eye on this place, still see it as theirs. So get yourself a hobby, fishing. Gorey, St Catherine's, Bouley, Bonne Nuit, who knows who or what is coming and going in those little harbours? Maybe nothing. But some day someone's going to see how many open doors there are in this Island, and I want to know about it. This is a nice place, a clean place, and I don't want any shit in it."

Vautier had offered his hand and the two had entered into an agreement.

★ ★ ★

It was just after half past eight when Christophe wandered up to the roof with a tumbler and his bottle of Forgeron. He needed to clear his head, and often clambered out of the dormer window of the loft, which was still waiting for the extra funds to turn it into the penthouse. Tonight he was warned off by the gathering gusts of wind and instead stayed holding on to the iron rail that ran round the rim of the roof. The hotel's five occupants had opted for room service, and once they had been served, he would dismiss the chef and close the kitchen for the night. Walk-ups were unlikely, given the turn in the weather; this was a night for hunkering. One couple had walked in at about a quarter to eight, but had been intimidated by the emptiness. Maybe they'd needed to discuss something best masked by the clatter of fellow diners. No matter. Christophe was confident things would pick up. And if they didn't, the Bretagne still presented him with a splendid opportunity. A high-end establishment with an owner desperate for numbers, but unwilling to put in the graft. Rob had not noticed that close to thirteen grand had gone out of his tills. He surely wouldn't question if considerably more were to be put through them.

He hadn't come to the Island looking to steal in such a way. He'd come to gather, to regroup, to buy himself some time. He'd found himself lulled by its small-time rhythms. Maybe it was enough to work in a bar, earn his way, and keep the skin of his knuckles ungrazed. Here was an opportunity for reinvention. Here he could be Christophe Fournier, sophisticated barman, maître d' and latterly hotel manager, keeper of another man's secrets while using them to mask his own. He found that his Frenchness conferred a certain status. Some of the Islanders clearly felt closer to the Normans than they did the Saxons, perhaps due to the ancient history that bonded them as kingdoms, or possibly due to the more recent history that stigmatised both as victims of occupation, who had, in popular parlance, "rolled out the welcome mat" in 1940. When the English spoke to the Jersiaise and the French, the question mark of "Resister or Collaborator?" still hung over them.

But, slowly, he had begun to feel he was destined to become a pet of the lunching classes, hearty handshakes, healthy tips, the veneer of friendship covering the statuses of serf and nobleman. This was never going to be enough. But he'd felt the same back in Marseille. Limited, boxed in, overlooked. Expected to use his fists, not his brains. He hadn't been lying when he'd said the French Connection had been the high point. After the American pipeline was shut down, the Unione had descended into infighting and was now a gang of street thugs making too much noise and drawing unnecessary attention to themselves. He'd been mocked as a pussy and a faggot for suggesting there were other ways of doing business so he'd done exactly what was asked of him until Philippe had pushed things too far. Philippe, who always liked to put him in his place, and who nicknamed him Le Hérisson, The Hedgehog, a taunt about his squat frame and hairy shoulders. He hadn't wanted to be a bit player in his new life so he'd started taking a little extra cash, then realised he could take more than a little. And then Louise had fallen into his lap, and he'd decided to reinvest his pilfered gains in his relationship with Rob. He had bought himself a surfeit of trust, and could now slowly begin working on the other part of his plan that had been gradually coalescing.

Christophe was a born watcher. That was how he'd started as a teenager, looking out for the cops, in uniform or out. He could spot a man's weakness, temperamental, physical, emotional. And he had been watching this Island. Money swilled under it like a drainage system. The tourists, the produce, the famous cattle: those were just window dressing. Sure, they made money, but underneath was where the real action was. He could see where things were going. Why did an island so small need so many banks?

He'd been watching the sea too, just as Vautier had asked him to. The Jerseyman was right: plenty of ways in with no one paying attention. He'd done some fishing in those little harbours, kept his ears open in the bars and cafés, the sailing clubs, discreetly tailed any of his fellow countrymen who had so much as a tinge of insalubrity. There was nothing going on. A bit of cannabis was floating around, but he didn't know how it was getting in and Vautier didn't seem too fussed about him drawing a blank on that. All of which had given him an idea.

He looked down now at Rob's boat, lying at an angle on the sand of the low tide. Were his eyes playing tricks or was it being rocked by the wind even as it sat with its full weight? Aged fifteen, he'd moved to Marseille, the drugs hub of Europe, where the heroin came in from Turkey and Afghanistan, the cannabis from the Middle East and the cocaine from South America. A container ship sailing from Marseille to Portsmouth, Bristol, Liverpool or Glasgow was a big red flag to a Customs man. To the ones who hadn't been bought off, that was a challenge. But a little boat like Rob's, meandering up the coast, would attract little attention. A chain of little boats relaying round the coast of France, each doing a fifty-mile cruise, according to the log book. And from there a hop across the Channel to Weymouth, Cherbourg, Amsterdam, Hamburg. More little boats, or people on foot boarding the ferries. Or, if he could find a farmer as hands-off as Rob, at the bottom of sacks of good old Jersey Royals. And then the profits being slowly rinsed in the Bretagne. If it all went to plan, this hotel would be permanently full on paper, with everyone ordering champagne on room service. When that got too big, with everything looking so rosy, it would be easy to persuade Rob to open other establishments. And when they, too, became full, well, he was in the right place for hiding money. This Island was built on a bottomless pit that you could just shovel it into.

This plan was his way back in, his lifting of his sentence. His boss, Raymonde, couldn't live for ever, and Philippe was too unstable to be accepted as a successor. When the time came, he would reach out. Only he wouldn't be going back on the street: this time he'd be the one giving orders, from a respectable office.

In the meantime, there was Barney Vautier. Christophe had to bide his time carefully. Back in Marseille a cop like him would be taken care of with a stream of cash or a spray of bullets. In his experience, a cop on an off-the-books lookout for criminals did it because he himself was the biggest criminal. Christophe knew there were few hard drugs in the Island; he'd want to keep it that way. Jersey would strictly be a transit route: the market wasn't big enough to justify the risk. Harder to hide the trail to the dealers on an island so small. So maybe Vautier could be persuaded to look the other way. Tricky to know — he needed to get closer. Bringing him this Scouser would help. He might even go looking for him. But not tonight, not with the weather worsening. There was an almighty storm coming.

CHAPTER
FIFTEEN

EMMA

Friday, 16 October 1987

Emma was marooned. A sudden deluge of rain was lashing the phone box, driven by a wind that seemed to be coming from 360 degrees. The rain had started as she walked from the car, hitting the letter she had written with four drops even as it nestled in her handbag. She hoped Colin would not mistake the stains for tears. She doubted it. Despite its import, it was not an emotional letter, and she had written it as calmly as if it had been a shopping list. She looked up at their flat. As far as she could tell, through the watery haze, there was still no light behind the curtains. The phone rang unanswered. None of this guaranteed that Colin was out — he could be wallowing in the dark, listening to his terrible music on headphones. She'd caught him like that before. He was pathetic, emotionally stuck in his teens; the wild-eyed declamatory nature of his early courting should have warned her of that.

Earlier, three days into her voluntary exile at her parents' house, she'd found herself ringing, wanting to scream at him for forcing her to be the first to make contact — contact she'd longed for, if only to spurn. Emma wanted to scream at him because she couldn't scream at Rob. Her rage against him had swollen when she realised it had no vent. Part of her appeal to her former lover must have been that they were stuck in a mutually assured destruction pact. He was banking on her silence. She couldn't blow his marriage apart without blowing hers apart too. She felt duped and bitter that she could only hurt him by refusing the sex she craved. But Colin she could wound and, to her, his transgression was equivalent to Rob's within their relative moral frameworks. For Colin even to think of erring, to have dipped but a toe into the pool of betrayal, was clearly on a par with Rob cheating on her even as they both cheated on Sally.

Jack and Joyce, her parents, knew none of the specifics of why she had turned up with a small suitcase and recently dried eyes, just that she and Colin were having problems, although she'd mentioned to her father a dalliance with a colleague. She knew her mother would steer her towards reconciliation, especially should the facts be presented to her; there had been no affair with Debbie, only the poor girl's projection of affection on to Colin's relentless courtesy. She made it clear that she did not want to talk to Joyce about it by going to work early and staying late, and making abrupt changes in conversation should the issue be so much as distantly alluded to. Jack was different: he had taken her out for lunch on the Thursday and encouraged a separation, asserting that Colin had gone "completely off the bloody rails" and confessing to long-held doubts, "always something odd about him", as well as portentous fears about his daughter's long-term happiness with a man "who so clearly lacks the nous to get to the top of anything". But Joyce had always seen Colin as some kind of saviour. She had never said so directly, but Emma sensed she felt that if her daughter couldn't find happiness with Colin, it would always elude her. She had taken her aside on that Christmas Day of the engagement and, squeezing her hand, had told her tearfully that she was glad Emma was "out of the tunnel".

"What tunnel?" Emma had laughingly responded, while wiping away tears of her own. She couldn't recall the last time her usually phlegmatic mother had cried, and it had proved infectious.

"You've seemed so lost these last years," Joyce had said, "and now you've found your rock."

"My rock on the Rock," smiled Emma, looking at Colin, on the phone to his own mother.

"You think you'll stay here, then?"

"Why wouldn't we?"

"Because you've tried to get away so many times before."

"Twice, Mum. And once was because I had to find Colin."

She had smarted at the memory when she arrived back in that room on the Tuesday night. She wanted to deny that she had ever felt such simplistic euphoria. On Wednesday she'd been relieved he hadn't contacted her — it had made her think he was feeling guilty, that he was scared of her. She'd felt unshackled and carefree.

On Thursday evening her father had told her that Colin had been suspended for aggression in the staffroom, and as she fell asleep, she rehearsed telling him how sad it made her that he showed more passion for some petty dispute over a pupil than for his marriage. He had always put her second — to his mother, to his neighbour, to his work. By Friday his silence had meant she'd had no option but to harden her position as the victim. She couldn't concentrate at work and came home early, wondering if there would be a message of contrition waiting for her, absolving her of any rashness in her departure.

There was no message, so she'd sat on her bed, clenching her fists and listening to the wind rattling the windows. She stood up and walked over. A grey dusk, the sort of low cloud that cast spirits down, all colour drained from the rocks, the sand and the sea. The Christmas morning of Colin's proposal had been blue and clear, crisp and vivid. She wondered if he would have ventured out in the rain to write his proposal in the sand. Would it have been more romantic if he had had to brave the elements? Perhaps if confronted by today's monochrome weather he would have baulked at asking her. And perhaps if those shells had remained scattered randomly by the tide, rather than assembled by Colin to bind the two of them together, she would be somewhere else, at peace with the world and her place in it. Had her life been shaped by the weather?

The phone had rung. She bounded downstairs and snatched it up.

"Hello."

"Emma, are you okay?"

"Yes, Mum, fine."

"I was in town and I popped in to say hi, but they said you'd gone home."

"I had a headache. It's gone now."

"When they said 'home', I didn't know whether they meant our home or yours."

"This is my home."

"Yes, of course, you know what I mean."

"Besides, no one at work knows anything about me and Colin."

"Any word from him?"

"No, thank God."

"Maybe he's waiting for you to call him."

"Why should I?"

"You might have asked for space, told him not to contact you."

"I didn't. I know what I said."

"What did you say?"

"It doesn't matter."

"Pardon?"

"I said it doesn't matter."

"Sorry, the line's a bit crackly here."

"Where are you?"

"The phone box outside Voisins. I'm sure the pips are going to go any moment and I don't have any more change, but I've done all my shopping so I'll head back."

"Great, see you in a bit."

"Maybe we can have a proper chat, before your father comes in."

242

"Maybe, although my headache's quite bad."

"I thought it was better."

"It comes and goes."

"Dr Paterson's surgery is open till five."

"If I wanted to go to the doctor, I would go to the doctor."

"Okay, I'll come home and make us a cup of tea. Perhaps we can try and talk things through."

The pips went before Emma could reply, which was just as well: she couldn't work out what she could say that would suggest her condition was beyond a motherly heart-to-heart, and at the same time not in need of medical attention. Either of those options would lead to a constricting form of caring that she just couldn't face and, worse, to an implied admonishment. Although Joyce thought of herself as a non-interventionist parent, a billowing safety net, ready to catch and comfort her children before setting them off again on the high-wires and trapezes of their choice, she could still convey "I told you so" with a cock of the head. Her opinion seeped from her, like water through rock. Joyce tried to temper her advice and reproaches because experience had taught her that Emma would veer off in the opposite direction almost as a reflex. She had always been a difficult child to help, whether it was stubbornly cutting the hair of her favourite doll, defiant in her belief that it would grow back as her own did, or insisting she would travel the world for three years only to return with a fiancé-in-waiting and an assertion that she had never really wanted to go away in the first place. Emma had sat stewing in anticipation of her mother hinting at the lack of harm in an attempt at rapprochement, desperate to avoid her unasked-for advice.

Her breathing had quickened, her jaw locked and she had grabbed the phone so tightly she felt she could snap the handset. She dialled with such clumsy ferocity that her finger stuck in the hole. She breathed deeply, depressed the buttons to return the dialling tone, and began again, with controlled determination.

"Were you ever going to call me? What the fuck have you been doing?" was how she planned to begin, but there was no answer. She had slammed the phone down. Her mother would be home in ten, fifteen minutes. Colin was out. It was a sign, an opportunity. She had sat down and written a letter, which spewed forth with such ease that she'd thought she must have been composing it subconsciously for some time.

Dear Colin,

I take your silence to mean that I am not worth fighting for. I know that you're a complete emotional coward so, rather than waiting for you to speak your timid mind, let me speak mine. You are no longer what I want in a husband. I'll send someone to collect the rest of my stuff once I'm in my new place. Bonnier's will be in touch. You had best find your own lawyers, and in the long term a new place to live (I will petition for the sale of the flat — I know you can't buy me out). I hope there's enough room at Debbie's for you, although

I imagine it will be hard making do on two teachers' salaries.

Emma

Seeing her feelings on paper made them real. This was what she wanted. She had jumped into the car and driven the long way via the inner coast road to avoid passing her mother on the way.

She'd darted into the phone box to double-check he was still out — she didn't want to see him. If he couldn't be bothered to speak to her, let alone face her, she would do him the same discourtesy.

There was a break in the rain so she put the receiver down and stepped out of the phone box, pushed on to one leg by a gust. She walked in a stoop to the block, having decided to listen at the door and slip the letter underneath, should Colin be at home.

Mrs Le Boutillier's door opened as she neared the landing. Emma wondered if she'd set off some invisible tripwire.

"Oh, hello, Mrs Bygate, I haven't seen you for a few days."

"I've been staying at my parents'. My mother's not been very well."

"Oh, I'm sorry to hear that. Mr Bygate must have been missing you — that'll be why he's not been himself."

"I'm sure he's fine."

"Well, he was quite abrupt with me this morning. Didn't introduce me to his friend and he wasn't very helpful about Marmalade. Now, he's either in the cattery because the Ozoufs are away — it's not right to keep an animal like that in a cage — or, and this chills me to the bone, he's gone missing. I've knocked on their door and there's no reply, but sometimes they both work very long hours . . ."

Emma had zoned out. *What friend?*

"I heard the front bell last night around one, but that wouldn't be them. Maybe it was your husband's friend . . ."

"Sorry, what friend?"

"The young lady."

"A young lady was here this morning?"

"Yes, they left together."

Emma, flattened and empty, turned her back and opened the door to the flat.

"Oh, I'm sorry. I wasn't suggesting anything. I thought she was a friend of yours too — she was wearing your jacket."

Emma shut the door and stood motionless in the dark for several minutes. She heard Mrs Le Boutillier muttering to herself, then shuffling back into her flat.

Another woman had been here. No, it wasn't possible, he wouldn't do that. But wasn't that what she'd wanted? No, the letter was a taunt, not a wish. This wasn't Colin. A woman had spent the night? And left wearing her clothes? That was bizarre. Had Colin picked her up naked? It didn't make any sense. But her coat wasn't on the peg. Could it have been Colin's mother, over here to console her son and claw him back to her? She could make out a blanket on the sofa: that was where Patricia slept when she visited. Emma

246

turned on the light and looked around the kitchen. There was no large tin of shortbread biscuits, a sure sign of her presence — "A fresh supply of your favourites, Colin," she would say. She opened the fridge: no meat from the butcher. The old woman always stocked up on fresh meat, a silent criticism of Emma's fondness for supermarket ready meals. Old woman. Of course! How could it have been his mother? Mrs Le Boutillier had referred to the stranger as young and, in any case, she had met Colin's mother a few times. Colin had hoped they might become friends and give him and Emma some peace, but there had been instant mutual antipathy when the war had come up, with the Mainlander insisting it was terrifying under the threat of bombs, and the Islander contending that occupation was worse. No, the mystery woman was not his mother, decided Emma, with relief — until she realised that this meant it had been someone else.

She ran to the bedroom. The bed looked unslept in, freshly made. She pulled back the duvet and fell on the mattress, smelling the sheets and looking for signs of an intruder. Nothing. The sheets hadn't been changed since she left. She let out a laugh. What was she worried about? This was Colin, her rock. A lifeless piece of dull stone who would never betray her. Silly old Colin. A man for whom a ruck in a rug hurt like a pebble in a shoe, and whose favourite band from the punk era was Dire Straits. He was not a man to cheat on his wife. She lay back and let her head hang off the side. Whoever had stayed here must have slept on the sofa, and Colin in the bed that he had made as soon as he'd got up, just as he always did. Or vice versa. The stupid old cow next door was just stirring things: there was nothing of which to be suspicious.

Emma noticed a pair of heels and a skirt left on the stool by the dressing-table. She rolled off the bed and crawled towards them. They weren't hers. She couldn't touch them — she felt sick. She pulled herself up, holding on to the door handle, and staggered through the hall, bursting out of her front door and finding herself pounding on her neighbour's door.

"I know you're there! Come on, you're always butting in when I don't want you!"

A confused and hesitant Mrs Le Boutillier opened the door. "I was just seeing to my dinner."

"What did she look like?" spat Emma, pushing her way in.

"Who?"

"You know exactly who! The woman this morning!"

"Please, Mrs Bygate, you're frightening me."

"For Christ's sake, normally you won't shut up. Come on, this is your big moment!"

"I am not a gossip."

"You are when it comes to bloody cats!"

"Have you seen him?"

"No, and he's not yours. He's nothing to do with you!"

Mrs Le Boutillier fell back on to her settee. "My chop will be burning!"

"I couldn't give a shit about your chop. Tell me about the woman!"

"Your language!"

"The fucking woman!"

"Not even the Nazis spoke to me like that!"

"That's not what I've heard. My aunt said you were a Jerry Bag."

"I don't know, she was maybe thirty, shoulder-length hair, light brown, shorter than yours," sobbed Mrs Le Boutillier. "Now please leave."

Debbie. Of course. Who else could it have been? Emma looked down at the frightened old lady and felt ashamed. She walked through to the kitchen, turned off some overboiled leeks and took the pork chop out of the oven. Then she tore off a length of kitchen roll, went back to the lounge and handed it to her snivelling neighbour.

"I'm sorry."

Emma fled back to her flat. Her own tears were flowing now and she scrabbled in her bag for a handkerchief. She pulled out the letter for Colin, which goaded him to run into Debbie's arms. But that wasn't what she wanted. He had found her at her lowest point. She'd been sinking down and he had raised her up again, her rock on the Rock. He was hers, not Debbie's, not his mother's, not anyone else's. She crumpled the letter and wept silently on the sofa.

CHAPTER
SIXTEEN

LOUISE

Friday, 16 October 1987

"What's the matter, Lou? Not got a kiss for me?"

Louise had frozen at the sight of Billy when she opened the door. Needing to mask the fear and panic, she broke into a beaming smile and wrapped her arms around him, kissing him with as much passion as she could muster. His breath stank but, then, Billy had once boasted that the only use he'd ever found for a toothbrush was as a shiv, with a razor blade stuck to the head.

"You're shakin', girl."

"I just can't believe you're here — it feels like a dream. Come in, quick." She pulled him inside and shut the door. She kissed him again, but he pushed her aside to walk further into the room. She knew he was checking for signs of another man. She'd not answered his question about Danny, and she quivered at the knowledge that eventually she would have to.

He turned round and stood with his arms folded, while she remained in front of the door. Best place to be, she figured, although she knew he was quicker than her. He was spindly and narrow-hipped, but that didn't preclude strength. Besides, as he had often demonstrated, it wasn't how strong you were, it was what you were prepared to do, and there was no move too low for Billy in a fight. He certainly didn't recognise the "never hit a woman" rule, which, to her shame, she'd enjoyed when a former school-friend had sneered at her in a club.

"Not got nothin' to say? Been a long time, girl. Didn't come all this way to be stared at."

"Sorry. I guess I'm just in shock. Good shock, happy shock."

"Sound like you lost your accent."

"When'd you get out? How'd you get out?" she said, trying to restore it.

"Couple of weeks ago. Good behaviour. Turns out slashin' a nonce is good behaviour." He gave a rasping laugh. "Screws put me up to it, looked the other way, then returned the favour." He wandered over to the window and peered round the corner of the curtain sheet. "You took a bit of findin', not in the phone book."

"I don't have a phone."

"So what you been doin', apart from not comin' to see me?" He was prowling round the room now. She'd forgotten the way he edged from foot to foot, like an animal trying to puff itself up to deter a predator or intimidate a prey.

She took a step towards him, hands clasped in penance. "I'm sorry, Bill, I just couldn't cope with seeing you inside, caged up."

"Worst place to put me, a cage. Nowhere for the other people to run. What's with the briefcase?"

"It's for work. I've got a crappy office job." She pulled him down on to the bed, putting the case under it with one hand while stroking his face with the other. "I can't believe you're here, that you're real." She kissed him again, wanting to distract him with sex, but terrified that she wouldn't be sufficiently aroused, and that he would know something was up.

"Shit job, poky bedsit, but a nice posh briefcase. What's that about?"

She was worried her voice would start to quaver. "This place is all about image, got to look the part."

"Looked heavy when you lugged it back."

"You been spying on me?" She smiled to convert her tone from accusatory to flirtatious.

"Not laid eyes on you for a while, wanted to check if you'd lost your looks."

"So, what do you think?" She stood and gave him a twirl, a wink and a curtsy, resenting how small he was making her feel.

"I'm here, aren't I? Otherwise I'd have just driven off."

"You brought a car?"

"Picked one up."

"Bill, you got to be careful over here. People notice things like that, cars going missing. Is it flash?"

"Yeah, but that's not gonna make it stand out. You didn't clock it across the road. Missin' Merc? Every other car's a Merc."

"The cops will be looking . . ."

"Cops? You really have forgot how to speak."

"Bizzies, then."

"The bizzies here are fuckin' yokels."

The one who'd come to see her wasn't. He was smart.

"What's your plan?" she asked, praying to hear *Thought I'd scoot round the Elizabethan fortifications, maybe check out the zoo, then head home and let you get on with your life*, but knowing that a very dark net was drawing around her.

"Just wanted to check in with my girl and bring her back where she belongs. But while I was trackin' you down, I saw a lot of opportunities. There's a bit of dope here, but it's run by pussies. And I don't think the bizzies'd know the difference between brown and fuckin' Marmite."

"Isn't your supply, you know, restricted?"

"What d'you mean?"

"Big Gaz took your patch and your dealers."

"You think I don't know that?" He sat up, gripping her wrists. "I fuckin' gave 'em to him, in return for his boys watchin' over me inside."

She sank down to her knees, brought his hands up to her mouth and kissed them. "You don't need watching over — I've seen what these hands can do. And they can take back whatever they want from Gary Hutchinson."

"Gaz's fuckin' small-time. Two square miles, that's his empire. He can have it. There's a whole fuckin' world out here." He let go of her wrists and stood over her, his eyes glittering. "Made some nice new friends

253

inside. Some Turkish fellas with big connections. They're sittin' on Skag Mountain. I just need a sea route from Marsay, it's a Froggie town. Plenty of boats here and no one watchin'."

"Why not just sail it straight back home? Stick it in one of the containers." Please, Billy, don't come and infect my paradise.

"Big fat Customs hands to grease. Nobody bothers here. Fancy yachts in and out. Plus I've been sittin' in bars, listenin'. I hear a lot of Scousers, Mancs, Jocks and Micks. They're back and forth on domestic flights. Split it up from here, small-scale distribution on a route the bizzies think is too poxy to check up on."

"Big plan."

"Yeah, just need some start-up funds. About fifty to buy in on a small supply, and with the profits from that I can go back for a larger chunk. Builds and builds. Be enough to get me off the streets and maybe into one of those houses on the beach. Imagine that. Not a beach hut, a fuckin' house on the beach!"

"Where you going to get the fifty grand, though?"

Billy smiled and sat down on the floor, sliding the case out from under the bed. "You tell me."

Louise swallowed hard, to counter the sensation that she was about to throw up. She moved closer. "I've been a busy girl," she purred, nuzzling his hair so that it wiped away the tears she couldn't hold back, "getting ready for you."

"How was runnin' over here gettin' ready for me?"

Her mouth was dry. This was never an issue that was going to be resolved quickly. "With you away, Bill, I had

254

no one to protect me. Mickey Delaney was eyeing me up, the McCallister brothers threatened to cut me so you wouldn't want me. It wasn't safe."

"You sayin' I couldn't protect you, that I don't have no reach?"

"I didn't know you had Gaz's backing. I thought he was another one to watch out for."

"Fuck Gaz. Him and the rest of those cunts would piss their pants at the thought of me givin' 'em a smile."

"It's not about you being weak, love. It's about me being scared and panicking, and being wrong. But maybe this will make up for it." She opened the case. He leapt on to the bed in delight.

"Fuck me, Lou, how much is this?"

There was no point in being anything other than direct. "Ten."

"How'd you get it?"

Further honesty suddenly seemed incredibly dangerous: it would involve confessing to sleeping with another man. Danny would buckle under such a revelation; Billy might throw her out of a window. But she was pausing for too long and her usually agile mind was so paralysed by his venomous leer that she found herself saying, "Honey-trap. Local businessman bored of his wife but not enough to want a divorce."

He gripped her head with both hands and leant over her till they were nose to nose. She felt sick and chilled. She thought of screaming, but who would come? No one who could stop what was about to happen.

"Ten grand for my girl's pussy. Seems cheap to me."

She smiled as strongly as she could. "I did it for you."

"And I say you're worth more. What's he do, this guy?"

"Owns a hotel. Flash one."

"Is he a madhead?"

"Course not. But don't fight him, Bill."

"I'll only fight him if he won't open his wallet."

"He won't pay any more."

"I need fifty, not ten."

"Maybe I can pull the scam again."

"What am I, your fuckin' pimp? I'm pissed off you whored yourself out once. I don't want it happenin' again. You fuck anyone else while I was away?"

"No."

"Don't lie, Lou. You and me, we was always honest with each other." That was bullshit. Louise knew for a fact he'd slept with her cousin.

"No one to worry about."

"What about this Danny?"

"He's just a friend."

"Rich? Worth a squeeze?"

"He's a chef."

"Let's meet your hotel owner, then." Billy stood up and clapped his hands.

Louise reached up and held his waist. It was worth a try. "Wait, Bill," she said. "Just hear me out. There's another way."

He looked down at her and spread his arms wide. "Another way what?"

"To get your house on the beach. With this money here, we could buy a place now."

"Serious? That's enough for a mansion? Which estate agents you been talkin' to?"

"Well, not quite a mansion. But there's this property up in Rozel. It's this sweet little bay, Bill, not like the coast back home. Blue sea, pink rocks. It's beautiful."

"I'm confused, 'cause you said this cash was for me. Sounds like you been lookin' for a place for yourself."

"For us, love. While I was waiting, I got thinking. This could be our way out. You and me in a big old place on the beach. More than Gaz has got, or any of the big guys back home."

"You and me? *Homemakers?* I need fuckin' stuff to do, Lou. I need challenges. I'm not gonna sit around watchin' you knit."

"This place would give us stuff to do. It needs doing up, and it's a bed and breakfast, but we can turn it into a nice little hotel. Open the doors to the tourists six months a year, sit on our arses the rest of it."

Billy's jaw dropped. Then he grinned. "A hotel. It's the answer to everythin'."

"Really?" Louise was flushed with relief and excitement.

"Sure. I want nothin' more than to spend the rest of my life washin' sheets and cookin' breakfasts and cleanin' shit stains off toilets. What the fuck you talkin' 'bout?"

"I'm just scared about you going back inside. I want you to play safe. Don't hate me for wanting you," she murmured, in a frantic bid to avoid a slapping.

257

"Is it that, or you want to save this prick a beatin'?"

"No, I don't care about him."

"'Cause I'm gettin' the urge. You know how I get. Need to get me rocks off. Someone's gonna fuckin' get it tonight, Lou. I reckon there's three candidates. I'm still sore you didn't visit, you can understand that, plus there's ten grand there you wanna piss away on a fuckin' B and B, rather than lettin' me expand me business with it. So you are a prime fuckin' candidate. So far, I've been fuckin' soft. Remember what Degsy did to his old lady when he got out and found she'd been foolin' around?"

Louise nodded, eyes down, praying for all the world that Barney Vautier would walk back in.

"Number two is this guy who paid under the goin' rate for a night in your hole. Even if he pays, he's gonna have to take at least one punch to the face for fuckin' me woman. And you know what I'm like when me blood's up. I can't stop meself. But we can forget your shitty hotel, we can forget his big flash one, and we can just wait here for option number three. Your friend Danny. You seemed to be expectin' him and I'd love to meet him. What do you say, Lou? Who deserves it most, out the three of you?"

"I'll take you to Rob."

"Rob, is it? Crackin'! Let's rob Rob!"

CHAPTER
SEVENTEEN

COLIN

Friday, 16 October 1987

"Are you sure you know where it is?" Colin yelled in Debbie's face.

She jabbed a finger out into the night. She might have said something back — he couldn't tell because of the noise of the wind that belted them as they walked through the rocky gully, and also because Debbie had drawn the string on her hood so tight against the rain that her mouth was obscured. She pulled his arm to get him moving again and they staggered on, heads down, beams from their torches picking out glistening black rocks, sand and dark tidal pools that they often had to wade through. Colin's trousers were sopping, his toes numb in his boots, every atom of his overcautious body telling him that each step was not only futile but potentially dangerous. He looked back: he could no longer see the lights of the Island. He prayed that Debbie's insistence that she knew a safe path out to Seymour Tower was folly, and that she was leading them round in a circle, back to the car park. They'd passed a few hours there, listening to the radio and eating chips while waiting for the tide to allow them access to the tower a mile out to sea.

His enthusiasm for the search had waned throughout the day as they had traipsed round various fortifications, starting with those on land. L'Etacquerel Fort on the north coast had been unlikely. It was reached via a wooden bridge across a dry moat off a steep coastal path, which didn't guarantee the total seclusion for which they assumed Duncan had opted. La Tour de Vinde, a circular structure at the base of Noirmont Point, was also a long shot, given that there was no access or platform around the base to use as partial shelter, but it passed the time until they could walk out first to Portelet Tower in the next bay, which they reached via a small sandbank, and then La Rocco Tower, in the southern curve of the vast sweep of St Ouen's Bay. With no sign of Duncan, they had headed to St Aubin's Fort, built on a small reef, and again left empty-handed.

He felt relaxed with Debbie. The air had been cleared, so he attached no significance to the occasional hand clasp used to steady each other walking over rocks or across fissures. At first conversation was minimal and practical, then became more expansive. He learnt that she had taught English in Japan before training as a history teacher, which she insisted she had told him before. At the sight of rabbits lolloping round the Noirmont grass he had confessed that, such was his childhood obsession with *Watership Down*, his mother had taken him on a pilgrimage to the very Down.

Debbie had laughed long and hard. "Oh, my God, that's kind of sweet, but so uncool."

He had been mildly taken aback: she normally treated him with more deference. He supposed that now the boundaries of the friendship had been clearly delineated, she felt she could mock him. She had no need to flatter him since what she wanted he couldn't provide. He decided it was healthier, although when he had warned her away from the edge of the cliffs above Portelet Bay, her response had had a confusing tinge of flirtation.

"Are you worried I'm going to fling myself off because we can't be together?" It had come with a smile rather than rancour, which made him overlook her insensitivity in referring to a suicide leap, given his fears for Duncan.

The easy company they made with each other, now that they each knew where they stood, meant that they had prolonged the comfort of the car for as long as possible before setting out for the tower. Also, as the tide had gone down with the sun, so the wind had come up with the rain. Even as they set off, he had tried to dissuade her from another fruitless trek, especially after she'd told him the incoming tide rose eight centimetres a minute.

"We don't have time to debate it, Colin. At this rate we have a half-hour window to get him off. If you don't want to be out here in this weather, how can you leave *him* out in it?"

"We don't even know he's there."

"I told you, I saw something."

Earlier they'd driven along to Gorey Harbour to buy some binoculars from an outdoors shop. Colin had hoped a close scan of the tower would rule out having to walk to it, but Debbie had sworn she'd seen something flapping above the walls at its base. Colin had been unable to make out anything in the grey, and posited that it could be a fishing net, flag or coat.

"Coat. Which means someone's out there."

"Or they were. Or it got blown out there."

"It got blown from the shore all the way to the tower without landing in the water?"

"It could have come off a boat."

"I thought you wanted to get to the bottom of this."

"Of course I do, but maybe tomorrow when the weather's better. It's been a long day."

The weather had got worse with every step. He tried to check the time but when he held up his wrist he couldn't work his watch out from under his sleeve. He knew low tide was at nine, and they had about fifteen minutes after that before they'd have to turn back. At least the wind would be behind them then, but it would be blowing the water in too, and eight centimetres a minute was already walking pace. It was dark — they might take a wrong turn. He started to panic.

He pulled Debbie to a halt, tugged her hood outwards so that she could hear, then yelled, "How much further?"

"Nearly there! Couple of hundred yards!"

Colin couldn't make out anything, apart from the silhouettes of rocks that were more likely his eyes playing tricks. "Are you sure?"

"Yes. Come on! You've risked your job over this! Are you going to be put off by a bit of wind?"

"This is a bloody hurricane!"

"You wait here, then. I'm going on to the tower."

With that she staggered onwards, a tiny gutsy figure putting him to shame. He knew he couldn't turn back without her, if only out of self-preservation: he was in her hands.

The sand was soggy and his feet were sinking, making his thighs burn with each step. Suddenly his left boot refused to accompany his foot and he found himself pitching forwards, grazing his hand on a small barnacled rock and landing on his right side in a pool. Debbie came back, hauled him up and helped him hobble back to his boot. He looked down at her. Her eyes were set. There was still no turning back. He grabbed her hand and they went forward together.

As he spun his torch around him, it seemed that the maze of rocks they'd walked through was flattening out, leaving them in the midst of sandbars. Debbie tugged his arm and pointed. Her beam picked out a large rock, above which loomed a structure with one white wall. Now it was his turn to pull her forward: they needed to get up there and down again fast. He didn't bother checking the time: even if they had an hour's grace, he didn't want to spend a second longer out there than was necessary.

The water-logged sand gave way with his weight so that he felt as if he was taking three steps to travel the distance of one, but he kept going, slipping and lurching forward.

They reached the base of the huge rock upon which the tower was built, which sheltered them from the slam and slice of the wind.

"How do we get up?" he yelled, then realised there was now no need to shout.

"This way," she said, leading him round to the right, where once more they were hammered by the wind and rain, coming at them in horizontal sheets. Large slabs of granite had been laid into a groove in the rock, making steps, slippery in the wet. They reached the platform at the base of the tower, which was shielded by a low L-shaped wall with an open end at the top of the steps. Debbie's torch picked out a figure next to a rucksack, huddled in the far corner where the wall met the tower. Colin ran forward.

"Duncan!"

The boy blinked in the bright light, then shielded his eyes, which helped conceal the tears that, no doubt, were falling — heaving sobs jolted his body up and down.

"It's okay," said Colin. "I got your letter too late. I'm sorry."

"I didn't know what to do . . ." he whimpered.

"You need to go home. Everyone's worried about you."

"Can't go home. He's going to tell them."

"About the drugs? Is that what he said?"

"Yes. Unless I did stuff. Let him touch me. He tried. I ran. When you found me, you stopped me —"

"Colin," shouted Debbie, her hand on his shoulder. "We need to go."

"Yes, come on," said Colin, pulling Duncan to his feet. The boy's legs wobbled and they fell down together. "Are you okay?" Colin asked.

"Haven't eaten for a few days" — Duncan was shivering — "and I'm cold. Can't feel my hands and feet."

"He could have hypothermia!" Colin called to Debbie. "We need to go."

"I know! The tide's going to start coming back in."

"Have you been here all week? Outside?"

"I had a tent, couldn't use guy ropes on rock, weighted it with some stones, blew away this afternoon."

"Here, put your arm round my shoulders."

Duncan clasped Colin's neck. Colin stood up and put his arm round the boy's waist, stooping so Duncan could hang on. The three of them staggered back towards the steps. Colin helped Duncan down sideways, bracing himself against the boy's weight.

"We need to hurry!" he heard Debbie bellow.

Colin reached the bottom and scanned the ground with the torch in his free hand. He couldn't remember which direction they'd come from, so instinctively headed for the higher sandbanks to the left, that were less lapped by the water than the rocks and bars at the base. He heard Debbie yell something — to go quicker, he thought — as he dragged Duncan along. She yelled again. He turned. He saw her torchlight but couldn't make out what she was saying. She waved the beam away from her. He couldn't be going the wrong way: there was more water behind her than him. He plunged on. She sounded closer — good, she was following.

"Wrong way!" he heard. Shit, he was still walking into the wind. Unless it had changed direction, he was heading out to sea. But the sea wasn't there. She caught up with them.

"What are you doing? Didn't you hear me? You're going the wrong way!"

"But it's dry!"

"It's higher up. The tide fills up the side closer to the land first. We need the white side of the tower behind us."

Colin took off again — quicker to go right round the tower than double back.

"Wait! We won't get round!"

Suddenly Colin realised that he and Duncan were walking through water, only ankle-deep but flowing so fast that it built up over the top of his boots.

Debbie was upon him.

"Can we get through this way?" he yelled.

"No! There's a shelf about two feet in front of you, you'll go up to your necks. This way! Quick!"

She pulled them towards her and, with Duncan in the middle, the three lurched back the way they'd come, past the rock base of the tower. The sandbank they'd walked up from was now a spit. They hobbled along it, slipping into knee-deep water either side as the sand slid from under their feet.

"We have to go back to the tower!" Debbie screamed.

"We'll never make it!"

"We won't make it to the Island!"

"But —"

"For once in your life, Colin, just accept that someone knows better than you!"

Colin swung Duncan round, they were now wading against a waist-high current and a blasting gale. The sand rose slightly as they reached the rock base, water flooding round from each side, then they rounded the corner for one last push against the water, fast-flowing and freezing against their knees. Colin pushed Duncan up the rocks towards the steps. Debbie followed the boy, then braced herself in two footholds and held out a hand to Colin. He kicked himself up the steps with her help and landed with his head on her crotch. They scrambled up behind Duncan, crawling up the steps on all fours, frozen by the wind as it lashed their sopping clothes.

They reached the top of the platform in a shivering heap, cut off by the water and at the mercy of the wind.

CHAPTER
EIGHTEEN

LOUISE

Friday, 16 October 1987

"Jesus, Bill, that was another red light."

"I don't see no bizzies."

"I told you, they've got honorary bizzies over here. They're just local twats given a badge to check the hedgerows don't overhang, but they can stop you for traffic stuff."

"Burn 'em off in this bitch."

He speeded up, then braked sharply as he came upon an unexpected bend. "Fuckin' hell! Where's a good stretch of road in this place?"

"Out west. Five Mile Road. It's not even five miles. Just seems it to these inbreds."

"Is it on our way?"

"No. Let me check where we're at."

Louise turned on the interior light and peered between the open map and the passing turnings. "Can you slow down? I can't see the names." He didn't respond. "For fuck's sake, it's a thirty-mile-an-hour speed limit! You're clocking fifty."

"You been here too long."

"Slow down."

"Wanna get there before he goes out for the night."

"We're not going to get there at all if you don't let me check the road names."

"How many times you been there?"

"Once. To threaten him. His wife was there. He damn near shat his kecks when he saw me."

"What's he gonna do when he sees me?"

"He might not be there. Like you said, he might be out."

"Then we'll wait."

"Okay, there's a left coming up . . . here . . . Fucking slow down!"

Billy wrenched the steering wheel and, as the car swung towards a lane, the back end slid round and clipped a garden wall. Billy gunned the engine and skidded off, whooping and punching the horn.

Louise had originally hooked up with Billy for status and power. Being his girl meant she was somebody. She had thought they were equals, that in time she could control him. Before he'd been put inside that notion was already sliding away from her. Now it had vanished. Billy was living proof that prison was not a corrective, she thought. He was like a difficult dog sent off for training that had come back knowing how to rip out a throat. She had been sure he would get up to no good inside, and have his sentence extended to the point at which, when he came out, he couldn't reasonably express any claim on her, preferably being a frail old man. But he was here now, next to her, desperate to prove himself the harder man, the bigger man, the richer man. But the really big men, Louise thought, the so-rich-they-couldn't-spend-their-money-in-a-lifetime men, well, you never knew who they were. Billy was small-time, would always make too much noise to get away with anything bigger.

"Take a right here."

"Where?"

"Here!"

It had started to rain harder than the wipers could cope with. That, and the lack of streetlights, meant Billy turned too late and smashed the left headlight into a granite gatepost.

"Fuck! These stupid fuckin' pissy roads." He reversed back and carried on.

"There'll be nothing left of this car by the time we get there."

"He got nice wheels?"

"A few."

"We should take a new ride, then."

"Let's not push our luck, Bill."

"You what?"

"We don't want to push him to the point he'd call the cops . . . bizzies."

"I thought you said he wants to keep his missus."

"Keep it to threats, don't actually touch him. And, honestly, let's not go too high. Maybe another ten."

"I told you, I need fifty. And another car."

"What if he comes after you? With the law?"

"He won't. I'll know where he lives."

Louise realised this was not going to end tonight. Rob would never be free of Billy, which meant she would never be free of either of them. "Let's think for a moment."

"I am thinkin', and it seems to me you might still be a bit sweet on this guy."

"No."

"What if it wasn't a honey-trap? What if you're his fuckin' bit on the side?"

"Why would he give me ten grand?"

"Buy yourself a nice flat, set yourself up, so he can come and fuck you somewhere other than that shithole bedsit you're livin' in. Or does he take you to his hotel?"

"You've got it all wrong."

"We'll find out, won't we?"

"He's not going to tell you anything I haven't."

"I'm sure he'll play along with your story, but I'll be lookin' at your face when I open him up. See if you shed a tear for him."

Louise felt sick to her core. She knew that whatever she said, whatever Rob said, didn't matter. Billy was going to half kill him. He would be hospitalised. His wife could be at home. There was no way to avoid questions and investigations, which would end where it had begun, with her and a blackmail charge. She'd thought Billy might scare Rob into upping the money, and she had no problem with him taking a few slaps — he was still a prick. But he didn't deserve what was about to happen to him. And, crucially, neither did she.

Rob's house was coming up on the right. She recognised the ludicrous lamps that blazed over the too-short drive. Lights were on. Someone was home.

271

"Keep going straight for a while."

"Me and straight don't go too well!"

They had passed Rob's house and she could send Billy round in circles while she thought of what to do — she doubted he'd recognise the road when they came back on to it: he wouldn't twig she'd played for time. No, they couldn't come back on to this road. She had to get through to him.

"Another right here, then keep going till I tell you."

He turned, this time without damaging the car.

"Bill, you've just got out. I don't want you to go back inside." She put her hand on his upper thigh and stroked it, hoping to disguise the shake that had set in.

"Yeah, you were pinin' for me big-time, over here suckin' some rich man's cock for money."

"I told you, it wasn't like that."

"I were against you doin' it again, but if it's what you like, maybe you should. Maybe I should put you to work, suckin' cocks. You like cocks, I like cash. We both win."

She mustered some of her old fire. "You don't own me, Billy McCaffrey. You went away. What I did then is not your business. I don't know what you did inside — for all I know you were sucking cocks for ciggies and taking it up the arse for an extra go on the table football. I don't give a shit. What's done is done. We're here now. If you want me, you better treat me with some fucking respect."

"That's better! That's my Lou! You fuckin' scared me back in your room. Folded like a little girl. Fine, you're forgiven, but he fuckin' isn't."

"No."

"No? Watch it, girl, you're still my old lady. I ain't bein' told what to do."

"They're on to you."

"Who?"

"Bizzies. They know you're here."

"How the fuck d'you know?"

"One of them came to see me."

"What? Why the fuck you tellin' me now?"

"Because I knew you'd be like this."

"What'd he say?"

"That a Scouser stuck a knife in a bloke's mouth. Jesus, Bill."

"This Island has one dealer — one! Imagine how easy it'll be to take over."

"They won't put up with it here, same as they won't put up with you beating the shit out of some local businessman. They'll come down on you like a sledgehammer. Best thing you can do is get on a boat in the morning, and get the fuck off."

"Best thing *I* can do? Thought we was back on. Thought you didn't want me back inside."

"If I wanted you back inside I'd take you straight to Barney."

"Who's fuckin' Barney?"

"The cop."

"You on first names with a bizzie? You fuckin' him too?"

"You're paranoid."

"Go on, then. Take me to Barney. I don't fuckin' believe you. I don't believe he exists. And you should be fuckin' glad of that, because if I thought you were talkin' to the bizzies, I'd put you under the fuckin' wheels of this car."

"Yeah, 'cause it's really easy to get away with a murder on an island this small."

"You just want me off so you can go back to your fuckin' boyfriend 'cause he's got money. Well, I'm gonna take his money."

"Calm down —"

"Shut your fuckin' whore mouth! Do not speak unless it's to tell me where to drive."

Louise gripped the side of the seat to stop herself quivering. She was out of moves. She could direct Billy down to Rouge Bouillon police station. There was no way he'd drive in, but she might be able to jump out, run in and yell for Barney or anyone who was around. But then what? If they caught Billy, best-case scenario they'd confiscate the ten grand on the back seat and blame him. Worst case, she'd be done for blackmail, either because Billy would land her in it out of spite or because, knowing her luck and this spider's web of an island, someone at the station would recognise the briefcase, the initials or both and call Rob in to have her stuck in a cell next to Billy's, from which he'd find a way to get to her. She'd be the rat who'd landed Billy in jail: there'd be no shortage of volunteers to fuck her up.

"Well?"

"You told me not to speak unless it was directions."

"And you haven't given me any for a while."

"There's only about four roads on this place. You're on the right one. Up to the top."

Rain, dark lanes, the outlines of trees waving, like a giant toddler had grabbed them by the root and was trying to shake off the last leaves of autumn. Louise eyed the lock on the door and wondered if she could unlock and open it before Billy guessed what she was up to. She didn't have her seatbelt on, but neither did he — he'd be straight after her. Unless she jumped out while the car was moving. But if she landed badly she had no doubt he'd just reverse over her.

"Where are we?"

She had no idea. They were banking wildly to the left and the right on a downhill lane barely the width of the car. "Nearly there," she said. "He owns all this."

"Where the fuck's his house, then?"

Billy slowed the car as the headlights picked out a small gravelled car park and a sign that said "Saie Bay". They were out of road.

She clenched her jaw, took a breath and turned to him, putting her arms round his neck. "Billy," she murmured, "I'm sorry."

He turned to her, clearly expecting a kiss, but she pulled him towards her at the same time as she brought her forehead crushing down on the bridge of his nose. He reeled backwards, gasping.

"Fuckin' bitch!" One hand covered his face while the other grabbed towards her, but she had opened the door and jumped out.

She ran as fast she could across the car park and up a small field. She felt herself pushed on and lifted by the wind, which was battering everything around her. Up the slope was a small wood. There were no house lights to be seen. She needed a phone. Between Barney Vautier and Billy she had made her choice. Billy didn't know where he was but she had a vague idea. Somewhere on the north coast. Just keep moving. A path ran in front of a series of large rocks and she spotted a small brick hut. Suddenly she felt a blow to the back of her head and fell, colours dancing before her eyes in the dark.

"Cunt!" she heard Billy yell. A fist-sized rock lay next to her on the muddy ground — he must have thrown it.

"Fuckin' cunt!" he screamed, as he approached. "Although respect, that was a fuckin' great headbutt!"

She felt his hands on her waist. He turned her over, sitting astride her, trapping her arms by her sides. Blood was streaming down his face, giving him a macabre red beard.

"Please, Bill, no . . ."

"I'm not gonna kill you, Lou. I'm gonna do somethin' worse."

He leant his head back in the rain, and gave it a shake. "Why'd you have to fuckin' do that, Lou? Why'd you have to do any of it? I fuckin' loved you! And now you're makin' me do this . . ."

He pulled out a knife.

"No! Stop! Help!" screamed Louise.

"He's not here, Lou. Not Rob, not that Danny, not your bizzie mate Barney. Just me. I don't know if you fucked one or all of them. But I know this. None of them's gonna want to fuck you after this."

He fish-hooked her mouth open with his left hand and brought the knife in front of her face. She pushed up with her hips and jerked her head round to bite down on his fingers as hard as she could. She tasted blood and heard a crack. He dropped his knife, screaming, and tried to pull his hand free, bucking on top of her, which allowed her to free her arms. She scrabbled around as he leant closer, no longer struggling to free his damaged fingers, but using his palm to push her chin up, exposing her neck.

"I am going to piss down your slit throat," he rasped, picking up his knife and waving it in front of her eyes. Her flailing hand found the rock that had knocked her down. She clasped it, then smashed it as hard as she could against the side of his face. He fell off her, his head hitting one of the large stones. She crawled over to him, and raised the rock again, but dropped it. She could see from the hole in his temple that it wasn't needed. Billy was dead.

CHAPTER
NINETEEN

EMMA

Friday, 16 October 1987

Emma blinked and peered around the room. She looked at her watch, but couldn't make out the time in the half-light thrown from a street lamp, which was wobbling like a bamboo cane in the wind and casting frenetic shadows on the window and the ornaments on the ledge. She didn't want to turn the light on: that would make things real, and she didn't want that. She didn't want to be lying alone in her flat, longing for the return of the husband she'd spurned, and she didn't want to have to think that maybe the only reason she wanted him now was because someone else did. That was too much for her. She could deal only with the here and now. And right now she wanted the man she'd married and, perhaps more importantly, wanted him to want her.

How could she lose him to nerdy Debbie? She'd really not seen that coming. This would be the second time she'd lost a man to a lesser woman.

She hauled herself upright. She could see the clock on the video recorder — 21:13. It made her think of

Colin. He always got annoyed if she unplugged it to use the socket for some other device, which reset it to a flashing 00:00 that she never corrected. They'd had a row about it once: she said it didn't matter as he rarely used the timer. The flashing irritated him, he said. It was a reminder that someone had failed to do something. Next to the machine was a stack of neatly labelled video cassettes that included not just the titles of the items recorded but a colour-coding system (blue ink for film drama, green for TV drama, red for film comedy, orange for TV comedy, black for documentary) and also timings. She'd found such attention to detail endearing, then suffocating. Now she didn't care. It was him. And if he cared that much about the little things, imagine how much he cared about the big things, like her. Or used to, before she'd pushed him away for not being enough like a man who'd betrayed her. Ironic, she thought, that if Colin left her for Debbie, he'd be more like Rob than ever.

She was hungry but felt unable to move till he returned; she was on pause. But what if he wasn't coming back? All his stuff was still here: of course he'd be back. And when he showed, she'd make a move, bring him back where he belonged.

She shut her eyes. The wind was howling, making the phone lines sing; she might have mistaken the sound for a cry. She opened her eyes and frowned, turning to the window. Maybe it had been a cry. She stood up and went to look out. Everything was bowing to the gale's fury: dustbins lay on their sides, refuse zipped along the street, cars rocked from side to side and a roof tile lay smashed on the pavement. The bins for the flats were still upright, shielded behind a wall that enclosed a yard to the right of the front door. Something was lying in front of them. At first she thought it was a full bin bag, then made out a hand clutching a thigh.

She went to get her waxed jacket, then silently swore at Debbie for its absence. She could keep it, but Emma would have her husband back. She made her way cautiously down the stairs, not knowing who was out there. She didn't want to get entangled with a drunk who'd got lost on his way home, however bad the weather.

She peered out of the small window to the right of the door that looked out on to the yard, but the outermost bin now lay rolling backwards and forwards against its handles, obscuring whoever she'd seen on the ground. She opened the front door, having to push hard against the wind. As it slammed behind her, with a crack that she wondered didn't shatter the glass, she remembered she'd left her keys upstairs. A neighbour could let her back into the block, but she couldn't get into her flat or drive the car, not that she'd want to in these conditions. The rain was hitting her face like hail, and her hair was whipping at her cheeks. She edged down the few steps that led to the yard, keeping a hand on the wall. She left it to inch round the fallen bin, and saw Mrs Le Boutillier, pale and grimacing.

"Are you okay? What happened?" said Emma, dropping to her haunches.

The old woman turned her head and spoke through gritted teeth: "I thought I saw Marmalade, all wet and frightened. I came to get him in, slipped and hurt my leg."

"Let me help you up."

"I'm fine."

"How long have you been here?"

"Just needed to gather myself."

Emma knew this was pride at accepting help from someone who had insulted her earlier. "Look, about before —"

"I can manage." Mrs Le Boutillier pushed herself up on her right elbow, then sank down again with a gasp of pain.

"You've really hurt yourself."

"I'm just bruised."

Emma tried to lift the calf-length navy mackintosh to assess the damage, but Mrs Le Boutillier brushed her away.

"Just help me up and I'll be fine."

She put an arm round Emma, who helped her into a sitting position, which provoked more wincing. From there Emma hauled her to her feet, but she couldn't put any weight on her right leg.

"Lean into me, I'll be your right leg," said Emma, and Mrs Le Boutillier hopped a few steps towards the entrance. Every time her thigh touched Emma's, she yelped, so Emma came round the other side and put her arm round her waist. Once at the steps Mrs Le Boutillier steadied herself with the handrail and they made their way up to the door.

"I shut myself out. Have you got your keys?"

"Yes, wait . . ." Mrs Le Boutillier fumbled in her coat pocket. "Aah, Jesus fucking Christ," she muttered, handing them over. "I'm sorry, my language."

"It's fine. I've heard worse and I've said worse. Okay, I'm going to need both hands to open the door. Can you get behind me, and just grab hold of my neck or shoulders?"

Mrs Le Boutillier pulled herself round behind Emma, who opened the door, and shuffled forward, towing her neighbour behind her. The door slammed.

"Phew, that's better. What a wind — never known anything like it. I'll keep hold of the keys so I can let you into your flat."

"Yes. Good. If you can let me in and set me down, I'll be fine. Thank you."

They made their way up the stairs in a silence broken only by Emma's "One, two, three" and the corresponding grunts, intakes of breath and occasional curses of Mrs Le Boutillier. At points she made a kind of low gurgle, almost a growl, clearly suppressing a howl.

They reached the door and Mrs Le Boutillier leant against the frame, shallow-breathing, while Emma opened it.

"Thank you. If you can just get me in a chair . . ."

As Emma helped her through the hall, she realised from the increasing stench why the old woman was so insistent on managing alone: she had clearly soiled herself.

"Why don't I take you to the bathroom?"

"I'm fine. Just leave. Please."

"It's okay."

"It's not okay. I'm so embarrassed. I can't . . . You mustn't . . . Oh dear me . . ." Mrs Le Boutillier was weeping.

Emma moved round in front of her. "Edna . . . Edna, I won't tell anyone." It was the first time she had used her Christian name.

"Those things you said about me. This will be your revenge on me."

"I don't want revenge. I'm sorry for earlier. I was unhappy about what you told me, but you didn't mean anything by it. And I took it out on you. What's happening in my marriage isn't your fault, and what happened outside isn't yours either. Now I'm going to clean you up and get you comfortable."

"You really don't have to."

"I'm locked out of my flat so you'd be helping me by letting me stay. Otherwise I'm just going to be hanging about in the corridor."

"Oh, but I can't let you clean me."

"You can. It's good for me to be useful for a change."

Mrs Le Boutillier smiled, then sadness reclaimed her face. "I'd ring my Bradley, but he never picks up. Why would he? He's heard all my stories."

"Come on, the bathroom."

"I think I might be all right to . . ." Mrs Le Boutillier tested the weight on her right leg as Emma moved back to hold her round the waist, but buckled, nearly taking Emma down too.

"Get me down . . . Now, please . . . here."

"Okay, okay, I've got you." Emma guided her, whimpering, to the sofa.

"Put me down on my left side, not the right."

Emma did so. Mrs Le Boutillier sighed and clenched her eyes shut.

"Let me just take a look at your leg."

"It's still bloody sore."

"We need to get your clothes off anyway before we get you in the shower." Emma unbuttoned the coat. "If you can just lift your bum up I'll slide your skirt off." She undid the clasp and zip. "Ready? One, two, three, go!" Mrs Le Boutillier pushed herself up, then screamed as Emma started to pull the skirt down. "It's okay, nearly there," said Emma, working as firmly and quickly as she could, which prompted more screams and a retch.

Once the skirt was round the other woman's knees Emma nearly gagged when she saw the source of the agony. A two-inch piece of bone was sticking out of Mrs Le Boutillier's thigh. It had pierced her stocking and Emma had been pulling against it. She edged the skirt off altogether and draped it lightly over the woman's thighs.

"Okay, Edna, listen. You need to go to hospital. You've broken your leg."

"Oh, my, no. Oh, goodness, it hurts."

"Don't look at it, and don't touch it. Just lie there. I'll call for an ambulance."

Emma strode to the phone, but there was no dialling tone. She jabbed at the top button but it was dead.

"Your phone's not working. Will you be okay while I go up and use Ian's or the Powells'?"

Mrs Le Boutillier nodded with a groan.

"I've still got your keys, okay?"

Emma ran up the stairs to the two flats above and rang both bells simultaneously, then banged on the doors when there was no response. Ian Mourant finally opened his.

"Can I use your phone?"

"It's down, must be the storm. Why?"

"I need to call an ambulance. Mrs Le Boutillier fell outside and she's broken her leg."

"Oh, Christ, no — have you tried the Powells?"

"No reply."

"You'd better drive her round. Shall I give you a hand getting her into your car?"

"I've locked the keys in my flat. We'll have to carry her."

"Right. It's just . . ."

"What?"

"They're saying not to go out unless it's absolutely necessary."

"She's broken her bloody leg — how much more necessary could it be?"

"Yes, yes, you're right, sorry, I'm not thinking straight. Let me get my coat."

Ian grabbed a mac and followed Emma back down to Mrs Le Boutillier's flat. "Maybe you could run over while I stay with her and get them to send an ambulance. Or the other way round," he suggested.

"We may as well get her there. It's only five minutes' walk."

"Yeah, normally, but carrying her in this weather . . ."

"We're taking her, all right?" said Emma, firmly, as they reached the doorway. "And don't say anything to freak her out, okay? Her leg's not a pretty sight."

"Yeah, yeah, of course."

Emma led the way in. "Okay, Edna, the phones are all down, so Ian and I are going to carry you round." Mrs Le Boutillier was staring blankly at the ceiling.

"Is that smell . . .?" Ian began.

"They'll clean her up when we get there," whispered Emma. "Now, we have to be careful of this," she continued, lifting up the edge of the draped skirt.

"Ooh . . . aah . . . no . . ." Ian sank to his knees as soon as he saw the bone sticking out of the woman's thigh.

"Take a moment, and remember what I said about not f-r-e-a-k-i-n-g people out," said Emma, authoritatively.

"Sorry, not good with things like that," panted Ian, buckling. "Not sure I can . . . Sorry."

Emma pulled him to his feet and he staggered out of the flat, with her help.

"Get back upstairs," she said curtly, "I can't deal with two invalids."

"Yeah, sorry, I'm just a bit squeamish, and . . . sorry." Emma sat him on the bottom step of the stairs leading to his landing, where he bent his head between his knees and breathed deeply.

Emma went back into Mrs Le Boutillier's flat. She felt her forehead, which was damp, from rain or sweat Emma couldn't tell. The immediate buildings around them were offices and there was no time to go banging on the doors of strangers further down the street. For one, she didn't want to leave Mrs Le Boutillier alone, and second, any help she raised might turn out to be as useless as Ian.

"Edna? Edna, listen . . ."

"It's all right, Maman, I'm fine, Edna's fine. I just had a fall."

"Edna, it's Emma."

"You think I'm a Jerry Bag . . ." muttered the old woman.

"That doesn't matter."

"We did what we had to. We were occupied. Do you know what that's like?"

"I'm going to have to take you to hospital."

"We've no food, Maman. I thought you'd be happy."

"I can't get my car keys so we'll have to walk. I'll carry you as best I can. Hopefully a passing driver will help us."

"A few smiles and a peck on the cheek for some extra meat and butter. Where's the harm, Maman?"

"Come on, let's go. I'm going to do your coat back up, it's still blowing a gale out there."

"Johann was nice. Only nineteen. Better here than Russia, he said. Like a holiday. But the other one, his friend. He forced himself."

"I'm not sure you should be telling me this."

"Telling you what? I never told you anything, Maman. It would have broken your heart."

"I'm not your *maman*, Edna. It's Emma from next door. Now, I can't carry you, and you can't walk . . ."

"I told you I fell outside in the storm, but he'd hit me."

"Please, stop . . . I don't want to . . ." Emma shut her eyes to head off a tear, hoping she was listening to delirium rather than memories.

"No one would have done anything anyway."

Emma opened her eyes and saw the ubiquitous shopping trolley in the hallway, an umbrella sticking out of the top. "Come on, let me help you up. I'll get you down the stairs. Then we'll figure something out with this."

"Get off me! Leave me alone. I just need a few days in bed!" Mrs Le Boutillier swatted at Emma as she pulled her sideways and up, trying to keep the weight off her right leg. "Aah! Stop hurting me! Help! Someone, help!" She broke into a sob on Emma's shoulder. "I just want to die. The shame! The shame!"

"I'm going to slide you along . . ."

"I've disgraced myself! I do apologise."

"It's fine, honestly," said Emma, relieved to be talking in the present.

"I can't move. Where are you taking me?"

"The hospital. Come on, it's not far. I'll help you."

She hooked her arms under Mrs Le Boutillier's shoulders and walked backwards through the hall, dragging the woman behind her. She opened the door with one hand, then grabbed the shopping trolley and hurled it on to the landing. The old woman hissed as her right foot bumped over the doorframe.

Shutting the door behind her, Emma kicked the trolley down the stairs. Ian had disappeared.

"The stairs are too difficult so I'm going to try to ease you down the banister."

Mrs Le Boutillier grimaced. Emma took her down a few steps to where the gap between the stairs and the landing began to widen. She then laid her over the banister as carefully as she could so that her feet were off the steps and, descending first to take her weight, slid her down.

The woman's eyes were bulging and her face reddening, so Emma tried to hurry to minimise the discomfort. She heard a faint splatter above the wind and looked down to see that Mrs Le Boutillier had vomited. She emitted a low gasp and shut her eyes. They were now at the bottom of the stairs. Emma held Mrs Le Boutillier steady to stop her falling off the banister as she pulled the trolley towards her with a foot, then leant down to grab it.

She brought the older woman upright. "Edna? Are you okay?" Her head was lolling. Emma took movement as a positive sign. "I'm going to try to keep your left leg straight to take all the weight off your right." She pulled the umbrella out of the trolley and used a stowed plastic rain hat to tie it to her neighbour's left thigh. She took the belt off Mrs Le Boutillier's raincoat and completed the splint by tying the brolly to her calf, then put Mrs Le Boutillier's left leg into the shopping trolley, leaving the right outside.

"Okay, Edna, here we go," said Emma, stroking the woman's hair. She leant forward and pulled Mrs Le Boutillier behind her, wrapping her free arm around her.

"It'll be a bit windy, but it looks like the rain's stopped." Emma pushed the door open, blocking it with her foot, and hauled the woman out behind her. The wind made every step a lunge, and by the time they'd reached the gate Emma's left arm was feeling the strain of holding Mrs Le Boutillier in place. If she leant too far forward her back was in agony, but if she stood upright her passenger would lean over to the side.

As they set off, the streets were deserted, save for refuse and a lone dustbin that rolled along and smashed into a parked car. The way ahead was increasingly hazardous. There was zero chance of meeting a passer-by on foot unless they were also making for the hospital, and she couldn't see a single moving vehicle. She heard a smash and turned as far as she could behind her to see that some scaffolding had come down. She blocked out the terror and pulled forward against the gale.

The streetlights juddered, and every time she passed one, she worried that it would come down. The General Hospital lay ahead and to the left, but she decided to cross Parade Gardens rather than run the gauntlet of lights, roof tiles and television aerials.

Twenty feet into the park she knew she'd made a mistake: fallen branches of varying sizes were catching under the wheels of the trolley, and the trees were whipping around violently. She decided to leave the path and walk across the grass, bringing them nearer to one of the hospital entrances. The wheels of the shopping trolley were locking. Emma felt herself sinking to her knees. She bent forward as far she could and lifted Mrs Le Boutillier and the trolley on to her back, gritted her teeth and staggered forward. Her foot caught in something and she tripped forward, then crashed sideways into a raised flower bed, jarring her hip as she tried to stop the two of them toppling over.

The road was in sight now, so she bent forward again, took the strain and lurched towards it. Inexplicable strength flowed from within and she found herself stepping into the road, not thinking to check for traffic. A car hooted and swerved round her. She reached the pavement. A&E was on the other side of the building, but she just wanted to get inside, so she dragged herself to the door twenty feet up the road and collapsed on the floor of the ENT reception area, where Mrs Le Boutillier startled a security guard with a tortured scream.

Moments later, a doctor and three nurses were lifting her on to a stretcher, and Emma was helped to a chair, where she sat in a daze, clutching her side as a nurse said they should probably check her out.

"How do you feel?" asked the nurse.

"Good," Emma replied. "I feel good."

CHAPTER
TWENTY

LOUISE

Friday, 16 October 1987

"Where's the rock?"

"I don't know — out there somewhere."

"We should get rid of it."

"It's a rock."

"It's a murder weapon."

"How do we get rid of a rock? Throw it in a volcano?"

"Throw it in the sea," replied Danny, with what Louise extrapolated from the gloom would be a piercing glance.

"Yeah, sorry. Of course. Getting rid of the rock's easy. He's the problem."

Danny and Louise were crouched inside the clump of roofed rocks that he had identified as a dolmen. If Debbie had been there, she would have been able to tell them it was Le Dolmen du Couperon, a late Neolithic Gallery Grave from 3000 BC, and the adjacent hut was a guardhouse from 1689, which had served as a magazine for a long-disappeared battery that had once commanded Rozel Bay. Minutes after she had killed

Billy, Louise had pulled his body inside, panicking she might be discovered, discounting the doorless guardhouse, unable to still her somersaulting mind enough to grasp the unlikelihood of ramblers venturing out in such flattening winds. She had then sat hyperventilating, not knowing what to do. She hadn't the strength to drag the body to the water and couldn't dig a deep enough hole with her bare hands to bury it — in any case, there wasn't anything approaching a wilderness on the Island that would allow a shallow grave to remain undisturbed. Ironically the one man who could have helped her with the disposal of a body was lying dead before her. There was only one other person to turn to, the only person she knew would do anything for her, although she couldn't be sure his love would stretch to this.

She had gingerly made her way back to the car, her legs feeling like they might give way at any moment. The wind knocked her on to her back and she lay there, staring at darkened grass blades and willing the whole world away. She could just lie there and let the night take her. With a bit of luck she'd be blown clean off the Island and bounced like a skimming stone all the way home across the sea. Except home was now even less of an option than it had been before. She sat up and half slid, half crabbed down the slope towards the car.

Billy had left it running. She had never driven before, but understood the basic principles. A few shudders and clutch burns later, she had managed to turn round in the car park and was heading up the hill. She drove in a straight line so she could be sure of finding her way back, and where a T-junction forced her to make a turn, she memorised an English version of the name of the road she was leaving. La Rue des Pelles became Pellet Road. Soon after the turn she came to a hamlet with a phone box. She pulled over, and found herself having to push the car door open with both feet against the wind.

She called the restaurant he worked in first, but there was a recorded message saying they had closed early because of the weather.

She called his home and his flatmate, Vicky, who always scowled at Louise for giving him the runaround, took delight in telling her he was asleep.

"Wake him up. Please." Louise had to be careful.

"Don't you think he deserves a little peace, after what you did to him today?"

Shit. "What do you mean? What's he said I've done?"

"Nothing. He didn't even say he'd been with you. But I can tell when he comes home with that hollowed-out look that you probably led him on and broke his heart again."

"Please, just get him on the phone."

"No. You're not good for him."

Louise kicked the base of the phone box in an effort to lance her rage, but it only seemed to stoke it.

"What goes on between Danny and me is none of your fucking business. You're not his mum."

"And what are you?"

"If you want him, have him. It's not my fault he doesn't want you. That's the fault of your fat ankles and shit perm."

"Oh, piss off, you Scouse bitch!"

294

Louise could feel the dial tone about to come on, when in the background she heard Danny's voice. A hand was placed over the receiver and muted the raised voices. There was then a bang and a clatter, which she imagined was the handset being flung down against the wall, and Danny was on the line.

"What do you want, Lou?"

"Danny, I can't explain on the phone. Something bad's happened, something really bad. You're the only person can help me."

"Are you okay?"

"No, I'm not. Just come."

"You come here."

"I can't."

"Don't mind Vicky."

"It's nothing to do with Vicky. Just come. Please. Please."

"I don't want to go out in this weather — it's not safe."

"If you don't come, that's it, I'm over. I'm gone. You won't see me again. Because I'll be . . . Just come, please . . ." Louise bit her lip. "If you love me, come."

"Where are you?"

"Saie Bay, up from the car park. There's a bunch of rocks and a hut."

"There's no phone box there."

"I found one up the road."

"Why don't I come there? The address will be on the phone somewhere."

"I need to go back to the bay."

"Why? How are you going to get there? Are you walking, in this wind?"

"Driving."

"Driving? You? Whose car? You don't have a licence."

"I'm running out of money, just come."

"Couldn't you drive to me first?"

"I don't know the way."

"Look, stay by the phone box, tell me where it is."

"No!" said Louise, but the pips sounded and the line went dead. She smacked the handset against the wall of the box. She couldn't wait here — what if someone came and offered help, thinking she had broken down? What if a police car passed? She was blocking a lane in a banged-up car with ten grand cash in the back. She couldn't risk being picked up five minutes' drive from a corpse, whose blood she could still taste in her mouth.

She drove slowly back to the car park, the most hazardous part being the three-point turn she attempted by the phone box. It ended up as a ten-point turn, the last two points of which were witnessed by a waiting Mini, whose driver wound down the window as he passed to say something, insult or a warning, that was lost in the gusts.

She parked the car and sat. She shook from panic and cold; the vehicle shook from the wind. She prayed that Danny would come. Her breathing had calmed and she worked out how to run the heating. She tried to think of how to explain things to Danny, where to start, what to admit, what to avoid, what to embellish, what to falsify. What if he freaked and wanted to go straight to the police? She could imply that she would expose his part in Rob's blackmail, and his plans to subvert the housing laws, although that would be her blackmailing him, not a good move with respect to their long-term relationship. She was still going over the options when a light appeared down the lane behind her. She sank down in the seat, wary of an encounter with a stranger.

The light came closer and Danny banged on the window, holding his bike with the other hand. Louise moved into the passenger seat and gestured for him to get in. He disappeared round the back to put his bike in the boot.

He opened the door and jumped in. "Sorry, the weather's fucking terrifying. Didn't want the bike to blow away."

"Danny . . ."

"I nearly got killed twice coming over here, Lou."

"Thank you."

"Before you tell me why, just know this is the last time I'll help you. I'm doing this because I care about you, and to prove I don't just do things because I want to sleep with you, like you said earlier. You treat me like a mug, Lou, and this is the final favour I do for you."

This did not sound promising. God knew what he thought she was going to tell him, but the reality was so far off the scale that she daren't risk it. Better to invent a milder peril, get him to take her home, then go on the run. What could tie her to Billy anyway? Nothing. Her prints were on the car, though. Torch it? Drive it into the sea?

"Well?" he said. "What is it? I'm not buying your fucking hotel for you, I'll tell you that. I don't want your money, not the way you treat me. You want me to drive this stolen car back where you took it? Is it Rob de la Haye's? Or did you buy it with your hush money and you need me to show you how the wipers work?"

"My ex came back. He just got out of prison. He found out about the money. I had to tell him."

"You've an ex out of prison? I don't want to know any of this. If you're back with him, fine, suits us both." Danny reached to open the door.

"He tried to cut my face open. So I hit him with a rock. I killed him. His body's up there . . ." Suddenly Louise was crying and struggling for breath. "He puts knives in people's mouths, Danny. That's how he gets his kicks . . ." She paused, staring at her knees and hoping for a hug, a word of comfort, of understanding, a declaration that all would be made right. Danny remained silent. "I was taking him to Rob — he wanted more money. Otherwise he was going to wait for you to come round and fuck you up, or he'd just take it out on me. But I couldn't take him to Rob — the police would have got involved — although maybe I should just have fucking taken him there and he'd be in a cell by now. Me too, but not for murder, and Rob would probably want it hushed up anyway, although Billy would have yelled about it and landed me in it and — and — and just fucking say something!" she screamed. "Or go, just go! I'll sit here and wait for the cops!"

"If it happened like you said, that's the best thing to do. Call the police. He came at you with a knife, you hit him with a rock."

"I can't do that."

"You might not go to prison. But the longer we leave it the worse it looks."

"Whether I go to prison or not, I'm dead if this gets out. If Billy's family know I killed him, they'll come for me."

"What — are they like Mafia or something?"

"Yes. They're gangsters, Danny. That's the world I grew up in. It's what I came here to get away from."

"Jesus, Lou. I don't know what to . . ." Danny tailed off. "I mean, me being here, you telling me this. If I don't tell the police, I'm . . ."

"If you tell the police, I'm dead. Billy's family'll kill me, Danny! I may as well jump off a cliff right now. Jesus Christ, shit fuck fuck!" She beat her fists on the dashboard.

Danny grabbed her wrists. "Shut up! Get a grip!"

Louise snapped back into the moment. She'd never seen Danny exhibit command.

"You're not bullshitting me?" he said. "About what'll happen?"

"I swear."

"Where's the body?"

"I told you, up there, under some big stone thing. I dragged it inside."

"Show me."

"What are you going to do?"

"I don't know."

They helped each other up to the dolmen, the light from Danny's bike showing the way, then crawled inside. Danny scanned Billy's corpse, then sat staring into space.

299

"We need the knife too," he said eventually.

"To cut him up?"

"Jesus, is it that big?"

"Probably not. You'll know, you cut up meat. Should we get your kitchen knives?"

"We're not cutting him up. It would take ages, it's fucking disgusting and then we've got ten little bits of body to get rid of instead of one big one."

"Chuck the bits in the sea, feed them to something?"

"You can't fart in this Island without everyone you know smelling it. You think we can go round chucking feet and hands off breakwaters and no one's going to spot it?"

"Not tonight they won't."

"It's lethal out there. Besides, I'm not cutting up a body. I feel sick just thinking about it."

"Why d'you want the knife, then?"

"I don't want some kid finding it. Plus it's evidence. Would he always have it on him?"

"Yes, why?"

"We leave it with him, don't want his family suspecting anything."

"We're just going to leave the body somewhere?"

"Yeah, I tried to cut down La Rue des Fontanelles on my way here . . ."

"Where's that?"

"Starts as a road, goes down to a dirt track, comes out over there, it doesn't matter. The main thing is, I couldn't get through. A tree's come down and it's blocking the way. I nearly went into it — it's on a bend.

300

So we put him in the car and roll it down the hill. It'll hit the tree and look like an accident."

"That's fucking brilliant. Unless someone sees us."

"You said yourself, no one's going to be out tonight. We've got to risk it, it's our only chance. Take the light, find the rock and the knife. Don't touch the knife — fingerprints. I'll pull him out."

Danny crawled out and started dragging Billy by the ankles, while Louise scoured the ground for the weapons. She found the knife easily; the rock took a bit longer. She was looking for a stone with a bloody edge, and was beginning to assume the rain had washed it off when she spotted it. The sight of blood and what might have been a chip of temple made her fall to all fours and dry-heave to the point at which she thought she would pass out. Danny pulled her up and held her.

"Oh, my God, I killed him. I killed him. I used to love him. And I killed him."

"He tried to kill you, Lou. He deserved it."

She put her head on his shoulder.

He held her away from him. "We don't have time for this." He looked down towards the car. "We can't drag him all the way because he'll get covered in mud and grass — it'll look weird when he's found. Rain's fine, no one can avoid that tonight. We have to carry him."

She nodded. She didn't have the energy to shout a reply over the wind.

"Can you manage it?"

She shook her head.

"Okay, where's the rock and the knife?"

Louise pointed them out and he kicked the rock towards the knife. "I'm going to get my bike. I can wheel him down on that."

He grabbed her hand and they began walking. When they got to the bottom, he sat her in the car, reached in and rummaged in the glove compartment for a cloth, then got his bike out of the boot and headed back up the slope into the storm.

Louise sat still, on the edge of elation that Danny could make the situation right for her, but not daring to believe it just yet. Ten minutes later he emerged from the dark, straining to keep the bike upright as he leant into the wind. Billy was bent over the crossbar, his arms hooked behind him and his feet dragging on the ground. His head was covered by one compartment of a double pannier that Danny had removed from the rack. He opened the back door. "What's that doing on his head?" asked Louise. "Is it so I don't have to look at him?"

Danny silently heaved the body into the back, then put the bike into the boot. He ran round to the driver's side, got in and started the engine. "Don't want to get his blood on the back seat. It's got to look like he died on impact, driving the car."

"Jesus, Danny, you sound like you've done this before. Either that or you're a natural."

"Just common sense."

He pulled off and they went back up La Rue de Scez, which was now strewn with small to medium branches. He wore a look of unflinching concentration that, for some reason, reminded her of her little brother playing Mousetrap.

"Fuck, I hope a tree doesn't fall here and trap us."

"We can make him crash into that."

"Uphill? Not likely. Why don't you shut up, Lou, and leave this to the professionals?"

They neared the top, and pulled out. "We're going to go round in a square, two rights in a row basically."

"Shit — oh no oh no oh no," gasped Louise, at the sight of oncoming headlights. "Fuck, no."

"Calm down. I'll let them pass," said Danny, pulling into a field entrance and waving as the Land Rover went by.

"Why did you wave? They'll have seen your face! You should have turned away."

"Fucking act normal, okay?"

They pulled out again. The road was canopied by trees bending as if their trunks were elasticated. Louise was hyperventilating again, worried that everything was about to collapse on them, that the world was falling in on itself.

Danny took a right turn. "This is the road." It was steep and narrow, again with a carpet of small fallen branches. He inched along as they came to a bend. As they rounded it, it straightened out as it plunged further, then was blocked about twenty feet ahead by a huge beech that had stood on the bank, where its roots had gone down vertically rather than spreading out to steady it. Danny braked, then reversed and stopped, leaving the car in neutral.

"Okay, this is as far away as I can get it on the straight. It's bloody narrow as it is. We don't want it getting stuck against one of the banks. Out."

Louise did as she was told. She went round to the boot, where Danny got his bike out and laid it on the road. Nothing was going to stay upright for long in these conditions.

"Hold the door open. The wind's going to push it shut again."

Louise opened the back door while Danny pulled Billy out and put him over his shoulder.

"Okay, shut this and open the front one."

Danny heaved the corpse into the driver's seat, struggling to get it upright. Eventually he pushed Billy's forearms through the spokes of the steering wheel and let his head fall forward against it.

"Does that look right?" asked Louise.

"It'll help keep the wheel straight, maybe it'll look like his arms slipped in there on impact."

"Maybe?"

"Have you got any better ideas? Because I don't want to hang around."

"No. Let's just do it. Have you put the knife in?"

"It's in his pocket," said Danny, tugging off the pannier that lifted Billy's head up straight before it flopped forward, unsupported. "I've got the rock in the other pannier. Right, I'm going to lean in the other side, jam it in second and take the handbrake off. It's going to start rolling, but don't push till I've shut the door."

Louise nodded and followed Danny round to the back of the car, stationing herself at the boot while he opened the door and reached in. He was out in a flash, the door was shut and the car was rolling. Louise pushed and it was away from her too fast for her to keep up. Danny ran after it, giving it a shove, then stopped as they watched it graze the right bank before slamming into the tree.

Danny stood there, staring down at it. Louise walked in front of him and took his hands. "You okay?"

"It's just hit me. There's no turning back now."

"It's okay. We're together on this. Together."

She lifted his arms wide and leant into an embrace that felt to her like the safest place on earth. Then they turned to walk back towards his bike and the long and dangerous road that lay before them.

CHAPTER
TWENTY-ONE

COLIN

Friday, 16 October 1987

Debbie had told him earlier that the tower had stood since 1782, and that L'Avarison, the rock upon which it was built, had been there since the lava had hit water millions of years ago. Tonight it felt like the wind might upturn it all and the sea splinter it into sand. Until now, Colin had always found Victor Hugo's assertion in "The Archipelago of the Channel", that Jersey had become detached from France during a terrible storm in AD 700, rather fanciful. Now he felt the Island could easily be being shifted out into the middle of the Atlantic.

He and Debbie cowered in the dark, Duncan between them, clutching his rucksack against himself. They were back where they had found him, as far away from the steps and the open side of the platform as they could get, sitting against the tower where it cornered with the short edge of the wall. The wind was blowing into them, screaming at them, the chilling breath of an angry demon. There was no hiding from it. It was whipping up the rising tide that was hitting the steps to their left with a ferocity that rose by the minute, lashing them with spray. Colin, the closest, was getting the worst of it. With another three hours till high-water, there was every likelihood that soon their current perch would be submerged.

Soaked, shivering and terrified, they had no choice but to sit it out. They were silent. Where before they might have let out the occasional cry at an unexpected dousing, now it was a whimper.

"We have to get inside!" yelled Colin to Debbie.

"I told you, locked!" she shouted back.

"We're going to get washed off!"

Debbie said nothing, just looked at him. There was no longer fear in her eyes, but neither was there hope. Instead there was simple acceptance that this was where things would end.

He craned his neck to look up at the tower behind him, its white outline looming ghostlike out of the dark.

"Window!" He gestured, turning on his torch and holding it with both his numb hands to keep it steady. The door to the tower was in the centre, ten feet above them, accessible by a steep set of hand-railed iron steps. A foot above the door there was a small window, about two feet square.

"No!" Debbie replied. "Too dangerous. Too high. Duncan's too weak to climb through."

"I'll go through, open the door!"

"Deadlocked!"

"I can open it!"

"How?"

"Break it down. Duncan, I need your rucksack."

The boy stopped hugging it and put his hands over the back of his head, his elbows knocking the bag forward. Colin grabbed it and tipped everything out, then stood, stashing his torch in a side pocket.

"Please, don't!" implored Debbie, gripping his arm. "You'll fall."

Colin shook himself free and crouched his way along the wall to the base of the steps, holding the frame of the rucksack, side on to the wind — it would fill like a sail if the blast got hold of it. He reached the base of the ladder, realised he would need both hands for the ascent and slung on the rucksack. He began to climb, his sodden trousers flapping. His fingers ached from the icy metal, so when he reached the top, he hooked one elbow over the rail, then opened and closed them fast to get the blood flowing. He looked up. It was madness. He'd be blown clean off if he stood up. But he couldn't just go back down.

He shrugged off the rucksack and unclipped the sack from the frame, then wore it on his front like an apron. He went down two steps and wedged the frame against the doorway at the top of the railings. Taking out his wallet, he tied it to his palm with his handkerchief. He took out the torch and put one foot on the handrail, pushing up to stand leaning into the tower. He stared ahead: if he looked down he would freeze or fall. He braced his arms inside the top of the doorframe as he moved his feet on to the bottom of the rucksack frame. From there he felt up with his left hand to the window ledge above, the torch in his right. Then he moved his feet to the top of the frame. He felt it buckle slightly,

308

which gave him the flood of adrenalin he needed to reach up and smash the window with the torch.

His left hand gripped the base of the window frame, the improvised pad protecting him from the shards of glass. He bashed at the rest of the window, clearing it from the frame with his head down in case it fell into his face. He dropped the torch on to the ledge and pushed up into the window, the rucksack frame bowing then clattering away once his weight was removed. He felt a sharp pain in the back of his head and ducked. His left hand was still on the wooden frame, but the right was now inside, gripping the window ledge. He pulled himself in as far as he could with his right hand, his legs kicking in the gale while his head was in the comparative stillness of the tower. He wriggled forward, the rucksack on his front protecting him from the broken glass over which he was sliding.

He was now half inside and picked up the torch to see where he might land. It looked like an eight-foot drop to the stone floor. To the right and two feet below was a row of large coat hooks set on a plank fixed to the wall. He reached down and along and gripped the first, then pulled himself further in. He felt himself sliding out of the window ledge and swung down like a pendulum, his left arm flailing. The plank came away from the wall and he fell on to the cold floor. He let out a sob, only now giving in to the terror of the climb.

He felt around for the torch, found it and examined the door. As Debbie had said, it was deadlocked. Of course she was right: she brought tours out here. He looked around the room. There were three bunk beds, a chemical toilet and a sink with a foot pump. He clambered up to the next level and found a small sofa, a hammock strung between two beams, a kitchen area, a table and chairs, and a fire extinguisher. He lugged the extinguisher back down to the door, lifted it and tried to smash the lock. He misjudged the strength needed and it arced to the floor with a clang and a spark. This time he held it like a battering ram and ran at it, winding himself. Of course. The door would open inwards: swinging in the other direction would mean a visitor had to step back and fall off the steps.

He sank to his knees. Maybe Debbie and Duncan could climb up as he had done. They might have picked up the rucksack frame. He could move a bunk bed to the window, stick his head out and beckon them. Maybe haul them up using one of the blankets folded on the beds. He doubted he had the strength.

He looked round the walls: a sextant, a spyglass and a small anchor. He pulled down the anchor, rusted but solid; he could hold it in two hands. The door looked thick and old, planked, with a horizontal beam across the middle below the lock. He swung the anchor above his head, aiming one of the hooks at the join of two planks in the top half. The impact rattled his wrists. He swung again. Chips of wood flew off, but nothing more.

He stood back. That door needed to come down. He shut his eyes. It was Rob de la Haye; it was Aidan Blampied; it was Barney Vautier. He swung the anchor again and again and again, seeing Rob taking Emma from behind, Blampied touching Duncan while Vautier looked on, but it was the idea of Rob with Debbie that stoked him to a frenzy. By now he was just grazing the door.

He sank to his knees and burst into tears. The woman he loved was out there, soon to be swept away. He leant his head and fists against the door, crying as he hadn't since he was a little boy. His father had been taken from him and there was nothing he could do about it. But he would not relinquish Debbie.

He got to his feet, wiped away the tears, and swung the anchor with a strength that matched the storm. The head of the hook stuck fast, an inch or so deep. He worked the shank back and forth and began to feel the wood split. The anchor came loose, but the join in the planks was now a crack, and there was a golf-ball-sized hole. He jammed the flat end of the hook into the crack and loosened the planks till they began to buckle. He threw down the anchor, picked up the fire extinguisher and battered the split again and again till the wood finally gave way. There was now a passable vertical rent in the top half of the door.

He stuck his head out into the storm. From the luminescence of the white wall he could see Debbie and Duncan holding each other in a crouch, six inches of water sloshing back and forth under them, as big canopies of spray hit them from above. He yelled but they didn't respond. The wind was too loud, and their heads were turned to each other, eyes probably closed.

He pulled one of the bunk beds towards the door and used the top bunk to lower himself feet first and sideways through the hole. As soon as he was on the outside ledge he was almost knocked off by the wind.

He was halfway down the steps when Debbie spotted him. She slowly stood and waded over, dragging Duncan.

Colin reached them at the bottom. "Up!" he yelled to Debbie, pushing her on to the first step. He bent down and slung Duncan over his shoulder as she began to climb, then felt his legs buckle as a wave broke against his knees. They both went down, Colin holding on to the rail with his right hand. The wave hit the far wall and began traversing back towards them, pushing Duncan against him and loosening his grip on the rail. They could both be sent rolling down the steps into the swell. He felt Debbie's hand on his wrist and, as she took the strain against him, he wrapped an arm around Duncan as the water drained back. He staggered to his feet and hauled Duncan up the steps backwards.

Debbie climbed through the hole first, then pulled Duncan in by his arms, as Colin lifted his legs. As Colin clambered in he saw, from the corner of his eye, a large red navigation buoy propelled on to the platform. It hit the bottom of the iron stairs, knocking the base loose and leaving them sticking up to the side at forty-five degrees, then wedged itself in the corner where they had been, smashing a hole in the wall and opening up a second front of spray.

An hour later they were upstairs, warmth returning to their bodies. The blast from the hole in the door was too much for them to stay on the lower level, more because of the noise than the cold. Their nerves just couldn't take any more of the roaring. There were no beds upstairs but, given the circumstances, comfort wasn't on the agenda.

They had helped Duncan up first and left him to take off his sopping clothes, until he called for help, his fingers too frozen to manage buttons. Colin and Debbie helped him down to his underpants, then wrapped him in blankets and heaved him into the hammock, where he fell asleep.

Colin had started to shiver so they agreed to undress on separate landings, then settled, blanketed, in their underwear on the sofa.

"I don't suppose there's a radio here?" asked Colin.

"No."

"Not that anyone would come out in this anyway. But it would be good to let people know we're safe. I mean, the tide will go out tomorrow. Hard to imagine now, I know . . ."

"Yes."

"Are you okay?"

"Yes . . . It's just . . . seeing you on the stairs in the wind, I thought you were going to fall, and then when you were inside I thought you'd never be able to get the door open, and that we'd drown."

"I would never have let that happen."

"Intentions are all very well, but you could have been hit by that buoy. We all could."

Colin caught himself just as he was about to confess to the same fears of losing her. An awkward silence descended amid the noise.

"I'm sorry I brought us out here," murmured Debbie.

"I'm sorry I nearly drowned us, going the wrong way," replied Colin.

"It was stupid of me. Selfish."

"What are you talking about? You found him, Debbie. Without you, he'd have been out here alone. He'd have been swept out by now. Or dead from cold."

"We're safe thanks to you. You saved us from being drowned or crushed. I was the reckless one."

"You were sure you saw something."

"I was sure that, once we finished looking for him, you'd go home. That's why I left my clothes at your flat. So I could go back with you. And why I kept us looking," she said, reaching for his hand. "All I do when I'm with you is try to eke out every single moment. I want to keep being with you."

"I want to keep being with you," he whispered, pulling her towards him to press his forehead against hers, then giving her the kiss he'd been dreaming of for longer than he dared admit.

CHAPTER
TWENTY-TWO

BARNEY

Saturday, 17 October 1987

What a fucking mess, Barney thought, as he made his way along the coast via multiple detours resulting from newly created dead-ends. The Island had been picked up and given a good shake. Trees were down everywhere. Tiles lay smashed on roads and pavements, as plentiful as fag butts. He doubted there was a bin left upright. Pity the poor bastards having building work done: you'd be lucky to keep a finished roof, let alone one where tarpaulins or plastic sheets substituted for wood and stone.

He'd been woken at half six with a call about a dead body in a car halfway down La Rue des Fontanelles. Not that he'd slept — Barney wasn't good with storms. Eileen had found him grunting through sit-ups in the lounge at two a.m., trying to take his mind off the noise.

"You all right, Barn?"

"Sure, love. Sorry, did I wake you?"

"How would you wake me above this racket?"

"Yeah, sounds like a bad one out there."

"What woke me was you not being beside me. Come back up."

"I don't know, there's something about being high up in this wind. I don't like it." Barney hated feeling at the mercy of something else. It was why he'd never got into sailing: you couldn't trust the sea.

"There's no lightning."

"Yeah, yeah, I know."

"Just a gale."

Lightning scared the bejesus out of him. A bolt of electricity from the heavens that could smite a man on the earth. He had committed too many sins to risk being overlooked by God's wrath.

"Besides, Barn, look at the size of you! You're not going to get blown away."

"Cheeky cow!" He sat on the sofa next to her. "Mind if we stay here for a bit?"

"Wherever you want, *mah coq*, eh."

They'd snuggled under a blanket on the sofa until the phone rang. The winds had died down to a strong bluster and he was looking forward to a lie-in on one of his off-duty Saturdays. But duty called. Some honorary had reported the body, and while Uniform would normally attend a traffic accident, there were so many roads blocked it was proving hard for anyone to get there. He lived close by in Trinity, and the control room added that the honorary felt there was something suspicious.

As he drove through the refashioned landscape he was surprised there'd been only one fatality recorded. After endless double-backs he finally made it to the top of the road. He eased the car down till he nearly hit an incident sign that had been thoughtlessly placed on the bend. He put on the handbrake and got out. There was still a hell of a squall blowing, but the high banks sheltered him from the worst of it. He looked up at the trees, still being buffeted, and hoped nothing was about to come down on him, then beat away the fear. Time for business.

A VW Golf was parked behind a Mercedes that was wedged against a massive tree trunk blocking the road. A short man eased himself out of the Golf, then stopped self-importantly to fix his cap. He approached Barney, saluting as he walked. His eyes were set in narrow slits, giving him a permanent squint that made people feel they were being continually sized up.

"Detective Sergeant Vautier, well met . . ."

Barney remembered his name just in time: Sean Houellebecq, pompous little twat. "Sean, move your fucking hazard sign before there's another crash. You stuck it right on the bend." He had little time for the honoraries: they were amateurs searching for status but unwilling to put in the graft.

"Is there any need? This road doesn't get much traffic on a good day. It's barely a road."

"Move it."

"Will do," said Houellebecq. "But can I ask you to wait for me to accompany you before approaching the victim? So as I can talk you through my observations."

Fuck off, thought Barney, as Houellebecq sprinted up the lane while he strode down towards the crash. A Merc, flash car, probably a lawyer. Well, the Island could afford to shed a few of those. Barney reached the driver's window and looked in. Young man, face smashed against the windscreen, which had itself been shattered by the tree or his skull or both.

Houellebecq returned to stand the other side of the car. "Do you see what I see?"

"Tracksuit bottoms, sweatshirt, Merc. This isn't his car."

"I meant the injuries."

"The car hit the tree, his face hit the windscreen. That's what happens if you don't wear a seatbelt."

"Observe." Houellebecq opened the door and crouched on the passenger seat.

Barney blew out his cheeks and looked at his feet, mentally cuffing Houellebecq round the head. "You called in the plates? A man dressed like this does not own this car."

"You may be correct." Houellebecq stuck his head out.

"Of course I'm fucking correct. No disrespect, I'm the detective, you're the bloke who organises the parking at the parish fête. Wait here."

Barney made a note of the number plate and walked back to his car, where he radioed in to the control room. "Vautier here, can you run a plate for me?" He rattled out the number.

"Sure thing, Barney. What's it look like out there?"

"Like Ted's wife sat on the Island."

"Ha! They're saying it was a hurricane."

"Fuck me. It'll only be the palm trees left, then. They're from that part of the world."

"Just be a few minutes. I've sent Joault off to look it up."

"Be fucking hours, then."

"You okay to wait?"

"Yup, it's either yack with you or stand around with Houellebecq."

"Oh, Christ! Is he running it like he's chief of police?"

"If his uncle wasn't the tourism minister I'd be slapping him with a fake DUI right now."

"Got that plate for you. It belongs to Eric Le Maistre."

"The Jurat?"

"Yup — reported it stolen yesterday morning."

"And just to be double sure, he's still fifty-five, bald, with a beard?"

"He was last time I saw him. So he's not the goner?"

"I can confirm that he's definitely not. Give him a call and tell him we found his car. But he'll be getting a new one on his insurance."

Barney hung up. He felt a tingle. Could it be? That would be handy, very handy indeed. Tie things up without any unnecessary attention. Get this dose of arse-ache off the Island without anyone knowing why he was there. He made his way back to Houellebecq, who was taking photos of the car.

"Cut that out."

"Could be useful."

"This is Jurat Le Maistre's car. Does it look like Jurat Le Maistre?"

"No. Who is it, then?"

"I'm just about to confirm that."

Barney leant in and pulled the corpse's head back by the few non-bloodied strands of hair he could find. The nose was gone, the eyes swollen shut, but it was a good fit for the faxed mug shot he had in his pocket. He tried to roll up the right sleeve of the sweatshirt, but the blood had dried against the skin, so he ripped the fabric and tore it loose. On the forearm he could make out the tattoo "Anfield Ani . . .". Barney was pretty sure the word that had been obliterated by the bone-showing gash was "Animals".

He stood up. Houellebecq stared at him disapprovingly from the other side of the car. "I assume you'll be calling the coroner."

"There's nothing suspicious about this death. He stole the car and crashed into a fallen tree. For once God stepped in and administered justice for us."

"But his head injuries —"

"Consistent with a collision."

"He hit the tree head on. That doesn't explain the injury to the left temple. Look."

"He could have bounced back and forth, hit the rear-view mirror."

"You haven't looked. He's got a huge gash to his left temple. The rear-view mirror is on a swivel. It would have given way."

"Who knows what shit was flying about here last night? The strength of that wind, there could have been manhole covers zipping around like frisbees."

"What about the arms in the wheel?"

"He slipped, lost control, got them stuck. Frankly, I don't care. The world is not going to miss him. This is a known Scouse criminal."

"And you can tell that how?"

"From my twenty-two years' experience in the police force. And the mug shot I'm about to show you."

"What about the fingers?"

"What about the fingers?"

"There are bite marks on the left hand."

"All right, fucking Sherlock," Barney spat, through gritted teeth, as he stomped round to the passenger side. He climbed in and took a look at the left hand that dangled at a sickening angle from a break in the arm. He heaved himself back out.

"Like I said, this is one Billy McCaffrey." Barney pulled out the mug shot and handed it to Houellebecq, who unfolded it, struggling to stop it flapping around in the breeze. "Now I know it might not be that obvious, as he's lost half his face since that picture was taken, but there's also the tattoo on his arm. And when they heave him out of there on his way to the morgue I'll bet my left bollock he's got a knife on him, a knife he used to carry out a very ugly attack the other night."

"Why would a man like that be driving down this track? All that's at the bottom is a dolmen."

"Got lost, wrong turn."

"Something about it doesn't feel right. I'm not sure he'd have picked up enough speed after he exited the bend to sustain such injuries. They're not commensurate with the force of the impact. And we can see from the dents on the right side he hit the bank, which would have slowed him down considerably."

"Could have got those dents anywhere."

"There are paint flecks on the stones in the bank. And look at the rear sides, how do you explain them?"

"I don't have to."

"Really? I rather think we do."

Barney took a deep breath. One punch to the throat and this prick would be on his arse. Nope. Barney was going to have to do some good old-fashioned shit-eating. He had been handed a lovely little tied-up parcel of a case, and he was not about to let this part-time busybody undo it.

"Sean, I got to tell you, you are wasted in the honorary ranks. Most of your lot are just donkeys in fluorescent jackets, but you have the makings of a real detective. I can't pull the wool over your eyes, so I'm going to have to break protocol, and let you in on operational information that, on paper, you absolutely should not hear. But, frankly, you're proving yourself an equal to me in the field, and so you know what? Fuck the rules. But you're going to have to promise me it goes no further."

Houellebecq's eyes lit up. Those were the words he'd been dying to hear for most of his adult life.

"First thing you need to know is that Billy McCaffrey is a big player in the Liverpool underworld. Just got out earlier than he should for GBH."

"What's he doing over here?"

"Who knows? Lot of Scouse over here, could be visiting friends. The point is, the victim of that GBH was the right-hand man of another rival player. Maybe those rivals heard he was here, maybe they came over. Maybe they had something to do with this. And maybe they didn't. Maybe they tried to give him a kicking and he escaped with a fucked-up hand and crashed into a tree because he couldn't keep a grip on the steering wheel. Or maybe he got in a fight with a Manc over the footie, nothing to do with the beef back home, same result."

"Shouldn't we try to find out? Otherwise someone is getting away with something they shouldn't."

"We could do that. We could explore all these variables. But is that going to do the Island any good? Publicising a gang hit? Do you think that's good for tourism? You think your uncle wants that on his plate? I mean, fine, if you want to be the guy who starts a grockle drought. Over what in all probability is just a lucky traffic accident. Lucky for the enemies a bastard like that makes, lucky for his victims past and future, and lucky for us. Because there's one less criminal to deal with, and hardly any paperwork."

Houellebecq nodded, then cocked his head with a leer. "Okay. On a completely separate note, I believe you know I'm looking to make Centenier as soon as I can."

Seeing this tool as the top honorary in his parish was a small price to pay. Barney extended a hand. "With my support, I promise you that won't be before too long."

CHAPTER
TWENTY-THREE

COLIN

Saturday, 17 October 1987

The clinging chill Colin felt as he trudged across the sand in his still damp clothes was countered by a glow from within, which he hadn't experienced since he'd strode down to the beach that Christmas morning to ask for Emma's hand. He was now half a mile out on the same beach, walking towards the Island he planned to leave for good, taking with him the woman whose hand he clasped behind Duncan's back.

He and Debbie had kissed and talked in a confessional outpouring till they had fallen asleep in each other's arms. Spurred on by the possibility that the malevolent sea was not yet done with its deadly plan, Colin didn't want to die with things left unsaid. Once said and reciprocated, his hopelessness fell away with the storm, and he promised Debbie a new life away from the Island.

Having made the journey only once and at night, he wasn't aware of any changes wrought by the weather but, according to Debbie, the oyster beds had been torn up and sandbanks shunted. This led to an occasionally improvised route, but they had started as soon as the waters fell away behind the tower just after half past nine, and though they were going at a slower pace than when they had walked out, they were not fighting the wind or the time quite as tightly as before. Their main concern was Duncan, who had not drunk any water for thirty-six hours or eaten for forty-eight and was stumbling along between them. The magnitude of the storm had become apparent as they left the tower: there was no sign of the buoy that had crashed on to the platform — it had been swept back off by the sea. There were, however, other things on their minds, particularly Duncan's.

"What happens when we get back?" Duncan had muttered.

"We contact your parents and the police. So they can call off the search. Steady, let me climb down first. Stay here on the ledge."

"I don't want to talk to the police."

"They're going to ask you where you were, and why you were there. Okay, get yourself down the steps — do it sitting if it's easier."

"I'll be arrested, expelled."

"Blampied's the one who's going to be arrested. That's it, keep going. Debbie! You can come through now, but stay on the ledge. We don't want to put too much weight on the stairs." Debbie had clambered through the hole, flinching at the breeze. "We'll warm up when we get moving," Colin said. "Right, Duncan, lower your legs off the end. I'll slow your fall if you push yourself off."

"The school won't want me back."

"You don't want to be at the school after the way they've treated you."

"I can't . . . It's my family's school."

"Duncan, you have to come home. You can't live out here. Was that your plan?"

"My plan was not to . . ." The boy had trailed off.

Colin reached up, almost touching his waist. "Come down, Duncan, come on."

Duncan had jumped and Colin caught him. "This will be dealt with, I promise. But you can't run away, and you can't . . . You can't do what you might have done at Grosnez."

"I won't. Not after what you did, coming out here for me. You're right, this is a second chance."

"Exactly. We get to start again. Now can you come over to the wall there? Sit down while I help Miss Hamon."

Debbie had climbed backwards down the stairs, then leaped into Colin's waiting arms as Duncan had done, except she pushed herself forward to ensure body contact. Colin looked down at her as she gazed up from his embrace, longing to kiss her, cursing his insistence that they behave professionally in front of the boy. He stood back. "Okay, off we go. Duncan, you can put your arms round our shoulders . . ."

As they neared the coast, weaving between rocks and the occasional stoved-in lobster pot, there were more obvious signs of a changed landscape: some of the boats moored in the bay had broken loose to hole or upturn their neighbours and end up dashed against the sea wall. The cover of a workman's hut blew past them. Behind the sea wall, several trees lining the road had fallen into each other in a lattice. A chimney on a nearby house had fallen through the roof — Colin shuddered at the idea of an occupied bed or sofa being in its path.

Duncan's head lolled forwards and he began bicycling his legs weakly against the sand.

"No, I can't, he's there ... I can't face my parents ..."

"Nearly there. You'll feel better for some warm clothes and food."

"Let me go!"

He writhed between them, working his way free to sink down to his knees, then fell into a ball. Colin knelt at his head. "Duncan, we've all got things to face when we get back. I've been as good as sacked because I stood up to Blampied and because I kept looking for you. If you don't go back, that was all for nothing. He's won. They can get rid of me, but not you. Whatever you did, he did something far, far worse. So we're going to stand up, together, and we're going to walk up that slip and we're going to tell the truth."

"There's no proof of what he said, how he tried to touch me. It's just my word against his."

"And mine. I believe you. I will stand by you. I will vouch for you. Your family might disown you, but I will not." Colin pulled the boy to his feet.

They staggered up the slipway, and heaved Duncan on to the back seat of the car. Then Colin headed over to the phone box at the edge of the car park to call the boy's parents.

"Arthur Labey speaking."

"Mr Labey, this is Colin Bygate. I found Duncan at Seymour Tower. He's a little weak but fine."

"Oh, thank God! Thank you. Where are you?"

"The Seymour slip car park. We just walked back — we were stuck out there in the storm."

"We'll be down to get him now."

In the background Colin could hear Duncan's mother wanting to know to whom her husband was talking. The phone was now held at the father's side. "That teacher, Bygate, he's found Duncan, down at Seymour Tower. I've told him to wait."

"I've heard the roads are hell with all the trees down, Arthur."

"I don't trust Bygate not to set up a press conference."

"For God's sake, Arthur, let's just get him home."

"Mr Labey," Colin said, as loudly as he could without shouting.

The man came back on the line. "We're on our way."

"If the roads are bad it might be better for me to take him along the coast, where there are fewer trees, to the hospital."

"You said he was fine. Why does he need the hospital?"

"He's cold and wet, probably suffering from exposure. They should check him out."

"Listen, I can't thank you enough for finding him, but kindly do not involve the authorities any further. I don't want to sound ungrateful, but haven't you done enough damage?"

"I have to call the police to tell them he's been found."

"Leave that to me."

"They're searching for him, they need to be informed."

"I will speak to them."

Colin hung up and immediately rang the police station. Detective Vautier was out, dealing with an incident, but the message would be passed on. The duty sergeant didn't seem particularly moved by the news.

"Don't you want to interview him?" Colin asked. "He has some serious allegations about a member of staff."

"All in good time, sir, but we're a bit busy right now. You might have noticed that the Island was hit by a hurricane last night."

Yes, and I was right in the middle of it doing your job, thought Colin. He would ring Vautier again later and make sure things were followed up properly. He rang Duncan's parents back.

"Lab —"

"It's Mr Bygate again. I'm taking Colin to the General Hospital. You can pick him up there. Bye."

Someone had to look after the boy's interests. He needed medical attention and, besides, his parents were less likely to bawl Duncan out in front of doctors and nurses. He got back into the car.

"I'm going to drop him at the hospital. By the time an ambulance has driven out here, we could have got there."

"Did you speak to his parents?" whispered Debbie.

"Don't ask," muttered Colin. "You okay, Duncan?"

"Yes."

"We're going to take you to the hospital just to warm you up, get you on your feet. Your parents will meet us there." He turned to Debbie. "I'll drop you on the way."

"Oh. Right," she said, clearly disappointed.

Colin squeezed her hand, smiled and mouthed, "I love you." She beamed.

Everything was slightly askew on the coast road. Colin had been right about the lack of trees: it was built-up pretty much all the way. But greenhouses were shattered, conservatories cracked, sheds upturned and the flagpoles leaning.

He pulled in to the driveway of Debbie's small bungalow just before Green Island.

"I'll just see Miss Hamon in," he told Duncan, getting out of the car.

"Will you come back when you've dropped him?" she asked at her doorway.

"Maybe. We all need to warm up."

"I know a way to warm up," she said, pulling him inside for a stolen kiss.

"You know I want to, more than anything, but I need to tell Emma first. You understand. After all she's said about us, all she's inferred, I can't let her be right."

"That's one of the reasons I love you. You're so fair, so . . . I was going to say decent, but it's so unsexy."

"I was worried you'd think I was being petty."

"No. You're doing things right. That's what you do. So when can I expect you?"

"As soon as I can make it. But she's not likely to hear me out and shake on it. There could be a protracted debate."

"But the outcome will be the same?"

"Absolutely."

"Just let me know when to hand in my notice."

"You're sure about leaving the Island?"

"Yes — why? Are you?"

"Yes, of course, but you've spent your whole life here. It's a big thing."

"I took myself off to Tokyo for three months, which you insist on forgetting."

Colin smiled. "Okay, I'll stop patronising you. I'm sure you'll cope with the Big Island. But we should wait till this business with Duncan is settled. I can't leave him in the lurch."

"You're not changing your mind, are you?" She frowned. "Because if you are, tell me now. I couldn't take it if those things you said were just . . ."

Colin kissed her and she melted into his forceful enveloping tenderness. "I have not changed my mind. I just want to do things . . ."

"Properly," she said, laughing, kissing him again. "I'll wait for you. Although I can't wait, I will."

He broke off from another kiss. "I have to go now, otherwise I'll stay for ever."

He bounded back to the car.

"She's great, Miss Hamon," Duncan said, as he got in.

"Yes, she is."

"When you were in the tower and we were stuck out there with the waves coming in, she told me it would be okay. She told me you wouldn't let anything happen to us."

The tunnel was closed due to a rockfall, so they skirted the harbour, where masts and rigging were tangled as though they'd been stored in a giant's toy box. "Jesus," said Colin, "this'll cost the Island a fortune."

Five minutes later they were at the hospital. Colin helped Duncan in to A&E and explained the situation, adding Vautier's name to the contact list and writing that the officer should "be kept informed of progress and discharge by order of the Bailiff". He thought about staying, but decided Duncan's parents would not be best pleased with his actions and demand he be removed. He was also hit by exhaustion and, cold to his core, felt he'd better go and lie in a warm bath, then crawl into bed. He shook hands with Duncan, renewing his promise to be at the boy's side throughout any investigations, and drove the short journey home.

He parked, feeling as if he could just sleep right there at the wheel, but gathered himself to climb out and walk slowly to the flat. When he woke he would speak to a lawyer, he mused, as he opened the door to the block. Although it was Saturday, or was it? Either way he should meet Emma first and set her straight. He wished he could do it all in a phone call, but she'd want a full autopsy into their marriage, even though she had already hinted it was as good as dead.

His contemplation was punctured by a pair of familiar feet that came into view as he neared the top of the stairs, legs stretched towards the door, and a ginger cat on a lap.

Emma jumped up when she saw him. "Where have you been? Are you okay?" she asked, putting her hands to his face.

He held her hands and moved them away. "It's a long story, but I'm okay. For the first time in a long while. We need to talk, about the future, about us."

"Yes, we do. Can I go first?"

CHAPTER
TWENTY-FOUR

ROB

Sunday, 18 October 1987

Rob found himself eyeing up the air hostesses as they came through the arrivals gate. Randy little bed-hoppers in his experience — why else would you do the job? It was like the Navy, but for straight young women: see the world, and while you're at it, suck dicks like they're about to be discontinued. Concentrate, concentrate, he urged himself. His wife would be here at any moment and he had to get his story straight. Well, not his story — he couldn't change the facts, just the way they were presented.

She'd called him yesterday afternoon after the storm. Her early-morning flight had been delayed, then cancelled, the previous night's cancellations having led to a backlog, so she was now looking at a full twenty-four-hour wait. This included a night at one of the airport hotels, which, coupled with her day in the departures lounge, meant the call had been exceedingly fractious.

"They should have cancelled it straight away, instead of letting us hang around in this dump. The toilets stink. Probably because the food is so bad. God, I'd rather have taken my chances in the bloody hurricane than stay another moment in this place — screaming kids everywhere."

"I hope they're going to pay for the hotel."

"I'm sure it won't be worth paying for. I'd be better off in a tent than whatever dismal hovel passes for a hotel out here."

"Why don't you go back into town?"

"And stay where? It's Saturday night. Anywhere half-decent will be booked."

"There's a big new Trusthouse Forte near Marble Arch."

"I am not staying in a Trusthouse Forte — I might as well stay in a stable. Oh, there's no point in talking to you. I'll ring you when the flight's called tomorrow."

It hadn't been the moment to lay some groundwork for her sympathy, which he had planned to do by relaying what he'd heard from Christophe that morning: his boat had been torn from its mooring and hurled through the windows of the restaurant. He'd succeeded in assuaging his initial panic by proclaiming it a great photo-opportunity, one of the most dramatic and telling images of the night. Sure enough, later that day it graced the front page of the *Island News*, along with pictures of the flattened trees in Millbrook Park and a headline about the return of that missing boy. He'd wondered wildly if the boat could be retained as a feature, the restaurant rebuilt around it, or at least the bar renamed Dry Dock, until Christophe had grounded him in his practical Gallic manner.

"I'm afraid the damage is a good deal more serious than your solutions allow for."

"Yeah, yeah. I'll come down and take a look later today, or maybe tomorrow. I'm trying to get Sally back from London right now."

"My assessment is that we will be closed for some time. This will necessitate a rethinking of our business plan."

"Fuck it, be fine, insurance will cover it. In many ways, it's a godsend, go back through the books and cook 'em up so we had a full house every night. Let's jack up our loss of earnings. Many rubberneckers?"

"A steady stream on the beach."

"Reckon we can charge them? Rope it off, let them in closer for a fiver?"

"I doubt they'd pay it and, besides, we do not own the beach."

"You sure about that?"

"Yes."

"I think there's some ancient cockling right my dad mentioned. May be worth checking out."

"As you wish."

The fact that he couldn't face going down and seeing the damage for himself was perhaps a clue that not even he was convinced by his bravado, wary that it would wither in the face of reality. He was also distracted by the further damage that he had to inform his wife about, and found himself playing down the carnage at the restaurant to himself but exacerbating it to Sally. In the call before she finally boarded her plane, he didn't pitch outright ruin, just enough gloom that she wouldn't be too hard on him when he presented her with Friday night's other disaster. He would imply that he had heard of it while she was up in the air. Sally didn't like secrets — at least, she didn't like the ones she found out about.

The arrivals doors opened again and she appeared, behind a luggage trolley that to him seemed excessively laden for one planned night away, dressed in a lime-green jumpsuit and powder-blue blouson jacket with a matching beret, none of which he recognised. This sent him into a low-grade panic: should he compliment her on the new outfit and risk ridicule for not clocking an established ensemble, or say nothing and be held up as the kind of ape who wouldn't notice if his wife came down to breakfast missing a limb? Marriage! What a fucking minefield. Juggling mistresses and one-night stands was a comparative walk in the park.

Sally was now upon him, and mistook his paralysis about her clothing for trauma over his loss. "My poor, poor boy's boat's broken."

He clicked back into his loosely planned narrative. "And the bloody restaurant, just when things were picking up as well." He took over the trolley. "Aren't these more bags than you left with?"

"I stayed an extra night so I needed extra clothes, which meant I needed another overnight bag. Don't pull that face. I've been through absolute fucking hell."

"But . . . Never mind."

"What? Go on."

"That bag's new as well."

"There's a Selfridges and a Liberty at the terminal. Would you rather I put my purchases in plastic bags in the hold?"

"Glad you made the most of it, then."

"What's that supposed to mean?"

"Nothing."

"I needed to cheer myself up."

"Exactly. Lovely jacket."

"I've had it for ages! You men, if it's not a car you don't see it."

"I meant it went well with the jumpsuit," he gambled, "which is new. Sorry, I'm a little out of it." That was better, remind her of his own agony. "What with the boat and the restaurant."

"You said insurance will cover it, though," she said, with a frown.

"Oh, yeah . . . It's just . . . You know how bloody long those buggers take to come through with stuff. Still, might exaggerate the loss of earnings a tadge."

"You dirty dog. Always come out on top."

Rob cursed himself for eroding the brief resurgence of her sympathy. He was now struggling to find a way to break his news. Maybe blasé was the way to go. They were approaching the exit.

"Pretty much everywhere suffered damage . . ."

"Oh, my Lord, I can't walk in this wind." They'd come out into some still strong flurries on the pavement that led to the car park.

"This is nothing. It was ten times stronger last night."

"I don't care about last night, Rob. I care about now, and I can't walk through this with my hair."

"You've got a hat."

"I've also got a hundred-pound fringe cut by Nicky Clarke that I don't want ruined. Go and get the car."

"Sure. Wait here."

"I'll go inside."

"Okay. Look for me to pull up."

"No, I won't. I'm going to sit down. I'm not standing in front of automatic doors — they'll keep opening and I'll get blown away. Come in and get me."

"I'm not supposed to leave the car in the waiting zone."

"I don't care. I'm not standing around. I'm exhausted."

"Fine. I'll come and find you. See you in a minute."

"Ah-ah-ah, where are you going?"

"To get the car."

"Well, take my bags, why don't you?"

Rob walked back to the abandoned trolley and began pushing it as best he could against the wind and the sideways slope of the pavement. For Christ's sake, how come she was the one who'd had a hard time flying over for a stupid haircut? He'd lost a boat and a restaurant. Not to mention ten grand to that bitch Louise. What a bloody week.

He fitted the luggage behind the front seats of the bootless Morgan. How did she always manage to have one bag too many for the space? They had so many bags now that their spare room felt like a left-luggage office. What the hell was in this new yellow monstrosity? He was about to cram it between the Delsey and the back of the car when he saw the corner of something hard poking out at the bottom. He sat back in the front seat and took a breath. Do it properly, he told himself. No point in incurring needless wrath by scuffing her pristine purchase. He leant back into the storage space and unzipped the bag. He started feeling his way gingerly through the clothing, past tissue-covered bras and panties, blouses, through a seeming forest of price tags, till he approached the heel or the handle or whatever it was that was threatening to puncture the leather. It was a small box. Normally he wouldn't care about a jewellery purchase, but most days he wasn't having to contend with a boat being flung through a window. Not that it wouldn't work out fine and to his advantage, and not that he could tell her to take back whatever overpriced junk she'd bought.

He snapped open the box and immediately felt guilty. A pair of silver Concorde cufflinks. She'd been shopping for him too. What a sweetheart. Really cool cufflinks. He couldn't wait to put them on. But he had to maintain the aura of surprise, so he worked the cufflinks back down to the base and squeezed the bag into the space, hoping that the unavoidable but minimal disruption to the contents would be put down to transit.

He got behind the wheel and pulled out, heading back to the waiting zone outside the exit. He honked, but of course she didn't come out. He glanced around. There were no parking attendants about, and he could afford a ticket, but it was more about making Sally meet him halfway. He hopped out and ran in. She was sitting sulkily on a plastic chair next to the newsagent. "Come on, let's go."

She walked silently back to the car with him.

"They found that boy."

"What boy?"

"The one that had gone missing."

"From where?"

"Home. Normandy College boy."

"Oh, yes, I know the one you mean."

"He'd got stuck out at Seymour Tower with a sprained ankle. Luckily a couple of fishermen found him."

"Good. I suppose."

Rob waved away an approaching attendant as they got into the car, and she apologised as he drove off. "Sorry, darling, I landed in a right grump. None of it's your fault. The hotel was just ghastly. And the breakfast! I asked for Eggs Florentine, and this girl just stared at me and said, 'Scrambled or fried?' Another night and I would have killed myself, although God knows how. There was no way I could have drowned in a bath that size."

"Well, you're back now."

"Good God, what happened here?" They were passing the Aero Club, where the smaller private planes had been flipped over in the night.

"The storm. It was horrific. There's loads of trees down — you won't recognise bits of the Island. A guy was killed by one, drove straight into it. In a way it's a good job you didn't fly back last night — could have been me smacking into a tree on my way to pick you up. Christ, imagine if I'd gone down to the bar to watch the waves last night. I could have been killed by my own boat."

"It doesn't bear thinking about," she said, patting his knee. "When did the boat crash?"

"Not sure. Some time after three a.m., they think."

"Well, you wouldn't have been there that late."

He'd already taken a breath to slide into the other bad news and pushed on: there was never going to be a perfect time. "They're still discovering all sorts of damage. I got a call just before I left to pick you up. There's one tree in particular that came down. You're going to be very cross about it."

"What?"

"The oak."

"What oak?"

"The one in front of the farmhouse."

"Oh, I don't care about that. That's great news. I win. I can have my fountain."

"I'm afraid it fell down on the house. Crashed through the hall."

His eyes were firmly on the road, but he sensed her jaw clenching. "Oh, bloody hell, Rob! This is all your fault."

"How is it my fault? I didn't cause the storm."

"I hated that tree. It's a curse."

"Yes, but as you say, you get your fountain."

"How much is it going to cost? In time and money? I wanted to be in by spring. Oh, this is a disaster."

"It might be summer now."

"I can't move in any later. I won't. I want the house-warming to spill out into the garden. I suppose now you're going to tell me we can't afford the fountain. Just to spite me."

"Don't worry about the money. Insurance will cover it, plus I've got a new arrangement with Rick. Money's going to roll in from the shares. We can soak this up."

"Soak up what?"

"The cost."

"You just said insurance will cover it."

"It will."

"Well, which is it? The insurance or the shares?"

"Both. I mean, insurance. But if they take their time filling in their forms I can cover it in the short term."

"What about the long term?"

"Short term, long term, medium term, it's all fine."

"That bloody tree."

"What are you doing up there?"

"Unpacking."

"You're taking ages."

"I'm cutting off labels and hanging things."

"Catarina can do that."

"She's not in till Tuesday."

Sally had just reached in for a tiger-print blouse and her hand had hit something hard. Puzzled, she had pulled out the cufflink box, which now sat on her lap. How had that got in there? They'd paid together after they'd got talking in Cartier's. Had the cashier given them the wrong boxes? Or had the swap happened at dinner when they'd compared purchases, or in the hotel room after the bags had been suddenly dropped to the floor and kicked over in the lurch to the bed? She had no way of getting them to him now, or of getting her diamanté champagne-flute brooch back. She could send it to BA headquarters, but all she had was a first name, and she imagined a lot of pilots were called Peter. No, best that it was a little adventure that had never happened. She would give these to Rob, although that in itself was dangerous: it would remind her of a new truth that, for the sake of her marriage, it was best to forget.

Her husband was a dreary fuck.

CHAPTER
TWENTY-FIVE

COLIN

Monday, 19 October 1987

Colin drove up to the school in silence. He had been summoned by a phone call from Le Brocq the day before, to discuss "a resolution to the difficult issues of the previous week". The meeting was set for ten a.m., so the playground and corridors were deserted as he made his way to the headmaster's office.

"Morning, Mrs Bisson. I'm seeing Mr Le Brocq at ten."

"Thank you, Mr Bygate. No need to explain. I am well aware of the headmaster's diary," she replied, the curtness so customary that it could easily have nothing to do with the fact that he had been suspended for nearly getting into a fight with a member of staff whom he had since exposed as a nascent pederast.

Le Brocq's door opened as soon as Colin sat down, and he emerged with a baffling jollity. "I thought I heard your voice, Mr Bygate. Good to see you're in one piece after your adventure."

Colin smiled weakly. "Yes" was all he could summon in reply.

"Well, come in. Can I get you some tea, coffee?"

"No, thank you."

Colin went in and sat down, not knowing what to expect. He had spoken briefly to Vautier the day before, demanding to know who had told the *Island News* that Duncan had been found with a sprained ankle by two fishermen inspecting damage to the oyster beds. Vautier had denied all accusations of a cover-up, blaming the error on the shortcomings of a local paper overwhelmed with a deluge of stories about injuries and rescues from the storm. Had not Colin's wife helped a neighbour with a broken arm? A leg? Well, you see how these things get mixed up. He talked Colin down from correcting the paper himself and, assuring him that matters were in hand, thanked him for his involvement, urging him to allow the relevant authorities to carry out a full and proper investigation into exactly how and why Duncan had ended up alone on that tower. Colin's parting shot had been that Mickey Rouain might not be as clean as Vautier thought, but he had backed down when the detective suggested he would interview Duncan about the matter under caution. Colin knew he was being strung a line, that Vautier was counting on him not wanting to link Duncan to a drugs purchase, but he smarted at the knowledge that this was also suiting Vautier's agenda.

"So," began Le Brocq, "I trust that you are properly rested."

"Yes."

"I thought it best to bring you up to speed as to where we are vis-à-vis the Duncan Labey situation."

"Just as long as you're up to speed yourself. Aidan Blampied tried to molest him."

"'Tried' being the operative word. There was no actual molestation."

"Duncan told me Blampied tried to touch him. And blackmail him."

"That's not what he told me."

"You've spoken to him?"

"Yes, and to his parents."

"When?"

"Yesterday morning."

"You asked him about all this in front of his parents?"

"Yes."

"Well, that's not proper procedure in these cases. He's unlikely to admit it in front of his parents. There are issues of shame and embarrassment. Plus his father was already on Blampied's side, him being an old boy and all that. You know, I can never tell if you people are incompetent by design or through ignorance."

"Have you finished?"

"No. Have the police spoken to Duncan yet? Or Blampied?"

"They have not."

"Right. I will, then."

"Sit down, Mr Bygate."

"I am under no obligation to you."

"But you are under obligation to Duncan. Would you like to hear his wishes?"

"From him, yes."

"He will be coming along at first break."

"He's back at school?"

"Yes. That is what he wishes. That is what we all wish."

"And is Blampied still here? Because that is outrageous."

"Mr Blampied has resigned. As you know, he is a keen sailor. An opportunity has come up to crew in the Tall Ships' Race, something he has always wanted to take part in. We wish him all the best."

"You've stood by him all week, why the change of heart?"

Le Brocq hesitated. "This is not the first time that such allegations have surfaced."

"Jesus Christ, he's done it before?"

"Allegations are not the same as —"

"Whatever you need to tell yourself."

"It's best for all if he moves on."

The bell for break rang.

"He just gets to walk away from this? This is disgusting. You are disgusting."

"You would rather tarnish the reputation of the school?"

"Heaven forbid that the cost of protecting the pupils in your charge should be your precious royal visit."

"And what about protecting Labey?"

"That's what prosecuting Blampied would involve."

"It would also involve a drugs charge for the boy."

"Whatever Blampied produces, there's no proof he found it on Duncan. Maybe he planted it on the boy."

"The accusation will be made. In court. And Duncan will also have to bear the stigma of having been the subject of an attempted interference, if indeed that's what happened, on an island where nothing remains secret for very long."

"So how are the actual facts going to remain secret?"

"Because all parties aware of them have agreed that it is in everyone's wider interest to forget them. Mr Blampied will forget that he found cannabis on Labey, and in return Labey will forget whatever he thinks Mr Blampied said or did in relation to the discovery of supposed cannabis."

"So why is it in my interest to go along with this?"

"Because that is what Duncan Labey has requested. The price of his silence is that you are given your job back. Believe me, I wish it were otherwise."

Colin's head sank. "Why? Why does he want me here?"

"He said he believes you have been treated unfairly. And he believes you saved his life."

Le Brocq's intercom buzzed and Mrs Bisson announced Duncan's arrival. Le Brocq strode to the door and ushered him in.

"Come in, Duncan, looking even better than yesterday. Got some good hot meals in you, I hope? That Sunday roast was certainly smelling good in your mother's kitchen."

"Yes, sir, thank you, sir," said Duncan, giving a brief half-smile to Colin and settling in a chair beside him.

"I was just telling Mr Bygate here about our little agreement," said Le Brocq, settling himself back behind his desk.

Duncan nodded gravely. A silence fell.

"So," said Le Brocq, "*ça suffit*."

Colin didn't know what to say.

"You may both return to your classes."

As Duncan rose, Colin grabbed his arm. "Wait. Duncan, is this what you want?"

"Yes, sir. I just want things to go back to the way they were," he said.

"There you have it," beamed Le Brocq, "straight from the horse's mouth!"

Colin signalled reluctant agreement.

Colin emerged on to the front steps as the bell ending morning break rang. As the flood of pupils began to ebb back into classes, he spotted Debbie emerging from the staffroom and crossing the quadrangle. She saw him, too, and paused, smiling quizzically. They began to walk towards each other, but as she saw the anguish etched on his face, her smile faded and she turned away, running for a hiding place before the tears broke. He was left with the gutting consolation that she had reprieved him from saying the words that would wound him as much to say as they would her to hear.

CHAPTER
TWENTY-SIX

ROB

Monday, 19 October 1987

Betrayal, that was what it was. An utter bloody betrayal. He'd not only paid his premiums, he'd put up with his insurance agent's tedious anecdotes about sea kayaking and puffin spotting. And he'd always given him free drinks at the bar when he'd shown up with women he described as clients — but who the hell meets clients at nine o'clock on a Friday night? Men whose wives are off the Island, that's who. Except Le Gresley wasn't married, was he? Hadn't he dated Emma for a bit, before she'd hooked up with Colin? Maybe that was why Le Gresley was stiffing him: revenge. Although how could he know Rob was fucking his ex? Which he wasn't any more. At least, not for a bit. Nope, actually that one was probably over. It was all so confusing. Maybe he could have a little nap here on the bar. Rob was very, very drunk, and had been for several hours. This was definitely the worst day in the worst week of his life, quite a feat considering that the competing low points included losing a mistress, paying ten grand to a casual fuck, and being told his finances were running on fumes.

The slide had begun that morning when he'd rung Dave Le Gresley to register the indemnity period from the Saturday morning. He'd finally gone down to the Bretagne, having decided that confronting the double heartbreak of losing his beloved boat and dream restaurant was ahead in the fun stakes over sitting at home basking in his wife's hate rays. It was dawning on him that his earlier flippancy was a symptom of shock. As he walked through the back entrance, he experienced the kind of "I can't face this" dread he imagined people felt as they headed into a morgue to identify a loved one. Christophe was there to greet him, calm and grave as ever: this was the kind of situation for which he was made.

He'd only glanced at the picture that had made the front of the paper. When he thought of his boat coming to rest in his hotel, he visualised it more as the kind of surreal image one might find in flicking through the poster racks at Woolworths.

"Fuck me with a bag of spanners," he gasped, as he walked across the damp carpet strewn with broken glass. The boat was on its side. The cabin had shattered the mirrored Manhattan drink display that ran against the far wall, the stern was hanging out over the sea wall and the hull had been torn open like the top of a sardine can. Before the boat had come to rest, a part of it — the bow, the four-foot mast on top of the cabin, what did it matter? — had punched a hole in the ceiling. A toilet from the room above had fallen down and shattered the end of the black marble counter. A bath was hanging through the hole at forty-five degrees.

The central chandelier was splayed under a bullseye of what looked like human shit that radiated out in dissipating splatters.

"Wow. The Queen's not going to like this."

"When the toilet came down it exposed the pipe, so anyone using the toilets above was flushing their waste directly on to the floor here. Until we shut off the water, which we had to do because the flow to the bath was flooding the room. Although it was already flooded by the seawater. I think the carpet is unsalvageable."

Rob had had that carpet designed with the parish crest and his initials woven into it. "So we've got no running water."

"We're waiting for a plumber to isolate the supply to that room, or if necessary the floor."

"Right. Fuck. This is more than just getting a crane to lift the boat out and putting the windows back in."

"It is."

"Well, I'm not going to get stressed. This is why I pay insurance. Over to them. I'll get Dave on the blower. Let's pull some boys in to patch up the holes, stop any more weather damage, and once Huelin's have done their assessment we can get some quotes in, get back up and running."

"You still want me to massage the takings, maybe create some winter bookings we will have to cancel?"

"Um, yes. I mean, might be a bit tricky. Dave's a regular . . . He'll know we haven't been on full steam. And everywhere slows down for the winter. But, go ahead, do some fiddling. I'll talk to him, have a feel for how much we can get away with."

Rob turned away, then swivelled back. "Hang on, sorry, I'm just getting up to speed with all this. We're shut as a hotel, and as a restaurant, bar, hang-out, whatever?"

"Yes."

"The staff, are we . . .?"

"Paying them? Yes. I've told them all not to come in . . ."

"Apart from security. There could be looters. What am I talking about? This is Jersey, not Toxteth. But we need someone here all the time."

"It has been arranged. And I am here."

"You're still staying here? But you can't wash or crap."

"I am the manager. I am not going anywhere."

"Sure. But I'm just thinking of the wage bill. We were going to sack a third anyway, but we'd better sack everyone."

"Will the insurance not cover their wages?"

"Not sure. Not big on small print. I'll ask. But if not, everyone goes."

Christophe stared impassively. "Not you," Rob blurted. "You're safe. You're still my overall business manager . . . We need to work things out. I'll speak to Dave."

Rob headed to his office. The windows were not only intact but also cleaner, following the storm, than they ever were after that stupid Porko had washed them.

He called Huelin's Island Insurance. The line was predictably engaged: pretty much everyone in the Island would be claiming for something from

354

somebody, but he knew as soon as he got on the line to Le Gresley he could jump the queue, being an important client and a Normandy College alumnus. He got through on his third redial.

"Dave, Rob, how are you? Still got a roof?"

"Yes, but not a greenhouse. Could be worse. I saw the paper. You seem to have suffered a double whammy."

"Yes, right fucking mess over here. 'Fraid your regular table's been smashed in. And there's the house, but we'll get to that after." Dave had put together the policies for pretty much all of Rob's portfolio: houses, cars, boat and hotel.

"I'll get someone down as soon as possible. Then you get your quotes in for repairs and loss of income."

"Cool. And with regard to loss of income, would you believe me if I told you we were looking at a packed winter?"

"If the bookings are there and verifiable — names, numbers, deposits — you will receive compensation." That seemed enough of a nod for Rob. Would they really ring the numbers, check the names?

"Great. We can have that over to you tomorrow. About the assessors, when you say as soon as possible . . ."

"Today will be tricky. The L'Horizon took a lashing."

"Nothing minor, I hope."

"Windows and tiles but, you know, royal venue and all that, they'll expect first dibs."

"Not for long, believe me."

"I do believe you. Now, do you have the details of the boat owner's insurance?"

"Yeah, it's me."

"No, the boat that went through the window. We'll get to your boat in a bit. Harbour's a bloody mess."

"It was my boat that went through the window."

"How come? It's moored at the marina."

"I moved it. Took a buoy in St Clement's."

"When?"

"Last week."

"Ah." There was a long, agonising silence.

"Dave?"

"Yeah, still here, just checking your boat policy and . . . You didn't tell us you'd moved it."

"So. I'm telling you now."

"The policy is predicated on a specified mooring."

"The boat is insured wherever I sail it."

"Drive, it's not a sailboat."

"All right, drive. Jesus, you sound like my dad. The point is, that boat is insured wherever I take it."

"Yes. But permanent moorings have to be specified."

"What about when I take it over to Carteret, or Saint-Malo?"

"Well, those aren't permanent moorings, are they?"

"Well, we can just pretend I was using a temporary mooring."

"Not sure about that. Although, I suppose . . . You still have the mooring at the marina?"

Rob felt like he had stopped breathing. "Not . . . as such . . . I mean, can't I say I still do, or do you need proof?"

"I need proof, Rob. They'll ask for it. I can't lie about this stuff. I'd lose my job. It's actually illegal."

"So I'm just supposed to eat the cost of an eighty-grand boat?"

"Can it be salvaged?"

"I think the helm's okay, and a couple of the seat covers. No! It can't be salvaged, not for much less than the cost of a new one. It's got a big bloody hole in it where it scraped over the sea wall and smashed up my fucking restaurant. Are you going to stump up for that, or is it on me as well?"

"Look, the problem is that you —"

"Oh, you are fucking kidding me!"

"If it was your boat, and it wasn't secured properly, on an unregistered mooring, then, yes, I'm afraid the damage it caused to your, or any, property is on you."

"It was secured, but in case you hadn't noticed, the Island was hit by a fucking hurricane!"

"Whether or not you secured it effectively on the mooring will be difficult to ascertain, but the fact is —"

"The fact is, you can go and fuck yourself!" yelled Rob, slamming the phone down. He called straight back. "Dave, sorry, that was out of order, but you can understand how bad this is for me."

"I know, mate, and I'm sorry. My hands are tied."

"A tree came down at the farmhouse. Can we at least get that sorted out? It came through the roof. If it rains again it's going to fuck up the floorboards . . ."

"Sure, sure. Let me ring you back in five."

Rob had then driven up to the farmhouse to meet some beardless gnome whose opinion he immediately distrusted, not least when he told him the company wasn't liable for the damage caused by the tree.

"What do you mean, not liable?"

"Look at the trunk. That thing's been dead for years, or at least dying. Should have come down ages ago."

"What's that got to do with it?"

"You have a responsibility to check that no overhanging vegetation is in danger of causing damage to your property."

"It wasn't overhanging. It was blown there by a bloody hurricane. Look, the stump's over there, and that's where it landed."

"I'm very sorry. There is a plus side. It means you don't have to hang around waiting for us to approve quotes. You can just get straight on with sorting it out. We're going to have a hell of a backlog."

"What are you talking about?"

"Well, I presume you've already got builders working on the conversion, they just tack this on to the job."

"Tack it on? I've got to pay for a new roof and wall! This is bloody months of extra labour!"

"We're all suffering. Think of the payouts we're going to have to make."

"Oh, my heart bleeds! I'm so sorry that you actually have to honour the obligations you've made. With the exception of those to me, of course."

"There's no need to be sarcastic."

"There's no need to be as fat and bald as you are."

"That's just rude."

"Waddle off before I get ruder. Go on, back to your toadstool. I hope it didn't blow away in the wind. Actually, I hope it did, but you're personally liable for the damage because you had it registered as a mushroom."

He'd left the Bretagne without telling Christophe the appalling response of his insurers to the hotel. Now he felt unable to go home and relay to Sally their equally galling attitude to the farmhouse, their coverage of which he had assured her was a "done deal".

He had got into his car and driven north. A walk along the beach: that would be good. Plemont was lovely — should be low tide: he could let the breeze clear his head, or he could just crawl into one of the caves, like a hermit. There was a diversion on La Route du Nord while they chainsawed up the trees that had come down there and he ended up going in the wrong direction on La Rue des Platons, which was itself blocked off by a collapsed wall, so he found himself driving back towards Bouley Bay. He surrendered to it, feeling drawn to what he saw as the epicentre of his bad luck, the Black Dog.

He parked as drizzle began wafting over the bay, and abandoned the idea of a walk in favour of a drink. In any case, he didn't much fancy a wet stroll across the stony beach where he'd given in to Louise's demands.

As he sat at the bar, with a bag of cheese and onion crisps and a double shot of Famous Grouse, he realised the starkness of the choice before him. It was the hotel or the house. He would have to sell one to save the other. He wasn't even entertaining the idea of replacing the boat. So, who to disappoint? Sally, who would sulk till the grave, or Christophe, who had lent what was doubtless to him a small fortune in return for a stake in the business he was about to close? Actually, he might have to let them both down. Selling the hotel would still leave him with a sizeable debt and no cash-flow to fund the farmhouse. He could always sell Le Petit Palais, the house they lived in. But then they'd be renting somewhere till they could move into the new place, which he didn't want to do because it was money with no return, and Sally didn't want to do because she wouldn't be able to decorate a rented property and was convinced whatever he found them would be aesthetically abhorrent. He didn't know which he dreaded most: his wife's reaction to losing her dream home, or the crowing of Carrière and his cohorts at the news of him having to sell his hotel because it had been wrecked by his boat. When he thought of the latter, he decided he would rather tear off his balls with a lobster claw.

There had to be another move.

His shares. Rick might have pulled some magic already. Maybe not: it had only been a few days. But it was still a substantial portfolio. Play safe, sell now, repair the hotel, stave off the creditors, keep the farmhouse on ice till the year after next. Sally would just have to see sense. And if she was dead set on moving in this coming summer, then they would have to sell their current abode and live in a tent in the garden while the builders finished their work. He hoped it wouldn't come to that. He pitied the builders if it did, having Sally on site.

He jumped up and headed for the payphone. He dialled Rick's direct line and the reception desk five times each, but got the engaged tone repeatedly.

360

He bought the rest of the bottle of whisky and retreated to a booth. The only other customer was an old man, with nicotine-stained grey hair, by the dartboard.

When he'd finished the whisky he went back to the bar and started on pints. As the old man lit another cigarette he stumbled back to the payphone. Rick was still engaged. Bellend must have left it off the hook. As he swayed back and forth against the wall he was struck by an idea, and left a message on the Bretagne office answerphone.

"Christophe, Rob, I'm at the Black Dog, having a great time. No, it sucks. Sucks like my mother. Not my actual mother, my slut of a stepmother. Anyway, had a thought. The boat might have leaked diesel. Have a fag, toss it in, arson, can we claim for that? Maybe not. I don't know."

Once he'd returned to his bar stool, which he clambered on to with difficulty, he noticed that a new pretty barmaid was serving. "You could be a model."

"Thanks."

"Got a boyfriend?"

"Yes, thanks."

"Is he rich? I am. Was. Will be."

She ignored him as two men in dungarees carrying bags and oilskins entered the bar. "All good, guys?"

"Yes, thank you," replied the older, squatter man, in a French accent. "Repairs all done. One more night and we'll be off."

"We'll miss you — they gave us free lobsters," she added, to Rob.

"Good job it wasn't crabs," he quipped.

The men were now next to Rob at the bar. "Easy," he said, "I saw her first."

"Two ciders?" she asked them.

"Fishermen, eh?" slurred Rob.

"Yes, we sheltered here from the storm. Some damage to the mast and the winch."

"That's nothing. I lost a bloody hull. And the rest."

"I'm sorry to hear that."

"Good living?"

"Is okay. Some seasons good, some seasons —"

" 'Okay' — that's one of the words you nicked from us. Like *la télévision* and *la radio*. What's that about?"

"*Pourquoi parlons-nous à cet ivrogne?*" asked his younger, taller, wiry companion, whose eyes narrowed with contempt.

"Why are you talking to this drunk?" translated Rob. "Yeah, we learn your language over here. Not like you guys."

"We both speak English." The man sighed, as he and his friend tried to move off with their drinks.

"Yeah, but you pretend you can't. I've been to Paris. Fucking rude, all of them."

"And what are you being?"

"I'm just being honest, pal."

"Excuse us."

"No, no, no. Let me buy you a drink. What'll it be? Cointreau? Armagnac? *Une bière?* Another word you nicked from us. I'm joking. Come on, my shout."

"No, thank you, we have drinks."

"You think I'm not good for it? Probably not. Lost a boat today. And a house. And a hotel. How much your boat cost? Fuck it, I don't care. Go on, go forage for snails, pick some limpets off the rocks. I was being friendly, I'm bored of that now . . ."

Rob turned back to look at the TV in the corner of the bar, and missed the restraining hand the older man placed on the younger one's shoulder as he stepped back towards Rob.

"Ah, look at those legs! Beautiful!" The video for Robert Palmer's "Addicted to Love" was playing. "Turn it up, love!"

The barmaid was about to comply when the young Frenchman leant over and changed the channel.

"Hey, what'd you do that for?" leered Rob. "I was enjoying that."

"No one was enjoying you."

"You're just jealous. I've fucked plenty of women as hot as them. Hotter. Little tip, you're not going to get your cock wet wearing wellies."

"Ignore him," said the barmaid. "He's drunk. I'm not serving him any more. He'll be gone soon."

"Who's drunk?"

"You."

"Says who?"

"Me. Drink up and go."

"Only if you put the Robert Palmer back on."

"No. No TV."

She switched it off just as a newscaster delivered the phrase "biggest day of losses since the crash of 1929". Rob found himself marginally sobered by this.

"Turn it back on!"

"No."

"Fucking turn it on! What crash? What's happened?"

"I don't care."

"The stock markets have crashed. Twenty-six per cent drop in the UK," intoned the weary Frenchman from the corner. "Yes, fishermen can know things too."

"What do you fucking know?" spat Rob. "Twenty-six per cent? Bollocks. Not possible."

"While you've been molesting women, we have been listening to the news."

"I'd rather molest women than boys. Like you lot. Fuck it, I'm going. I'm gone. Fucking fucks."

Rob swayed out into the car park, thinking about where to throw up. Maybe the front seat of whatever lawnmower those two Frog pricks had driven up in. Wasn't a car, though, it was a boat, wasn't it? Look out for a pedalo, then. Twenty-six per cent losses? That newsreader was talking absolute bollocks.

He felt a blow to the back of his shoulders and fell down on all fours. Fuck, it hurt. He was wondering how he'd walked backwards into something while moving forwards, when a kick to the ribs disabused him of the idea that his injury had been self-inflicted.

Someone picked him up by the lapels of his jacket, spat in his face and kneed him in the balls. He had never known pain like it. From toenails to hair follicles, every cell was screaming.

His head was spinning and he was slow to translate the phrases that were being yelled at him, but he could tell from the tone they weren't complimentary. A foot pushed at his shoulder, trying to turn him on to his back. He vomited an afternoon's worth of booze and bar snacks on to it, which didn't go down too well with the owner of the shoe. Rob laughed bubbles of puke and blood. The only fight of his life and all he'd managed to do was cause damage to what looked like a two-pound shoe. He pulled his arms over his head and began to cry, knowing the beating he was about to take, when another French voice joined in the chorus. Oh, Christ, the whole fleet was about to pile in. Except he recognised this voice.

"*Laissez-lui seul.*" Christophe was telling them to leave him alone.

He felt feet step over him and, peering out from between his shielding elbows, could see Christophe's silhouette under the harbour lights. His assailants seemed to be nonplussed by the appearance of a countryman.

"*Reste en dehors de tout ça!*" spat the older man. *Keep out of it,* Rob worked out he was saying.

"*On dirait que vous venez de Marseille?*" asked Christophe. *You sound like you're from Marseille, yes?* Did he hope they had some friends in common?

"*Qu'est-ce que ça peut te faire, putain?*" hissed the younger man. *What's it got to do with you . . . bitch?* Yes, that was it. Bitch or whore. Either way the mutual-friends angle was looking pretty hopeless.

Christophe took off his jacket and hung it on a railing. Oh, Christ, they'd kill him. Maybe Rob could crawl back to the bar and get help while they laid into him. In fact, why didn't Christophe run for help now? Too late, the men were circling him, but he looked as though he didn't know they were there, unbuttoning his shirt as though he was getting ready for a swim.

"*Voulez-vous chercher la bagarre, ou voulez-vous baiser, pédé?*" *Are you looking to fight or fuck, faggot?* The younger one clearly favoured the former, and lunged at Christophe. Even though he was looking down as he fiddled with his shirt, the little man managed to sidestep his attacker and deliver a mighty punch to the side of the neck that left him gurgling on the ground. Christophe calmly put his foot on the side of his throat and opened his shirt to the older man, who was about to rush him.

The Marseillais saw something that made him stop and hold his palms wide, signalling surrender. Christophe took his foot off the groaning man's neck, rebuttoned his shirt as he went to retrieve his jacket, then walked over to help Rob up as the two Frenchmen scurried into the night.

"Are you okay, Mr de la Haye?"

"Not really. I'm fucking ruined, Christophe. Ruined."

"It could be worse. Imagine if you had not liquidated your shares. Bad news today for investors."

So it was true. No wonder Rick's phones had been engaged. Rob laughed long and hard, then winced at a pain in his ribs. "Yes, imagine! It would be fucking terrible." Especially for the kind of fool who'd reinvested fifty per cent of whatever junk he'd had in the first place, he thought. He laughed again. If you're going to go down, go down big.

"Let me get you home."

"Thanks. I think I'm a bit over the limit."

"Sleep it off. Things will be clearer in the morning."

Christophe helped a hobbling Rob to his car. "Did you speak to your insurance friend?"

"Yeah, not good."

"We will work together on this."

"You're quite the brawler."

"I used to do a bit of door work in the rougher part of town."

"Well, if I ever sack you, I'll do it by fax."

He eased Rob into the back seat. Rob felt something hard next to him. "Where did you get this?" he asked, recognising his briefcase in the flare of the interior light before Christophe shut the driver's door.

"Someone dropped it in this afternoon," he replied. "You must have left it somewhere. You see, your luck has not completely run out. I know how much that case means to you."

"Yes. It did," said Rob, stonily, as he wound down the window and flung the case on to the verge as Christophe sped up the hill.

CHAPTER
TWENTY-SEVEN

COLIN

Monday, 19 October 1987

Colin sat on the ledge, his feet dangling two hundred feet above the same wave-lashed cliff base into which Duncan had contemplated hurling himself the week before. He let the sea calm him, while he idly stroked some yellow lichen on the rock next to his thigh, watching its colour bleach into grey as the light fell.

Bathed in the half-light, he no longer felt like a ghost on the Island. Now he had a purpose, a reason to be here. His baby was growing inside Emma. He knew what it was like to be fatherless, and he would never allow that to happen to his own child.

He had known that morning he would remain on the Island, but he hadn't known he was going to remain at the school. But he had a responsibility, not just to Duncan but to all the pupils. If not him, who would help the future Duncans? Who would stop the other Blampieds? No one had been there before. He would be there now.

At first he'd been angry: if he hadn't made such an effort for Emma's birthday, she wouldn't be pregnant.

Now he was calm. A part of him always felt more comfortable with a path of expected behaviour, no matter that it involved a degree of privation. And painful as the situation was, it was less painful than leaving Emma, with or without a child. He only had to renege on a promise made at a moment of extreme crisis with Debbie, as opposed to the vows he'd made to Emma before God, family and friends. He wanted to explain to Debbie that the qualities she cherished in him were those that meant he could no longer be with her. How could she love a man who would leave his pregnant wife? He knew this would be scant consolation. He had a letter in his pocket, already rewritten after he had baulked at the mawkish sign-off "in another life, we would be together", which he had changed to the formal but heartfelt "I wish you nothing but happiness".

He knew it was cowardly to slip a note through her door and run away, and he knew that they would have to speak at some point, especially if they were to continue working at the same school. He couldn't leave, but he knew it wasn't fair to force her out so somehow they would have to reconcile. Perhaps she would leave anyway. In her shoes, he would.

Already he felt closeness returning between him and Emma. He had seen a change in her since the news. She was calmer, more at ease, relaxed yet focused. She said she had felt reborn in the storm. The doctor at A&E had told her that Mrs Le Boutillier had been in deep shock when she had brought her in, and that she had probably saved her life. She had saved one life, was about to create another, and was finding meaning in her own.

He had asked his third-year English class that afternoon to write down their favourite song lyrics for discussion. A solemn boy who normally said very little had picked "Jigsaw" by Marillion, a band about whom Colin knew little, other than that they had a penchant for a jester on their album covers and a lead singer called Fish, but he had been struck by the opening lines, so much so that they had distracted him for the rest of the lesson.

We are jigsaw pieces aligned on the perimeter edge,
Interlocked through a missing piece.

Maybe his and Emma's child would be that missing piece. He had to hope so.

The baby would be born in the spring, when the Island would be thronging with new life. The ferns on the north coast would be unfurling; the western commons and headlands would be gold with gorse flowers; the lanes would be vaulted by the trees and fringed by the hedgerows in advance of their biannual trim, the Branchage. The sun would begin to warm the sea, and then the tourists, the lifeblood, would return. It was a beautiful place, one worth fighting for.

He looked up at two vapour trails, one current and sharp, streaming out behind a plane invisible in the dusk, the other older, billowing into nothing. He often wondered who was on the planes, where they were going and whether they were aware they were passing over an anomaly, which, the week before, he had begun uncharitably to think of as a crumb left over from a Continental shift. It was an odd place, neither English nor French, a nominal part of the United Kingdom, a defiant abstainer from the EEC, seemingly on the edge of so much yet at the centre of everything. There were worse places to make a stand, to stake a claim.

He stood up, took one last look at the heaving sea canopied by the first of the night's stars, and made his way back up the path to the car.

Acknowledgements

My thanks are due to the following people:

Reuben Grove was the first person I trusted to read the early chapters. If he hadn't reacted so positively, I might not have continued.

Isabel Lloyd was my second reader. She was not only greatly encouraging, but also provided advice and criticisms, which proved enormously helpful and were consistently echoed by my agent, editor and copy editor.

Ed Docx helped me to narrow down the voices of certain characters. His overall seal of approval meant a huge amount to me and gave me the confidence to submit the manuscript.

The enthusiasm and support of my wonderful screenwriting agent Abby Singer at Casarotto led me to my brilliant literary agent Jane Finigan at Lutyens and Rubinstein, whose excitement, guidance and faith have been invaluable throughout.

My boundless thanks go to my editor Clare Reihill for buying the book, and for then offering incisive and perceptive criticisms, which identified numerous fault lines that I have done my best to correct. Thank you

Clare, for bringing the ending a little further into the light, and for making me a better writer.

I was lucky enough to have an outstanding copy editor in Hazel Orme, whose impeccable taste and judgement have improved every aspect of the book.

Thanks to Stephen Guise for meticulous coordination.

Thanks to Tony Able for his memories of 19 October 1987.

Thanks to Derek Hairon of Jersey Walk Adventures for information about the tidal patterns around Seymour Tower. The website www.jerseywalkadventures.co.uk has details of all the fascinating tours they offer.

Thanks to Geraint Jennings of the Société Jersiaise for a prompt ruling on Jersey-English spelling.

Thanks to Sarah Robins for last-minute French corrections and for alerting me to the in/on Jersey pitfall.

Thanks to Richard Pirouet for a final adjudication on "in the Island".

Kevin Brace was kind enough to allow the use of his photograph for the cover. His excellent work captures the unique beauty of Jersey, and can be found at his website kevinbrace-photography.com.

Thanks are also due to the staff of the Fat Cat Café, Stoke Newington, who provided multiple meals and coffees throughout the writing and rewriting of this novel.

Love and thanks to Anne for waiting to read it.

Finally, my love and gratitude go to two inspirational teachers who had an incalculable influence on me that I still carry daily — Peter Fekete, to whom this book is dedicated, and Colin Benson.

LIFTED BY THE GREAT NOTHING

Karim Dimechkie

Max lives with his father, Rasheed, and doesn't remember his mother, who was murdered by burglars before father and son were forced to emigrate from Beirut to New Jersey. Rasheed is enamoured of his idea of American culture — baseball and barbecues — and has tried to shed his Lebanese heritage completely. He has a single purpose in life: to provide Max with a joyful childhood; though sometimes his efforts do more harm than good. When Max turns seventeen, he discovers that his father has been lying to him — about everything — and their peaceful universe is destroyed. As Max ventures on an uncertain journey to Beirut, he must ask himself, what happens when your truth is a fable? And can some lies be a sacrifice in disguise?

THE SHUT EYE

Belinda Bauer

When James Buck pops out to buy fireworks, leaving the front door of his flat open, his little son, Daniel, wanders outside and goes missing. Now James struggles to cope with his guilt, while his wife Anna spends her days guarding the small footprints her son made in the forecourt near her door. A flyer advertising a psychic, Richard Latham, offers Anna hope at last . . . DCI John Marvel knows Latham from another case of a missing child — that of twelve-year-old Edie Evans — but he was of no help. With two children missing, Marvel is astounded when his boss asks him to find his wife's missing poodle. He must also make a decision about Latham. Is he a visionary? A shut eye? Or a cruel fake, preying on the vulnerable?